THE CITY WANTS YOU ALONE

The Final Book in
the GIRL Trilogy

Published by Girl Noise Press

Girl Noise Press is a small press born out of bedroom culture. We publish books that are sharply witty, a little DIY, petty, pretty and profound. Written in gel pen by the glow of a lava lamp, then hexed and sealed with a kiss.

Visit us at girlnoise.net

Cover art by Lucille Groleau
Cover design by Andrea Martin

Girl (1994)

Rockstar Superstar (2004)

Paranoid Park (2006)

Recovery Road (2011)

Dream School (2011)

The Prince of Venice Beach (2014)

Boy (2017)

THE CITY WANTS YOU ALONE

The Final Book in
the GIRL Trilogy

BLAKE NELSON

GIRL NOISE
PRESS

To my fellow travelers.

PART ONE

IT WAS VALENTINE'S DAY—OR Valentine's *night* actually—and I was standing in the bus shelter, outside the Westridge Mall, waiting for the 57 Bus to take me downtown. A bunch of my fellow mall workers and I were meeting at The Deuce to dance and get drunk and feel sorry for ourselves for not having boyfriends. The trouble was, I had the closing shift, so it was already 10:30, which meant the buses were on the night schedule, which meant they took their sweet time coming. If they came at all. Plus it was cold and raining and I was dressed for a club—a skirt and light trenchcoat—not for standing in an outdoor bus shelter for half an hour. I had already been waiting twenty-minutes. I was beginning to shiver slightly.

And then things got worse: Eric Lutz appeared. He came waddling out of the big glass doors of Macy's and made his way toward the bus stop, bare-headed in the rain. Eric was a manager at Footlocker. He was famous around the mall for hitting on every female he encountered, regardless of age, ethnicity, or body type. People made brutal fun of him, sometimes right to his face. Still, he kept at it. Patiently chatting up the Cineplex girls, the food court workers, the bored moms with their baby strollers. I was only one month into my career here at the Westridge Mall, so Eric Lutz hadn't had a clear shot at me yet. So I guess it was my turn. And on Valentine's Day no less.

He came into the shelter. I moved away slightly. He was as unattractive as advertised: cheap parka, polyester Footlocker pants that dragged on the ground behind his heels, a three-dollar stocking cap which he eventually pulled over his large, balding head.

He turned and studied me for a moment. "You work at the mall," he said.

I nodded that I did.

"I thought you looked familiar," he said, arranging his stocking cap.

I stared straight ahead.

"Where do you work?" he asked.

"J. Crew."

"Oh, a J. Crew girl," he said, smiling calmly. "I like J. Crew."

"Yeah?" I said. "What do you like about it?"

He shrugged. "Just the nice clothes ... the nice people ..." He turned to me again, a gleam in his eye. "What's your name?"

I sighed to myself. "Andrea."

I'd been kicked out of college. That's why I was talking to Eric Lutz. That's why I was standing in a bus shelter. That's why I worked at a mall, two miles from my old high school in Beaverton, Oregon.

Getting kicked out of college wasn't the worst thing that could happen to a person. If you'd been kicked out for political or philosophical or artistic reasons (as I was), that could be cool. When you thought of how many brilliant, creative people had parted ways with various institutions over the years ... it was a long list. In a way it was a badge of honor.

But that's not what it felt like standing next to Eric Lutz. I felt like I'd never gone to college at all, like I'd been shifted into some alternative universe where I was a "working girl," born to chew gum and wear cheap makeup and complain about my shift schedule to the night manager. Or until I could trick some mattress salesman into getting me pregnant and marrying me. Suddenly I was in one of those British working class movies I used to watch in my *Language of Film* course, where at the end the characters realize they are trapped by their lower class birth, doomed to an endless cycle of drudgery and obligation. And worst of all: they had no one to talk to but the Eric Lutzes of the world.

The bus came. To avoid further conversation with Mr. Lutz, I took a seat in the far back, near the back door, where I was treated to blasts of cold night air at every stop. My feet were wet, which didn't help, but in Portland your feet are always wet.

More people got on the bus which further insulated me from Eric Lutz, and eventually made me forget about him altogether. Yeah, to be out of college ... it was scary. It gave your life a special ring. Like you were really *in it* now, you were facing down the nothingness of human existence. Even when you were out partying with your friends, you'd feel this low-grade, underlying desperation. And all that stuff in college, all that history and literature you had pondered so leisurely, that was a distant dream. It was the bottom line that counted now. Get a job. Buy a car. Find a boyfriend. And then try to trade up in whatever way you could.

And the worst part: the way time changed. Suddenly, there were no semesters or winter breaks or summer vacations to stop and think and consider your next move. There was just the continuous flow of bills and paychecks and work schedules and rent ... and maybe a free Saturday here and there. Or a holiday. Like tonight. Valentine's Day.

2

KATE, my roommate, was standing outside the Nordstrom downtown, stamping her feet in the cold. She and I shared an apartment together just up the hill from downtown. She also worked at the mall. She was a hairdresser and a beautician and was made up in her professional way: precise eyeliner, pinkish lipstick, a suburban, pixie-ish haircut that one of her co-workers at Wild Cutz had talked her into.

The two of us headed right off, up the street toward The Deuce, our heads lowered in the mist, our shoes clicking along the wet sidewalk. In our trenchcoats and skirts, we could have been 60s London girls off to the pub, or maybe punk chicks in San Francisco, circa 1979. But I didn't say that to Kate. She wasn't smart in that way. She didn't think about history or different eras. We were just girls without boys, which we would drink over and complain to our friends about.

Everyone was at The Deuce: Gretchen and Christina from Macy's, Amber from Cinnabon, Rachel and Chelsea from PacSun. Several of the girls were dancing already and people had drinks. Our gang had claimed two of the booths in the back and the seats were strewn with wet coats and bags and hats and umbrellas. The "two drinks for the price of one" special was about to end, so we needed to order right away. I ordered two rum and Cokes, and when they came, took a long warming sip of the first.

Eventually, Kate and I wove our way onto the jammed dance floor to join the others. We bopped around as best we could. Gretchen drank while she danced, sipping through her stir straw as she slowly rotated her ass in a highly sexual manner. While I had been at college learning about economic determinism, these girls had been in bars learning how to make guys want to fuck them.

And it worked. Very quickly we were surrounded by boys. They tried to dance with us. They tried to buy us drinks. They screamed in our ears for the few seconds between songs. One of them got Rachel to follow him to the bar. Amber wandered off with two Portland State students. Kate and I danced with two boys who were somewhat cute, if you could overlook the one's gelled hair and the other's white jeans.

After a half hour on the dance floor, I retreated to our booth, only to be joined by the gelled hair guy. He'd bought me a drink, a Long Island iced tea, I guess in hopes of getting me plastered. I wouldn't drink it. I kept sliding it back across the table to him, saying, "You drink it." He asked me if I was sad on Valentine's Day, since I didn't have a boyfriend, which seemed like a weird thing to say to a girl. And then he wouldn't leave our booth. Which was a little creepy.

About that time, Amber came back for her coat. I grabbed her arm, hoping she would see my situation with Mr. Gelled Hair and not leave me alone. But she had no sympathy. She gave me a stern look of: *if you don't like him, get rid of him.* But I didn't know how to do that exactly.

Amber took off and I found myself stuck with my new friend. I tried ignoring him but that didn't work. I tried getting up to dance but he followed me. Finally I slipped into the bathroom and hid. That wasn't so great either. A girl was puking in one of the stalls while several other hard-faced Deuce girls stared me down in the mirror. So I snuck back out and peaked around the corner at our booth. Gelled Hair Guy was not visible so I made my move. I hurried forward, untangled my coat from the others and ran for it, ducking out the back door.

What a relief that was. Out of the sweaty heat and into the cool night air. But now I was standing in a dark parking lot by myself. I put on my coat, unsure what to do next. I felt conspicuous standing there, so I started walking, through the cars and out to the street.

The rain had stopped and there were people out, couples mostly, Valentine's dates. A pickup drove by and someone called out, "Hey baby!" which was then followed by a surprisingly sincere: "I love you!"

A few blocks later, a smaller car slowed down beside me. I immediately veered away but a voice said, "Andrea? ... Andrea Marr?"

I turned and looked and holy shit, it was Nick Pax! Nick Pax, local rock star from my high school days! I was so surprised I couldn't speak for a second. Then I laughed out loud. He was in one of those tiny Italian cars, with a friend driving. "What are you doing out here?" said Nick, hanging out the window. "Where are you going? Do you need a ride?"

I did. Of course I did. I hadn't seen Nick Pax in three years. I hadn't seen anyone like that since I'd landed back in Portland, I guess because I was embarrassed about getting kicked out of school. Or maybe because I thought my old "indie-rock Portland" friends might be a bad influence, and I couldn't afford to slip any lower in the social hierarchy.

But that was ridiculous I realized, the second I laid eyes on Nick's grinning face. Nick Pax! Oh my god, it felt so good to get inside that car!

Nick and his friend Matthew were heading to K Club where there was a big Valentine's Day party. Did I want to come? Yes, I did.

They asked me where I'd been and I told them I worked at the mall now, out in Beaverton, and that I'd been at The Deuce with some of my co-workers. Nick Pax couldn't believe I would go there. The Deuce? On Valentine's? That place was a meat market. It was horrible!

Then he asked me questions: When had I got back? Why was I here? The rumor he'd heard was that I'd moved back east and become an upper crust snob. I told him no, I'd failed at being a snob. And I'd been rejected by the upper crust.

We talked nonstop: about the music scene, who was still in town, where different people were, what they were doing. By the time we got to K Club, I was so happy. We went inside and it was packed with cool people. Why had I avoided this world? I was so hungry for it, I realized. My entire body sighed with relief.

Now I actually *wanted* to dance, and so I did, a big gang of us did, including some girls who I remembered from years before, who did double-takes when they saw me, like: *I remember you,* even though we hadn't actually been friends.

After that, I sat in the stairwell with Nick Pax and told him the long story of my career back east, making weird art movies in college, one of which got me expelled. And how freaked out my parents were, and how I'd come home in disgrace and then got a job at J. Crew and how I was supposedly going to transfer to University of Oregon in the fall, and try to get back on track, or at least that was my parents' plan. "The truth is, I hate working at the mall and I don't want to go to University of Oregon," I shouted in his ear, "I have no idea what I'm going to do." He nodded along to all of it. He was very encouraging and nice like he always was. Nick Pax. The *legendary* Nick Pax. When I was in high school, he was famous for writhing around on the floor during Pax shows or climbing onto the bar and hurling himself into the audience. But here he was, older now, and wiser, and a little worn in his face. He said Pax hadn't played in over a year. One of the guys had gotten married. Another had moved to San Francisco. He was a substitute teacher now, to pay the rent, though he still played some gigs with different bands around town. He said how great I looked and how he loved when Cybil and I and our little high school gang would show up at their gigs. The "HOP Girls," his band-mates had called us, because we bought our clothes at HOP Vintage downtown.

Nick tried to kiss me later. That was my own fault because I was being so nice to him and dancing with him and touching him a lot on the dance floor and by the bar. Also we were both kinda drunk. He and Matthew drove me home in Matthew's tiny car. It was three in the morning by then and Nick walked me to my door, and then went for the kiss and I kissed him back for a second, even though I could never see myself with Nick Pax, cute and fun as he was. He could tell I was hesitating and so he broke it off and said goodnight and slunk off with his hands in his back pockets in that cute boyish way he had.

Wow. Nick Pax! When I got into our apartment I plopped on a chair by the window and stared outside, with my trenchcoat still on, and my hair wet and my body tired but also so happy to have reconnected to the one part of Portland I could relate to. Could I be part of something here? It seemed like I could. I was supposedly trying to be a writer. I had written a novel in college. Were there other young writers in Portland? There probably were. But whatever. At least I'd had some fun for once. And I'd kissed Nick Pax!

3

THE NEXT MORNING I clocked in at J. Crew and checked myself in the mirror in the back room. You had to have a certain look at J. Crew. Not that there was an actual rule about it. It was just understood. *Look like your catalog* was the rule of working in the mall, which was why Elspeth at Hot Topic wore black lipstick and Rachel at PacSun wore surfer sandals in February.

It was slow that morning, so I did some re-folding to look busy. Then I vacuumed in the dressing rooms. I enjoyed these activities more than usual. I felt freer today, like I had other things going on, since I'd found Nick Pax. I would hang out with him more, I decided. I might even call him. I wondered if I would have anything to say to him in the light of day. But then I remembered that he was a substitute teacher, which gave me hope and made me feel like he was probably smarter than I thought.

At lunch, I got some noodles in the food court and talked to Amber and Rachel. The debauchery at The Deuce after I left, hadn't been too extreme. Nobody had been arrested. Nobody had sex without a condom. They had wondered where I went. I told them I'd run into some high school friends and got pulled away.

That afternoon, someone called the store and asked if we had any striped T-shirts. We did, and I asked what size and the person said they had to be *black and white* stripes because he was an artist, like Picasso. That was weird, but we did have black and white striped shirts and I asked what size and the person said they had to be *wide* black and white stripes because besides being an artist he was also a pirate. I was like, "oh-kay" and tried to act professional and then the person said, "Andrea, it's me, Nick."

He said he couldn't believe that I worked at J. Crew, I was one of the original HOP girls, who were the coolest! He threatened to come to the mall and rescue me, but I pleaded with him not to, the result being that I accepted his offer of a ride home from work. And an invitation to dinner.

So that's what happened. Nick Pax drove all the way to Beaverton and picked me up and took me all the way back downtown. We drove to the east side and ate burritos at his favorite Mexican place. Then some musician friends of his appeared and we got a pitcher of beer and we sat around talking and hanging out. It was funny how comfortable I felt and how instantly Nick and I became friends. It was like we'd known each other all those years between then and now. Like that time had counted somehow, and bonded us, even though we barely knew each other before.

That week, we went to more places. Nick knew the best spots for gyros or pizza or microbrew or donuts. He also knew everyone in Portland, which made each place we went to a social visit. Being with him I was suddenly seeing people I recognized, people who were around when I was in high school. I realized Portland was still here, cool Portland, and it had actually grown, it had exploded in some ways. Why had I been so bummed out to come back here? Portland wasn't so bad. Portland was pretty great.

The only problem came at the ends of these nights. Nick hadn't tried to kiss me again, but it was coming. Finally on Saturday we came out of a house party and he invited me to come over to his place but I said I couldn't, I had to work the next morning. So he kissed me in his car. Like before, I went along with it at first. But this time I kept going along with it. We started making out and things got pretty hot, pretty fast. It was totally different than making out with college guys. Nick Pax was a *rock star*, and the way he touched you and held you and took control, it sort of melted you. I was still determined not to have sex with him. But that didn't last. We did it right there, parked on the street, him on top of me in the back seat, tall and lanky Nick Pax.

When I got home, I was a mess, a happy mess, and Kate saw immediately what had happened and followed me into the bathroom where I peed and was drunk and I told her the whole story, including how Nick Pax was a local legend when I was in high school and now he was a substitute teacher. Could I like him? Could I go out with him? He was *twenty-eight years old!* I was barely twenty-one.

Kate was pretty impressed by all this. I had told her a little about my life as a teenager in the Portland music scene. She had listened but I don't think she understood. But now she was more interested than ever. Hot musicians taking you to cool parties, and then having amazing sex with you in their car? That sounded like the greatest thing ever. Kate was a hairdresser, after all.

· · ·

I went out with Nick Pax a couple nights later. We went to a movie and walked around downtown in the rain, and then ducked into a doorway and totally made out, like practically coming, rubbing against each other.

We went back to his group house and had sex in his room. Afterward we lay breathing side by side. I could hear someone talking on a phone somewhere and also the sound of the rain plinking on the windows outside. I looked at Nick's conked-out face, with its happy contented look, and the little wrinkles by his eyes and thought, oh my god, he's my lover! Like in the old school sense of the word. Like we're too different to actually go out, but we can't resist each other. Even laying there, I found myself wanting to touch him and feel him against my bare skin, which turned out to happen by itself without much effort.

This was the end of February, the depths of the gray wet Portland winter. My mom's birthday came and my parents and I went out to dinner at Shari's, which was a chain restaurant my mom liked, even though it was just a slightly better version of Denny's. Our waitress wore one of those frilly tops that showed off her cleavage. She was probably pretty sexy if you were a middle-aged guy with a bored wife and a couple of kids. My dad didn't notice her though. I did. She had orthopedic shoes for walking around all day. And a lot of makeup. And white tights like a nurse might wear. I wondered how old she was, and where she lived, and who she had sex with. Some mattress salesman I bet.

Anyway, so we talked, my parents and I, and they asked me how things were going, how was my job, how was Kate, who they had met and had liked. I told them about going to The Deuce on Valentine's and how lame it was and that I'd run into some guys I knew from the band Pax, which my parents didn't comment on. To them, my adventures with reckless artistic types had been my downfall. So I didn't go into it much more.

The rest of the dinner was pretty dull and even worse because for some reason it was my responsibility to make it fun. But I was feeling cranky and depressed and also hoping I could get home early enough to call Nick and have him come over for an hour before I went to bed. That was the other thing that was happening. I was staying up later. Not only to hang out with Nick, but also to do stuff with Kate and sometimes staying up to read or watch videos or write letters to my best friend from college, Sally Zimmerman. Sally had also worked on the student film that started all the trouble, which was about a freshman girl on ecstasy, and featured a freshman girl who really was on ecstasy. Sally Zimmerman would have been kicked out of Wellington too, but her father was a famous professor, so he made some calls and she was able to transfer to Yale in New Haven. Sally was extremely smart and cool and always had some new thing for me to check out, like the letters between Sartre and Simone de Beauvoir, or the erotica of Anais Nin or an article she had read about an anarchist collective in Oakland where everyone used the same bathwater because it helped strengthen your immune system. Sally's letters always made me feel connected to the larger world. That was the thing about Portland. You could have a great life there, and have friends and interesting things to do, but now that I'd gone to Wellington, and been to Boston and New York and DC, I knew Portland was just one place. There was so much other stuff. And I wanted to hear about it and know about it and not lose touch.

MATTHEW FERGUSON—THE guy who owned the tiny Italian car—was Nick's best friend. He had played bass briefly in a later incarnation of Pax and had also played in a bunch of different bands around town. He was sweet and goofy and he didn't talk very much, which probably made him a good band member, but also caused you to forget he was there sometimes.

For this reason, it didn't occur to me that he and Kate might like each other. Nick was the one who thought of that. It made perfect sense: Matthew had run out of local girls to go out with. And Kate had become very interested in the musician crowd. She was deeply impressed with Nick Pax and also with me, since I had snagged him. She would be thrilled to have a cool musician boyfriend.

So the four of us went bowling one night. Kate and Matthew seemed shy together, but in a good way. Kate was doing her "attraction cues" she had read about in *Glamour*, like touching her hair and laughing at Matthew's jokes and bumping into him a lot. It seemed to be working, as Matthew had the biggest grin on his face. Nick and I exchanged glances of: *this is totally going to happen.*

. . .

After bowling the four of us went back to Matthew's apartment which was basically one big room full of bass guitars and cords and amplifiers. There was also a small TV and a few items of thrift store furniture. Matthew immediately pulled out a huge plastic bong and everyone got stoned, me and Kate doing our best not to die of smoke inhalation. She and I took "baby hits." Nick sucked the whole two-foot cylinder of pot smoke right down like a vacuum. Matthew did too.

Then we settled in to watch *Risky Business* on a VCR on Matthew's tiny TV. Nick and I snuggled on a mattress on the floor while Matthew and Kate sat together under a blanket on the couch behind us. Kate was very stoned, despite mostly coughing her way through her bong hit. Her eyes were little red slits. I'm sure mine didn't look much better. Nick must have been stoned too, but you could never tell with him.

We watched the movie, Nick and I curled up under a smelly sleeping bag. Nick gave me a little back massage and then kissed my neck and eventually slid his hand sexily up and down my back. This seemed almost cruel though, since we couldn't really do anything and there wasn't any place to go.

I didn't notice Matthew and Kate at first. They were behind us and I was wrapped up in the sleeping bag, the back of my head cradled in Nick's armpit. But then I heard something. A slight gasp. I scooted myself around so I could discreetly take a peek. Kate and Matthew were totally making out. Also Kate's hand was under the blanket in the approximate area of Matthew's lap.

I glanced at Nick who had also noticed this. He grinned at me and then we both covered our heads with the sleeping bag and giggled to each other.

But I guess Nick felt inspired by Kate's boldness and a

moment later, I felt his fingers undo the top button of my jeans. A tingle of excitement passed through me and for a moment my desire totally overrode my modesty. He slowly pulled my zipper down and then with one firm push, sent his long musician fingers down my belly, under my panties and right to the spot. Wow. I felt a deep warmth spread through me and I gathered the sleeping bag and curled deeper under it, and also deeper into Nick, who slowly, gently began to move his finger around.

After that, things got pretty intense. Nick's fingers were completely intoxicating. And then I heard Kate moan. She tried not to, but the sound of her suppressing it made it even more sexy in a way. I was getting so excited. I peeked out again, and looked behind me, and now Kate was on top of Matthew, facing him and straddling him. They were totally having sex! Her T-shirt was still on and the blanket was still covering her ass, but it was totally obvious, especially when you saw Matthew's hairy legs, and his tangled jeans and boxers, bunched around his ankles.

I kind of couldn't believe it. But Nick seemed totally into it, and it was making him even more focused and erotic with his fingertips. Slowly, Nick began shifting us around until I was completely on my back, though still mostly covered by the sleeping bag. He rolled a condom onto himself and then we were doing it too, missionary style, on the mattress, while Kate continued to move up and down on Matthew's lap, not three feet away from us in the dark, blue-lit room. Every few minutes you would hear Tom Cruise say something, or the screech of tires, or some other movie sound. It was dreamy and sexy but also weird and sort of funny and definitely the most risqué thing I had ever done. I was already congratulating myself for it, and even telling Sally about it in my head. Oh my god, she would be so scandalized, I was practically having group sex!

This secretive, and then less secretive, grinding and moaning went on for several minutes, both couples wrapped up in our separate coverings. I was totally letting myself go with it. But then I opened my eyes for a second and saw Kate standing over me. She was off the couch and had come over to us. She was still wearing her tight baby tee but she was completely naked below that. She seemed to be in some sort of sex trance. But what was she doing? Why was she standing there?

She knelt down beside me on the mattress and watched us. We were pretty exposed by that point and I felt an urge to grab the sleeping bag and cover us up. Where was Matthew? He had apparently finished and was in some state of post-orgasm unconsciousness back on the couch. And now Kate was watching us, watching Nick especially, seemingly oblivious to the awkwardness, or maybe just totally high. It was a little disconcerting to say the least. Did she want to join in with us? And if she did what was I supposed to do?

But then Matthew came over. He was completely naked now and he came up behind Kate and started kissing the back of her neck and feeling her breasts through her shirt, from behind. She began moaning and lolling her head back, as he led her back to the couch.

When it was over, everyone was crashed out, naked and breathing, totally exposed and nobody really caring. Tom Cruise was still talking on the TV. I was still a little freaked out but I guess there was no reason to be. Nick was totally happy of course. As was Matthew. As was Kate.

The trip home, at one-thirty in the morning was one of the more interesting silent car rides I'd experienced, though by now I had got over whatever weirdness I had felt toward Kate. In fact she had apologized in Matthew's bathroom if she had done something wrong. I assured her she hadn't. She said she'd had a boyfriend in high school who liked stuff like that. Two couples together and switching around. That was a bit of a shock. She did that in *high school?* I had thought I was introducing her to the ways of the world. But maybe I didn't know as much as I thought.

5

AT SOME POINT in all these adventures I began to fall in love with Nick Pax. Which made me want to tell him things. One night we were driving around and I asked him about Todd Sparrow, my great teenaged love, and the one Portland musician who actually became sort of famous from the early days. Nick said the last he heard Todd was living in Minneapolis. I had heard that too. Nick said, "Those guys were gonna be huge." And I was like yeah, and sighed. Nick heard me and asked me if I knew Todd. It occurred to me that my legendary affair with Todd Sparrow was only legendary in my own mind and maybe with a few of my friends at the time but not with the world at large. I didn't want to sound like a groupie, so I just said I'd had a big crush on him, like everybody else. Nick asked if I had done anything about it, and I didn't answer at first. But he got curious and started asking me more. So I told him the truth, how Todd and I had hung out and had sex a couple times but it wasn't really like that, it was more of a friendship, and how we would talk for hours and how sometimes in certain situations I would get anxious and he would say, "It's all right Andrea, everything is all right ... "

Nick was quite surprised. He had not known about this. He had not known Todd well. Their bands had been competitive with each other, so there was not much communication between them. Nick said how jealous he had been when Todd's band Color Green appeared on MTV's *120 Minutes*. He cried himself to sleep that night. It was the first moment he realized that Pax had become as big as they would ever be. And that they were not going to make it to the next level.

I leaned over and touched his arm when he said that. And then I undid my seat belt and crawled over and kissed him on his stubbly face and stroked his hair and rubbed his neck and almost told him I loved him. But that seemed risky so I didn't say it and eventually I went back to my own seat and buckled my seat belt again. But I wanted him to know I understood. Mainly, because I felt the same way. Even at my age, it seemed like other people were already doing big things and having big successes while I just worked my stupid retail job and didn't do much of anything.

It was after that conversation that I decided I had to start writing again. I bought a new notebook and wrote a journal entry about my relationship with Nick. It didn't go very well. I tried to write about the sex stuff. I wrote a whole page describing the night at Matthew's apartment. But I was too bashful to really describe it. I kept trying though. It seemed like sex scenes were something I'd have to get comfortable with, if I was ever going to write another novel.

That plan had been on the back burner for a while. I had written a novel in college which I still thought about some-times. I couldn't imagine doing that again. Not now, with my busy Portland life. Still, every time I got a letter from Sally Zimmerman, or wrote to her, I felt this weight hanging over me.

Sally had read my novel and liked it and always encouraged me to keep writing. It probably made her sad to think I'd gone home to Portland and stopped doing anything. It was like in that R.E.M. song:

Don't go back to Rockville
And waste another year

6

ANYWAY, so more time passed and Nick and I hung out. Sometimes with Kate and Matt, other times just the two of us. Then one night, I came home and I noticed a note on the kitchen table in Kate's girly scrawl: "Message for you on the answering machine!!!" I looked over at the blinking red light and felt an unusual excitement in my stomach. Which didn't make sense, since who could it be? It wasn't Nick, I'd just left him.

I hung my coat up. I kicked off my wet shoes. I stood over the answering machine for a moment and felt another strange pang of anticipation. I hit the play button. There was an old message from my mom. I skipped it. Another old message for Kate. I skipped that. Then a third message came on, a new one. I didn't recognize the voice. "Hello Andrea, this is Will Soren calling. I'm an agent here at the Ruth Goldman Literary Agency in New York. Your manuscript *Manifesto* was passed on to me. I would like to talk to you about it. Can you call me tomorrow? My number here is 212 ... "

The message ended. The machine beeped. I felt around for the chair behind me and lowered myself into it. I glanced around the room, my eyes quickly returning to the answering machine. I pushed the button again. "Hello Andrea, this is Will Soren calling. I'm an agent here at the Ruth Goldman Literary Agency ... "

I felt this *brimming* feeling. Like I was going to overflow. I felt a deep alteration in the universe. But I did nothing. I sat.

The message ended. The machine beeped. The house went silent. My eyes moved across the room again, bouncing from object to object. I reached over and pushed the button again. "Hello Andrea, this is Will Soren calling ... "

Manifesto was the novel I'd written in college. It was a love story about a suburban punk rock kid and an environmentalist barista. I had worked on it off and on during my sophomore and junior year. I'd given a copy of it to Sally, and a few other copies to friends, but most importantly, I now realized, I had given a copy to my writing teacher, Professor Greeley, at Wellington. He'd published two novels himself. Was that how it got to a literary agent? It must have been.

I resisted pushing the play button again. I sat. I stood up. I sat. Then I was seized by an unstoppable urge to call my friend Sally, in New Haven. I grabbed the phone but it was past midnight, west coast time, which meant three in the morning back east. No. I would have to wait until the morning.

I hung up the phone. I realized I was breathing funny. Then from behind me, I heard Kate's whispery voice. I turned and there she was, sleepy-headed, in her pink flannel pajamas. "You heard the message?" she said, touching her lips in the darkness of the hallway.

I nodded that I did.

"Is that good news?"

I nodded that it was. She grinned sleepily, skipped forward

and gave me a big hug. "Why didn't you tell me you wrote a book!?" she asked.

But even as she congratulated me and gushed over me and wanted to make hot chocolate to celebrate, I felt a sense of separation. What was going to happen if I got a real literary agent? Suddenly the life I had started here in Portland seemed unreal, pointless, a momentary distraction. My real life wasn't here at all. It was somewhere else.

I called Sally first thing when I woke up. But she wasn't home. So then I called my mother at work but she was away from her desk. So then I called Nick but he was substitute teaching. So I would have to call Will Soren with no preparation, no advice or support. And I had to do it now, or I'd be late for work.

I dialed the New York number. A receptionist answered. Her phone voice was incredibly polished and professional. She sounded like a talk show host, or like a person who narrates TV commercials. "Who may I say is calling," she asked. I told her. A moment later a new, equally rich and resonant voice addressed me. It was Will Soren.

He instantly took charge of the conversation. How was I? I was fine. Where was I? I was in Portland. Didn't I go to Wellington? No, I didn't go there anymore, I was in Portland now.

Will Soren got to the point. He enjoyed *Manifesto*. Had I sent it to any other agents? I said no. That seemed to make him very happy. He felt there was something fresh about the style and the outlook. "I feel like you're one of these young people. That you're speaking for them ... "

I didn't hear anything too clearly after that. He said something about the book's structure, and some problem with the ending. But by then I was in a daze. I had left my body. I also felt afraid. Will Soren's voice was not only resonant, it also possessed a tone of utter superiority. He sounded like an actor. Or an aristocrat. Was this really his normal talking voice? And how was I supposed to talk back?

But even as I could barely believe I was having this conversation, in another way, I felt a rising confidence. *Manifesto* was good. It was funny. Other people had read it and genuinely liked it. Sally had laughed out loud. And so in that way, this was not a huge surprise. You write a good book and someone wants to represent it. So what's the problem? There was no problem. So why did I feel like I was going to be sick, or that I was going to squirm out of my seat, or that I might pass out?

I didn't remember hanging up. I assumed I said the right things. Suddenly the call was over and Will Soren was gone and I was sitting alone in my empty house. One thing I did retain from the conversation: Will Soren would send me editorial notes, and I would do a re-write. I had agreed to that. I thought. I wasn't sure what I'd agreed to. I had a moment of deep fear and panic.

Then I totally lost my shit. I sprang to my feet, knocking the chair down behind me. I jumped in the air and began to bounce around my living room. *Oh my god oh my god oh my god,* I chanted under my breath. *Oh shit oh shit oh shit.* My hair bounced in my face. I hopped back to the phone and tried Sally again and by some miracle she picked up. I flung myself on the floor and gasped and cried into the phone: "Oh Sally, thank god!"

"What!? What is it!?" she said

I told her what it was.

7

"THE CALL," as I came to think of it, would be a test of things with Nick. I had no idea how he would react, or even how I would feel telling him. Of course "The Call" was good news. It was great news. But it was also news that might change my life. Like my transferring to University of Oregon, which my parents were so convinced would save me and turn me into a normal person again. Suddenly that didn't seem like a good idea at all. What if my book got published? I wouldn't want to be stuck on a boring campus in Oregon during that.

Nick called me at work the next day and I told him I had some good news and made it into an "I'm not going to tell you now, but be prepared to celebrate" scenario. But that seemed weird so I just told him. Nick was shocked at first. He had forgotten that I wrote a novel, since I only told him once. But then he was super happy for me. He asked what that meant exactly but I couldn't talk to him about it from J. Crew.

He came and picked me up after work and we went to his favorite bar to celebrate. But it was awkward in a way. He bought a big pitcher of fancy microbrew and made a big deal about it and started to tell the bartender but I nudged him to stop and later told him, it wasn't for sure, none of it was for sure, the agent was just interested, I had to do a rewrite of the manuscript, and work on it and *maybe* then something would happen. So then we sat and drank beer in an uncomfortable silence.

The other thing I was worried about: I didn't want Nick to feel like here was another situation where he had worked his whole life on his band and his music and some young kid comes along and takes off with their career. That's what happened to him with Todd Sparrow. Nick's band was good, but Todd's band was better and it was Todd who ended up on MTV's *120 Minutes*, not Nick. It must have been hard for him to have that keep happening. It would be hard for anybody.

Later we drove around, and then he started asking me about it. That was when everything felt good again. I told him the story of my writing career, writing in my journals and writing my first short stories at the Winchell's Donuts by my parents' house. And then the annoying creative writing class I took at Wellington, but how that one Wellington professor had liked *Manifesto*, which was how the whole thing happened.

Nick listened to this very carefully. He was very impressed. He nodded and said, "You guys always seemed like that. You and Cybil and the HOP girls, like you would do big things someday."

"I haven't done anything yet," I said, but that was false modesty and wasn't true, since I had written an entire novel, which did take almost two years of my life.

That night when we had sex it was slow and intense and a little sad in a way, but also super close. Afterward while we lay in the dark, I held Nick close to me and breathed him in and thought about how great he was but how hard things could be, especially at this stage of our lives when everything could change in an instant, and everyone was finding out the truth about themselves. Were you talented? Were you lucky? Were you destined to make it big?

Or were you destined to be a substitute teacher?

I started calling Sally. I couldn't really afford the long distance charges and I wanted to go back to writing her letters again, because someday it would be fun if this was written down somewhere, how excited we were and our funny ideas of what we thought would happen if I got a real agent. But for now I didn't have the patience to write letters. I was going crazy wondering what Will Soren's letter was going to say, and what sort of changes he would suggest. Also, I suddenly had all this new energy and confidence. Like I felt so excited some days I could barely contain myself and I'd sneak away from J. Crew, or lock myself in the bathroom, or go for long walks around the mall when I was supposed to be eating lunch.

Sally was the best person to talk to. She knew a lot about publishing. Her dad was a professor and had written a best-selling book called *Doing It* in graduate school about how different societies deal with sex and courtship rituals and marriage. It was written in this humorous, easy-going style and he became an academic celebrity. So I would ask her questions and she would talk to her dad and he would have little tidbits of wisdom, like how the publication of a book was "a process" and not like winning a race. It was a series of stages and steps and the developing of something over time.

But mostly I would lie on the floor and daydream with Sally about what it would be like to be famous. I would never say it like that, I was pretty humble actually, compared to how some people might have been. But I couldn't help it sometimes. Sally told me about this new French writer, Sylvie Dussault, and her novel *Memories of Love*. She was twenty when she wrote it and it was about the affair she had with her poetry teacher when she was in high school. It was very French and intellectual and full of sex. It was a big hit in Europe and all the Yalies were reading it and it was on the cover of *The New York Times Book Review*. Sally and some friends even rode the train down to New York to see her speak. Sally said Sylvie Dussault was very small and her left eye wandered to the side like Sartre. "That's probably half the reason for her fame," said Sally. We both wondered if maybe I could be like her, or maybe I was too normal and needed something distinctive, like a weird eye.

Sometimes I would force myself to write Sally letters which was another way to daydream about what I should be like as a writer. Like what my actual persona would be (though I had no idea) and how maybe I needed to change my book because it wasn't very sophisticated or sexy and also, would it hurt me if *Manifesto* was my first published novel because wouldn't my later books be a lot better and not so obvious and not so suburban? And then I'd go through my own copy of *Manifesto*, reading through it and copying passages into my letters and asking Sally what she thought, but I suspected I was being annoying so I stopped. Sally even told me not to look at it. Her dad agreed. He recommended sitting tight and working on something else while I waited for Will Soren's comments. That was the only way to not go insane.

About a week after "The Call," I went home to my parents' to see my older brother James and his wife Emily who were visiting from Seattle. Baby Marcus was running around like a banshee. He was four years old now and was constantly breaking everything or throwing things or taking all the pots out of the cupboards so you would trip over them.

We had dinner in the main room and I guess my parents hadn't told James about "The Call" yet. When it came up he was so amazed. He immediately thought the book would be published and that I would become a celebrity. So then I had to explain that no, it meant it *might* get published someday in the future. But that it was good to have an agent interested, especially this agent, who I had looked up at the library and seemed to be well respected in literary circles.

But then during dessert, Emily got pissy. She never liked me, so that was nothing new but now she seemed even more perturbed, since her main complaint with me had always been that I was spoiled and indulged and irresponsible, especially after I got kicked out of Wellington. Now her attitude was: why does Andrea get everything? Why doesn't James get some success? But of course James never had success because he was married to cranky Emily who always told him what a loser he was.

But James liked it when Emily was unhappy so he kept getting another beer and toasting me and making a big deal about "his famous sister" and how much money I would make. He had the best time of all of us.

8

THEN ONE DAY Nick called and said a band he knew had lost their bass player. He'd broken his arm skateboarding. The other guys wanted Nick to fill in and go on tour with them for a couple weeks.

I got the feeling Nick was asking me if he should go, almost like asking permission since I was his girlfriend. I felt like I should say, "Yes, go" and not be clingy, though of course I would miss him terribly if he'd be away for several weeks. Especially now that I had my own exciting news.

He decided to go. The band was called the Kleptos and their first CD was getting a lot of play on college radio so they were playing all over the country. I took Nick to the airport, with his bass and a backpack of clothes. It was almost like we were a married couple, me making sure he had toothpaste and guitar picks and extra socks. And him promising to call, which he did, from Denver and Omaha and Des Moines. He'd tell me about the annoying lead singer or how cold/hot it was in the van, or how bored he was, and how he wished he were home watching videos with me and teaching third graders their times tables.

When the Kleptos played in Seattle, Matthew and Kate and I drove up to see them. We arrived a few hours before the show and whisked Nick away for some Indian food. He was so happy to see us. He was like, "I'm too old for this," and told us funny stories about how idiotic the audiences were and how the Klepto crew thought it was the funniest thing to piss out the window of the moving van, or piss out the window of the hotel, or piss out the window of the dressing room, etc.

That was the first time I'd seen the Kleptos and I had to admit they were pretty good and pretty polished. But they were no way as good as Pax, and not nearly as original. They were cheesy in a crowd-pleasing way. This made me feel sorry for Nick, that the Kleptos were actually selling lots of records and getting big crowds. But Nick seemed okay with it. He was having fun and making some money. And the thing about him was, he was a true musician. Watching him made you think of the middle ages and roving troubadours traveling from village to village playing songs on their lutes or whatever and doing it their whole lives, like literally until they dropped dead. That was Nick. Everything from his long hair, to his skinny body, to his long fingers. He was born to be on the road, sunglasses perched on his head, dirty Keds on his feet, on to the next town, the next show, night after night.

When I got home from Seattle, Will Soren's letter still hadn't come. So I kept hanging out with Kate and Matthew. Like Nick, Matthew knew everyone in Portland, so he always knew what was happening and where the best parties were. I continued to see Portland scene people I remembered from high school. Like Pauline, who was a famous femme fatale in the old days, and lived in a punk house and was a heroin addict. Now she ate raw foods and meditated and took photographs of puddles and old people, none of which were very good but at least she wasn't dead.

One night, Matthew and Kate and I went to this new martini lounge everyone was talking about. We sat on these low stools and got drinks and Matthew went off to talk to someone. That's when I saw this group of musician-type people sitting around a low table across the room. They didn't look like Portlanders, they had a different vibe about them that I couldn't identify. One of the girls had a red track jacket on with the collar zipped up over her chin. Another girl was tall and looked like a model. A guy with his back to us had dyed blonde hair, cut short in an English Mod style. I asked Kate who she thought they were and where they were from, but she didn't have a feel for stuff like that. I thought L.A., since the girls were so pretty. Or maybe Boston, since they had a big Mod scene. When Matthew came back, I asked him and he agreed with me, they were definitely not from around here. He thought maybe Chicago, since one of the guys wore an army jacket. He could tell they were important. They had to be a band or artists or something. But before we could think of an excuse to talk to them, they disappeared into the back somewhere.

The next morning I was having breakfast and the mailman came. I immediately threw on my raincoat and ran outside in my bare feet to check for my editorial letter from Will Soren. No luck. The older guy who lived across the street waved at me from his yard and I realized what young hipster girls we must seem to him, coming in and out at all hours, hanging out with scraggily musician boys, and now me with my bed head and my bare legs and bare feet standing in the wet road at ten-thirty in the morning.

I went back inside. One thing that Sally's dad said was that he always worked on something new while he waited to hear about a book or a project. So I got out my new notebook and tried writing a little bit, some character sketches at first and then a journal entry, but none of it was very interesting.

So then I decided I was going to force myself to write a story. It didn't have to be good. It didn't have to be long. But it had to be a real fictional short story, like in *The Best American Short Stories*, which my mother had bought me last Christmas, since I wanted to be a writer.

Nick was still gone, so I didn't have any distractions. I got home from work the next day and gathered my stuff and walked downtown to my favorite café.

I started my story. I started with a local musician guy, and had him meet a local girl who had been away at college. But it was too close to reality and got bogged down almost instantly. I tried another story about a bass player who meets someone at a party and they go home and have sex but then can't talk to each other for some reason. That went nowhere too. I tried some other things but nothing worked. Finally, I gave up and turned over another page and wrote "Dear Sally," and started writing about Will Soren's letter not coming and Nick going away and the other problems of my life. I had no problem writing about that, and got so deep into my various complaints, I didn't notice that some other people had come into the café. When I went to get a coffee refill, I spotted that same group of people from the lounge, the beautiful model girl and the guy with the army jacket. They were talking and eating sandwiches and drinking tea. I tried to listen to them, to hear if they had accents but they didn't seem to.

I went back to my seat and looked at my notebook. I had written three pages of my letter, which was a lot. And then as I read back through it, I felt an unexpected stirring inside me. I realized someone was standing beside my table. It was one of the lounge people. I saw his feet first, and then my eyes traveled up his pants and up his sweater and then all the way to his dyed blonde hair. That's when my heart nearly dropped out of my body.

"Andrea?" he said, in that familiar voice.

"Todd?" I said back.

9

TODD SPARROW WAS FAMOUS, of course. But he hadn't always been. He wasn't when I first met him six years ago, standing outside the Central Library with an old electric guitar in a shopping bag. But everyone knew he would be. Or they should have. I did.

Because he was such an obvious star, any relationships he had in those days, were always seen as temporary. *Soon he will be famous and we will all be forgotten*, was the prevailing attitude among most local people, both guys and girls. Some people hated him instantly but even that was a form of acknowledgement of his eventual rise to bigger and better things.

For that reason, despite our little romance/friendship, I never claimed any special connection to Todd. When he moved to Seattle, I never claimed he'd been my boyfriend, even though some of my friends would say that, and insist on it, saying: "You guys were together!" And I'd be like, "No we weren't." And they'd be like, "Andrea, Todd really liked you!" And I'd always say: "He liked a lot of people."

But the truth was, I did think something had happened between us. I didn't even have to think it, I knew it. We had amazing times together. And the best part of it was the talking. We could talk forever. We could talk for days. And we did. And even if it was nothing I would lay claim to later, when he was in *Spin* or on MTV, I knew how much we had connected. For a brief period of my life Todd Sparrow had been my best friend.

And now here I was, with no warning or preparation, suddenly facing my moment of truth. Had Todd Sparrow really cared about me? Had I made any impact on him at all? I had no idea.

He stared down at me. A slow, knowing smile crept onto his face. He looked older, and different in a way, but still good. In fact, he was better looking than he had been, as if his success had altered his face into its best possible shape.

Thank God I'd worn a skirt to the café. And had my cute sweater with lightening bolts on it that Nick had found in a thrift store in Indianapolis and brought all the way to Seattle to give me.

Finally, Todd spoke. He asked me what I was doing in Portland, he thought I'd gone back east. I said I'd been kicked out of college. I had moved back home.

He nodded.

I asked what he was doing. He was recording. He was working on a project with a singer named Edith Monroe. They were working at Bedtime Studios down the street.

I was like, "Oh."

Then we just stared at each other. But there was all this tension. There was all this unspoken stuff going on.

His friends began to leave. Todd said he had to leave too, but would I walk to the burrito place down the street with him?

I packed up my stuff without a word, my hands shaking and my insides churning and my brain pretty much turning to mush. But I was definitely going. The sudden feeling I had of not wanting to let Todd out of my sight was so strong it was scary. There was no way he was leaving that café without me, no way in the world.

It was dark outside and we walked down the wet sidewalk under the streetlights. What did we look like, I wondered? Like a classic indie rock CD cover: me in my trendy skirt and my grey raincoat and my tights, and him with his suit jacket, with the collar up and his Mod haircut. But what a relief it was to be with him. I felt like I'd been holding my breath for half my life and now I could finally breath again.

We were both so nervous and excited we walked too fast and we both realized it at the same time and we laughed and slowed down and we still hadn't said anything. We were both paralyzed I guess, at least in terms of talking.

He finally said how whenever he was in Portland he thought of me and wondered if he might see me, though he always assumed he wouldn't since I'd gone back east. He figured he'd never see me again. I answered, "I know" to everything he said. It made for an awkward conversation and we eventually shut up again, since neither of us was making much sense.

We walked into the burrito place and the girl behind the counter brightened at the sight of Todd. All the burrito people did.

I was still trying to catch my breath and my heart was pounding and someone said something to me and I shook my head no, not knowing what they were saying. Todd asked me if I was okay and I said I was. "Do you want something?"

someone asked me again and I couldn't speak and I shook my head no.

I sat down at a table while Todd ordered his burrito to go. He came and sat too, but then we lapsed into silence again, both of us looking away and not knowing what to do. Finally, our eyes came together and he stared at me with this intense look in his eyes. It was almost like it was hurting him to see me. And maybe I looked like that too because I felt this surge of sadness pass between us. He said, "You look older." I said he looked older too.

Someone called out "Todd!" His burrito was ready. We stood up and he took it from the girl at the counter and we went outside. He had to go back to the studio. I wanted to walk there with him. Of course I did. I wanted to handcuff myself to him but I knew I should probably go, I needed to get away and try to regroup and figure out how to talk and what exactly I wanted to say. So we said goodbye on the sidewalk, outside the burrito place. For some reason, I blurted out: "Nick and I hang out now … " And he was like "Oh yeah?" and then I couldn't say anything else. He seemed baffled by this and everything else and he said, "Okay, I'll see you," and he walked away and I walked away too. I forced myself to not look back.

A block away, I went into a convenience store and went to the back of it, by the candy, and I started to cry and shake and tremble all over. Because, oh my god, I had loved Todd Sparrow so much when I was young. And now we were older and we had changed and gone our separate ways, *but I still loved him just as much*. It had never stopped. My love for Todd Sparrow had never stopped.

10

MATTHEW AND KATE and I went out the next night. I spent an hour getting dressed. Portland was not very big. If Todd was out, we would most likely see him.

We went to Bradley's, a new place where bands played, and then drove over to K Club and then went to some other places. I told Kate about the situation, and Matthew too, but I made it sound like more of a fan thing, so Nick wouldn't get jealous. I said I knew Todd back in high school but had frozen up when I saw him at the café. I was looking for him, to hopefully redeem myself from that, and also because I wanted to catch up and have a real conversation.

As the night wore on though, Kate could tell something was up. In the bathroom she was like, "You're in love with Todd aren't you?" And I had to admit I was. The rest of the night was so painful. Like every place we went, I was like, "Is he here?" and if he wasn't, I felt hopeless and bored and had no interest in anything.

We never found him and then we went to shoot pool at this dive bar and some local guys came in who knew about the Edith Monroe project. All the Portland music people knew about it, since Edith was this singer from Los Angeles who everyone hated for being an L.A. model type or whatever. I didn't say anything about knowing Todd to them, and they dismissed the whole situation, and made fun of Todd and Color Green as being "so five years ago."

The next day at work, I looked up Bedtime Studios in the phone book and found the address. When I rode the bus home that night, I got off nearby and innocently walked past. It was a gray, windowless building on a quiet industrial street, surrounded by warehouses. You couldn't even tell if anyone was inside it.

So then I went home and by now, I had calmed down, and I called Sally to ask her if I should do anything about Will Soren because his editorial comments had still not arrived. She said not to worry, that wasn't unusual. And so then I told her about Todd and seeing him and I cried a little. She didn't know much about him, but she could hear how devastated I was, and she talked to me deep into the night, which was three hours deeper where she was, back on the east coast.

That weekend Matthew and Kate and I went out again and this time we found Todd. He was at that same lounge place. He was there with those same studio people, including the tall beautiful girl who was probably Edith Monroe. I was totally freaking out from the moment we got there. I wanted to run away but I wouldn't let myself.

Matthew fortunately knew one of the guys from Bedtime Studios and that gave us an excuse to join them. So the three of us went over to their table and jammed ourselves into their party. Todd was talking to Edith intensely and didn't even see us and then when he did, I was stuck far away at the other end of the group. Todd stared at me for a second. I stared back and smiled and drank my microbrew too fast, since I was so nervous.

What a weird night. So nothing happened and we sat there and I talked to Kate while Matthew talked to his musician friend and Todd talked to Edith. Then me and Kate went to the bar so I wouldn't have to sit there feeling stupid anymore.

At the bar I was thinking we should leave but then Todd came over. Kate immediately disappeared and Todd stood there for a while and then asked if I wanted to go for a walk.

I got my coat and we went outside. It was wet and drizzling and we walked down the street and it was strange but not as bad as at the burrito place. And now, even though I was glad to be with him, and glad to know him, I also felt a certain distance. Like our lives were totally different and we'd grown apart and it was okay if we couldn't be friends anymore. He had been super nice and super happy to see me, and I felt the same way and if we didn't have anything else to say to each other, that was okay, it was just what happens sometimes in life.

But then he started talking. He told me about Edith. Where she grew up and what she was like and how she had an evil showbiz mom who made her do baby food commercials when she was one year old. Edith had escaped by moving to Montana and living in a trailer with her dad who drove race cars and eventually killed himself. He said how interesting she was even though everyone slagged her and thought she was an L.A. sell out. His record company guy had suggested Todd produce her new album. Todd had never done that, worked for hire on someone else's record. He didn't know if it was the right thing for him. Color Green would be recording a new album in the summer, that was his real gig. But he believed in Edith and loved her lyrics and wanted to help her.

I was so glad he was talking about this stuff. He totally relaxed. And then I totally relaxed. It was cold though, so we went into the lobby of the Benson Hotel, which I wouldn't have thought to do, but Todd knew about that from touring. You can sit in hotel lobbies any time you want. So we went inside and sat on a couch by a fire and he looked kind of tired now, but also relaxed and happy to have someone to talk to, and who understood, and I guess that was me.

Then I told him I wrote a novel. He was like, what? He was so impressed. And so excited for me. He was like, "What's it about?" So I told him about the suburban punk boy, who was kind of a jerk and pretty conservative, and the eco-barista girl who was totally earnest and a do-gooder. He thought it sounded great. He totally wanted to read it. And I told him about the agent and he couldn't believe it. He was like, "Does that normally happen to someone so young?" and I shrugged and said I didn't know. It hadn't actually happened yet. I was waiting for the letter.

So then he was totally into me again and was so excited. He sat there thinking about it, me as a writer, as a published writer, as a famous writer, and he smiled so big and laughed to himself. He said: "Of course you became a writer. You were always watching people!"

Then he scooted closer to me and pulled me toward him and stuck his face in my hair and said: "Sorry, I just wanted to smell you again." And I was like, "You can smell me if you want," and so he did, burying his face in my hair again, and then in my neck. It was a little awkward sitting in the hotel lobby. Then he stopped and sat back on the couch and smiled and gazed into the fire.

11

TODD WAS STAYING in a small rented house off Burnside. We took a cab there. We didn't talk, I didn't want to talk, I wanted to feel myself, and the electricity flowing through me and the importance of what was happening. It was too much in a way, I couldn't process it, so I didn't even try. I just stared out the taxi window at the wet streets of Portland and the occasional people on the street, or on their bikes, or walking in their rain ponchos.

The cab pulled over and we ran through the rain up the steps to his house. Todd found his keys and I felt calm suddenly as he hunched over to put the key in the lock. We got the door open and went inside and it was cold and dark. Todd apologized because he'd just moved from a hotel to this house and didn't have anything to drink or any food. He found one old beer in the back of the refrigerator and poured us both a little bit in coffee mugs.

He figured out how to turn the heat up and we stood there, in the small kitchen, cold but excited and I smiled up at him and took a tiny sip of the beer. Todd stood there for a long time, both of us did, enjoying what it felt like to be with each other.

Then he put down his mug and moved toward me and slipped his arms inside my open coat. At first he just held me, and we rocked together and he rested his chin on the top of my head. I let my face slide down sideways onto his sweater and I breathed him and felt him and felt the solidness of his arms and his shoulders and the taut muscles of his back as I gradually slipped my hands further around him.

When he kissed me, it was warm and milky and familiar: the way his lips moved and what he did with his tongue and the smell of his face and his breath. And the meaning of it, the meaning of Todd Sparrow liking me and wanting me and kissing me and the fact that all this time this had been here, waiting for me, and how different this made things, how I would talk to people differently after this, how it meant that I really was someone, not the someone I already was, but something else too, a person who Todd Sparrow cared about and had never forgotten and wanted now, again, after all these years. And the main thing was: I had been right. I had suspected this love was real, and it was. It also meant that I wasn't a mediocre person who daydreamed all this. It was real, my life was real, and my life was so much bigger than I ever let myself realize ...

We went into the bedroom. You could see he'd just moved in, his bags were on the floor unopened. It was cold and he started to unbutton my shirt but we were both shivering. He said we should probably take off our clothes and get under the covers, so we did. I stripped down to my panties and bra and he did the same, to his boxers and T-shirt. The bed was nice and big, a married couple's bed, I learned later. We got into it, on opposite sides and for a moment we didn't touch. I shivered all over and he did too and then I moved my foot over until it touched his shin and he put his foot over toward me, against my bare leg, which I shaved because I worked at ridiculous J.

Crew, but I was glad because it was smooth and it felt good against the hairs of his leg. Then his cold hands found me and pulled me close and began to lightly caress my shoulder and chest. We both sighed.

Later, he rolled his weight onto me and now the urgency was there and the pressing need of it. We both let it happen, letting the craving of it push us forward, each nerve or zone being activated. And then the murmuring, the sounds of my voice and his voice and the slightness of it, the airy heat of his breath on my neck and my chest and my shoulders. Our faces found each other again, and our lips touched and everything was opening and coming together. And then later, the main part, the machine part, the repetition and the gradual glow of pleasure that grew and spread out and slowly erased everything else from consciousness ...

I woke up at some point, late in the night, in that special darkness of a Portland night, as if you were under a thousand layers of mist and rain and moss and earth. I felt my way, naked, to the bathroom and found the light switch which blazed mercilessly through my eyeballs and brain and forced me to blindly reach around for the toilet seat and fold it down and sit. I leaned forward, my torso over my bare thighs and very nearly fell back asleep as the pee gently, effortlessly flowed out of my body.

Only then, half asleep on the toilet did a creeping feeling of dread come over me. It began to form above me and gradually gained weight and depth so that I found it a great effort to lift my head and wipe myself and stand up. It was Nick Pax who was there in that bathroom. Not so much his physical image, it was more his voice, the casual innocence of it, the calm "whatever" vibe, the easy, non-judgmental, non-committal, weightlessness of it. That quality was why he was Nick Pax, substitute teacher and fill-in bass player. It was also why I'd ended up here, naked, in a different man's bed.

Nick Pax had been fucked over again. Just like always.

I guiltily flicked the bathroom light off. In the dark, I fumbled my way back to the tangle of blankets and musky maleness and burrowed my way back into the warmth. Now though, I couldn't sleep and lay there in the oppressive blackness, alone with myself and the sleeping, breathing body of a person I seemed to believe was going to change my whole life, change everything about me. Why did I think that? I knew it wasn't true.

And later, with the first traces of light outside, I found myself not so willing when Todd awoke and pressed himself against me again. But I was persuaded, of course, and I let him grow and touch me and penetrate me again and satisfy himself, this time the physical release being the most pressing need, nothing to communicate now, the act simply repeating itself like it does, until its not terribly mysterious purpose has been fulfilled.

12

THERE WAS a message from Nick when I got home from work the next day. He was in Texas somewhere, calling from a hotel, a few hours before a gig. I called him back thinking I'd probably missed him but Nick answered right away.

It had been a few days since we'd talked and he sounded cheerful and happy to hear my voice. He launched into a story about the show the night before, there'd been a problem with the sleazy Houston promoters, and then a wild party at an abandoned gas station. I listened to his voice as he talked, I could picture him there, lanky Nick Pax, sitting on a cheap hotel bed, his trusty bass lying beside him. He sounded younger than me as he talked. And not very smart. And naïve.

After a while I said, "There's something I have to tell you." From then on, he remained silent while I explained as clearly and simply as I could what had happened. I told him everything. He asked if Todd and I were together now and I said I didn't know but repeated what I had started with, which was that Todd had been a huge person in my life and I felt a closeness with him that was different than any guy I'd ever known. And then, before I was quite done explaining, when I'd just gotten warmed up with my justifications and rationalizations, Nick said with sudden authority that the van was there and he had to go. He hung up. And that was that.

The mall was quiet and empty the next morning, almost church-like. At J. Crew, there were no customers and nothing to do, so I swept up in the back room and folded sweaters that had been folded a hundred times.

After work, I went to the bus shelter and rode the 57 back downtown to our apartment. I got off but didn't go home, and instead walked around, my head empty, my chest feeling heavy and awful. I told myself that I had done what people do all the time. I had changed romantic loyalties based on the fact that I loved Todd in a deep way, and I only liked Nick. And also because Todd was cooler than Nick and affected me in a way that Nick did not. And, if I was totally honest: because Todd was such a *star* and Nick was so not. Switching boyfriends in this way was what girls did. They did it all the time. You were supposed to do it, people expected you to. Now I had done it and life would continue and everyone would heal eventually, except that Nick would be even more beaten down and Todd would be even more legendary. And I, the girl, the prize, had ended up with the more "successful" male, the world being endlessly cruel like that. But of course I would get my comeuppance, and would eventually lose Todd to some new girl who was cuter than me, or cooler, or both, which was another way in which the world was endlessly cruel.

I went out drinking with Kate the next night. Todd was working late at the studio, he was pretty much always going to be working late at the studio. And so we hit the bars and played pool and goofed around. Everywhere we went guys paid a lot of attention to me. I didn't know if it was a new confidence I had, or a special glow, or maybe word had gotten out. Portland was such a small town, if I was Todd Sparrow's new girlfriend, however temporary, it would be big news and it would travel fast.

Then, on Tuesday, I almost got fired at J. Crew because I screwed up the registers and lost a hundred dollars. They said, "We know you didn't steal it but you might as well have." That was creepy and I was starting to hate riding the bus to the mall, way out in the suburbs, when I could probably get a better job downtown. It was April now, and I was going to be in Portland until August, when I was supposedly going to University of Oregon. That was the plan anyway, though it was a pretty loose plan now. All my plans had gotten pretty loose.

And naturally, after breaking up with Nick, I was barely seeing Todd. I had slept over at his place twice that first week but then not at all the next week. When he finally had a full day off we drove up to Mt. Hood and rented snowboards and rolled around in the snow for a couple hours.

And also he wasn't going to be in Portland very long. When the recording was over he was going straight back to Minneapolis to start rehearsing the new Color Green record. The first time he mentioned this, the possibility of me going with him seemed to exist. But almost immediately, we both stopped talking like that. We both realized that we didn't know what was going to happen.

Then, right in the middle of everything else, a thick manila envelope appeared in my mailbox one morning. It was from Will Soren at the Ruth Goldman Agency. I was like, *holy shit!* It had been almost five weeks since we'd spoken, which seemed like a lifetime ago. I tore it open and found the manuscript of *Manifesto* and a long letter with "The Ruth Goldman Agency" printed at the top.

I had to go to work so I squished the huge envelope into my backpack and continued to the bus stop. At work that day, I was a good employee for a change. I sold a bunch of summer crap and didn't screw up the cash registers. And all during the day I got happier and more excited knowing the Ruth Goldman envelope was waiting for me in the back room.

My plan was to ride the bus home and then go somewhere fun to read the letter, a café or something, but I couldn't resist and before I'd even settled in my bus seat I had the letter out.

It was quite long I saw, six pages, which I found alarming. I flipped through to the last page and realized it wasn't written by Will Soren but by someone named Jessica Friedman. I wondered what that was about. But then I read the beginning of the letter and she explained that she was Will's assistant, and it had been her pleasure to read my manuscript and in conjunction with Will, offer some ideas and suggestions on how to make *Manifesto* a submitable manuscript.

This was even more alarming. I had got the impression Will Soren really liked it. Now they were talking about how we "might" make it "submitable"? I read the entire first page of the letter. Then the entire second page. The comments were very general. Almost vague. The main thing the novel needed, Jessica Friedman seemed to suggest, was to be significantly different than how it was now.

I finished the letter in a panic and called Sally immediately when I got home. I read her the first three pages and she agreed it didn't sound good. She told me not to freak out. She called her dad and then called me later and her dad agreed that it was unfortunate that they wanted such a complete overhaul. On the other hand, at least they thought it had potential. But I didn't feel like that. I felt angry and confused and like *what happened?!*

The next time I saw Todd I told him about it, and he wanted to see the letter and it was one of the weirder moments of my life watching the great Todd Sparrow read a letter about something I had done, from a real literary agency in New York. It changed his perception of me, I thought. But he agreed about the letter. It seemed oddly unspecific. It gave no indication of what they actually wanted me to do.

So then he wanted to read the book. So the next day, I left my extra copy for him at his house. This was also extremely nerve-wracking. For three days, I was all squirmy at work and feeling super anxious that Todd Sparrow had my novel. Would he actually read it? And in my heart, it wasn't even the best thing I could do. It was old! I felt like I knew a lot more about the world than I did when I was a sophomore in college.

On Wednesday night Todd called and I met him downtown for sushi. He had to go back to the studio that night but he seemed genuinely excited. He said: "Your book was really funny. I actually laughed!"

Which pretty much caused my brain to explode.

13

LATER THAT WEEK, I ran into Nick Pax at Gobby's Pizza. He was back from the tour and he looked a little worse for wear, I thought.

Because he'd first brought me to Gobby's and introduced me to everyone, I thought of it as his place and not mine and when I saw him come in, I slunk away and took my pizza slice to the back. But he saw me and came over and was super nice. He wanted to know about Todd's record and what Edith Monroe was like, but she was staying with different people so I never saw her. "I barely see Todd," I said, and smiled at him in this bashful way, like *things haven't exactly worked out like I thought.* He shrugged.

Then a girl appeared. She came up to Nick and asked if he wanted a coke. She was ordering for them. Nick introduced us. Her name was Crystal. She was really cute and very young and trendy in a new way I'd never seen before. Like her hair was this odd geometric cut, and also she was wearing a neon colored skirt which if she hadn't been so young and cute I would have said was the ugliest thing I'd ever seen.

When she went back to the front, I asked Nick about her.

He said she was a singer and had her own band. He said, "Have you heard of electro-clash?" I said, "No, what's that?" He laughed. It was the new thing. It was like punk rock mixed with techno mixed with disco mixed with horrible neon colors. All the high school kids were into it. I was like, really? He laughed again and I had the very weird sensation of realizing there was cool new stuff that I didn't even know about. I wasn't a teenager anymore.

It was funny that I ran into Nick that day because I ran into him again that night at K Club with Kate. Crystal, the electro-clash girl, was there. He was showing her around and mentoring her I guess, since she was the new cool thing. I asked Kate if she had ever heard of electro-clash but she hadn't.

A band played that had three girl singers who stood in a line in matching skirts and go-go boots while looping beats played on a synthesizer. Was this electro-clash? I didn't know and went to find Nick to ask him and eventually found him in the stairwell smoking a joint with Matthew. Nick explained more to me about electro-clash and told me not to feel bad. He said: "I didn't know about it either, I'm old too." And I was like, *I am not old*. But I sort of was. At least compared to the Crystals of the world.

Later, Crystal and her two-person band went on. She sang and played a small keyboard while a boy, who looked about fourteen, played guitar and keyboards and other things. They were very cool though. A drum machine started each song. And they danced around in this dorky, electronic way.

Nick sidled up to me at one point and told me they were still in high school and they were about to get signed to Matador, which was one of the best labels.

Crystal was great, I had to admit. She played up her innocence, but also totally took charge of the stage and the music and the entire room. I had this interesting feeling, and also scary, that there were millions of creative people in the world, waves of them, and they were always arriving, in a continuous flow, the new cool kids, the new cool world, the new cool thing. And I guess it made me respect Nick Pax because he had found a way to understand it and remain part of it and even help the new people when they needed it.

Meanwhile, all that week I agonized over Jessica Friedman's letter. I must have read it ten times. And then one day I got so mad I wadded up one of the pages and threw it in the garbage. Then I had to dig it out and un-crumple it and smooth it out. I couldn't see how I could change my whole book. Wouldn't it be easier to write a different book, if every single thing in it needed to be changed?

But at the same time it was still exciting. I carried that letter with me everywhere. And sometimes on the bus I would get it out and look at the top where it said:

The Ruth Goldman Agency
250 West 57th Street
New York, NY 10107

And I'd imagine this huge building and people in suits and briefcases hurrying around and jumping in limousines or whatever they did. I actually had no idea what a literary agency would look like, or how many people worked there, or how the office would be set up. For some reason I imagined it like a dentist's office—since my dad was a dentist—like you'd have to sit in the waiting room and then they'd call your name and you'd go inside to talk to the agent in some private room, like getting a cavity filled.

Sally tried to explain what her dad's agent was like. His was a "boutique" agency, whatever that meant. Once Sally sent me a newspaper clipping she'd found of Will Soren and Ruth Goldman dressed up and standing next to people in tuxedos at the National Book Awards. That made me feel better. I'd look out from the bus I was riding, stuck in traffic in Beaverton and think, I was part of that world now. I wasn't a big part of it, but I was attached. I had my foot in the door. I had found a tiny crack of an opening. Now, I had to find a way to get through it.

It was funny too about Todd. After that super intense sexual beginning, we lapsed into this casual, almost "friends" feeling between us. Like one night he was tired and I slept over and he put his arms around me and pulled me close and then fell right to sleep. And I could tell he was thinking about Edith Monroe's record all the time. He would get up in the middle of the night to write things down. Or he would talk on the phone to Edith in this certain way, super focused and intense. It was hard to be with someone when they were working like that. But it was good too, because I could observe him and see how he lived and how he dealt with things. He hadn't gone to college of course, I wasn't even sure if he went to high school, but he had these systems to keep stuff organized and he was very methodical and you could see him *compartmentalize*, even with me he did it and I guess I should have minded that—a normal girl probably would have, but I mostly watched it and tried to understand it and saw that he had no choice, he was getting paid to make this record, and Edith Monroe was this big deal, this controversial figure in the music world. The whole thing was a big risk for him, even though everyone tried to make it seem lowkey. You could feel the effort it required. It was such a good thing for me to see. The way you had to be in the world. The way Todd was. The way he'd always been.

But the really interesting thing was how he treated the letter from the Ruth Goldman Agency. He read it that first time, and found it perplexing, and tried to give me advice and even one time I went to his house and saw that he had been re-reading my book, like he'd started it over again.

He agreed that the letter was unclear about what exactly they wanted me to do. But he thought they must have some purpose for writing it. People at this level wouldn't waste time working on a project they saw no possibility in.

So then *my* mystery became *his* mystery and we talked about the letter sometimes, laying around in bed, which was a good thing, since sometimes we didn't have much else to talk about. And of course on those nights, the sex was amazing. I loved him so much on those nights and would do anything for him and did. He was the best teacher I ever had, the kind of teacher I sure never got at college. All of which was made even more profound and important, since our time together was running out.

That was the catch. I was not going to Minneapolis. We never talked about this but that part was clear. For all I knew he had a girlfriend there, though it seemed unlikely. So I had to continue on and do what I could and prepare myself. I had the manuscript to worry about too, as I was now going through it, taking "baby steps" in my revision, which Sally's dad had recommended. I had asked Sally's dad if I should call the Ruth Goldman Agency and ask for explanations. But he said no. Do the revision as best you can. And send it back. And let them respond. That was the professional way.

Then one day Kate and I ran into Nick at K Club. Nick and I had a nice talk. I told him that Todd was about to leave and how strange it was, how fast it had happened, and now it was going to end. I told him I was sorry for breaking up with him like I did.

He shrugged. He told me he was sleeping with Crystal, the electro clash girl. I was like, what? He said yeah, and that she was seventeen, she was still in high school. He was worried about that. "I could lose my job," he said. I told him he could *definitely* lose his job and it was against the law and he should stop doing it! He said he couldn't. She was so magical. And she loved him. She needed him. She wanted him to manage the Crystallines, which was their new name.

I was quite shocked by this. And a little jealous. This girl had a band and a record deal and was sleeping with Nick Pax, and she wasn't even eighteen? It didn't seem right. Or fair. And it was illegal!

I FINISHED my revision for Will Soren on June 2nd. Matthew told me I should email it back, that was becoming the big thing, emailing people on their computers. Kate had got a laptop computer for her birthday which we fiddled around with occasionally. She had an email account and she would unplug the phone and plug it into her computer to send emails to people. But then we'd miss real phone calls which seemed counter-productive.

Sally's dad advised me to do it the old way, type it up and send the complete manuscript back. So I got my mom to help type it and then took it to Kinko's and Xeroxed it. Then I went down to the big Portland post office and bought a special bubble envelope for manuscripts, and carefully wrote the address across the front:

Will Soren
The Ruth Goldman Agency
250 East 57th Street
New York, NY 10107

Then I put the stamps on and dropped it through the big slot for packages. Later, under that date, I wrote in my new, Todd-inspired day planner: SENT MANIFESTO REWRITE in big block letters.

A week later, Todd called and told me there had been a change of plans. They were supposed to be at Bedtime Studios through June, but they had finished the basic recordings and the record company wanted them to come back to Minneapolis and do the remixing there. It was unexpected but, as Todd explained, it was good news for Edith because the guy had listened to the rough mixes and really liked them. Which meant Todd had done a good job.

I took the news like I was supposed to. I had been practicing, actually. Some part of me had known Todd was always telling me the best possible version of things. Making it sound like he'd be in Portland forever, so we wouldn't have to deal with goodbyes. So I was ready for it, in a way. As ready as I could be.

That night, we went to the twenty-four hour IHOP on the eastside. Todd used to hang out there in the early days, when Color Green was first taking Portland by storm, and then Seattle and then the whole country, all in the course of about nine months. It had happened so fast, Nirvana and Pearl Jam on the highest level, and Color Green on the next level down, and all the other stuff: the zine movement and the Riot Grrrl phenomenon and the politics and the fashion. We had watched it explode right in front of us, all around us.

I felt lucky I'd been part of it. And I felt lucky now too, sitting here with Todd Sparrow, with his thick watch and his black T-shirt. He'd gotten his hair cut somewhere professional, somewhere Edith had found, so it wasn't the Mod style anymore. All of this in preparation for his return to Minneapolis to start their next record and get Color Green up and running again. The great unstoppable Color Green, though I knew that Todd was not assuming that. They had released three records and the word around Portland was that each had sold less than the one before. So Color Green was like every other band in the end. Bursting out of the gate and then trying to stay relevant once the initial thrill wore off. Well, it didn't matter to me. Todd was Todd and always would be, it wouldn't matter if he was pumping gas or bagging groceries. Though of course it mattered to him, it mattered more than anything, which was why he could not bring me along on the next leg of his journey.

There was a small going away party and I got to meet Edith finally. She was shy and definitely burdened by her good looks and her troubled childhood. We didn't have much to talk about. But we stood together for several minutes. And I liked her.

I think Todd thought he owed me one big sex blowout or something, since he was the "leaver" and I was the "leavee." But then it turned out we never even got to sleep together again. Not overnight. We had sex once, but it was quick and was part of the general confusion of everyone having to leave so fast.

Matthew and Kate and I drove Todd to the airport. Todd and I had an awkward, not very conclusive goodbye, walking through the airport while Matthew and Kate waited in the car. I went with him to his gate. It seemed like he was relieved to be going. Portland was small and people were possessive of him, and jealous sometimes. He always had to be careful to not appear "big time" in any way. But he was sick of that. He *was* big time and he wanted to go back to a place where he could act like it.

We stopped at the gate and he told me he loved my novel and wanted to hear everything that happened to it, and to send him anything else I wrote, he needed stuff to read and he thought I was real writer and had no doubt I would be published if not now, then eventually ...

I told him I would probably write something about him someday. He said he would be honored. Then he kissed me goodbye and gave me a long hug and then pulled back and looked at me. It was a strange look. I wanted it to be a look of deep love but it wasn't. It was more of a "Who is this interesting girl that I always run into?" look. Like he really did like me. But he did not love me. Not like I loved him.

When he was gone I cried. And I walked the length of the airport concourse, even though I knew Matthew and Kate were waiting. I gave myself some extra time. And I thought about Todd at first, but then after I'd cried myself out, I thought about airports and all the places there were in the world and wondered where I would end up when it was all over.

15

IT WAS weird that first year living on my own, with Kate, in our apartment in downtown Portland. Some unbelievable thing would happen, some momentous event, like hooking up with Nick Pax and I'd think my life would never be the same. But then two weeks later, something else would happen and I'd forget about the first thing and it was like the entire world was new again. And meanwhile those life-changing events got pushed aside and filed away. Whatever power they gave you, whatever lessons they taught you, you had to trust that they would remain inside you. You couldn't dwell on them, or sit around *reflecting*, there were too many other things happening.

It was, in fact, exactly two weeks after Todd left that Sally and Carol Smith showed up in Portland. Carol Smith was my other best friend from Wellington. She had directed the ecstasy movie that got us all kicked out.

Sally and Carol Smith—who went to USC film school now —were driving up from L.A., filming stuff and goofing around and eventually ending up at the Seattle Underground Film Festival where one of Carol's short films was playing. Carol Smith was already a rising star in the student film world, which was no surprise to anyone, but was still difficult for me since I got the worst of the punishment for the ecstasy movie. Not that I cared that much, but an apology, or even a little sympathy would have been nice, especially from Carol Smith. But I guess she assumed I'd figure it out, which was what I was doing. Also, she was such a real artist herself and so relentless, nothing would prevent her from accomplishing her goals. So I guess she thought if I was going to do something, I would do it, and it wasn't up to some college dean, or my "official transcript" or whatever. It didn't matter what happened at Wellington. Which I agreed with in theory. But it still freaked me out sometimes to realize I would never get a Wellington diploma. Not to mention what it did to my parents, who had paid all that tuition money.

Anyway, so the two of them arrived one day in their rented car and parked outside my apartment. They were staying in a cheap hotel, but they wanted to see my place and meet Kate. I could tell they were a little surprised by her. Kate was not at all like a Wellington person, she was a twenty-two year old hairdresser from Beaverton. You could tell Kate was thrown off by them too, especially Carol who had this silent forcefulness about her, and could be pretty intimidating if you didn't know her.

So then I drove around with them in their rental car and showed them the sights of Portland. They wanted to see where I grew up for some reason and so we went there, to the suburbs, to my parents house and we walked in on my mom and dad unannounced. That was awkward. Carol took some pictures and then got out her video camera and shot some stuff in the back yard. My parents were polite and they were naturally very curious to meet Sally and Carol in the flesh. These were the people who screwed up their daughter's college education but were also, supposedly, my best friends in the world. Sally was super nice and great but Carol was being her usual intense self and my parents had no idea how to react to her. They probably thought she was a lesbian. They seemed utterly baffled and possibly offended by her.

When we got back in the car, I felt sad that my parents didn't understand my friends. But then as we drove away, Sally was like, "I love your parents. They're just like you, Andrea. Super sweet and nice and cool."

The next day I had breakfast with Sally and Carol and we sat in a booth at this cafe and had a long talk about everything that was going on in the world. I told about Todd and his record with Edith Monroe. And the emergence of electro-clash. And the crazy colors the teenagers were suddenly wearing. Sally told about the new French "retribution feminism," where women wrote books about murdering rapists in gruesome ways. Carol Smith was reading this new novel about jaded New York City art kids, called *Electra Rising*, that everyone at film school was reading.

Carol then told about living in Los Angeles and USC. None of the film people could do anything by themselves. Everyone wanted to collaborate. But there were some cool video artists there. And Cal Arts was basically ground zero for future art world stars.

It was so interesting to listen to Carol. She was becoming something, I saw. Not a star, exactly. Maybe an anti-star. She had this weird charisma. No wonder she got into every film festival she applied to. She was someone you would pick out of a crowd and think: that person is important.

Which made me wonder if I needed to be like that as a novelist. Maybe I didn't. Writing was so different than other art forms. But maybe you still needed that aura around you of: *Pay attention to me.*

After that, Carol and Sally left for Seattle and were gone for four days. That was extremely hard for some reason. Without Todd around, and no contact from him. And no word from The Ruth Goldman Agency. And then going to work at the mall and having to eat lunch with Gretchen and Amber and talk about TV shows or some new boy that worked at the Cineplex.

When Sally and Carol came back through Portland, I met them at their hotel and now they had a bunch of new stories about the film festival and all the politics and intrigue and how one kid from NYU had spent a million dollars on his student film and it was terrible and everyone made fun of him.

It was so fun being with Sally and Carol. I needed that contact so much. I called in sick and spent the day with them and slept in their hotel and had breakfast with them in the morning. But they couldn't stay because they had to drive to Weed, California where some photography students had a compound in the woods and all these people were there for the summer, eating berries and hanging out and running naked in the woods. It sounded so fun and I think Sally saw that I wanted to go with them. She said, "Andrea, you can come too, you can take the bus back." But I didn't think I could because I had my job, and I'd have to tell my parents and I didn't know if I could do something like that. Even though it sounded like the greatest thing ever.

As the summer continued, I started to freak out about the agent situation again. I'd heard nothing about my re-write. I had asked Sally over and over what I should do and I felt like she was getting bored with my problems. Her final answer seemed to be: if I wasn't comfortable with Will Soren, I should send *Manifesto* to some different agents.

I didn't know what to do. After four weeks, I had called the Ruth Goldman Agency and got a different Will Soren assistant, not Jessica Friedman, who told me Will was very busy and he would get back to me soon. Two more weeks had passed. So now I had to call again, it seemed like. That was one thing everybody said: you had to be persistent.

So one day, before work, I got up early and took a shower and took several deep breaths. Then I picked up the phone and called the Ruth Goldman Literary Agency. When the receptionist answered I explained the situation and got angry a little bit and said it seemed like they should have responded by now, and it wasn't fair to string me along like this. The woman listened carefully and said she would pass this on and she was sure they would get right back to me this time. So I said, okay, and apologized for losing my temper, but the woman said no, it was okay, I had a right to stand up for myself. She wished me luck. Which seemed nice and like something she didn't have to do.

So then I went to work and for some reason I called Nick Pax but he wasn't home and then I called the number I had for Todd Sparrow in Minneapolis, which I'd done before, even though he hadn't called me back.

I ran into Nick a couple nights later, and we drove around and I told him the whole story of the agent. He didn't say much, but I knew he understood. Of course he did. He'd been screwed over a million times.

We ended up at my place, and I invited him in, and he gave me a back rub, which turned into an erotic massage which turned into sex, which was nice. I guess I needed to be close to someone. And Nick was so nice and felt so familiar, even though he was still going out with the seventeen-year-old.

Then one day, I came home from work and there was a letter from the Ruth Goldman Agency waiting for me in our mailbox. It was an ordinary sized envelope. I sucked in my breath and took it out. It was the usual elegant stationary, with my name and address typed neatly on the front. I took it inside and set it on the table and put on some water for hot chocolate.

So then while the water boiled I sat down at the table and picked up the envelope and opened it very slowly and carefully. I had no idea what it was going to say. It was a single piece of paper. I unfolded it ...

It was a form letter. It had been copied a million times and was so faded it was hard to read. It said that though my manuscript had merit, the Ruth Goldman Agency was not interested in representing me at this time, and that they wished me luck finding representation elsewhere.

That was all it said. The person who had signed it, with one squiggle, was a name I had never seen before.

I didn't panic. I didn't cry. I took a deep breath and I felt a strange sense of relief. At least I got my answer.

I dialed Sally's number. She picked up the phone, thank God. And then I very calmly told her what happened. I told her I thought I would cry, I had expected to cry, but I mostly felt relief. I didn't like Will Soren anyway. Or Jessica Friedman.

Sally said it was for the best, and that their confusing comments showed they were incompetent. Now what I needed to do was talk to some other literary agents. And find someone

I did like. And not to take the first agent who would have me. But to consider several of them and learn what they were like, and choose the one that was the best fit for me.

I listened to this, and somewhat believed it, but now I couldn't talk because despite Sally's support, my vision was blurring and my face was sinking down and I could feel a single tear running down my hand as it gripped the phone.

Sally comforted me as best she could. "Do you know what the best part of this is?" she said. I sniffled and said I didn't. She said: "Now you have to move to New York."

PART TWO

16

I COULDN'T GO DIRECTLY to New York. I didn't know anyone there. I wouldn't have known what to do. So I flew first to Connecticut and stayed with Sally for a week at Yale as we plotted and planned and strategized. Mostly she tried to keep my courage up. And I tried not to cry too much or freak out. I was pretty much terrified of New York. I mean, not really, but moving there, I just had no idea how you did that.

Plus I really liked being back in Connecticut. It was September by the time I got there. School had started. Yale was all Ivy-ish and full of cute, smart people. The quiet Connecticut streets were bright with the first fall foliage. And after a week, we had a nice routine going. Strong coffee each morning, dinners with her Yalie housemates and for me, during the day, a walk through campus to people watch and read the paper at one of the local cafés.

After a week though, it was time to go. Thanks to Sally, I had found a room in a shared house in Brooklyn. Where this house was, I knew only theoretically. It didn't matter. Sally drove me to the train station in the afternoon. The Metro North. A big silver train of destiny. I was so scared.

. . .

It was a painfully short drive. I had just gotten warm, just gotten cozy in the seat of Sally's car when I was forced to get out again, forced outside, into the chilly afternoon air. I wrestled my huge rolling suitcase out of the backseat, dropped it on the ground and extended its handle. Sally handed me my equally weighty shoulder bag, which I heaved onto my shoulder. We gave each other a quick hug goodbye since Sally was late to a class. "You have your directions and your phone numbers and your subway tokens?" she asked. I did.

She gave me another hug; a deep, loving hug and then pulled back, gripping my elbows for a second as if to transfer her own strength and courage into me. "This is going to be so great," she told me. "You just wait."

I nodded numbly and hugged her one last time. Then she hurried back to her car and drove away.

I rolled my heavy suitcase into the train station and bought my ticket to Grand Central. From there, I followed the signs, lugging my stuff up and down several sets of stairs. On Platform Three I spotted a sign: *NEW YORK CITY* it said, in firm, sophisticated lettering. I positioned myself beneath it, pushed down the handle on my suitcase and let my heavy shoulder bag fall off my shoulder and thud on the ground at my feet.

There were a dozen other train riders spread across the platform. Yale people, they must have been. Professors possibly, or other serious-looking professional types: a man in a suit, a dignified older woman with round glasses. I dug around in the peacoat I had brought, and found a half-finished bag of M&M's and ate several of them, one at a time.

On the wall beside me there was an advertisement for

Vermont. A large photograph showed a quaint country store with a dazzling autumnal forest in the background. Underneath it said: *Revisit the Simple Life.* I wondered if someday I would need to do that. If I might find myself on this very same train going the opposite direction. I tried to imagine some future version of myself, gray-haired, conservatively dressed, worn out by my high-powered, New York life. But that would be decades from now, a lifetime away, I would be an entirely different person.

I finished the M&Ms and threw the wrapper away. I looked up and down the platform. I thought about the opening scene of J.D. Salinger's *Franny* story, the train platform full of Ivy League boys, smoking cigarettes in the cold, waiting for their dates on the big football weekend. I had meant to read that again while I was here ... but no, there wasn't time. The pressures of finding a New York apartment had become overwhelming. Among other things, I had to keep calling my mother with updates. My parents were naturally apprehensive about their twenty-one year old daughter moving to New York City without even a completed college degree for protection. And moving into an apartment with people they didn't know, and that I had never met, all of it happening in a frantic rush of phone calls, rent negotiations, cashiers checks, and all dependent, in the end, on the last-minute cancellation of a girl from Pennsylvania who had suddenly threatened to re-appear, claim her precious room and send me back to Portland in defeat.

But things had worked out. I would be living with a girl named Naomi Cohn, a friend of a friend of Sally's from Boston. Naomi and her friend Liz needed a third in their bachelorette pad in a Brooklyn neighborhood called Greenpoint which I had never heard of but which I was told was not as dangerous as the really dangerous neighborhoods, whatever that meant.

· · ·

The train finally appeared. It came around a long curve in the distance, straightened with steely precision and eased into the station. The doors opened. A conductor, with an old-style cap and uniform, stepped off the train and called out, "All aboard" to his new passengers. That was me. I grabbed my stuff.

Getting on, I created a little problem with my too-heavy suitcase and oversized shoulder bag. I knocked into people and finally worked my way into an empty seat by the window. I began to sweat, and my arms already hurt, but that was to be expected. I scooted closer to the plastic window and stared out through the scratched surface, at the trash and weeds and industrial ruins beyond the train tracks. I was officially city-bound.

Two hours later, the train shuttered to a stop in the dim gray basement of Grand Central. The full train car sprung to life instantly, myself included. I gathered my stuff, nerves tight and adrenaline flowing. The doors opened, releasing a thick surge of people onto the platform. That's when the jostling started, the pushing, the racing, the maneuvering. And yet even in the midst of it, a certain East Coast *politesse* was observed. It was nothing personal, this mad rush. It was just how they did things here.

We emerged from the dust of the lower tracks into the airy splendor of Grand Central Station. I had been here before, during college, so it wasn't totally new. Still, I stopped to gaze once at the towering ceilings and to feel the moment. Then I was back to business. I was supposed to be at the apartment by 7:00 to meet Naomi and get my key. It was already 6:00 and I still had three subway trains to connect to.

I spotted a sign to the subway and rolled myself through the rush hour chaos of the concourse. People were literally running in every direction. When I found the subway, it was the opposite: a slow clog of people had formed around a single escalator. It was a total log-jam.

So I bailed on that and maneuvered my way around to the stairs where I thumped my poor suitcase down several flights, bumping a few people, and arriving in a whole new area of congestion and confusion. Thank god I already had subway tokens. I dug one out, almost dropping it when someone ran into me from behind. I pushed my way to the turnstiles and plowed through and then entered the even more frantic vortex of the actual subway station.

Speed was the thing. You had to move fast. And so I did, trying to avoid hitting people with my suitcase, but not stopping to check the damage when I did. "Sorry! Sorry! Watch out!" I said loudly as I dashed back and forth, not knowing where I was going, or where my subway line was. When I did find the 6 Train, I couldn't get down the stairs to it. There were too many people coming up. They came up like a wall. They came up like an army.

During a momentary lull, I crashed down the stairwell like it was a mosh pit, my suitcase bouncing down the steps behind me. At the bottom, a train was just pulling in and I snaked my way through the swarming platform and by some miracle ended up inside. When I dumped my exhaustingly heavy shoulder bag on the ground, it landed on somebody's foot.

Transferring from the 6 Train to the L Train was another crazed race. The desperation that people moved with made no sense. Did they hate the subway this much? Nobody was chasing them. There was no fire. But still they ran. They flew. And so I did too, lowering my head, clenching my teeth, powering forward. I found the L Train, which I had been told about. It was the "cool kids" train. And sure enough, it was here I saw my first bohemian New Yorkers. The artsy types. The people with weird shoes and coats and abrasively colored sweaters. But the L Train was late. Or delayed. Or something. As I descended the stairs, I saw that the platform was so densely packed, it seemed impossible that nobody had fallen into the tracks. I nudged and squeezed my way onto the platform, the strap of my shoulder bag now cutting painfully into my shoulder. And how would I get on the train when it actually arrived? I could barely move. I could barely do anything.

But I did get on, forcing my way with a newcomer's desperation. Getting off in Brooklyn, the energy level seemed to lessen slightly. All I knew about Brooklyn was that it was not in Manhattan and that it was where young people like me lived when they first landed in New York. "It's where you go to have your dreams crushed," someone had jokingly told me on the phone at Sally's.

My next objective was the G Train to Greenpoint. I followed the signs and found myself rolling my heavy suitcase through long underground passageways, up and down, to the right, to the left, up, around, down, through. I finally arrived at the correct platform. Here, there was a profound shift in the subway population. The cool kids disappeared. Suddenly everyone looked poor, downtrodden, like they probably didn't speak English. I had been told that Greenpoint was a Polish neighborhood and that I would be able to tell the difference. And so I could.

The G Train came and I got on. It seemed dirtier and more depressed than the other train lines. There were no weird people to spy on or strange clothes to gawk at. It was just people coming home from work, from not very interesting jobs.

Two stops later it was time to get off. I rolled my now battered suitcase out of the subway car and consulted Naomi

Cohn's detailed directions which told me to walk toward the exit on my left. At the end of the platform, I got tangled up in an ancient floor to ceiling turnstile. When I got through that I was confronted by yet another set of unforgiving stone stairs. I gripped my suitcase and the straps of my shoulder bag, and prepared myself for this final climb.

But just then a pile of garbage in the corner beside me came to life. It lifted itself up. It reached out toward me. I screamed and jumped nearly out of my shoes. The pile of garbage was a person. It was a woman. She was trying to sit up. I stared into her reddened, swollen face. Her tiny, squinty, pig eyes met mine. I nearly fell over my suitcase. I felt myself gag.

Other commuters—coming up behind me—pushed by, angry that I'd been stupid enough to get caught in this little eddy of misery. And so, like them, I tore my eyes away, gripped my suitcase with my rubbery arms and forced myself forward, dragging myself and my things upward one painful step at a time. At ground level, I was so spent and traumatized, I tripped on the last step and fell forward, dumping my shoulder bag and landing face-first on the filthy sidewalk.

I was sweating now and my arms were burning and for a moment it was all I could do to get to my knees and then, slowly, to my feet. I had skinned my palms and they stung. I brushed off my jeans and pulled my sweat-damp hair back behind my ears. Then I looked up and saw where I was: on a dark corner in a *ghetto*. To appear vulnerable in a place like this was probably suicide. In fact, the first pair of craggy-faced Polish men who came around the corner stared me down so brutally, that I immediately dragged together my crap and went staggering down the street.

I lurched forward several doorways and then ducked into the doorway of a dirty Chinese restaurant, where I tried to study Naomi Cohn's directions in the dark. But now I was in the way of people leaving the restaurant. Stepping back onto the sidewalk I nearly collided with a gang of hispanic girls who cursed me in the darkness. This place was impossible. You couldn't stop. You couldn't go. You couldn't get out of the way.

I gave up on the directions, re-gripped my suitcase and began a blind march down Manhattan Avenue. This turned out to be the correct choice and four blocks later, I came to Wilton Street. I turned right and found myself in a quieter, more residential environment. For the first time, there were not constant pedestrians to avoid or swerve around, which was a welcome relief.

I limped along under the street lights, watching the numbers rise and waiting for my new home to appear. Finally it came: 191 Wilton. A plain, green, three-story building of no distinction whatsoever.

I let myself through a little iron gate and walked to the door, dragging my hated suitcase up those last couple steps. I stopped then for a moment, and looked around at my new street, the crumbly pavement, the stone stoops, the broken sidewalk.

And so it begins, I said to myself.

17

I BUZZED THE BUZZER. Nothing happened. I looked up at the second floor window, but nothing happened up there either. I didn't want to buzz again, but I was in New York now, and a New Yorker would buzz again. So I did.

Finally, there was a slam inside the building and the sound of feet descending. A moment later, an inside door was unbolted. Then the front door opened. It was Naomi Cohn.

Naomi was about my height, thin, with cute fashionable hair, a stylish skirt, a grey cardigan sweater. She had an attractive, intelligent face but I felt a certain restraint immediately come over her. She apparently had to check you out first, before she decided about you.

"Did you have any trouble finding it?" she said, staring at my battered suitcase.

"No, no," I said. "It was just a lot more stairs than I thought."

"You could have taken a taxi," she said, holding the door open for me. She turned and headed up the stairs, realizing half way up that I might need help. She came back and took the overstuffed shoulder bag from me.

"Wow, this is heavy," she said.

"Yeah," I agreed from behind her.

Even burdened with my shoulder bag, there was a gracefulness in her movements. But that made sense: she was from Sally's nice neighborhood in Boston, and after that, had gone to Bard, which was an artsy, private school.

"Are you going to have your stuff sent out?" she asked.

"I guess so," I said, which was a lie. Pretty much everything I owned was in my suitcase and my shoulder bag.

We reached the second floor landing. Naomi gripped the door knob: "Get ready ... !" she said, with great sarcasm.

The door opened into the kitchen. It was extremely small, and oddly shaped, but it was neat and clean. Against one wall was a small table, two chairs. A single flower stuck out of a vase on the windowsill. A small painting hung on the wall.

It looked very "liberal arts," was my first thought.

"And back this way is where we sleep," said Naomi, leading me through a series of rooms that was almost like a hallway. There weren't doors. It was just one room, then another room, then another. The last room, at least, had sliding doors that shut it off. This was Naomi's room. Liz's room was next to hers. She had a small bed and a dresser but no actual closet that I could see. Standing in the doorway to Liz's room was when I realized where my room was. I was standing in it. There was a futon there, as promised, which took up two thirds of the total space. There were no windows.

"There's this curtain thing Megan rigged up," explained Naomi. She demonstrated by pulling a curtain across the room on a small cord. It created a wall of sorts between the "hall" part of my room and the "bed" part.

"I know," said Naomi, watching my face. "It's small." I agreed that it was. She asked if I'd ever lived in New York before and I said no. She said it was a good deal by New York standards.

Naomi took me to the bathroom, which, like everything else, was tiny and cramped. There was a shower at least and a bathtub. She opened the cabinets which were so jammed with stuff I couldn't imagine where my stuff would go.

"Some of this is Megan's," she said, daintily removing several plastic containers and dropping them into the trash. There was still no room for my stuff.

She went to the kitchen and got me my keys. She handed them to me.

"Liz is visiting her family upstate," she said. "I'm not sure when she's coming back. You guys can introduce yourselves."

Naomi disappeared then, moving through my room, through Liz's and into her own where she appeared to be dressing up for something. I remained in my "room." I gripped my suitcase in both hands and heaved it onto the futon which was at least elevated on a platform, almost like a real bed.

"Megan asked that you mail her a check for the futon to her parents," called Naomi from her room. "Her address is on the fridge."

"What happened to Megan?" I called back.

"She moved back to Pennsylvania."

"She didn't like New York?"

"She followed a guy here. She didn't really know what she was doing."

"Oh," I called back.

"You don't last long here if you don't have a plan," said Naomi. "In my experience."

Now Naomi came through my room wearing a sleek black dress that was only partially zipped up in the back. She went into the bathroom, put on makeup, came out again. She was quite beautiful, in a sharp, severe sort of way.

"Would you mind," she said, turning away from me.

My brain was so fried by this point it took me a second to realize what she wanted. I zipped up her dress.

"Where are you off to?" I said, carefully.

"Dinner party," she said. She was wearing black tights, flats.

"Are you going to ride the subway dressed like that?"

"No. I take a car service. That's the best thing, at night. The number's on the fridge."

She got a coat from her room. It was very stylish, very *chic* was the word that popped into my head.

I stood there, stupidly, and watched her arrange a light scarf around her neck. She fluffed out her hair. She looked great. She looked like an adult. She looked like a woman who lived in New York.

"Gotta go," she said, a slightly more sincere tone in her voice. "Help yourself to whatever!"

With that she left.

I was sore, and tired, but in another way I had never been so awake in my life. And now I was alone in the apartment. I went back to my bedroom. If you could call it that. I wanted to make fun of it to someone, to laugh about it, but I was by myself.

A cheap lamp was on the floor next to my bed. There were also some plastic storage container things stashed under the futon platform. These I used to put away some of my clothes. Then I pulled the curtain closed and laid down on my bed. I stared up at the white ceiling which wasn't very high. No windows. And a curtain for a wall. This was weird. This would take some getting used to.

I poured a bath. This was a little bit nerve-wracking as I expected Liz, who I knew even less about than Naomi, to show up any minute. But I would have to take a bath at some point, wouldn't I?

Steam filled the tiny room, as I tried to find a place for my toothbrush and toothpaste and other basic toiletries. Where was I going to put things like tampons? Under my bed? I'd already run out of room. And I hadn't even finished unpacking my one suitcase.

The hot bath was heavenly. And the tub itself was old-style and generously shaped so that I was able to lower myself down to my chin, my hair floating around my head. I thought about how great Naomi looked. I would need a new haircut. I would need a new coat. I would need a new everything.

An hour later, after some nervous testing of my keys to make absolutely positively sure I could get back into the apartment, I ventured outside and walked up the street to the small super-market I had noticed by the subway. Inside, I had no idea what to get. Pasta and pasta sauce? That seemed safe. And some juice. What would Naomi and Liz think of my food prefer-ences? I got some green beans out of a dirty bucket, then put them back when they appeared diseased. Then I wandered into the canned goods aisle. The brands were all different. Many of the labels were in Spanish or Polish or Hebrew. And why was there a thin layer of oily dirt on the floor?

I got in line with my paltry collection of items. Nobody in the store seemed to be American, or at least what I thought of as American. The checkout girl looked like she was from Transylvania: thick black eye makeup and her hair gelled and sticking up funny. And then the prices. Everything cost twice as much as it usually did, the few items I bought were nearly twenty bucks.

Back in the apartment, the refrigerator was thankfully half empty. I put away my stuff. Then I found a pot and boiled some water, and eventually made myself some pasta, borrowing somebody's salt and a little butter to season it. It tasted weird. But I ate it. Then I washed out the dishes and went back to my room. But it was only 9:40 and I was wired. I couldn't sit on my bed all night. So then I put on my peacoat and went out again.

Manhattan Avenue had changed in the couple hours since I'd lugged my suitcase down it's dirty sidewalks. It was less crowded now, and the people who were out were closing up their shops or putting their cardboard recycling on the sidewalk. I was surging with energy for some reason. Because it was New York, I guess. Because I now lived in New York. I couldn't quite fathom it. Starting right this minute: *I lived in New York.*

I reached the main intersection of Manhattan and Greenpoint Avenues. There I spotted a threesome of young people dressed somewhat like me. The girl was laughing about something, her breath making steam in the light of the Dunkin' Donuts they were walking by. I continued in that direction, discreetly following them for a while. The boys looked like Portland boys in their thrift store overcoats and Converse sneakers and jeans. I wondered if it would be weird to introduce myself to them. And tell them I had just moved into the neighborhood. But something about the way they talked and acted, they seemed separate from their surroundings. Like they were a self-contained unit, and would not appreciate being interrupted by some random person. Which made sense I guess. And so I let them go.

.   .   .

Back at 191 Wilton, I let myself in the front door and walked up the creaky, narrow stairwell, noticing the over-painted wood hand railing and the partially rotted posts that held it up. Everything was dusty, flimsy, old. Inside the apartment, I dumped my peacoat on my bed. I noticed there was light coming from Naomi's room. This was because her two windows (hers was the only bedroom that had windows) were facing the streetlight outside. I pulled her sliding doors open enough to creep into her room. I looked out the window. Beyond our street I could see a tiny sliver of Manhattan's skyline. It was far away but glittered impressively, especially the Twin Towers, its red lights blinking steadily in the darkness. Since no one was home, I took the opportunity to snoop around Naomi's room a little. Mostly I looked at her books. She had sophisticated-looking editions of things I'd never heard of. Art theory, literary criticism, feminist texts, Russian classics. It was instructive how she managed her lack of space. Several rows of shoes were lined up under the window. Her small closet was literally stuffed with dresses and coats.

Next I looked around Liz's room. She was more the organic type, judging from her stuff: a pair of Birkenstocks, aroma therapy candles, an unopened deck of tarot cards in her book-shelf. She had interesting books too, many with Buddhist or spiritual themes. Pretty much everyone in New York was going to have interesting stuff, I realized. How else would you end up here?

On the top of her bookshelf was a little personal area: family pictures, a small toy horse, some other sentimental items. This was apparently a shrine to her non-New York self, the real Liz, who she was attempting to protect, or at least stay in touch with. And then on her bed, with a small grouping of pillows, I saw a single, lonely-looking teddy bear. This struck me and seemed to be an omen of what I was in for. The toughness of the city. The aloneness. "Great city, great solitude," Sally had quoted to me in one of her letters. An ancient Greek philosopher had said that. Apparently it had been true forever.

18

THANKS TO SALLY, I already had a pretty good job possibility, which I followed up on immediately, and with great thoroughness, since I was terrified about money from the moment I arrived at Wilton Street.

A friend of Sally's uncle owned a fine art press, and needed a new assistant. I called twice, leaving messages, and then finally reached Richard Kinney, who invited me to come to the office the next day.

And so barely forty-eight hours after arriving, I found myself sitting on the G Train in my best J. Crew skirt and tights and flats and my peacoat, going to my first job interview.

I wasn't so sure about my peacoat. To me, the peacoat was an East Coast staple. You could show up anywhere in one and be fine. But that was based on being a freshman at Wellington three years ago. Nobody in New York was wearing them now, I noticed. But no sooner had I thought that, I spotted a very unusual woman, probably thirty-five years old, sitting across from me on the G Train. She wore an old peacoat, dirty jeans and old, paint-splattered work boots. She was an *artist*, I suddenly realized as I looked more closely. She was very good looking in a mannish kind of way. Her body language was like a defiant teenager, the way she slouched on the subway seat and chewed on a little red straw. She had a short, punkish haircut—expensive looking—which might not have worked on a normal person, but went perfectly with her strong features and sharp blue eyes.

So maybe you could wear a peacoat.

I transferred from train to train until I reached Tribeca where Richard Kinney had his office. The job, as Sally had described it, paid pretty well for publishing and I could probably survive on it, if I was careful with my money. Also, Tribeca was a good neighborhood to work in, according to everyone, which I found to be true when I got there, as there were lots of nice shops and cafes and well-dressed people walking around.

I found the address and punched in the proper numbers on a state-of-the-art intercom system. Mr. Kinney's voice came on and told me the elevator was out, but to come up to the fourth floor. He buzzed me in. The four sets of stairs weren't much fun but I dealt with it, resting and taking off my coat and trying not to get sweaty and flustered. This was New York life apparently: dirty subways and broken elevators on your way to a job interview for a fine art book publisher.

I knocked on the door. Mr. Kinney answered. He was a small man, with an intense face and greying hair that stuck up in different places. He wore a white wrinkly shirt untucked and old jeans but with expensive-looking loafers.

He led me inside, apologizing for the messiness of his offices. The reception area was small, there was a small sofa and a coffee table covered with books and papers and folders and envelopes. There were two other rooms, one where his desk was and another where a young man with red plastic eyeglasses was sitting at a computer. He introduced me to this person, Andre, who seemed to be foreign and barely looked up from his screen.

Richard Kinney offered me coffee, juice, water, tea. He stared at me for a moment, with obvious curiosity, then smiled warmly and gestured for me to come into his own office. In this slightly larger room was a big desk which he sat behind. The chair across from him, had several heavy coffee table books stacked on it, the top one entitled *Moroccan Tile* which I had to remove and place carefully on the floor.

"You'll get used to that," said Mr. Kinney. "Moving books around, that's what we do here, try not to drown in our own product."

I nodded and smiled and sat and undid my scarf and tried to smooth my hair a bit. I could feel that it had become static-y in the dry east coast air and was probably frizzing out. Lastly, I took off my peacoat and pulled up the sleeves of my sweater and felt a fresh, lightness come over me. I looked over at Richard Kinney, who was again staring at me as if he found me unusual and amusing in some way. I was apparently not what he expected. But what did he expect?

He asked me about Sally. He knew her uncle very well. They'd grown up in the same neighborhood and had both gone to Dartmouth. They skied a lot there. And drank too much scotch. Did I like skiing, being from out west? I said I hadn't skied very much but yes, I loved the mountains and the snow and being outdoors. Did I like the city? I confessed I had only been here two days.

"*Two days?*" he said, smiling. "Well that explains it."

I didn't know what that meant, but I smiled. Richard was quite handsome, and youthful-looking despite his grey hair.

There was something very direct and attractive about him, an easy confidence. He appeared to enjoy his life immensely. It occurred to me that I had never met an adult who seemed so energetic, and so happy.

He described the job to me. I would work with Andre mostly. It was not challenging work. It was mostly clerical stuff. Inventory. Shipping. Talking on the phone. Andre would show me how to use the computer. With Christmas coming, things would get a little crazy, but then they would calm down again afterward.

He asked where I lived and I told him but he didn't know anything about Greenpoint. He asked me about Wellington. I said I had liked it very much. He asked me what I wanted to do in New York and my chest contracted and my heart raced and I squeezed out the words: "I was hoping to become a writer."

He took this statement totally seriously. Or appeared to. Then a wry smile spread over his face. "Well you could do worse than this job. It will give you at least a small taste of the publishing world."

His phone began to ring after that. He spoke to most of the people as if they were old friends. His voice was rich with warmth and friendliness. Again, I thought, *what an extraordinary person.*

But he had work to do. It was time for me to leave. As he led me to the door, he told me what the job paid—slightly more than he had told Sally—as well as the hours, and some of the benefits, like flexible hours and use of the computer and the long distance telephones. At the door, he shook my hand and told me to think about it. I wouldn't need to start until next week. He repeated his warning about the dullness and simplicity of the work.

I nodded and smiled. And then with great control and dignity began the long descent back down the stairs. On the street, I maintained my reserve until I was safely around the corner. Then I stopped, looked up at the sky and was like HOLY FUCKING SHIT, I JUST GOT MY FIRST NEW YORK JOB!

Then I calmed myself, buttoned up my peacoat and walked quietly through the quaint cobblestone streets toward the subway.

That night, Liz came home. I was re-arranging my sleeping area when I heard clunking on the steps beneath me. The whole building creaked and groaned whenever anyone came up the stairs, including the two older gay guys who lived on the top floor, but who were rarely seen.

Our door swung open and I could hear movement inside the kitchen. I heard a long female sigh, and then the door shut. I pulled back my little curtain and looked out. I could see Liz's back. She had put her bags on the table and was undoing her scarf. She was taller and bigger than I expected. She looked a bit jockish, in sweatpants and her somewhat damaged blond hair in a tight braid behind her.

"Hello?" I said.

She turned and smiled. "Hello?"

I came out of my hiding place. I introduced myself and she gave me a hug. It was a little awkward but nice, and a lot warmer than with Naomi who I hadn't dared touch. Liz was very friendly, very down to earth. We began talking right away. She made us both herbal tea and told me about her family in upstate New York. Her older sister was getting married in a couple weeks, so she'd been up there, helping out. I was glad Liz was so open, but I could tell by the way she dressed and talked and conducted herself, that I didn't have that much in common with her. Like even though New York was this exciting cultural mecca, it didn't mean every actual person was going to be interested in the same things. But that was okay. Liz seemed solid and friendly and that was the important thing. She even helped me figure out how to arrange my room. She had slept there herself during her first months in the apartment. Later, she walked with me to a nearby Salvation Army and helped me find a little table that I could set up at the foot of my bed.

19

THE NEXT MORNING, I woke up in a state of having slept so deeply and for so long, I could barely get my eyes open. I was dehydrated and stiff in my joints and it occurred to me how stressed out I'd been, flying out from Portland, my week in New Haven, my new apartment, my first job interview, all these new people.

Fortunately, I had the apartment to myself at 11:30 in the morning. I stood up and stretched my leaden body and put some water on for coffee. I went barefoot into the tiny bathroom and sat on the toilet. I looked down at my pale naked thighs and said out loud: "Sorry to put you through this, body, but this is what we have to do right now."

I stumbled into the kitchen and attended to the coffee. It was quite cold for some reason and in my fogged brain state, I made the mistake of fiddling with the iron radiator which looked like it had been made during the industrial revolution. I promptly burned the shit out of my hand. Also, as I studied the radiator, I saw that parts of the wood floor were broken and rotting underneath it. I got down on my hands and knees to look closer. To my amazement, I could actually see—through various gaps and holes—into the kitchen of the apartment below.

Then, since I was down there, I put my face sideways on the hardwood and looked down the length of our kitchen. The whole floor was totally warped! And then looking up, I saw that the ceiling was crooked too. The entire building was sort of leaning to one side. Wasn't it illegal for an apartment building to be crooked and warped and rotting through to the apartment below? I guessed not. Maybe that's why the rent was so cheap. Maybe our whole building was on the verge of collapse.

These general investigations eventually led to more snooping around in Naomi's room, where I found several bottles of antidepressants and also a bottle of Xanax as well as some Adderall, which was supposedly the cool new studying drug among college students.

I then snooped around in Liz's room some, finding an *Artist's Way* notebook, which didn't have anything written in it except for several false starts, like: "I am trying this again," or "This time I am really going to stick with this … "

This reminded me of my own journal, which I had not written a word in since I had landed at Sally's ten days before. I hadn't even got out my notebooks, but I would do that today. Also to do: call Richard Kinney and tell him I definitely wanted the job. It had been almost twenty-four hours which seemed enough time. In fact, as my money fears again rose up inside me, I resolved to do that immediately.

I composed myself and made the call. Andre answered the phone in a professional voice and said that Richard Kinney had just left for Colorado for a couple days, to rock-climb, and so I left a message that I would like to accept the job. Andre said nothing to this, which was weird, since that meant we would be working together. But whatever. He was Swiss, Sally had told me. Which explained the red plastic glasses on a boy.

I took a bath and ate some lunch and began to feel like my actual self again. So then I decided it would be a good day to go exploring and write in my journal and maybe even try writing a story. So that's what I did, taking the G Train to the L Train to Union Square. First I went to the big Strand bookstore because that's where everyone told you to go. But it was a million books you never heard of, completely unorganized, though there was some interesting people watching. So then I walked through Washington Square Park and eventually ended up on Prince Street where I found a café. I got an overpriced coffee and got out a notebook and wrote on top: "October 14, 1997—NYC" which seemed very impressive to me. Below that I wrote a recap of my travels which wasn't very interesting but at least it was something. Then I watched out the window at the people walking down the street in their trendy clothes. I wasn't even sure where I was, somewhere in SoHo I thought. The sense of tiredness I'd woke up with was turning into a nice warm feeling of being *here* finally. I'd sip my super strong coffee and think: *I'm in New York City.* Which to the people walking past the window probably meant nothing but to me was a very big deal.

On Friday, Sally came down from New Haven on the train. I think she wanted to see how I was doing and also, I think she enjoyed sometimes how naïve I was, and liked being the knowledgeable one and teaching me things.

I met her at Grand Central and we walked on Fifth Avenue where all the clothes stores were. Sally agreed I needed something better than a peacoat, but now that I appeared to have a job, I didn't feel a pressing need to replace it.

Sally knew her way around New York somewhat, so she showed me some things, most importantly where you could go to the bathroom (bars and hotels).

Then that night, Sally, Liz, Naomi and I all went out for Thai food at the one nice restaurant in Greenpoint. Naomi obviously had high standards of restaurants and she seemed pretty bored by anything in our neighborhood. She really belonged in Manhattan, you could tell, but we had a pretty spectacular deal there at Wilton Street, as I was learning.

It was still a fun dinner, with Sally and Naomi talking about people they knew in common in high school and me getting a glimpse into their lives in the affluent suburbs of Boston. Naomi was a couple grades older than Sally and had been very popular and had a million boyfriends in high school. Sally had been the nerdy brainiac with a retainer. Liz smiled a lot but didn't say much. Her high school and college career sounded more ordinary. She told us about the non-profit organization where she worked. They did stuff like getting clean water to villages in Africa. She had invited me to one of their events and I had said I would go, but now as she talked about it, it didn't really sound like my thing.

Sally spent the night, sleeping on my futon with me and then the next day we went to a big Saturday flea market in Greenwich Village. This turned out to be super fun and there were a million cool people walking around. We kept bumping into these two guys in particular. Sally noticed them first. I was oblivious. I guess I forgot about boys, since I'd been in such a harried state the last couple weeks. But she was right to check them out: they were cute, and our age, and dressed in old Woolrich coats.

Sally dared to say something to them. Of course she did, she didn't live here! Mark and Brent were their names. We chatted for a few minutes, then separated, and then ran into them again as we were leaving. Sally suggested the four of us go across the street and get coffees. So we did.

They were film students at NYU. They were impressed that we went to Wellington. I didn't mention about getting kicked out, but then Sally brought it up and told the story to impress them with what rebel artists we were.

After that, the four of us walked around. It was such a nice day with the leaves turning colors, and the elegant city people, enjoying the crispness and the sunshine and the fullness of their New York lives. When it was time to go, I gave the boys my number, and the cuter one, Mark, said he would call me. Sally made him promise, joking about how I was alone in the big city and I needed someone to look after me. It was said like a joke, but as we walked away from them, I looked back and Mark looked back too, and we smiled at each other. I felt this sort of ... tug in my chest, which surprised me, because like I said, I hadn't thought about boys in weeks. As we descended the steps to the subway, I asked Sally if she thought he would call. She said she didn't know, and if he didn't, we had done our best, and that there would be other boys. This was New York after all, there was no place on earth with more cute and interesting boys.

20

I STARTED my new job the next week. Richard Kinney wasn't there so it was me and Andre sitting in our little room, my little desk behind his bigger desk. Andre started me out doing delivery logs and invoices. It wasn't so bad. All the bookstores we sent books to were very high-end and were in places like Malibu or Aspen or Tuscany, Italy. And then there were a backlog of requests people had sent, some of them personal letters to Richard. In one case, a woman wrote an elegant hand-written letter asking for several books, most of which weren't even published by us. I showed Andre the letter and he gave me a list of rare book dealers to call. I was to find the books and order them, no matter what the cost, and have them shipped to her directly. It was all very extravagant and posh, but also fun in an old school way.

Of course Mark never called. And when I told Naomi about it she laughed and said in New York, the guys never call. If you like a guy, you have to call him, or better yet, sleep with him, and that was your best chance of ever seeing him again. This sounded extreme, even though she was joking. Naomi looked at me then and said, "You've slept with guys, right?" And I was like of course, but even as I said it I knew that hooking up with people in Portland was not the same as hooking up in New York. I didn't know how it would be different, I just knew it would be.

It turned out I was right. The main problem being, how did you even meet anyone? That was the big surprise of my first couple months in New York. Without school, without a mall job, without old friends like I had in Portland, I had no starting point. And New York wasn't a place where you'd see someone at the one coffee shop everyone went to and then later could start talking to them at the one bar everyone got drunk at. There were millions of young people, and thousands of bars. You almost never saw anyone twice. And even if you did, there was this New York way people had. Like they already had their friends. They already had their lives. Why would they want to talk to you? Their social schedules were full. And even if they weren't, they would never admit it.

And like if you were sitting in a café, surrounded by cool boys, the only person who would talk to you was some total weirdo. And the nice guys you saw reading on the subway, they couldn't talk to you, even if they wanted to, because they were too shy or too afraid of seeming like a stalker. The only real way to meet people was to be introduced, but to do that, you had to have a little circle, or like a gang of people from your college that you moved to New York with.

One night Liz and I went to a bar in Manhattan to attempt to meet boys. We were playing pool and these two Australian guys started to play teams with us and for once it felt sort of normal and like we were actually hanging out. But then later they started drinking out of our pitcher and then ordered another one but didn't pay for it. And then one of the guys tried to kiss Liz by the bathrooms and then we realized they were sort of laughing at us. And then they admitted, right to our faces, that they were also doing the same thing to two NYU girls in the bar across the street. They were like, are you going to take us home and do us? And we were like "what?" and they were like "wrong answer" and they left us with the bar tab and went across the street to "do" the NYU girls.

So yeah, it was weird that first couple weekends when Sally wasn't there. And then after several more painful weekends, I decided to take a break and I took the train up to Sally's in New Haven to have a weekend of college fun. But that seemed lame too. Like the Yale undergrad guys seemed like little nerd-boys. And even the grad students Sally knew, seemed really obvious and predictable in their Yalie way.

That night, I started to think: *Get ready Andrea, because this next year is going to be one of the hardest of your life.* And then later, sleeping on Sally's floor, I thought about Nick Pax and Matthew and Kate and how easy everything was in Portland and how pleasant, and how people had time for each other and were relaxed and you could hang out, as friends, or lovers, or whatever. It wasn't this pressurized "minefield" situation as everyone described dating in New York. Or the endless worry about "stalkers." Those were the two words you heard continuously about being single: "minefield" and "stalker," which just made everyone even more paranoid and negative than they already were.

But there was another part too, and that was, in New York, everyone was ambitious. Everyone was working toward some personal goal. Which made you feel like you had to do that too. In my case, that meant finding a new agent. Or writing another book. Or getting involved in the literary scene. Or possibly doing all three.

And so one day, when Andre was at lunch I got out the

phone book and looked up literary agents and wrote down a couple names that I thought sounded familiar. I noticed many of them were at the same address as the Ruth Goldman Agency. 250 West 57th Street. That seemed to be where all the good agencies were.

And then one day I found a copy of a magazine called *Publishers Weekly* in our office bathroom. I started flipping through it and I was suddenly like, *oh my god, here it all is!* There was stuff about different agents and different writers. And it had pictures of them. And there was a separate page that listed all the book deals that had been made that week, and which agent did it, and who they sold it to. I grabbed up a bunch of *Publisher's Weekly*'s and took them home and that night wrote out a long list of which agents did which books, and also which books might be like my book. I was quite proud of myself for doing this and then a couple days later, I found this other book in Richard's office called *The Writers Marketplace* which had a chapter about how to write to a literary agent and ask them to consider your novel.

Anyway, so then, when I could clearly see what I needed to do, I felt energized and super excited about New York. I didn't care about boys or dating. Getting your career going came first. That was rule number one in New York. Me first. Then you.

IN NOVEMBER, as promised, my workload at Kinney Publishing began to increase. "The book business is a Christmas business," Andre told me in a rare moment of verbal communication. According to him, people bought the same amount of books between Thanksgiving and Christmas as they did during all the other months combined. And so, starting November 1st, Richard Kinney was there from morning to night, and Andre too. And then Richard Kinney's fifteen-year-old daughter started coming in too. She did some of the busy work that I was supposed to do, though she was much better at it, having done it before. Her name was Brooke and she was very serious and sophisticated for being a sophomore in high school. She wasn't pretty, which was strange, since Richard and his wife were both extremely good looking. But she was so adult it was unnerving. I was afraid to even talk to her, she seemed so smart. She also knew how to do everything and we fell into a pattern of her telling me what to do, which Richard seemed to approve of.

As November progressed, I was occasionally sent on errands upstairs to the Kinney apartment which was one floor above us and was huge and looked out over the Hudson River. This was where I first met Mrs. Kinney who was so icy and aloof I was afraid to speak to her. But I felt like I better, since Kinney Publishing was supposed to be like a big family, and it wouldn't look right if I acted too intimidated by her presence. So I tried to think of things to say when I saw her, like complimenting her earrings or saying how incredible their view was.

Another guy showed up one day, another seasonal worker, who I never talked to. He did something with shipping and was always driving to New Jersey and coming back with clipboards and boxes that usually disappeared again, but occasionally got stacked in the reception room or in the hall outside. I didn't understand a lot of what we were doing, which didn't seem like a good sign. Brooke especially seemed to think I was a little slow and when I told her I was from Oregon, that confirmed it. I didn't take this personally, but I felt bad sometimes, like one time I heard her asking her dad about a boy situation at school. I was like, *ask me, I'm a girl!* And I was a lot closer to her age than her dad. But she never did. That's how dumb she thought I was. And unsophisticated. Thank God I'd gone to Wellington. At least they knew at some point I had proven my worth to someone.

One of the job requirements at Kinney Publishing was to stay in New York over Christmas, since the office was still super busy right up to Christmas Eve. And so I stayed, and worked, and was happy to. All of December felt like a great adventure, especially as every day the city got wilder and crazier with holiday frenzy. One night, I walked up Fifth Avenue to check out the window displays. A light snow was falling and everyone was rushing around with their presents. I ended up helping this woman and her funny Pakistani cab driver (in white socks and sandals) try to pack a huge load of presents into a cab.

And then the day before Christmas, the city suddenly emptied itself out. Sally left New Haven for Boston. Naomi and Liz disappeared from the apartment. Even the Kinney's folded into themselves so that even though I had been working so hard, right up to the last second, and felt like I was practically a Kinney myself, they suddenly withdrew and I was a single girl again, going home like I always did, putting on my hat and scarf and walking through the quiet streets of Tribeca to the subway.

I spent my first New Years Eve in New York with Liz at a party for her Clean Water for Africa organization. It was not really my crowd, but I did my best, standing around and drinking champagne and talking to a young Indian man who was getting a PhD in Urban Planning in Developing Countries. I tried to find it interesting. But it was no use. And nobody even got drunk. At midnight I was afraid I would have to kiss someone and I hid in the stairwell during the countdown, sitting there on the metal steps with my dumb cone hat and my chin on my fist and thinking what fun things were probably happening in Portland at that moment and how many cute boys there were to kiss.

Sally visited me again in January and we went to the Whitney museum on Free Night, which Sally said was "art student" night. We cruised around and checked out the artistic guys. Sally, who could be very bold when she was acting on my behalf, started talking to some boys who went to The School of Visual Arts. They were pretty weird but one of them, Ian, was really smart and had a nice voice. He told us interesting tidbits about the art world and the different artists we were looking at. He seemed to know a great deal, even though he was from

Georgia. He'd lived in New York for three and a half years which to me seemed like a very long time.

After that, we rode the subway downtown with Ian and his friends and went to some cool bars they knew about. These were way better than the places I went with Liz. And the beer there was cheap and it was very "art student" with obscure west coast singles on the jukebox, stuff I didn't think New York people knew about, but then I remembered, New York people knew about everything.

When we left the last bar it was snowing really hard. It was the first real blizzard of the year and everyone was excited and looking up into the sky or running down the street and sliding on the snow. We walked Ian and his friend to their subway and we told them to call us and we gave them our numbers and for a second I thought I should ask Ian for his, so that I could call him, like Naomi said to do. But I chickened out.

When they were gone, Sally and I walked in silence through the snow, watching people throw snowballs at cabs. I said to Sally, "Ian's not going to call me is he?" and she said probably not.

Meanwhile, I had written five letters to five different agents, telling them about my novel *Manifesto*, and asking if they wanted to see it. I was very proud of myself for doing this and Sally also approved and I was quite happy when I dropped these "query letters" into the mailbox outside the Greenpoint Post Office.

But then later, I said something about it to Naomi and she thought I was wasting my time writing letters. I told her that's what you were supposed to do. She was like, "You have to meet them. Like in person. Nobody cares about someone who writes them a letter." I immediately saw that she was probably right and I was like, "But how do you meet them?"

"You have to get in with the right people," she said. And then added: "Isn't that why you came here?"

I had to admit it was.

That whole conversation was scary enough, but then a week later, Naomi pulled back my little curtain and looked in on my tiny sleeping area. I was reading *Anna Karenina* which was putting me to sleep. In fact, my eyes were closed at that moment.

She told me she was going to a dinner party with some writer types and she would take me, if I wanted to go.

That last bit, "if I wanted to go," was an unnecessary jibe. Of course I wanted to go.

"Well get ready then," she said. "I'm leaving in ten minutes."

22

WE GOT a car service to Brooklyn Heights. I sat silently next to Naomi Cohn in her black dress and a light blue overcoat she'd just got on sale at Barney's. I was, unfortunately, still wearing my peacoat, but at least I had a nice cashmere sweater one of Sally's Yalie housemates had given me.

We stopped at an upscale deli in Brooklyn Heights and bought a bottle of wine which I offered to help pay for. When Naomi refused my twenty, I offered to get something else and so she sent me for goat cheese and bread. I didn't know anything about goat cheese, so I picked the second-most expensive one.

We walked from there to the party, clipping along the cold sidewalk, Naomi's thin, competent legs striding at top speed. She was all business, all the time. Which was, I reminded myself, how I needed to be.

We rang the buzzer and an attractive woman let us in. We went into the apartment which was way nicer than ours, but still small and cramped, like everyone's except the Kinney's. We were the last to arrive, so I met everyone at once. They were mostly in their late twenties/early thirties, I thought. There was a couple who didn't talk much and the hostess Daphna who had an interesting artsy, preppy style. There was a cute guy with dark messy hair who was waiting for his first novel to come out. I was very interested to hear about that but I didn't want to pry or seem too self-serving. As it turned out, he barely said a word all night. He was quite anxious about his book and whenever he took a drink of his gin and tonic, he did it in this weird fast motion, like he didn't really want to drink it but had no choice.

Daphna's best friend Grant was a loud funny guy who had a refined tone in his voice. He seemed gay, but in New York I could never tell about that, and in fact, he was not gay, I figured out eventually. Then there was another woman, who was older, and had grey hair, who already had a book of short stories out but seemed quite miserable and depressed. One of her short stories had been in *The New Yorker* several years ago. The woman cringed when Daphna mentioned it.

So mostly we sat around and talked and drank wine for about an hour. Then we sat down for dinner. There was less talking while we ate, but it was a little scarier in a way, because everyone was right there, everyone could hear everything you said. I mostly kept my mouth shut. But that wasn't going to work either because if I didn't talk or assert myself in some way, I wouldn't get to know anyone.

Grant saved me by asking me about myself. Everyone went quiet and listened, which was nerve-wracking. I said I grew up in Oregon and went to Wellington and everyone nodded approvingly. They all went to similar colleges except the older *New Yorker* woman who went to the University of Arizona. It was funny because the minute she said that, I could see she was really a westerner and not really like the other people. She had sun wrinkles on the side of her eyes and she wasn't as good looking or as stylish as everyone else.

When the main meal was over, people loosened up and

began teasing the grim, silent, about-to-be novelist who seemed completely distracted and miserable, though it appeared that these people were his closest friends.

At one point people talked about agents. When that came up I swallowed and tried to think of something to say. Then Naomi announced: "Andrea wrote a novel about her hometown, and she needs an agent." Everyone chuckled and looked at me and felt sorry for me and someone asked me what my book was about and I told them, feeling embarrassed, that it was about a suburban punk kid who falls in love with an environmentalist girl. Nobody seemed interested, though they didn't make fun of me or anything. Mostly they just fell silent. I noticed the worried novelist was so preoccupied he hadn't even heard what I said. So then, since nobody else was talking, I said: "I had an agent for about a month but I lost him. I guess he didn't like my rewrite."

That got people's attention, at least a little. Grant asked me who it was and I said, "Will Soren at the Ruth Goldman Agency." Grant's eyes went wide and he looked at Daphna and she looked around the table and everyone kind of hesitated for a second. Then they all burst out laughing. Like Will Soren was a complete joke. I was confused and Daphna said: "We're not laughing at you, it's just that nobody takes Will Soren seriously." And then Grant launched into a story about Will Soren representing a young married woman, and having an affair with her and getting her pregnant. This had been at the beginning of his long and checkered career. It had been in the *New York Post* every day for a week. The married woman's novel had ended up on the bestseller list, partly because of the scandal of sleeping with her agent.

So everyone had a big laugh about that. Someone else said Will Soren had represented the ridiculous book *Electra Rising*, which I'd heard about from Sally. I laughed too, though I had noticed just that week *Electra Rising's* "pseudo-feminism" was still being argued about in the letters section of the *Village Voice*. Also Carol Smith had read it last summer. And liked it. And had told me to read it.

I'd livened up the conversation at least. Everyone had an opinion about Will Soren. Several people said how lucky I was to escape his clutches. "Getting rid of him is the best thing you could have done," said Daphna. But of course I hadn't gotten rid of him, he had gotten rid of me.

And then Grant told a story of a college friend who had been brutally canned by an agent he had interned with for months. Other people had similar stories of the ruthless world of literary agents. Daphna asked me if I had met Will Soren in person. I said no. She nodded that I was very fortunate.

The party began to wind down. I went to the bathroom and when I came out I found the older woman from Arizona in the bedroom, looking at Daphna's book shelf. I went and looked at the books with her. I asked her what it was like living in New York after Arizona. She didn't really answer. I watched her face. I had never stood next to someone that had been published in *The New Yorker*. It seemed like once you'd achieved that, it didn't matter what happened after. She seemed sort of tense though. And she had wirey, frazzly, grey hair, which seemed to mirror her mental state.

Back in the living room, as we sipped cappuccinos, I watched the anxious novelist guy. He still looked deeply anxious and unhappy. I didn't understand that. No matter what else happened, how could you not be excited if your book was coming out? I went and sat next to him and said hi, and he just stared at me. He was very drunk by now. And I said congratulations to him about his book and he said: "I met with Will

Soren." And I said yeah, what was he like? And he said he was an "arrogant prick" and was "dismissive" and that he "hurts your reputation." I nodded solemnly though I wasn't sure why he was telling me that. Shortly after, he got up and got his coat. He nearly fell over as he put it on. Everyone laughed and made jokes about how he was a real novelist now, since he was shit-faced drunk.

We rode back to Greenpoint in a car service town car. Naomi seemed bored but she admitted that I had done okay. That I had at least amused everyone with my stories about Will Soren. "He sounds absolutely horrible," said Naomi.

But I didn't agree. I didn't say this out loud, but deep down, something told me that to be hated by the Daphnas and the Grants of the world, might actually be a recommendation. I doubted Will Soren was sitting around criticizing them. I probably needed to learn more about him. And about all the agents, and all the different agencies.

And most of all: I needed to read *Electra Rising*.

23

ELECTRA RISING WAS about a girl from New York City who returns home from a liberal arts college in upstate New York. She parties with her wild Manhattan friends. This cool older guy wants to marry her but she can't figure out what she wants or who she is, and eventually goes a little crazy. It was short and minimal in style and had a lot of sex scenes, which were the parts people made fun of the most. In general, it seemed like it was trying to be shocking, like it was trying to be a book about "the new generation." It was maybe trying too hard I thought, but a lot of it was still really funny. The partying scenes were great. The rich-kids-on-coke dialogue was exactly right and totally hilarious. I liked it enough to go back and read certain parts a second time. When I was done, I found myself thinking about it a lot. Especially since it was about what real New Yorkers were like, like people who lived their whole lives here. It was a little painful in that way. Reading it, I felt like a total hick, and like the New York I saw, living in ghetto Greenpoint, barely counted as being there at all.

The other interesting thing that happened was Richard Kinney saw me reading it and asked me about it and I told him it was good. I said, "It's about the young sexy crowd," meaning that as a joke. But Richard seemed genuinely interested and wanted to borrow it and check it out. I told him the story of the dinner party and how everyone hated this one agent I had almost worked with. Richard Kinney, you could tell, didn't want to get tangled up in my writing career. Like he thought it was good that I wanted to be a writer but he never discussed it with me. I wondered if some other employee had wanted his help getting published or maybe wanted Richard to publish them himself. In general most people in New York seemed horrified that their friends might have novels they wanted them to read or wanted them to help get published. So I kept that stuff to myself mostly. But he asked. So I told him.

Winter continued, and since it was so slow at the office, I went on a little reading frenzy. I read *Tropic of Cancer* and *The Delta of Venus* and *The Secret History* by Donna Tartt. I read *Bonjour Tristesse* and an erotic novel Naomi kept hidden by the bathtub. I read *The Handmaid's Tale* and the first hundred pages of *American Psycho*. I did much of this reading sitting at my desk, which I felt a little guilty about but Richard didn't seem to care. He would take me to lunch sometimes and we would sit there, chatting about mountain climbing or him reminiscing about his own first years in New York. That was how it was in the book business, after Christmas, everyone relaxed.

February came and on Valentine's Day, Liz and I and her friend Jasmine went out drinking. We played pool and flirted with guys, though I was much more on guard now in those situations, unless the guys were super nice. But of course the super nice guys never came up to you and if they did, they never asked you for your number.

The whole dating thing in New York sucked so much in that

way. Everything had to follow this certain track. You met, you talked, then you gave him your number and he was supposed to call. Which he never did. One time a guy did call Liz. He was this creepy guy from some place in Indonesia we'd never heard of. He kept bugging her and she finally went to dinner with him and he tried to kiss her afterward in the cab. So then she had to get out, like at a red light, and he yelled at her and called her a whore and she lost one of her shoes in the escape. He gave her the shoe back though. He threw it at her, out the taxi window.

So that was the dating world of New York. Nothing natural or easy ever happened. Not like Portland. You never just hung out or "ended up" at somebody's house. I mean, some people did, people who knew tons of people I guess. Occasionally, I'd end up at some cool party and I'd realize, wow, if I knew *these* people I could have a real social life. But you got the feeling those groups were joined from way back, they were old friends, they had come from college together, and even their little groups would eventually dissolve and disintegrate. That's how it was in the big city. Nobody stayed together for long. The city didn't want that. The city wanted you alone.

In March, I bought my first laptop computer. I had to, it was 1998 now and everyone had one and everyone was emailing and when I would talk to other aspiring writers, they were all using email and writing their stories on their computers and now there were even websites that published fiction online.

The other thing was: there were computer dating sites, which everyone was excited about. Like *Swoon*, which was supposed to be for writers and publishing people and media types. And then *Nerve* got big, which was another dating site for the supposedly cool people, and everyone seemed to think the whole dating concept had been re-invented, or like now that it was on a computer it would actually work and people weren't going to be assholes, which of course was absurd. All the computer did was make you talk to the person by typing a message to them, instead of writing them a letter or calling them, like on the old-style personal ads, which only the most nerdy people used to do.

But in New York it was different. All New Yorkers were nerds in a way, so computer dating was huge. Liz went on a bunch of dates on *Swoon* that were all horrible sounding. And Naomi did *Nerve* because she said it was "the right kind of people." The thing about Naomi was, she got lots of male attention anyway. She'd figured out the formula, which was basically: always act impatient and annoyed, and always wear lipstick.

In the meantime, the five letters I sent to agents had done nothing, just like Naomi had predicted. I started to think I needed to re-write *Manifesto* for a second time, so I started typing it onto my new computer. This took forever, and was a pain, and it made me start to hate it. It was no *Electra Rising*, that was for sure. As I typed, I tried to change it, taking out the more corny parts and making it a little more sparse and less cutesy. That was one thing New York did right away, it made you eliminate all *cutesiness* from yourself. You could not be *cutesy* here. The pressurized environment would not tolerate bad taste.

Still though, this was not a bad time for me. My first spring in New York. I was settled in now, and even though there were difficult things I had to deal with, other positive things were beginning to emerge. Like *The New York Times*. I started reading it every day. Usually at the Kinney Publishing offices, but on weekends Naomi and I pitched in for the Sunday edition. Reading it every day, you understood the world in a new way. There was a general feeling of *excellence* in *The Times* and when you were reading it regularly, that superior feeling rubbed off on you.

One day in April, I left work and sat in Washington Square Park and I felt really calm and satisfied with my life. My brain was full of interesting things and I had a good job, and I spent time with the remarkable Kinney family, and I knew people like Naomi Cohn, and I still had my novel. I felt a sense of completeness. I was a real New York person now. I was doing it. I didn't know what "it" was exactly, but whatever, my life was genuinely interesting and exciting, which was all you could ever really hope for.

24

THEN ONE DAY AT WORK, Richard's daughter Brooke came downstairs in a rush and went into Richard's office and shut the door. I could hear something going on, a tense conversation, not yelling, but Brooke raising her voice and Richard saying something back in an angry tone. She left soon after, slamming the office door and then slamming the main door. I glanced at Andre but Andre kept his eyes fixed on his computer screen, as always. A few minutes later, Richard called someone, I could heard his muffled voice through the wall. He left immediately after and something felt very wrong. This was highly unusual. Kinney Publishing was generally the most cheerful, happy place on earth.

A couple days later, Richard Kinney called me into his office and had me shut the door. He asked me to sit down. I was like, *oh shit, I'm getting fired*. Richard sat there behind his desk. He looked terrible, like really old suddenly and tired and gaunt. What was happening? Then he said to me, in a very careful voice, that his wife was leaving him and that things were going to get a little crazy. He might need me to run some personal errands and do some other things for him, if that was okay. I nodded that I would do whatever he wanted. Of course I would. He said the first thing he needed was for me to take Brooke to her weekend Dance Camp, which meant driving her to Connecticut on Friday afternoon. To myself, I was like, *drive a car? In Manhattan?* Richard was like you know how to drive don't you? I swallowed silently. I said I did.

Two days later I found myself in a secret underground garage. I didn't even know the Kinneys had a car, but of course they did. It was a shiny clean Mercedes station wagon. So then Brooke and I had to drive out of this secret parking garage, where you had like three inches on either side as you pulled out. We survived that and made it to the street and then I had to follow the directions Andre had written out for me, super simplified, as if I were a complete moron, thank God. Brooke helped. She was great like that. She was probably the most competent fifteen-year-old girl on the face of the earth. So off we went, me driving a Mercedes through Manhattan and then getting on the expressway and people driving like maniacs all around us. But I went slow and Brooke talked me through it, and told me not to worry. She then confessed that she and her friends often snuck their parents' cars out and drove around at night in Manhattan. They'd even taken this car out. I was like: "Don't tell me things like that."

A week later, movers showed up at the Kinney apartment. They were slick and fast and they had all of Mrs. Kinney's stuff out of there in four hours. We could hear them from our office pounding up and down the stairwell. They looked like commandos, young and with crewcuts and uniforms and barking orders at each other in Russian or wherever they came from.

Later that week, Brooke was in the office and we were going

through the mail and she slowly began to tell me the story of what happened. Her mother had been having an affair with a man in the Mayor's office, he was a very high-profile person, so she couldn't say his name. That was basically the problem: her mom thought her dad lacked ambition. She thought the art press was silly and a vanity project. Brooke added that her mother was power hungry and was never satisfied with anyone or anything. "Basically, she's totally evil," Brooke said.

I never saw Mrs. Kinney again. All those useless compliments I had wasted on her, none of which she had even bothered to acknowledge.

Not that I cared. I considered knowing Mrs. Kinney a crucial learning experience. I had never met someone who cared so little about other people. She literally had not allowed me into her brain. I did not exist. And I had shut her out too. If she'd dropped dead right in front of me, I'm not sure I would have felt a thing. It was scary and inhuman, but that's how certain people were in New York. They didn't care if you lived or died.

Meanwhile, the drama continued. Mostly I tried to stay out of things. I went to work and tried to find stuff to do and read *Prozac Nation* during my extended lunch breaks. In June, I had the office to myself when Andre took a month vacation with his boyfriend. It was interesting how Andre did not get involved in the Kinney breakup in any way. He had good boundaries. That was probably the best way to handle it, instead of doing what I was doing, which was always offering to help. But I didn't know. I'd never been around a marriage breaking up before.

As the summer began there was other news too. Like Sally— now graduated—was moving to New York to go to the Columbia School of Journalism. Also, Carol Smith was leaving

USC after winning a bunch of student film prizes. She was hoping to come live in Brooklyn. I was very excited about that but I was also careful to remember that Carol and Sally would have their own New York lives, like I had mine. I couldn't assume the three of us would be instant best friends again.

Besides, I had friends of my own. Liz and her friend Jasmine and I had become pretty close. Jasmine had an actual boyfriend which seemed so strange and exotic to us, we always liked to hear about that.

And then Vanessa, another old college friend, showed up in New York. This was going to happen a lot now. People from my class at Wellington, having just graduated, would be landing in New York that summer and the next year. A lot of them would just go home to their parents' apartments in Manhattan. Most of them would not be living in places like Greenpoint.

Anyway, so Vanessa took me out to dinner at this nice restaurant, since I was a starving artist, in her mind. She had been pre-med at Wellington and had just started working on a research project at NYU Medical School. She seemed different than she'd been at school. She was more adult and mature but she also was quick to make fun of herself for ending up in the sciences. It was "dork central," she said, but she loved the blood cell research she was doing, even though it probably sounded boring to someone like me.

As June progressed, I ended up staying at the Kinney's overnight a couple times. This happened the first time when Richard wanted me to house sit while he was in Europe on business. I was supposed to look after Brooke, which was unnecessary, but I did it anyway and fed the cats and slept in their guest room the first night (their apartment had two floors). The second night Brooke and I both curled up in the big master bed and watched a movie and then fell asleep there together. It was so fun to be around Brooke, she was such a fascinating person. That night I watched her sleep and thought about what a strange life she would have, this super child, so adult and mature, but also, not very pretty, or popular and sort of dour in her personality. How was she going to survive in her world of rich kids who were gorgeous and charming and perfect social beings? It made me think of *Electra Rising*, though Brooke was no party girl, that was for sure.

Another time I came to work but Richard had me come upstairs to help clean up his apartment from a party the night before. The housekeeper hadn't shown up, so he and I did the cleaning. It was like the middle of the day, and after a while, he found this half empty bottle of fancy wine and he was like, "to hell with cleaning, let's finish this wine." There was just enough for a half glass each, and so we sat by the window of his apartment and looked out at the Hudson and took sips of it. At first Richard didn't say anything, but then he started talking. He told me the whole story of how he met his wife and chased her around the South of France one summer and finally stole her away from an investment banker, telling her there was more to life than money and a house in the Hamptons, and how he wanted to publish the great neglected artists, the *real* artists of his day.

He talked on and on. It all came pouring out. And the problems with Brooke when she was little, how Mrs. Kinney became more and more critical of her daughter when she realized she wasn't beautiful and wasn't going to have the right friends.

Richard at some point opened another bottle of wine and we sat there all afternoon. I even talked too. Though my life story wasn't as interesting or dramatic, but I still told it, or parts of it. Richard listened and I had this nice sensation as the sky got dark, that Richard liked me and respected me in some way.

He had trusted me with his daughter, and trusted me to be part of his family.

I never went back to the office that day. We ate dinner there, together in the apartment, fancy pizza delivered, since he knew I liked that and afterward he called me a car service back to Brooklyn. When the car arrived, he gave me a hug and told me how much it helped him to have me around. I said thanks and then I gave him another hug, because I liked him so much and because I'd had a lot of wine.

25

FOR FOURTH OF JULY, Liz and Jasmine and I had an unusual predicament. We had *five* different party's to go to. None of them were super amazing, not like the GQ party Naomi was working on in Central Park. She had just begun a new job organizing celebrity parties and corporate events. Still, five Brooklyn parties was pretty good, for us.

Then earlier that day, while Naomi was making us do a group clean in the kitchen, Richard called and told me that Brooke and her friends were going to watch the westside fireworks from their roof, and I was welcome to come over too, and bring friends if I wanted. I thought that sounded great and said we might, but I hadn't talked to Jasmine and I couldn't decide for everyone.

But later when I told Liz and Jasmine, they were like: if there aren't any guys what's the point? To hang out with some fifteen-year-old girls? So I was like, okay, and we went ahead with our original plan and went to the Brooklyn parties.

. . .

The first party was terrible. It was these redneck people from Philadelphia who were totally drunk by the time we got there. They were in this garage space, which smelled like oil and they didn't have any beer left.

At the next party there was no one home. Like, literally, no one answered the buzzer.

The third party was mostly hip-hop people and this woman dressed in traditional African garb. Several people stood in their bare feet in a wading pool and drank beer, and other people cooked tofu burgers. After an hour we left.

The next party was the good one. It was near the L Train Bedford stop and it was on the roof of a huge old warehouse building. There were about fifty people and music and there were grills and coolers and food. But later, as the sun went down, this one guy came around and said, "You guys! You won't be able to see the fireworks, that building is in the way!" He said he'd been there last year, on that exact same roof, and the view of the fireworks would be blocked by the new apartment building they were building on the next block. Liz and I had noticed this when we first got up there.

By this time there were even more people there, drinking beer and sitting around on the gravel roof. It was getting dark, and the fireworks would start soon. So then some of the people decided they better go down to the East River, or they'd miss the fireworks. They started gathering their stuff and heading down the stairs. And as soon as some of the people started leaving, then everyone decided to leave and it became this big rush of people hurrying down the stairs, carrying beer and hot dog buns and lawn chairs.

Liz and Jasmine had been talking to some boys they knew and volunteered to carry their big cooler. I ended up carrying someone's bag of ice. So down the stairs we went, with everyone else.

Down on the street, there were other people coming up from the subway station and they were doing the exact same thing: rushing toward the East River since it was dark and the fireworks were about to start. My bare leg was getting wet, carrying the ice. I wasn't even sure who the ice belonged to. Jasmine and Liz had gotten ahead of me too, but hadn't noticed since they were so preoccupied with the two boys.

Suddenly, I realized I didn't care about the fireworks. Or this mob of sweaty people. Or any Williamsburg boys who I didn't really like and who would never call you anyway. I wanted to be with Richard and Brooke, having a glass of wine and doing something civilized like sitting on their roof in Tribeca, eating fancy cheese.

I dropped the bag of ice in the street and found a pay phone and called Richard, quickly, before I could think about it. When I heard Richard's voice I knew I'd made the right decision. He sounded so relieved to hear from me. And I felt the same, instantly relaxed and calm and like he was the one I wanted to hang out with and I knew he felt the same way.

He repeated his offer, though he didn't know where Brooke was, he might have lost her to some new friends. He laughed and said she was getting to that age, she didn't want to hang out with Dad anymore. I said something corny like, I still liked hanging out with him. He laughed and said I was welcome to come over. I said I would, and I hung up the phone.

From that moment on, the whole night changed into something else. I walked back toward the subway, against the flow of desperate fireworks seekers. I watched them and felt nice feelings for them. I felt nice feelings for everyone, so completely happy and content and excited was I for my new plan.

The L Train was just pulling in as I entered the station. I was wearing cut-off cords and an old striped T-shirt and blue Vans. My hair was pulled back in a scrunchy and I was sweaty like everyone else, but when I sat down in the air-conditioned subway car, a delicious chill went through me, which helped me freeze my thoughts and stay as I was, in a perfect mood of anticipation and non-thinking.

My subway luck continued and I caught the 9 Train just as it was pulling in. I got off in Tribeca as the westside fireworks were starting. People were doing the same thing in Manhattan as in Brooklyn, hurrying toward the water, looking for the best places to watch. Suddenly the first whistling explosions lit up the sky. Everyone stopped what they were doing to stare upward. The whole city seemed mesmerized. I kept walking though, weaving through the people. What a happy adventure it felt like, to be running through the streets of New York on this balmy night with these great bursts of color filling the sky overhead.

Richard buzzed me in and I ran up the stairs, holding my breath and not letting myself think about anything. The truth was, I just wanted to see Richard. I just wanted to sit with him, and breath in the summer air, and talk to him and be able to look at him and be where he was. And even though I hoped Brooke wasn't there, it would be okay if she was. I liked Brooke as much as Richard, in a way. Still, it would be better if she wasn't there.

Richard let me into the apartment, which was dark. I was like, "It's starting!" He grabbed some champagne and we climbed up the stairs to the roof. Brooke wasn't there. So it was just Richard and I. We pulled the folding chairs toward the westside and opened the champagne and watched the fireworks which were the biggest and most spectacular that I'd ever seen. New York really did have the best of everything.

It went on for an hour. When it was over, we sat there and

didn't talk and I drank more champagne in little sips. Below us you could hear the craziness on the street: people screaming and setting off their own fireworks, or cars getting stuck in post-fireworks traffic and honking their horns. I stood up and looked off the roof at the people down below and Richard did the same and I felt my whole body tingle and come alive as his elbow touched my arm on the cement wall. Then I went downstairs to pee and alone in the bathroom, I felt this strange thing come over me, like I knew what was going to happen, and I guess I had known all day, I had sure known when I was running down the street to get here.

When I came out, Richard was in the kitchen, standing among the granite and the stainless steel. He looked so happy, fiddling with another bottle of champagne and I came close to him and leaned against the counter and he stopped what he was doing and looked at me. I saw him hesitate. I let him hesitate, and didn't do anything to encourage him, but I didn't pull back either.

He set the champagne bottle down and put his arms around me. He said something I didn't hear and then gently kissed the side of my head. Then he held me. I suddenly felt angry at him because I loved him so much. I wanted to hit him almost. It was a strange feeling and I loved the confusion of it. But I knew also that I loved him. I loved him so much I could barely stand it.

I was so wet when we got in his bedroom. When he lay down beside me I hated him again, because I knew this was fucked up somehow, but I wasn't sure why. And the thing I was mad about the most was that he hadn't done anything. I had done it. I had called. I had come over. I had made the move in the kitchen. Or maybe he had maneuvered me into doing it somehow. He had definitely made me fall in love with him.

Whatever it was, I felt the need to take control. I wanted

him inside me, and insisted he do that, instead of doing what he was going to do, a lot of foreplay or whatever. I wanted that because I wanted it over and done with. But then once he was inside me, I was okay again, and I wasn't mad at all and I pulled him close and squeezed myself around him, and everything was fine and perfect, just as I had dreamed it would be.

26

THE SEX WENT on and on. We'd do it for a while and then doze off and then wake up and do it a different way and then talk for a long time and do it in some other way. We went like that until morning: fading in and out of sleep, fading in and out of each other, me wrapped around him, him wrapped around me.

In the morning he made coffee and brought it in and before I could even lift the cup off the tray, he was on me and we were doing it again. This was the best of all, this late morning part, where I was half asleep and the air conditioning was on and it was cool, almost chilly in the bedroom and my nipples got hard and other parts of me were sore but also wanting to keep going, to keep adding more layers to this amazing thing we had started.

I guess we didn't get bored with each other which is what eventually makes you stop in those situations. Or you've just had enough. We never seemed to reach that point. I wondered if that was because we were so different in age, and different in other things, our bodies, our backgrounds. There were so many differences we needed to constantly connect. So we spent a lot of time connecting.

I left around three in the afternoon, in those same cutoff corduroys and T-shirt. Richard offered to call me a car service but I knew I needed to walk around, and in fact, I spent the next couple hours, wandering the humid streets, drinking iced tea, and trying to get used to this new person I was, this new person who had affairs with her boss, who fell in love with her boss, if that's even what had happened. In all honesty, I had no idea what had happened. That's why I needed to walk around.

Later that evening, I called Jasmine from the Bedford subway station and told her what had happened. She came running to meet me at a bar in Williamsburg where I blabbed out the whole thing to her for several hours. Which didn't really make me feel any better. I was pretty shell shocked really. But also weirdly happy. And also kind of terrified.

Later that night, I finally lurched into my tiny bedroom and collapsed into my bed. I lay there for a second, feeling the totality of everything that had happened ... and then burst into tears. Liz heard me and came into my room and I was like, "No, no, I'm fine, I'll tell you about it tomorrow."

It happened again, on Tuesday, in the office, while Brooke was upstairs. Richard and I had sex on the little couch in his office. And then I went upstairs to the Kinney apartment after work on Thursday when Brooke was staying with her mom in their house in Connecticut. We did it in his super comfortable bed, another marathon session, six hours of laying around and doing every sexual thing we could think of.

Brooke, meanwhile, began having nasty fights with her mother and wanted to come back to her dad's. Mrs. Kinney wanted Brooke to live with her, which seemed ridiculous since

Mrs. Kinney didn't even like Brooke. But Mrs. Kinney was a fighter, and was going to fight Richard in whatever way she could.

I stayed in Brooklyn all weekend and went to work on Monday and Richard was out meeting with lawyers all day. That week I barely saw him except for a few short stops in his office. A lot of stuff was going on and I laid low. On Friday he took me out to dinner and told me we needed to cool it. This was at Rudy's, the lowkey fancy Tribeca restaurant we always went to. But then after dinner we went right back to his apartment and did it more intensely than ever.

Liz and Jasmine were pretty freaked out by all this. I would say, "It's not like I planned it!" But then I'd tell them about the hours in bed and they would shut right up. Like as questionable as it was, my situation with Richard still had this incredible allure to them. They were mesmerized. Maybe every young woman wants to do that once in her life. If for no other reason than to learn all the different sex things, the "ways of love."

One night I talked to Naomi about it. She was brutal, as always. She said I had to get as much out of him as I could. Especially when we broke up. Because this was his fault, and I could sue him. I had not considered this and didn't want to. But I still listened to her, since I was definitely worried what would happen if I couldn't keep working there.

"He has to help you financially when it's over," said Naomi, looking directly into my eyes. "Or at least get you a new job. He *has to*. Remember that. And don't be shy about it when it happens."

· · ·

But we didn't break up. We kept having intense sex and then laying around talking and then having more intense sex. And I would ride back to Greenpoint in car service limos, with multiple doggie bags from Rudy's that Liz and Naomi and I would share in the dark apartment, the three of us thrilled by the delicious morsels and the illicit way they had come to us.

But what was going to happen? I didn't know. I didn't want to know. Obviously it couldn't last. But that made it better. Each time Richard touched me the futility and tragedy of it all, made me quiver with anticipation. And the best part of all: I was so young. I was so blameless. I never had to plan, or scheme, or talk, or explain. Richard was in charge of everything. He would decide. All I had to do was close my eyes and open my arms and feel his warm breath on my neck as he eased himself inside me once again ...

In August, Brooke was enrolled in a boarding school in New Hampshire since nobody knew what to do with her. But then at the last minute Richard's excellent lawyers figured out a way to have her live with Richard for the school year even though Mrs. Kinney was threatening all sorts of crazy things. Also, according to Richard's lawyer, her powerful new boyfriend from the Mayor's office was balking and might not be so enamored of Mrs. Kinney as was originally thought. This further weakened her position.

Richard briefed me at Rudy's. We always went there now. I knew all the waiters. I knew my favorite things to order. At the end of dinner, Richard became very serious. He started to rotate his water glass thoughtfully. He said: "We have to stop. This is not something we can have going on around Brooke ... "

I agreed, totally, but I still assumed we would have sex that night. And we did. I couldn't imagine two people loving each other as intensely as we did that night. He went down on me for half an hour. Tears actually streamed down my face as his tongue caressed me with so much love. I closed my eyes and actually felt myself rolling over velvety waves of pleasure, just like in Naomi's erotic bathtub book.

And then, to add to the weirdness, Sally arrived in New York. She moved into an apartment uptown by Columbia and prepared for the start of grad school. She called and we made a dinner date. I had told her about Richard Kinney on the phone. Mostly telling her a more guilt-ridden and ambivalent version of what was happening. But at the restaurant I gave her the other side of the story: how much I loved him, how ecstatically happy I was, and how this affair was pretty much the most incredible thing I'd ever done in my life.

Sally was shocked. I mean, like *shocked*. And not in a good way. Richard was her Uncle's best friend! But she didn't judge. Or she tried not to. It was a weird conversation.

And then a couple days later, Carol Smith arrived in town. So then it was the three of us hanging out, but even with asexual Carol there, all conversation pretty quickly turned to Richard Kinney. I gave Carol a pretty bare bones synopsis of what had happened. By now though, I had noticed the pointlessness of describing it to people. Nobody believed Richard and I actually loved each other. Everyone saw it as a purely sexual transaction. I was the cute young girl and he was the horny old man. I needed validation. He needed to prop up his middle-aged self-esteem. We were both there for our own selfish reasons. We were both taking advantage of each other in our own way.

All of which I understood. All of which I accepted the logic of. But none of which I believed. Not in my heart. I loved

Richard. Fucked up as it was, temporary as it was, doomed as it was: I totally loved him. Some of those nights, holding his sleeping head against my chest, I wouldn't let myself go to sleep, because I didn't want to miss *one second* of our time together.

Richard broke up with me at Rudy's. Which was fitting. He said he loved me and respected me and I had been a great friend to him, and a great lover, but to continue would hurt too many people, Brooke first and foremost, but also me, and him. He needed to be a father now, and regain his equilibrium and deal with Mrs. Kinney from a position of confidence and not guilt, which sleeping with me was causing him. And I needed to return to my own life as well: building my career, being with my friends, finding a man my own age, who I could eventually have my own family with. It was a nice speech, warm and full of love and I began to cry halfway through it, my tears dropping into my butternut squash soup, which was my favorite thing at Rudy's, along with the lobster ravioli.

And then, in one of the strangest emotional shifts that ever occurred inside me, I went from deep genuine sadness and grief, to thinking about Naomi's advice. *Get as much as you can.* I dabbed my eyes with my napkin. I looked around at the elegant room and the lavish meal in front of me and the beautiful people at the adjoining tables and I knew it might be a long time until I was in a place like Rudy's again. *Get as much as you can.* When had I become a person who considered such things? The thought of it sickened me. And yet, there it was.

"As for you working for me ... " said Richard, oblivious to my own inner turmoil. "I think we need to rethink that as well. I happen to have a good friend who needs someone right now. She runs a fantastic photography magazine. It's a much bigger operation, lots of young people on staff. It'd be a great job for you. I can talk to her if you're interested ... "

With tears in my eyes, I nodded that this was probably for the best. And so it was, that the ancient rules and obligations of clandestine New York love affairs had kicked in. I didn't even have to ask.

27

AND SO AUTUMN began with me in a state of blurry emotional numbness. I was quite devastated. My friends rallied around me as best they could. People advised me, consoled me, told me what I should have done, and what I should do in the future to prevent such a thing from happening again. Not that I listened to any of it. But it made everyone feel better to talk.

In mid-September I walked into the offices of *In Focus,* Richard's friend's photography magazine. There, without trying very hard, I was given a job. This I showed up for, on Monday, on time, like I'd always done at jobs.

Then, as the weeks went by, as Richard began to fade from my immediate day-to-day existence, I gradually realized I was not just okay, I was quite happy. I felt like I had done something serious for once. Serious and profound. And now I would move onto new things, having learned and been transformed by this experience. And wasn't that why I had come to New York? It felt like it was.

.　.　.

With Sally at Columbia, she and Carol Smith and I became real friends again. I had a new standing with them, since I had an entire year of New York experience and they were just starting. Now I was the one who knew certain things and for once I could help them.

Not that Carol Smith didn't get up to speed instantly. She was making a movie within a month of landing in New York with her friend Libby Schulman from USC.

Sally got right into things too, making friends with different Columbia Journalism people, who we hung out with and whose parties we got invited to.

By October I had settled into my new job, which turned out to be pretty great. *In Focus* had a real staff, a dozen mostly young people. Veronica Haycox, the editor and founder, was funny and eccentric and seemed to like me instantly. The whole gang at *In Focus* were artsy and smart. They were constantly telling me about events and parties and people I needed to know about, as if they could tell I was cool, I just needed a little coaching.

Also they knew everything about computers and internet stuff, which was all anyone was thinking about in 1998. Every twenty-something in New York was frantic to become rich, creating a website that hooked you up with babysitters or could pay your parking tickets or would find you a one-night stand. Not that the *In Focus* people were totally like that. They were genuinely artsy, mainly because Veronica had worked at *Interview* magazine when she was young and hung out with Andy Warhol. So she only hired people that understood that world and would respect her for being part of it.

On October 15th, Liz moved out and I moved into Liz's room which was twice as big as mine, and a little more private.

Naomi found a new girl, Mari Tamaru, to replace her. Mari was Japanese American and had just graduated from Sarah Lawrence. She complained a lot at first, and was kind of spoiled, but she calmed down after a couple weeks and became a good roommate. She found a good cheap Mexican restaurant we all started going to, and she was funny and crude and talked endlessly about how she needed to "get laid."

The other thing that happened was I started writing again. My schedule at *In Focus* included two half-days, so I was able to get some pretty good chunks of time to myself, sometimes at home and sometimes at the magazine office, where I could stay late and have the big computers to myself. The first idea I tried seemed to work right away and before I knew it I had sixty pages of a novel. The story was about these two sisters growing up in Portland and the younger one is really hip and cool and the older one is more normal and wants an average life and doesn't want to rock the boat. It started with their childhoods and then proceeded into high school and then into their twenties. I really liked it. It had a lot of the same stuff as my first novel, *Manifesto*, lots of references to youth culture and the current times. But unlike *Manifesto*, the characters seemed less like a joke and more real. The general style of it seemed more mature.

Anyway, I loved working on it. It flowed so easily, which was how the best parts of *Manifesto* had felt. And it was fun to see the characters develop: the more reckless younger sister who so casually rejected her suburban upbringing, while the older sister worried constantly about how people perceived her and never wanted to get into trouble and thereby defeated herself by her own tentative approach to everything.

So yeah, that autumn sort of flew by with me working on *Sisters* and then running around with Sally, and also meeting up with Carol Smith and Libby and hanging out with their

USC friends, the so called "indie film mafia," which they jokingly called themselves, the joke being they had no power, they couldn't get hired anywhere, and were constantly taking temp jobs at the Pets R Us or whatever.

One night, Sally and I went to a party for a new magazine called *Context*, that someone at Columbia had told her about. *Context* was supposed to be like an intellectual journal, but for the new generation. It was full of long articles about semiotics and meta-fiction and the new modes of interpreting literature. I almost refused to go because of my bad memories of English major types at Wellington, but Sally had heard their parties were pretty wild so we went.

It wasn't as pretentious as I expected. It was basically a two-bedroom apartment full of people in their twenties, most of them drunk, all of them standing around in this dorky way. They were trying to be intellectuals I guess. But they weren't trying very hard. We started talking to people and nobody was talking about semiotics, they were talking about how insane their rent was or some guy who slept with all his roommates or someone's friend who had invented a velvet pocket thing a boy could put his penis in and his computer would give him a hand job. At one point one guy started arguing loudly with this girl and she poured her drink on his shoes and everyone thought that was great fun.

I started talking to a cute guy with messy hair and black plastic glasses. He told me about a short story he was working on and I told him I wrote a novel once and had an agent briefly but the agent dumped me. He told me he wrote a novel in college, but everyone in his workshop criticized it, so he never submitted it anywhere. So we talked about writing novels and how daunting it was to start one, but how fun, once they started to roll. His name was Rex Keating and we kept jabbering away. We both got a little over-excited actually and so I moved away at one point and got another drink just to calm down.

Copies of the magazine, *Context,* were stacked on a table. Sally and I flipped through it and talked to some other people and I snuck looks at Rex Keating, to see what he was doing and if he was talking to anyone else. Eventually he came over and showed me his *Context* article about first novels written by young people of privilege. There was a section about *Electra Rising,* which he liked, even though everyone else made fun of it. I said I liked it too and I told about the pretentious dinner party I'd been to where everyone dismissed it, which made me like it even more.

So then we both got excited again and got going on another conversation where we both talked too fast and referenced a million things and got into a frenzy of connecting on different styles of music and books and what we liked and what we didn't like, etc. It made me like Rex even more, the fact that neither of us could shut up. I had to fan myself with a copy of *Context.* This was mid-November, so my affair with Richard Kinney was far enough away that I felt ready to like someone. And Rex was not only smart, and a writer and a critic and approximately my own age, and *he was cute!*

Sally saw me blabbing my head off. She came and dragged me away and I told her I really liked this Rex guy and she was like, don't overdo it. So I tried not to, drinking more and talking to other people and listening to another argument between the girl who poured drinks on people's shoes and two other guys. The girl was named Danielle and she turned out to be the editor. So that made me like *Context* even more, if the editor was this crazy girl who didn't give a shit and poured drinks on people's feet.

Finally, Rex came over at the end of the night and

awkwardly said goodbye. Sally jumped in and said, why don't you give us your number? Since she knew I really liked him, and was afraid he'd vanish forever, like every other guy. I said, "Better yet ... " and I grabbed his sleeve and walked him out the door and onto the landing. I turned him toward me and stretched upward and kissed him right on the lips. I don't know what made me do that. I was pretty drunk I guess. And all the excitement. And all the drama of the pouring drinks on people. But he didn't kiss me back! He pulled away from me, like really fast, and then I was like, *oh shit.* And then this girl came rushing out. She was his girlfriend!!!!

Sally was right behind her and coughed really loud and the girlfriend was like, "Rex?" and we all laughed it off and pretended Rex and I were arguing. I grabbed Sally and we ran for it, but as we skipped down the stairs, I glanced up and Rex was looking at me and not at his girlfriend, who had annoying cat-eye glasses and seemed seriously alarmed, though Rex was totally innocent and hadn't done anything.

Sally and I ran out of the building and into the streets of the Upper West Side and laughed and screamed and couldn't believe how funny it all was, and how exciting. And then we walked with big bounding strides, arm in arm, and it was misting slightly and there was that nice burnt smell of autumn in New York. Of course I was in agony to know that Rex had a girlfriend. But in another way, I didn't even care. I just loved everything right then: my life, my friends, my new novel. My tragic affair with Richard Kinney. And guys like Rex. And girls like Danielle. It was just what I wanted. All of it. It was exactly where I wanted to be and I pulled Sally close and put my forehead against her shoulder and she looked at me like, "What's got into you?" and I was like, "Nothing ... nothing at all ..."

28

THAT CHRISTMAS I FLEW HOME, since I'd missed the Christmas before. This became an ordeal. Blizzards were hitting the Midwest, and my flight got cancelled and I had to stay in a hotel in Chicago. It took two days to get to Portland. When I got there, my older brother James and his wife Emily were also visiting from Seattle and having a huge ugly fight. Emily had left and was staying at a friend's house and didn't want to spend the holidays with James or the rest of us because she thought James had a drinking problem and wanted him to get help. That made things awkward around the house because James was there by himself and looking old and not in the best shape and actually drinking quite a lot, I noticed, like not obviously drunk but more just always having a beer in his hand, and needing to have a beer in his hand, though my mom said that he was no different than he'd always been.

After I'd been home a couple days, I drove downtown and got some Christmas presents and had a hot chocolate in the Nordstrom café. I'd now lived in New York for fifteen months and I had to say, Portland seemed pretty podunk all of a sudden. And like, nobody looked very good and everything seemed dull and slow and like nothing much was going on. Which was a horrible thing to think about your hometown and the place where many of your friends still were.

I called Kate. She had moved out of our old place and back to the suburbs but she wanted to see me and hear about New York. So we went downtown and went to a couple different bars and eventually ran into Nick Pax. We just talked to him for a second. He looked a little burned out and I assumed something had gone wrong with Crystal and her band Crystalline, but he was like, no, everything was good. They were releasing a new record with a new Seattle label and doing sold out shows up and down the West Coast. I had not heard anything about them in New York but that didn't mean anything. I asked Nick if he and Crystal were still together, as a couple, and he nodded that they were. But he didn't say anything else. So that was a little awkward.

On my last night in Portland, I went to this cheesy bar with Kate and a couple of our old friends from the mall. Kate had completely reverted to that world and had this annoying boyfriend who was not cool at all. She didn't seem embarrassed about it and I tried not to be, but after a couple drinks I couldn't hang out with them. I couldn't take the suburban dumbness. They seemed so backward in a way, which I knew was snobby on my part, but I couldn't help it.

I was so glad to land at LaGuardia and get back to my New York life. I'd been home two days when Rex called me. He wanted to hang out and talk about writing. I hesitated at first, because of the girlfriend, but when I asked other people nobody seemed to think it was a big deal. So I met him for coffee. He was very professional and we talked about agents and what publishers were looking for and it was actually super helpful. I told him about my dealings with Will Soren and he was deeply impressed by that: he considered Will Soren one of the best agents for new writers. Soren understood the zeitgeist. He had launched Anna Madsen, author of *Electra Rising*.

Eventually Rex mentioned his girlfriend, Rebecca. I could tell he was pretty serious about her, which meant that everything between us was going to be on a "friends" basis. This was bad news of course. But I absorbed the momentary pain of it and kept up a good front: talking about writing stuff and life in the big city.

Later, back at Wilton Street, I told Mari and Naomi about the coffee date. They were both like, "You have to steal him from her!" I was like no way, I could never do that, but they were insistent: "This is New York, annoying girlfriends have to be challenged and you are in the perfect position, since he obviously likes you."

I still refused, but then he called me again the next week and this time he wanted to go see a new Hungarian movie, *Little Otto*. It was a movie adaptation of a Hungarian novel that all the literary types were into, which made it another literary situation, so that Rex could claim it wasn't a real date.

So we went. *Little Otto* sort of sucked and afterward we didn't really have time to talk. Riding home on the L Train, I found myself staring at Rex. He was so cute, and in just the right way. Like not obviously handsome. But more like smart and bookish and perfect for someone like me. Before I could stop myself I said: "What's the deal with your girlfriend?"

I got a short version of the story. They had met at Oberlin in Ohio. The original plan was to get married after college, but Rex had really wanted to come to New York and she had eventually followed him there. Four months ago they had moved in together, which hadn't gone smoothly at first.

This made me like Rex less. The whole girlfriend thing

sounded lame. And those cat-eye glasses she wore, they were terrible! And then when I got off the train first, Rex didn't even stand up or walk me to the opening doors or even do anything. He just sat there, staring at me.

A week or two later, I was laying in bed one night and I heard Mari come in with a guy. This was in February, around Valentine's and she had told Naomi and I that she was going to "fuck some dude if it's the last thing I do." So here she came with "some dude."

They went in her tiny little room and I could hear them giggling and taking off their clothes, though you could tell they were basically strangers. They got things going and I heard these little gasps and then the rhythmic thumping and then it got louder and thank God, stopped pretty soon after that. But it freaked me out. Naomi had had sex in her room a few times, but basically, I felt like it was understood that our place was too small for bringing random guys home except in emergency situations. I guess that's what this was. Still, I had to go to the bathroom later, so then I had to get dressed again and walk past some naked stranger's hairy ass to get to the toilet.

Rex called me again. This time he wanted to meet for Chinese food. I found this extremely confusing and frustrating.

I discussed it with various people. What should I do? What should I say? Should I even go?

I went. I felt like, fuck it, we're all grownups and Rex's relationship is not my problem and if he only wants to talk about writing, okay, we'll do that.

Also, we'd exchanged some of our writing. I had given him the beginning of *Sisters*. He had given me the first two chapters of a new novel he had started. It was pretty good. Which made me look at him differently, even though he was probably more clueless about getting publishing than I was. His problem was he believed in "good writing." You know, like Hemingway and "one true sentence" and having integrity and being super serious about everything. He didn't understand that sex appeal and humor and having an interesting author backstory counted just as much. Or better yet, being a tortured waif like Anna Madsen of *Electra Rising*. For some reason I had started reading that again, and staring at the author photo a lot. Anna Madsen was *mesmerizing*. Which probably counted more than anything.

That night I kissed Rex again. To see what would happen. To see if he would come to life in some way. We were standing outside a Chinese dumpling restaurant on Mott Street. He kissed me back. For a second anyway. But then he immediately started talking about Rebecca and how he felt guilty. I was like, break up with her then! But he had a bunch of reasons why he couldn't do that. She had supported him so much while he wrote his first novel, and had helped him work on it and had read it like five times.

I looked at him and I said, "So what? It's your life!" Which was pretty harsh, and not really like me. But I felt like he needed to hear it.

29

CAROL SMITH DID NOT HAVE Rex's problems. She had the exact qualities it took to be a star. She had great ideas. She had charisma. She never stopped working. She was also weird and distant and snotty to people at exactly the right times. She was the kind of person that anything she did, good or bad, was interesting in some way.

She was also a lesbian, or so Sally and I had always assumed, even though Carol never actually said it. She had never had to say anything since she never dated anyone or had sex. But that had suddenly changed. With Libby, her whole vibe was different. Maybe this had started in California and we just hadn't seen it. Now it was pretty openly on display: her and Libby sitting close together, putting their hands in each other's pockets, whispering little comments to each other at odd moments. Then one night, they actually kissed goodbye outside a reading, with Sally and me standing right there. So that was weird, though not entirely a news flash.

Another thing going on with Carol and Libby was the movie they were making had been selected for a "New Visions" grant. They got five thousand dollars. The movie was a short, about a bisexual girl who likes both a boy and a girl at her high school. The story was Libby's idea and it was much more plot-oriented than Carol's other work. But I had liked it when Carol showed us a rough cut of it. Now she was flying up to Boston to do "video transfers" and other important film things they could now afford with their $5,000.

We all had dinner at Sally's one night, Carol and Libby and Sally and I. But it felt weird. I couldn't tell what was going on. Carol had decided to move in with Libby so it might have been that. Carol was such a loner. I couldn't imagine her living with another person. Or maybe it was the big Sundance Fellowship they were now trying for, and seemed like they might get. I didn't know. You would think Carol Smith would be ecstatic with all the success she was having, plus an actual relationship. But you never knew with her.

A little while later, Rex emailed me again and wanted to hang out. I wrote back: "I can't hang out with you, you have a girl-friend." But then Rex called me at work and actually got angry with me. He said he thought we were friends, real friends, and why was I being such a classic New York person by being like, "If I can't have a relationship with you that exactly fulfills *my* needs, I won't even speak to you."

It was fun to be called a "New York person." I was secretly proud of that. And I did really like him. He was my favorite person to talk to. Plus, he was a good writer, his new book was good, and what if it got published? I might need his help to get my book published!

So I stayed friends with him for my various overt and covert reasons. And then one night Rex, Sally and I and his girlfriend Rebecca got drunk and played pool in Williamsburg. Rebecca turned out to be pretty nice. She had new glasses too, designer frames that were narrow and plastic and more normal, though now she looked like a manager at the Gap.

So that was my life. Hanging out and working at *In Focus*, and working on my novel which I was now calling *The Trouble With Sisters*. It was March 14, 1999 when I wrote in my organizer: FINISHED FIRST DRAFT. It had become more about the younger sister, the cool one, but that was okay. The tone of it was "the bumbling ways of young people." There was especially a lot of sexual bumbling, which was how Portland was, at least in my memory. There was even a scene of a threesome.

So then I was glad I was still friends with Rex and I gave him *The Trouble With Sisters* and he read the whole thing in a week. When he was done, he called and wanted to meet up in McCarren Park since it was a nice day. So we did. We got coffees and walked into the park, and he wouldn't say anything about *Sisters* until we were settled on our bench. I had no idea what he thought. He kept me in suspense. I was like, "So?" but he wouldn't answer. First he had to stir his coffee. Then he mentioned how nice the weather was. Finally, I was like, would you stop torturing me and tell me about my book?

He laughed and said it was great. He loved it! He thought it would get published. He had actually read it in two nights. "The pace of it," he said, shaking his head, "how did you do that?" I didn't know. But I was so glad. And so relieved. And then we both laughed and high-fived and he said, "I hope my new novel is that good."

So that made me super happy. So then I harassed Rex about different parts, like what did he think about this character and that character and wasn't it funny when so-and-so said that, or did this? I was being annoying, I knew, but he didn't seem to mind, he smiled really big and watched my face in this certain way. Like he really believed that I had written a good book. Like he believed in me in general. Not that that guaranteed anything. But it sure felt good.

A week or so later, Rex came to my apartment one night to look at Chapter Six, which I kept changing and couldn't get right. Naomi was there, and she knew all about our weird platonic relationship. She was adamant that I should steal Rex away from Rebecca. When he arrived, she welcomed him and gushed over him and insisted he join us for dinner. So then the three of us sat and ate pasta and Naomi was giving me looks and sideways glances. She opened a bottle of wine and forced a glass on him.

After dinner, Naomi insisted Rex and I go into her room, to look at my changes, so that we would have privacy and quiet. It was so obvious what she was doing, but Rex didn't seem to notice.

Naomi had left her room dark with just the desk lamp on for maximum coziness and intimacy. Again, Rex was oblivious. We sat side by side at Naomi's desk and I showed him my re-written Chapter Six on my laptop. I offered to read it to him and he was like, "go for it."

I put my heart and soul into that reading. I used my best voice, clear and articulate but also soft and intimate and warm. It really was so nice sitting there with Rex, side by side, the light radiating up into our faces, and my lips saying the words and his eyes and my eyes following the sentences across the screen. It was, in my opinion, extremely romantic. And the more I read, the more romantic it became. It seemed impossible that he wouldn't kiss me. Or do something. How could he not?

But he didn't, and I finished and I couldn't even talk for a second, I was so emptied out. Still, he did nothing. So then, I couldn't stand it anymore and I pushed my chair away from the desk and told him that I couldn't be friends with him anymore, I wanted to be with him, like all the way with him, and it was making me crazy.

I said this in a low, grave tone. I didn't look at him as I spoke. I stared at my laptop. He sat beside me, stunned. And flattered too, it seemed like. But he didn't know what to do. Then he said: "What about Rebecca?" And I got mad and I was like, "What about her?"

He had to think about that for a moment. Then in a calm, careful voice he said he was going to marry Rebecca. He wanted to marry her. He had told me that from the beginning. And why was I making things so difficult and lashing out at him and now giving him this ultimatum?

I didn't actually know why I was doing those things. But I didn't say that.

He sat there for a few more moments. Then he shook his head and stood up and got his stuff. I didn't move. I continued to stare at my laptop.

He made his way out, through Naomi's sliding doors, into my room and over Mari's messy floor. I heard him pass through the kitchen and out the door and I could feel his footsteps on the creaky stairs. A moment later the front door slammed as he left the building and walked away down the street.

30

ANOTHER MONTH WENT BY. And then it started to be real spring and it did that cool east coast thing where the weather gets violent and dramatic and the roof blows off some warehouse in Queens and almost chops somebody's head off. And everyone gets a little crazy and sex-starved and someone shoots up a McDonald's in New Jersey somewhere.

This was my first experience with spring fever, or at least that I noticed. I hadn't had sex in months and I was feeling seriously itchy and restless and like I couldn't quite contain myself. Maybe that's where the "April is the cruelest month" thing came from. Because not only did spring make you horny, if you lived in a big northern city, you were exhausted from the long winter and you'd gained five pounds and your face was sallow and pale and how were you supposed to meet guys when you couldn't even button your pants? Not that the guys were so discriminating. They were horny too. The "cruelest month" idea was probably based on the fact that despite everyone being desperate to get together, few people actually did, and everyone was therefore extremely cranky.

The real problem was New York. We were too good for each

other. We were too ambitious and neurotic and worried about our own personal ranking in the world to open ourselves up to another person. And so naturally, when we should have got drunk and fallen into each other's arms, we instead got drunk and judged each other and couldn't put away our pride or lower our standards or "settle" in any way, and so we went home and threw ourselves into our art projects or our novels or our websites or whatever, only to become even more frustrated and miserable than we already were.

Mari was the only person I knew who escaped this fate. She was "getting it regular" from a guy she met at the gym. He sounded horrible: a real estate guy, vain, rich, sarcastic, but somehow he and Mari got into a post-gym routine of sushi and beer and then intense fucking at his place. He would then pay for her cab back to Brooklyn. "He likes Asians," Mari explained, as she did her nails one day at the kitchen table. That sounded like an ideal situation to both Naomi and I, both of us smoldering with spring lust. Mari did her best to help us out, giving us detailed recaps of her trysts. He slapped her ass all the time, which none of us understood. It was a frat boy porn thing. But there was no real relief in these details.

Poor Naomi, despite her worldliness and a seemingly endless supply of interested guys, she continued to struggle in the romance department. Most guys were beneath her. Or just too stupid to bother with. So now at the height of spring, each night the streets below our windows were literally streaming with cute guys, singing, skateboarding and drunkenly carrying on; Naomi stayed in, eventually opening one of our paint-stuck kitchen windows enough to crawl onto the fire escape where she started a little garden. I joined her in this. Or at least talked to her, drinking wine with her and taking tiny hits from the skinny joints she occasionally rolled herself.

Another month passed, and it got warm, and people broke out their Brooklyn summer uniforms of cutoffs and sneakers and retro ironic T-shirts. On one of those days, I was sitting on the subway heading uptown to meet Sally, and I had the sudden and very deep conviction that I loved Rex Keating, like completely loved him, like more than I even consciously understood. I could *marry* him and have kids with him and could live my whole life standing next to him. This thought hit me so hard, and crushed me so thoroughly that I felt like I would burst into tears and collapse onto the filthy subway floor. But then I mustered my strength and pulled myself together, lest I become one of those crying people on the subway that everyone sees at some point if they live in New York.

31

REX REX REX. This turned out to be my mantra of the summer. I didn't see Rex for several weeks in June though I had emailed him with some small questions regarding my novel, which I was working on daily at this point. He always answered, and was helpful, but there was a definite reserve there. He didn't like ultimatums it turned out. But what boy did?

And so the summer continued. I'd wake up each morning, put on a cute skirt and ride the subway to Union Square with my fellow aspiring young city dwellers. I would hurry up the stairs from the subway, cut through the park and the leafy trees, toward the *In Focus* offices on East 20th street. Each day I'd vary my route slightly, enjoying the sunshine, and thinking about my life, until at some point, I'd start doing it again, muttering under my breath: *Rex Rex Rex.*

At work, I'd smile at the front desk guy, ride the elevator to the fourth floor, dump my crap in my cubicle. I'd get a coffee in the lounge and listen to whatever was going on, the office gossip, the new movies people had seen. Then back to my computer and my headphones and my couple hours of writing captions or copy editing or fact checking or whatever was required. But always, before the day was through, the muttering would start again:

Rex Rex Rex ...

I worked on *The Trouble With Sisters* continuously that summer. I did draft after draft. I didn't want another situation like *Manifesto* where an agent would think they saw a germ of something but it needed a million changes. I wanted *Sisters* to be ready to go. And it wasn't like I had anything better to do. I would take my laptop with me into work and then later go to interesting cafes my coworkers would tell me about. Or sometimes I'd just stay in the office, in the air conditioning, laying on the floor and working on my laptop and helping myself to the free *In Focus* coffee.

In August, my parents sent me a plane ticket so I could come to my dad's birthday. That was actually a great trip. Going to the airport, I felt like a big shot, with my new novel in the works and feeling so at home in New York now and having my friend Carol Smith getting a Sundance Fellowship (this had just happened) and Sally at Columbia and me at *In Focus*. Things were starting to happen for all of us, I thought. Even the thing with Rex felt good in a way, like it hurt but it was a good pain, like even though it wasn't working out exactly the way I wanted, at least I'd found a person like Rex, a quality person, that I could have my little friendship/unrequited love affair with.

I stayed in Portland two weeks, so my parents and I could get a nice big dose of each other. I missed them, I realized, despite all my exciting goings on. They were sort of amazed by me too, now twenty-three years old and living my big city life. I'd catch them staring at me sometimes, and we spent a lot of time sitting around talking, at the kitchen table or in the living room. I would tell them about New York, what people were like there. And like if my dad said something about politics or current events I would say, without contradicting him, "In New York, most people think that ... "

One night, folding laundry, I told my mom the story of Richard Kinney. I hadn't planned too, it just kind of spilled out. I had no idea how she would take it. But then she told me she had had a weekend fling with a visiting professor when she was at college. He was thirty-eight. She was nineteen. I had never heard anything about this. It kind of shocked me to my core. "Oh yes," she said, in her no nonsense mom way. "Charles Landau. Art Historian. I still think about him sometimes," she said, folding one of my dad's shirts for the ten billionth time.

I drove into downtown Portland one night, without calling anyone, and walked around and it was strange because a lot of *The Trouble With Sisters* was set there. K Club and the old Outer Limits space and Coffee Haus, and some of my other hang outs. The funny thing was, none of it looked like it did in my head, none of it was like I remembered. But that was okay, as long as the version I envisioned was consistent, it didn't matter if it was real or not. "A novel is an extended dream," Rex had said when we still wrote each other long pretentious writer emails. "It need only obey the rules of a dream."

Oh *Rex Rex Rex* ...

After that, I wanted to hang out in downtown Portland more, and spent several afternoons working on *The Trouble With Sisters* in various cafés. There was one gang of girls I kept bumping into, who circulated around those same places. They were young and fashionable in their Portland way. They'd sit at the outside tables, smoking and talking about boys and parties and the different bars. They called all guys "dudes" I noticed. They were a little rough around the edges, but they were the cool chicks of the moment, you could tell.

Near the end of my trip, I wrote an email to Rex telling him about my progress on *Sisters* and being super chatty and confident, but also nice and thanking him for his feedback. The next day I got an email back which said simply: "Good Luck!" Which made me mad, after I wrote him like five long paragraphs and told him about my entire summer.

But that wasn't anything compared to how I felt when I got back to Greenpoint and found a card in my stack of mail announcing the wedding of Rex Everett Keating and Rebecca Anne Green. What a horrible thing to send to someone! I was so mad, I jammed the card back in the envelope and threw it in the garbage.

32

AND THEN NAOMI FOUND LOVE. Or something like it. She met a guy at an event party for a new sports drink. Michael Grossman was also from Boston and they started talking and I guess they couldn't stop yakking at each other—like Rex and I at that first *Context* party—though knowing Naomi, who was much more socially polished, I'm sure she played it way cooler.

So that was the big news around Wilton Street. And because of it, Naomi and I went through a period where we talked every day. It was almost like we became best friends, though I don't think Naomi would have characterized it that way. Whatever it was, we spent a lot of time sitting on the fire escape, drinking white wine and watching the various goings on in the jungle-like backyards of our neighbor's buildings. And talking about Michael Grossman.

His most important attribute was his apartment. He lived in the West Village, on a leafy, cobblestone street, which Naomi fell deeply in love with instantly. After just a couple dates she began plotting how to move in with him. She "got" the whole Brooklyn thing, being broke and wearing old sneakers. But she didn't need to extend her adolescence any further. She wanted to live in Manhattan and be a grownup.

She never said that to Michael Grossman of course. To him she was bored, flakey, half-interested. The story he got was that there was another guy who she wasn't quite free of. This other guy, who was partially based on a past boyfriend, was solid, stable, rich, and wanted to marry her.

Naomi played the situation very artfully, pretending to be utterly infatuated with Michael for short periods, then bailing on dates for no reason and frustrating him in various ways. Thus she created a scenario where the only way he could achieve consistent happiness was to convince Naomi to move in with him.

I loved hearing Naomi's machinations. I would sit on the fire escape, sipping my wine and grinning mischievously. Often, like the writer/betrayer I aspired to be, I found myself encouraging her most devious maneuvers. I wanted to see how far she would go. And how much she could get away with. It was such a delicious story.

I'm sure she knew what I was up to, but she never edited herself in the slightest. She showed me her worst. She reveled in it. Maybe she thought I'd write about her someday. Or maybe she thought the truth should be known by someone. Whichever, she honestly didn't give a shit what anybody thought of her: which was, at heart, the basis of her whole personality. It was the source of her power.

Meanwhile, September arrived and Sally started her second year at Columbia, where she found more smart people to hang out with. This included Steve and Benton who we began to pal around with. They wanted us to go for a weekend to Vermont to see the fall foliage at some point and got us to commit to the second weekend in October.

It was during this time that I also began going to the art events the *In Focus* people were always telling me about. One notorious photographer had a big show and Sally and I went. It was my first real New York "art opening" and it was all these outrageous people being snobby and hilarious. There was free drinks and food and we met a woman wearing a Commes de Garcon jacket which had different length sleeves and pockets that were sewed on sideways.

We also went to things with Carol and Libby, and sometimes just Libby because Carol went back to L.A. to do some film stuff. We were becoming better friends with Libby and her crew of USC people who were artsy and fun but also very polite and agreeable, like you had to be in the movie business. Not like the art people who were super aloof or drunkenly falling down the stairs. Or the *Context* parties which we still went to sometimes but were never quite as fun as the night I met Rex.

That fall was also when I learned how to take cabs. Not that I could afford them, but I could afford them if five people crammed in. So several nights a week Sally and I ended up bouncing around to these different events and different scenes and different friends scattered around the city. I had become good friends with Walter, a gay Asian boy from *In Focus*. He was only nineteen. He'd skipped college completely and moved to New York straight from high school in Vancouver BC. He knew everything about nightlife and DJs and dance clubs. We'd run into him somewhere and he'd drag us to some huge dance party that would be like in a refrigerator warehouse in Queens. Or he'd take us to some new club in Chinatown with underground celebrities like this guy NEO who had platinum blonde hair and wore silver clothes. One night we talked to NEO, who turned out to be this goofy guy from New Jersey, with an accent, who said he started doing the NEO thing to score NYU chicks and then he kept doing it because he was famous in Japan now, he was in all the Japanese guidebooks as a tourist attraction.

In October, Steve and Benton and Sally and I did the Vermont foliage trip. That was super fun too, in a collegiate kind of way, riding in the back of Benton's Volvo, chatting about intellectual things and listening to music. In Massachusetts, we got hot chocolates from a Dunkin' Donuts and finally got far enough into the wilds of New England that when you stepped out of the car, you could actually feel the difference in the air. You could smell the trees and the dustiness of autumn and you could reach down and stick your fingers into actual dirt. Or pick up a leaf. Or throw a stick into a babbling brook.

In New Hampshire, we stayed in a little hotel on Friday night and then got up early the next morning to climb a mountain. This was fun too, though I got pretty winded, which was weird. I was twenty-three, why was I so tired? Sally said, "Maybe you party too much."

On the trail, I told Benton about my novel. He was very interested. I had recently changed the title to *Chicks and Dudes*, since *The Trouble With Sisters* sounded like a Disney movie, and the book had become more about the Portland music scene and not so much about the sisters anyway. When I told him the new title he laughed and seemed to think you couldn't call a literary first novel *Chicks and Dudes*, which made me think it was perfect, since Benton was pretty conventional in general and not really that cool. His idea of a good "literary" title would probably be something like: *The Wind That Blows* or some quote from the bible or maybe something like *The Highly Unusual Life and Times of Gertrude Bunch, Philologist* since everyone was doing old-timey titles right then.

. . .

After the hike, we had a nice dinner and then went to a local bar and ordered a pitcher of Stella Artois and sat by the fire and enjoyed the woodsy smells and rustic ambiance. Benton and Steve were great companions that weekend, fun to talk to and super nice and smart. But it was interesting because one thing I had noticed about Sally, she didn't dress any different than she did at college. Steve and Benton were the same, sticking to the classic WASP, grad student look: jeans and a button down shirt and Converse maybe, or more likely, Nike crosstrainers and some sort of practical rain-resistant parka. "Collegiate" or even "Young Journalist" was their basic style. I, on the other hand, had gone in more of a Naomi direction, sleeker, more *chic*, combined with my usual staple of thrift store dresses and whatever tennis shoes people were wearing at the moment. Basically, I looked like where I lived, Brooklyn, which made me a hipster I guess. One thing I knew though, I didn't want to look "college" anymore. This made me feel bad for Benton and Steve and their boring upper-middle-class-ness. They were so bourgeois. I mean, so was Rex, but he at least had clunky glasses and wore old sweaters with the elbows worn out.

So that was the one weird thing of the trip. The fact that our group was basically three normal people and artsy me. I found myself worrying a little bit about my friendship with Sally. Like what if she got more and more like that? What if she got a job at *Time Magazine*, or became a writer for *Good Morning America* like a friend of hers just did? Then she'd become a total yuppie and get that annoying tone in her voice. And she'd get more and more boring, while I would still be in the city, with gay Walter from *In Focus*, and Naomi, and being more "downtown" than ever. That would be so sad. But it could totally happen.

33

IN FOCUS always had one huge party every year in October. I had been hearing about this party since I started working there. In the past, many famous people had come, certain legendary things had happened, things that people still talked about, mostly Veronica, since it was her chance to be an important person in the art world again, like when she was young and worked at *Interview* with Andy Warhol.

The first people I invited were Rex and Rebecca. That gave me a little thrill for some reason, it was my attempt to insert myself into their lives. I had seen Rebecca a couple times on the L Train, but avoided talking to her. Now though, I decided I could deal with her. I missed Rex so much, plus I wanted them to see how cool *In Focus* was, so they would be jealous. And Naomi had advised staying close to Rex, no matter what. Where there was one awesome guy, there might be more.

Within a day though, I got an email back from Rex saying they couldn't come but thanking me anyway and asking about my novel. "I'm still working on it," I wrote back, adding: "I don't want them to have any reason to reject it." He agreed and said he had joined a writers group with some college friends. They read each other's stuff and that had helped him see some of the problems with his new novel.

Since he couldn't come to my party, Rex invited me to a dinner party he was having with Rebecca and some of their friends. "I'd love to," I wrote back instantly. And then I wasn't sure that was such a good idea. So then I emailed again and said, "Can I bring a date?"

I brought Benton. When we arrived, people seemed to make a little extra fuss over us. It turned out several of Rex's writing buddies were there and Rex had told them about *Sisters*, and how good it was, and how I almost had an agent for my first book. So that was the reason for the unexpected attention. It actually backfired because when we were sitting around before dinner, people seemed reluctant to talk. So then Benton told someone he went to the Columbia School of Journalism and everyone was impressed by that and asked him questions and that got the conversation going again.

We had dinner. I ended up sitting across from Rex. Of course Rebecca, being the tolerant fiancé, had allowed this and did nothing but smile at me as I gossiped wildly with Rex. We talked about Danielle, the *Context* gang, the rumor that *Electra Rising* was going to be made into a movie starring Fiona Apple, various other publishing news, different agents we'd heard about, new books we had read recently. *Oh my god*, I thought at one point, *I love talking to Rex*. But maybe that was just because I hadn't seen him in so long. And also, even as we chattered away, I had that same feeling with him as I did with Sally in New Hampshire. Like he was becoming so adult and serious now, with his marriage plans. And then while we were eating, I looked around at his college buddies and thought they were bland and predictable and maybe Rex was going in a different direction then I was. And he still hadn't finished his novel. So in a way, he wasn't going in any direction.

But then later while we drank coffee in the living room, I had the opposite thought. Now everyone seemed super witty and smart and well-adjusted and happy. These were the kind of people you'd want to be friends with for life. I suddenly saw how great Rex and Rebecca were going to be together and how successful Rex was going to be, either as a novelist or something related to it. He was the best of that liberal arts type of person, genuinely intelligent and funny but also humble and self-aware. And Rebecca was like that too, coming over and talking to me about Oregon and about her own redneck relatives back in Ohio.

When we left, I felt hollow and sad and like no matter what I did I would never be like Rex and Rebecca. And to make things worse, Benton was hitting on me and wanting to go for a drink. I said I couldn't, I had to get up for work and then he tried to kiss me at the subway entrance and then I felt stupid and like I was this slutty wannabe writer chick that people were always trying to sleep with but never wanted to marry.

34

THE BIG *IN Focus* party was on a Friday night at a beautiful townhouse of some friends of Veronica's near Gramercy Park. It was a super fancy party with expensive catering and fresh flowers and a DJ and a coat check and a person at the door only letting in people with invitations. God knows where the money came from. Not from *In Focus* where they barely paid anybody.

I went early, thinking I might help set up, but everything was being done by professionals. So then I sat around and drank Perrier water and ate cheese and crackers. I was dressed in a cute grey skirt of Naomi's with a red shirt under a black cardigan. I looked pretty dressy, especially after I'd put on lipstick and eye stuff, at the urging of Walter and some of the other staffers, who were going to show up in Prada suits.

Every stage of the party was fun. Also, to not be a random guest like I was at most parties, to actually be a host, and on the inside, that made it ten times better. Walter and some other *In Focus* people walked in soon after I got there. They looked stunning. So then we ran around as the first guests appeared, sneaking crackers and caviar and running last-minute errands for Veronica, who was decked out herself and kept fanning herself with the latest issue of the magazine.

And then Libby and Sally arrived. Carol still hadn't come back from California, and there seemed to be some confusion about what was happening between her and Libby. But nobody said anything about that now. I got them drinks and we goofed around and then Benton and Steve walked in, looking sheepish and frumpy with their tweed coats and ties. It was so fun to see everyone. And I swear I felt like the belle of the ball, being the hostess to my friends and introducing them to people and showing off how cool my boss Veronica was and how cute the boys were who I worked with.

And then Jim Jarmusch walked in, with his white hair sticking up and his beautiful eyes. Everyone tittered about that. And later Rick Moody, who everyone got excited about, since everyone loved *The Ice Storm*. Other people came too, people I didn't know, but who you could instantly tell were famous. Like this old guy who had short gray hair and pink glasses and an ascot. And then other writers and photography types. And then I saw the woman from Arizona, who had the story in *The New Yorker* a long time ago. She appeared looking even more agitated and overwrought than before. I went right up to her and re-introduced myself. She was with this bored looking older guy, who was possibly her husband. But she remembered me and asked how I was, and I told her I had written another novel and it was way better than the first, and what should I do with it?

She said: get an agent. And I was like, but who, and how? And she said I could send it to her agent. She gave me her email address and we made a vague plan to have lunch sometime. I was like thank you, thank you, thank you.

· · ·

The photographer David LaChapelle came. He was a huge star and a personal friend of Veronica's and she ran screaming down the stairs to greet him. Someone said that Anton Corbijn was there, or was coming, but we never saw him.

Then Sally ran into a cute guy she knew named Jonathan Resnick. She had met him in New Haven where he was doing something at the Yale Art School and also sleeping with one of the grad student women in her house. Sally had mentioned this to me at the time, because he had stopped to drink coffee with her one morning on his way out. They'd had a great conversation, despite how weird and possibly inappropriate it was for them to talk.

Anyway, Jonathan had recently become the photography editor at *Esquire*, which was why he was at Veronica's party. He was super nice and not even that old. And he was definitely happy to see Sally again, that was obvious. He told us he was writing a memoir, about being a chess prodigy when he was ten. He said the novel was dead and that memoirs were the new thing. But then someone else said: "Tell that to Rick Moody." But it turned out that Jonathan and Rick were old friends from prep school.

Throughout this conversation, it was very obvious that Jonathan Resnick liked Sally. He was very forward about it: smiling at her, and redirecting the conversation back to her whenever he could. Later, we snuck upstairs and discussed the situation, me, Libby and Sally. Libby said, "Wait, he was fucking your roommate? And now he's hitting on you!?"

But really, was that so bad? He didn't *try* anything with Sally. They just talked that one morning. Sally had seen him other times, around New Haven, and he had been super nice and totally not creepy. I was like: so what's the problem? He obviously likes you. You have to talk to him more!

Sally was hesitating. What if he just liked younger women?

And wasn't that mostly a sexual thing? They both looked at me, since I was supposedly the expert about older men. I didn't know what to say, except that I definitely didn't regret my affair with Richard Kinney. It had been painful when it ended, but what isn't? I sure learned a lot. And he was an amazing person. And the sex …

Eventually, we agreed that we would all go down and talk to Jonathan Resnick together. And see what his deal was. And if there was even a hint of sleaze, we would retreat immediately.

But before we could get downstairs, Sally had a little self-esteem meltdown. We had to go into the bathroom, just Sally and I. Sally thought she was too tall. And her head was too narrow. And her hair looked stupid. And she wasn't dressed right. I knew she could get like this, but this was extreme. I was like, *it doesn't matter, he likes you. He's liked you since New Haven.* Eventually she snapped out of it and we went downstairs again.

By now, there was a whole new bunch of important people at the party. Older art people and some writers and magazine people I didn't know. An older man in a suit who did something with the Museum of Modern Art was being gushed over from all sides. It was hard to keep track of everyone. We did our best though, us underlings, monitoring the fame and the personalities, so we could someday talk about these people like Veronica always talked about Andy Warhol and his friends.

Sally and I made our way through the crowded rooms. It had gotten warm even though the air conditioners were on full blast. The air smelled like elegant perfume and champagne and expensive wool suits. I had the thought, as Sally and I slipped through the people, that this was one of those nights you read about in old novels, where some brilliant remark or sideways glance changes the direction of people's entire lives.

We came into the kitchen and there was Jonathan Resnick, talking to a tall elegantly dressed woman. Sally and I both stopped dead. The woman was Marjorie Isaacs!

Marjorie Isaacs was huge right then. She had written a novel about three rich sisters and their romantic misadventures in Manhattan. It had been the biggest book of the summer, at least in New York, and Marjorie was constantly being written up and gossiped about, people usually saying she was an even bigger bitch than her characters. She seemed like that now, holding court in the kitchen, with a cruel, superior smirk on her face. Jonathan Resnick, Rick Moody and several men in suits stood in a semicircle around her, grinning stupidly and hanging on her every word.

When Sally saw this, she immediately pulled back. There was no way she could compete with someone like Marjorie Isaacs. We had to wait until Jonathan was alone, or away from her at least.

But we'd marched in there with great intention, and I had a feeling we couldn't stop now. Besides, we didn't have to compete with Marjorie Isaacs, we could just stand there and gawk at her like everyone else. I pulled Sally forward. And it worked, because when we got closer, Jonathan saw Sally and immediately grabbed her and pulled her into the group. "Marjorie, this is my good friend Sally Zimmerman," he said, introducing her. Marjorie couldn't care less, but she shook Sally's hand. She even shook mine as I had been pulled forward as well.

Somehow, Sally and I were brought fully into the circle. We were introduced all around: the first suit, then Rick Moody, then another suit. Jonathan Resnick worked his way around the group and then paused for a moment before he introduced us to the last of the distinguished suit-wearers. This man had hung back the furthest, maintaining on his face the most disinterested expression of all. He was clearly only here as an escort for Marjorie Isaacs.

I almost pulled back, to avoid bothering him, to avoid the withering stare he focused at Jonathan as he began his introduction.

"And this ... ," said Jonathan Resnick, suddenly nervous himself and obviously afraid of the stoned faced man. "... is Will Soren."

PART THREE

35

YEARS BEFORE THIS, way back during our sophomore year at Wellington, Sally went on an E. B. White kick. She made me read his book *On Style,* for my writing, and some of his essays, including one called "This is New York," which became a thing with her and me and Carol. It was about how difficult New York is, the prickly people, the cramped conditions, but how this was balanced out by the endless possibilities. At one point, White said something like: "You shouldn't come to New York unless you are willing to be lucky," which became our rallying cry back at Wellington, since we all kind of hoped to end up there.

The problem with luck though, is you have to do something to create it. And then, when it arrives, you have to do something else to take advantage of it. That "something else" typically being something terrifying and impossible and probably beyond what you think you are capable of. Also, it usually arrives at some unexpected moment when it's the last thing you're thinking about.

That's where I was now. Standing in front of Will Soren, my hand out, my eyeballs bulging, my nervous system momentarily paralyzed.

Mr. Soren was tall, wide-shouldered, with wavy grey hair, expensively cut. He wore tortoiseshell glasses, expensive looking and an unusual shape that made you think they were made in Paris or some other non-American foreign capital. He was wearing a dark navy suit and a white shirt with a dark tie.

"Nice to meet you, Will Soren," I said, using both names to make sure I didn't lose his attention instantly, which seemed highly likely. I had to do something. That was obvious. E. B. White's moment of luck had arrived.

"You used to represent me," I said loudly.

Everyone laughed. Will Soren smiled slightly, but ever, *ever*, so slightly. "No, I'm serious," I said. "You liked my novel *Manifesto*, and I did a re-write for you, remember?" He didn't seem to. "And I sent it back but you never responded. And then I got a Xeroxed rejection letter!" I said.

He grumbled slightly and glanced over my head as if looking for the easiest way to leave the room.

When I first spoke, I didn't have a plan. I didn't know where I was going with these statements. But then something strange happened. Everything slowed down. Like in a movie. And in the little gap of time that was created, I had a second to think, and then I saw exactly how to play it.

I let a pause develop, an awkward pause, during which I could feel the mood of these men, and of Marjorie Isaacs, the whole group, recoiling from me, the slighted writer, the young wannabe. I could tell what they were thinking: *Poor Will Soren.* He'd strung me along for some reason, maybe he'd met me somewhere, or I was a friend of a friend, or maybe he'd hit on me, after too many cocktails. They were all firmly on his side. They had all been in similar situations.

"But the good news is ... " I said, changing my tone to extreme brightness, happiness and youthful excitement. "... I wrote a new novel. And it's *better!*"

Everyone laughed again, and smiled and began joking around.

"Hear that Will?" said one of the suits. "She's got something new!"

Will Soren smiled with relief. He met my eye. "Good ... good for you ... I'm sure it's great."

"It is!" said Sally suddenly pushing forward. "I've read it! Andrea's the best writer of her generation! She's going to be huge!"

Somehow, the way Sally said this suggested that she barely knew me. She sounded like we'd just met and that this was not a friend's opinion, but the accepted wisdom of a new groundswell of brilliant young people who were about to rise up, and seize the publishing industry and dump all these suits onto the street. For this reason, they all took Sally completely seriously, Jonathan Resnick especially, since he seemed determined to leave the party with Sally's number, or possibly Sally herself. Thank God for men and their delusions.

Nature favors the bold. The whole thing worked. The other men studied me. They all looked at Will. He would be a fool not to at least investigate this "new generation." That seemed to be the instant consensus. Plus I was young and funny and I was wearing lipstick and a skirt.

Will Soren managed a pained smile, dug around in his coat pocket and produced a card. He handed it to me.

"I'm at WCM now," he told me. "Call my office on Monday."

"I will," I said firmly. Every ounce of electricity my young self could generate was now radiating out of me, finishing the job, executing the kill, finalizing the deal. I was as young and sharp and bold and brilliant as I would ever be at that moment.

Then I turned and walked away.

. . .

Sally found me upstairs, hiding in a closet. She came running into the room, calling my name. When I heard her voice I stumbled out from behind the door and we both went into a frenzy of hopping, squealing, laughing. Then we threw ourselves on our backs on the bed of the absent townhouse owners, who would probably never know what role their apartment had played in the course of these two young people's lives.

I thanked Sally. I thanked her and thanked her and thanked her. How many times had she come through for me? How many times had she saved my ass? Everything good in my life had come through her.

We both agreed that I had to leave the party. It was winding down anyway and all we could do now was screw things up. Sally would retrieve our coats from the coat check people. But then as I waited for her to come back, I realized she couldn't leave, she still had to talk to Jonathan Resnick. I told her this when she re-appeared with our coats. But she didn't care about him. "He can find me if he likes me so much," she said. I wasn't so sure that was the best strategy, but I was too excited to think about it.

We crept downstairs and then slipped down the hall with great stealth, passing some of my co-workers. "I have to sneak out," I whispered to Walter, without stopping. This prompted a conspiratorial glance. "It's not what you think," said Sally, following behind me. "*It's way better.*"

Outside, the air felt cold and fresh and sharp in my lungs. Sally and I dashed across the street and stood for a second arranging our scarves and getting our bearings. I was still shaking with excitement. Sally said, "Is *Chicks and Dudes*, ready to show to him?" I nodded that it was. "So that's it then," she said. "This is it."

. . .

Then Jonathan Resnick appeared. He came out the front door and walked halfway down the stoop and looked up and down the street. Sally and I both ducked behind a car and stared at him through the car windows.

"He's looking for you!" I whispered to Sally.

She did not dispute it. I was so glad for her. It would be so fun if something great would happen to her tonight too. But before we could do anything, he turned and headed back up the steps to the party.

"That's okay," I said to Sally. "We know he likes you."

But Sally was not the type to think about herself. She wanted to think about me. And Will Soren. And so that's what we did, skipping away down the street, and imagining all the amazing possibilities if we could get him to represent my book.

On Monday though, I did not feel all the amazing possibilities. I woke up in mortal terror. I had to call Will Soren! On the phone!! I decided I would do it from work.

I rode to Union Square on the subway and then made my way to *In Focus*. There, in my cubicle, staring at my phone, it occurred to me that Mr. Soren might not be as interested as he had seemed, that what felt like such a victory to me, might not seem like anything to him and his friends. To them, it was just another party, another Friday night, and as usual, some desperate writer had humiliated herself in a vain attempt to get noticed.

So I braced myself as I dialed my phone. But I did not hang up. I got an assistant of course, but I calmly explained who I was, and then nervously said, "He told me to call." A moment later, the deep sonorous voice of Will Soren came on the line.

"Hello? Andrea?" he said, as if we were old friends. We exchanged pleasantries. Then he apologized for the form letter and explained that he'd been leaving the Ruth Goldman agency at the time, and that many worthy projects had been lost in the transition.

Through all of this, I said little, but found myself adopting and maintaining a surprisingly professional tone with him. I don't know where that came from. I was apparently not as scared as I thought.

Will Soren told me he'd be curious to see my new project. Had I shown it to anyone else? I did a Naomi and lied and said another agent had asked to see it but I was still polishing it up. Again, I didn't know where this momentary courage came from, but there it was. I'm not sure Will Soren was fooled, but the fact that I attempted this lie seemed to impress him. He wanted to see it right away. He made me an offer: if I promised not to show it to anyone else, he would read it immediately, and get back to me within a week.

By now, my calm was beginning to crumble. I was having trouble breathing. But I took one short, shaky breath and managed to say: "Okay."

A moment later I was mercifully off the phone. My hand trembled as I put the receiver down. I put my fingers to my temples and breathed and closed my eyes for a moment.

And so it begins, I thought.

36

SINCE I SEEMED capable of anything at that moment, I picked the phone back up and found the number of the photography department at *Esquire Magazine* on my phone list. I called it and asked for Jonathan Resnick, holding my finger on the hang-up button on the phone, in case he actually came on the line. But, as I expected, I got an assistant. "Hi," I said. "I just need to leave a quick message for Jonathan … " The assistant seemed okay with that. "Tell him Sally Zimmerman's number is … " and I told her the number, carefully, but with a casual air, as if it was some small business detail, that someone had neglected. I thanked her and hung up.

I figured I had a day or two, to print out *Chicks and Dudes* and send it to WCM. So I decided to read through it one more time. Or at least through the first hundred pages or so. As soon as I got home, I started reading. The familiar first couple chapters seemed okay. But then Chapter Six still felt awkward and unfinished. I had fixed it, I thought, but now I could see that it still wasn't right.

I kept reading. There were other problems. There were several rough patches in Chapter Eight. And too much slang had crept in. The writing style, loose and conversational, was totally ungrammatical in places. Like way too much. Which was okay in a "whatever, Portland" way, but this wasn't "whatever, Portland" we were dealing with. This was Will Soren at WCM. Why had I been so lax about that? At several points, the style made things confusing and unclear. It was definitely going to distract a sophisticated reader.

I started to fidget a little. But I kept going. I kept finding bad sentences, unbalanced paragraphs. I scrambled to fix these, as well as clean up the slang and the weird constructions as best I could. When I looked up it was nearly 8:30. I had been doing this for three hours. And I was only on page 58! The whole book needed to be gone through. Whole chapters had to be fixed. And Will Soren thought it was on it's way!

I called Sally but she was out. I called Carol Smith in California, but remembered she didn't care about my problems. I called Libby who had become a sympathetic ear but she was not home either. I then realized who I really needed to call, the only person who could actually help me: *Rex*.

Thankfully, he answered. And even more thankfully, he told me to come over.

I burst into Rex and Rebecca's apartment at 9:45. What a mess I was: panicked out of my mind, the mangled hundred pages under my arm, my hands shaking, tears in my eyes. You'd have thought I'd been mugged.

Rex took the pages and then took my coat. I sat down on their couch and blurted out the story, how Will Soren had shown up at the *In Focus* party, how I had somehow managed to impress him and his friends, but now he wanted to see the manuscript and *it wasn't ready*. It wasn't even close to being ready. It sucked! And this was my last chance!

Rebecca was the first to speak. She asked me if I had eaten. I was like, "What?" But then I thought about it. I thought about my day. I'd had a power bar for breakfast on the subway and then a bagel with cream cheese for lunch. So no, I hadn't eaten.

She went to make me a sandwich. Meanwhile, Rex calmly took the manuscript from me and sat down at his desk. He understood the time situation, and also, he seemed deeply impressed by this accidental meeting with Will Soren. He was smart enough to know that fluke meetings sometimes launched careers.

Rebecca returned and put a sandwich in front of me. Rex began reading. I ate the sandwich. About four pages in, Rex chuckled. Then he laughed a little. Rebecca who was doing something in their kitchen nook, came out and took my plate away and then returned with a banana, which I thanked her for and peeled and ate, with quick nervous bites.

By now, Rex was a dozen pages into the manuscript. I studied his face as he focused and continued to read. He mentioned a couple tweaks I could make and I quickly wrote them down. At one point, he said quietly: "Yeah Chapter Six is still a little wobbly."

"But is it okay?" I said.

He didn't answer but kept reading. I lay my head back on the back of the couch. Rebecca appeared again with a cup of herbal tea. Which I drank down sloppily, spilling some of it on myself and their couch and the tops of my shoes.

It was 11:30 when Rebecca announced she was going to bed. She had an early day at work. I apologized to her, and thanked her profusely and gave her a huge hug and nearly started crying. She squeezed my hand and told me not to worry, I'd be fine, she was sure the book was amazing. Rex had told her it was.

I was so embarrassed. I was like, "I'm so sorry to barge in here … " Then I told Rex to stop. He could read it in the morning. But he insisted. And so Rebecca went to bed and I lay down on the sofa and he continued to read, making occasional small comments, little typos or things I could fix. They were small things. I wrote them down.

At 12:46, he stopped. He scooted his chair back. He continued to stare at the papers. He said: "If Will Soren doesn't like this, he's crazy. It's great Andrea. It's really great."

I sat there staring at him. I didn't know what to say.

Rex walked me out. He put on his down coat and his slippers and led me down the stairs and then decided to walk with me a little ways down the street. I had calmed down now, after Rebecca's sandwich and banana and herbal tea.

I asked him how his new novel was going. It was a stupid question but he said, "Okay." He said he hadn't done much since the engagement. He felt weird working on it when Rebecca was around; it felt like he was shutting her out in some way. "Which will be fine, once we're married," he joked. "But I don't want to scare her away just yet."

I said how great Rebecca was, how lucky he was to have her. He'd have plenty of time to work. She would make sure of it. That's the kind of person she was.

He nodded. We walked along breathing the cold air, absorbing the quiet of the street. Rex stopped. He couldn't go any further in his slippers. He suggested I get a cab but I needed to walk, to de-stress myself. He nodded and fell silent, in an unusual way. He told me again not to be afraid to send the manuscript. He said if Will Soren didn't want it, someone else would. I smiled with embarrassment through these compliments. I tried to make a joke. But his voice had grown quiet and serious in the dark. He really meant what he was saying.

Then he stepped forward and hugged me. We had hugged before, many times, but this time it was different, like not romantic, or even friends. It was something else, I couldn't quite put my finger on it. But then later, as I walked through silent Greenpoint, I suddenly knew what it felt like: a goodbye hug.

37

NAOMI HAD MADE progress with Michael Grossman and was sleeping at his place regularly enough that if she wasn't home after a certain time, 2am approximately, I knew not to expect her. Occasionally, on these nights, I slept in her bed. This was because she had windows, and a better bed, and it was nice to lay there and look out and see the sky, which you couldn't do from my room. The night of my manuscript panic, I did that, laying on my back and staring upward, a strange stillness filling my body and soul.

The next morning I woke up earlier than usual and had to wait for Mari in the bathroom where she had a whole routine. When she was gone, I took a bath and got ready for work. At *In Focus* I did my usual: in my cubicle by ten, music on my headphones, making my way through the day's work. I ate my cinnamon raison bagel with cream cheese from the deli across the street. I chatted with Walter in the lounge. He was breaking up with someone, and mulling over several new prospects, as he usually was.

When my shift was over at four-thirty, I casually pulled up the remainder of *Chicks and Dudes* on my computer. Rested, fed, encouraged by Rex and Rebecca, I cruised through the manuscript. Rex was right. It was fine. It was smooth, breezy. The characters were likable. The one nagging thought I had: would people take it seriously? Not that it was supposed to be super serious. But I did hope that it had some literary quality. What if people saw the word "Dudes" in the title and totally dismissed it? Which would probably happen.

The other *In Focus* people started to leave at six. I stayed. I had my own keys to the office. I read through the rest of the pages, drinking tea, sitting in my cubicle, the entire building now completely quiet and still.

It was done I decided, standing up suddenly. There was no point tweaking it any more. I went into the main office and loaded the big printer with paper. Then I went back to my computer and dragged the file onto the printing icon. The printer whirred to life. I sat, slouched in my office chair, watching the pages get spit out: *ka-chut ... ka-chut ... ka-chut ...*

I wanted to take the manuscript to 250 West 57th Street myself, to see this mythic literary address. But I thought it might seem pushy and I wanted to do everything absolutely by the book. Nothing weird. No indications that I was a stalker, or unbalanced, or would show up places where I was unwanted. I'd made my bold move at the party. Now it was time to look totally professional. I took the manuscript to the big post office on 34th Street and slid it into a special padded manuscript envelope and paid the five bucks to send it First Class the twenty blocks to WCM. I hand-wrote "WILL SOREN" and the WCM address with a Sharpie. I made sure to use my best handwriting, making the block letters look clean, neat, confident, destined for success.

The next day, Libby called. There were problems brewing

between her and Carol Smith. We met for dumplings at the Chinese restaurant on Mott Street. Carol had gone to L.A. and was working on a new project there. Carol had told Libby to get a new roommate, and had basically broken up with her, it sounded like. But Libby had decided not to find a new roommate and had waited, thinking Carol might change her mind. Now Libby was going to owe twice her usual rent.

I didn't know what to tell Libby. Carol was her first live-in girlfriend (and vice versa) and Libby seemed to think there was some etiquette or rule for how someone would act in that situation. Like how could Carol just not come home? Without talking? Without anything? Without at least discussing who owed what for the rent? The truth was, Carol was brutal like that. She didn't see herself as a normal person with normal obligations. I had seen that myself. But Libby was young and from the midwest, so I guess she still believed in certain things.

Later, Libby took me to karaoke at a nearby bar. A bunch of USC people were there. I knew some of them and we had drinks and people sang karaoke songs. I wasn't usually a big karaoke person, but tonight I didn't mind it, watching the people sing off-key and act dumb. I ordered my drink, a vodka tonic, which I'd recently learned from Naomi, who considered it a simple, elegant, always appropriate drink choice.

After a second vodka tonic, and in the middle of a Styx song, I was seized by a deep desire to call Rex and tell him the deed was done. *Chicks and Dudes* was in the mail. It was out in the world. He and I, its reluctant parents, could do nothing more ...

I slept with a guy named Evan that night. He was one of Libby's USC friends, a good looking L.A. boy who was slightly more forward than the others, and a bit more of an asshole. That was the thing with guys. In certain situations, the assholes were your only choice, because they were the only people who could move things along, who could steer you down the road to sleeping with them.

Evan was staying in his uncle's SoHo loft ten blocks away, so that part was easy. His uncle was an advertising person of some sort and was "bi-coastal." His loft was quite big and full of interesting art books and Japanese-designed furniture.

Evan himself was clean and neutral smelling and when we undressed and got into the beautiful bed, he went right to work on me with great skill and attention. Not that I really cared. I wasn't there for the sex. I just needed to do something different that night. It was post-partum something or other. I could not go home to my own bed.

In the morning, Evan made us cappuccinos on the shiny Italian espresso machine in his kitchen. I'm not sure I said more than five sentences during our morning together. He kissed me and took my number and then released me into the brightness of the morning.

It was November now, 1999, a weird time in the history of the world. What was going to happen in the next millennium? Probably a lot, judging from how fast things seemed to be going. In my post-sex daze, I let my brain bounce around randomly: the world, the city, my fate, my future. In the next century, would we have special machines that would clean the air? Would I ever have children? What would happen to newspapers? Maybe the world would actually get cleaner as the human race progressed. Was I a slut? Who bought this absurdly expensive stuff in the windows of SoHo? And didn't they realize if a pair of jeans cost $600, they were guaranteed to have some stupid bauble or weird pocket or something?

·   ·   ·

That night I slept in Naomi's bed, but then she came home at three in the morning. She nearly stepped on me, before she realized I was there. I apologized profusely and crawled into my own bed, and then I heard her swearing to herself and banging around so I asked her what was going on. A lot, it turned out. "Do you need to talk?" I asked. She did.

We made tea. She wanted to smoke, which she didn't normally do, so then we had to open the window. This made it cold, so we put our winter coats on, over our underclothes and shivered and held our warm tea mugs to our chests. She told me things weren't working out with Michael Grossman. They had visited his family in Newton and it hadn't gone well. His parents didn't like her for some reason. Michael told Naomi, that his mother described her as "hard."

Besides, she and Michael had nothing to talk about. He was an idiot. He was a sales executive for a stupid sports drink and hung out with jocks and played golf with morons. She hated people like that. She wanted to go to museums and galleries. She wanted to go to fashion shows. She needed someone who could talk about something real.

Then she lowered her head and started to cry. Which was shocking to see.

That Friday I went with Walter and some of his gay friends to a new dance club everyone was talking about, everyone who paid attention to dance clubs. It was funny how I'd become just like I was in high school: one finger in every scene, with no deep connection to any of them.

But the dance club was amazing. It had low ceilings and laser lights and this great underground basement feel. Naturally, the people were gorgeous and deadly cool and it sent this *zing* through your nervous system just to walk into such a place.

Pretty much everyone was gay though, so it wasn't like I was going to meet anyone.

Walter had promised me I would dance my ass off, and I did. As usual, he slunk off every once in a while, to do who knows what ... but I was okay, I knew his other friends by now too. One of them was giving us coke and we all danced, and lost ourselves in the *trance* of it, the different beats and rhythms and "soundscapes."

Afterward, I was all coke-buzzed and adrenalized but also wanting something more. So I called Evan from Walter's cell phone. Evan had a cell phone too so I got him immediately. I asked if he wanted to meet up and he definitely did. I said, "I've been dancing, I'm kind of sweaty." He said I could come over and take a shower.

So then it was back to SoHo, to Evan's loft, and into the luxury bathroom with its mirrored walls and clear-windowed shower. Then the clean bed and the clean boy and the attentive sex ... and the hiss of the espresso machine in the morning.

38

WILL Soren called me at work ten days after I mailed the manuscript. He said he'd read my novel and he wanted to take me to lunch. I said okay.

For the two days before this lunch date, I went to my job, did my laundry, didn't say much to anyone. Again, I wanted to check in with Rex, but thought better of it. Instead I called Sally, who called her dad, who was probably sick of giving me advice by now. His comment for the lunch date was: "Eat and listen." Sally reminded me to not talk with my mouth full, which I apparently did sometimes.

I remained remarkably calm. I had a half-day at *In Focus* on the day of the lunch so I went in early and did a decent three hours of work. I had told Veronica the situation and she was impressed and encouraging. She told me to give Will her best.

I left the office at 11:30. I was wearing jeans, a nice sweater, an overcoat. I wore no makeup, a little extra deodorant. I felt like I needed to maintain a certain nondescript quality, and let my best asset, my youth, do the rest.

I arrived at the sushi restaurant ten minutes early. I glanced inside. Will Soren was not there. So I walked around the block.

But that only killed four minutes so I walked around a different block and then wandered around inside a D'Augustino's Supermarket. I got back to the sushi restaurant five minutes late. Which was perfect.

Will Soren had just walked in. I walked in behind him. He was even taller than I remembered. He had to look down to greet me and shake my hand. Then we waited for the hostess.

He didn't say much. So I didn't either. We were led to a table. We sat. He asked me how my day was going. I told him I'd worked a half-day at *In Focus*. He nodded at that, and asked about Veronica. He said to give her his best. I promised I would.

We ordered. Will Soren had a very large head. He had long, wavy grey hair. He seemed too big for me, too important. I felt like nothing sitting there with him. I remembered Marjorie Isaacs at the party. She had radiated glamour, malevolence, genius. My main point of interest was what? My clear Oregon skin? And my book was about people even more clueless than I was. It had long strings of dialogue about bongs.

Soren told me his assistant had read my book. She had liked it a lot. He had read the first half but hadn't finished it yet. He said, "We might have something here." I nodded. He asked me where I'd gone to school and I told him my story again, I'd gone to Wellington and left without graduating. He didn't care about that. He looked at me closely then, a cold, evaluating gaze, that sent a slight chill through me. Then he asked me how I thought I would do meeting with editors. I said I thought I could handle that. He said editors always wanted to hear from the new generation. I nodded that I understood. He told me I'd looked good at the *In Focus* party and to wear something like that when we met with people. I said okay.

Our sushi came. We ate in silence.

Afterward, on the sidewalk, he shook my hand. He said he would set up some meetings.

. . .

I walked away in the other direction. At the end of the block, I realized I'd left my scarf in the sushi restaurant. I hurried back.

I had barely noticed the interior before and now, as I cautiously crept back inside, by myself, unprotected by Soren's hulking frame, I was shocked by the dining room's opulence and slick modernism. Had I just been in here? Meeting with a famous agent? It seemed impossible.

I tried to sneak back to our table but it had already been cleared away. The hostess woman, appeared instantly and without a word or any readable expression on her face handed me my five-dollar scarf.

A week later, a woman called me at work. "Hello Andrea, this is Liz, I'm Mr. Soren's assistant." I said I was pleased to meet her. She asked me if I was available to meet with Mr. Soren and Mr. Weintraub at Simon & Schuster next Tuesday at 11:30am. I said I was. She told me to meet Mr. Soren at 11:20 in the lobby at 1234 Sixth Avenue and he and I would go to the meeting together. I said okay. "Let us know if anything comes up," she told me. I assured her nothing would.

39

ON TUESDAY, I tried to sleep in. I wanted to be fresh and maybe a little bit sleepy for my big meeting. I even wondered if I should arrive with bedhead, to look "Portland," like my book. But in the end I decided to brush my hair and be normal and to wear the exact same clothes from the party, like Will Soren had said. Which meant Naomi's grey skirt, the red blouse, the black sweater. Then I added my one little embellishment: a plastic yellow barrette for that authentic "alternative" feel.

I rode the G Train north to the F Train, and rode that into midtown Manhattan. Standing in the subway car, I watched the other late morning commuters, their shopping bags and backpacks balanced on their laps. Some had earphones on, others read books, a few restless souls stood, clinging to the overhead pole, letting themselves sway slightly with the movement of the train. Real, actual, born-and-bred New Yorkers: what strange deformed beings they were. How strange to live here in this land of dreams if you weren't actually dreaming anything. What was the point of all this struggle if there wasn't something you were trying to get? If you were just existing? But of course real New Yorkers couldn't go anywhere else. The rest of the world would never accept them. They would be clownish caricatures, with their exaggerated faces and their honking voices. They would explode anywhere else from a lack of external pressure.

The subway stopped at 50th Street and I got out, making my slow way to the stairs, worrying that I would sweat too much if I walked fast or got too excited. *Calmness*, I found myself repeating. *Stay calm.*

I was ahead of schedule and when I reached the lavish, gold-plated lobby of 1234 Avenue of the Americas. I was so nervous and scared I turned and walked back down into the subway station again. I found myself standing next to the subway booth, watching people stream out through the turnstiles. When my watch reached 11:20 exactly, I forced myself to turn and walk up the stairs to where Will Soren would be waiting for me.

He was there, in his usual dark suit. He smiled at me. Not a warm smile exactly, but something like it. I greeted him and we shook hands and he stuck his hands in the pockets of his pants, making them bag out. He asked me if I was ready. I said I was and he said good and pushed the UP button.

When we were in the elevator, Will Soren told me that he wasn't sure how Weintraub would react to the book, or if he'd finished it yet. It wasn't his usual thing, but there was some restructuring going on and he might want something edgy, with a youth angle.

I nodded obediently to this. Then I almost asked Will Soren if *he* had finished reading my book, not in an accusatory way, but to see what he thought. But it occurred to me he probably hadn't and probably never would. So I said nothing.

· · ·

We exited the elevator into a beautiful reception area. Will Soren nodded to the young woman at the desk and we proceeded directly down a long hallway. Here, we walked beside a glass trophy case of Simon & Schuster classics, their bestsellers, their upcoming releases. I felt a twinge of near-panic pass through me, but I stayed close behind Will Soren's large protective shoulders.

We strode by several offices. I dared to peak into these tiny rooms, usually to see a single person at a cramped desk, the back of a head, a set of hunched shoulders, and the ubiquitous computer monitors. A voice suddenly rang out. "Will! Hey!" Will, in front of me, frowned and turned. He forced a fake smile onto his face and went back to one of the doorways. The man inside was already coming out to greet us. He was younger, with thick red hair, a bright shirt and tie. He greeted Will with fake warmth and shook his hand. Then he turned to me. "So who's this?" he said.

Will told him who I was. The man smiled at me, shook my hand. "Taking her into see the head man!" he said. Will nodded and touched the young editor's shoulder and told him he would be in touch, adding that he had a special project for him, waiting in the wings. The editor lit up. "Great, Will. Fantastic! Send it over. I can't wait to read it!" The two shook hands again, smiled fake smiles, patted each other on the back. *So this is how the world works*, I thought.

We continued uninterrupted down the hall, Will Soren falling into an even deeper silence than he'd been in before. He knocked on a door at the end of the hall. Someone said something and Will opened it and went in. I followed.

An older, balding man was sitting at a large paper-strewn desk. This was Ben Weintraub. He was my dad's age, I would guess. He was on the phone but wrapped up his call immediately and rose from his desk to greet us. I liked him instantly. He was warm, pleasant, there was a humorous shine in his eye.

The office itself was messy in an editorial sort of way. Weintraub offered us seats on a small couch along one wall. We sat. A cute female assistant, about my age, appeared and Weintraub offered us drinks, water, coffee, whatever we wanted. Will Soren didn't want anything and so I didn't either. The assistant and I made brief conspiratorial eye contact and she disappeared.

Weintraub stood in front of his desk. Then he sat on the edge of it. He studied me carefully for several seconds. I seemed to be different than what he expected. And yet he seemed pleased. He said he had not finished the book but he'd liked what he'd read so far and that his assistant loved it and could not put it down and now the other young people in the office were fighting over it. That sounded like good news. Weintraub asked me some basic questions about myself which I answered as succinctly as I could. Short answers seemed to be called for. Will Soren looked pleased.

Weintraub then went back around his desk and sat down and something changed slightly in his demeanor. He was out of ass-kissing mode. He and Will Soren talked briefly about a different book. There seemed to be some disagreement about it and for a moment, a subtle, unspoken negotiation took place. Then they spent several minutes reassuring each other that their differences were nothing. It would all work out. There was no real problem.

Since this issue did not concern me, I spent that time looking around at the office. Several small plaques and awards rested on a high shelf. There was a stack of rubber banded manuscripts on the floor. There was another stack on the windowsill. None of it looked very organized. Nor did any of these other manuscripts look like anything Weintraub cared about very much. That was what Will Soren had done for me. He had gotten me off the floor and off the windowsill. What incredible good luck it was that I was sitting on that couch next to him.

Two days later, we did the same drill with a Mr. Rosenthal at Random House. First, the nervous walk through the hallway, the younger assistants sneaking looks at me as Will Soren led me forward. Then into another large office where Mr. Rosenthal asked me some general questions about my novel. He had read it, the whole thing, but he seemed unsure of what the point of it was. He asked me if the characters in the novel were based on people I knew. I nodded yes. Will asked him if he thought it was ready to go, or did it need significant edits. Rosenthal shrugged. He didn't seem to know. His default reaction to everything Will said was: "Whatever you think" or "I'm probably too old" or "What can I say?" He was basically at our mercy, his body language seemed to suggest.

Will led me out ten minutes later. He smiled at me on the street as he hailed a cab. "You're doing great," he said, as one pulled over.

I watched him ride away. Then I went looking for the nearest subway station.

The third meeting was with a woman, Cynthia A. Dunleavy. "She's a piece of work," Will warned me as we waited to be admitted into her office. We sat in chairs, side by side, not unlike the waiting room at my dad's dental office. I picked up a copy of *Publisher's Weekly* and flipped through it. I noticed one of Cynthia A. Dunleavy's books happened to be on the cover. When I mentioned this, Soren pointed out that all the *Publish-*

er's Weekly's in Cynthia Dunleavy's waiting room featured her books on the cover. That's why some of them were several years old.

The receptionist appeared and admitted us into the office. It was much bigger and cleaner than the others. Except for one large bookcase along the wall, you would not have known it was the office of a book editor. Mrs. Dunleavy was a small, precise woman, with large alert eyes, gaunt features, a miniature body that seemed to have never passed through puberty. She felt sharp to me, and dangerous. I felt my chest tighten as I sat.

Like the others, she began with praise, followed by bland questions. She watched me closely as I spoke, she was not listening to what I said so much as watching my face, watching to see how I reacted to the intense pressure she was somehow putting on me, even though she wasn't actually doing anything.

Near the end of our twelve-minute meeting, she said to me: "So this is your dream, Andrea? To come to New York and publish your novel?" It was a trick question. Or so it seemed. I couldn't tell. There was no good way to answer it without sounding like an idiot. I found myself freezing up, then nodding, and then Will Soren interrupted to tell her that I'd attended Wellington where I had been a standout in the creative writing department. Cynthia A. Dunleavy was not fooled by this. She could see what I was: a child, a wannabe, a rube from the hinterlands, who was being cleverly exploited by Will Soren. Her eyes burned into me. I sat there and let myself be scalded. Thirty seconds later, Will Soren thanked her and guided me out.

40

MEANWHILE, during the two weeks that this was happening, Sally was in the early stages of a romance with Jonathan Resnick. For their first date, Jonathan took Sally out to dinner at a small Italian restaurant in Greenwich Village. After the meal, he took her to a bar on 19th Street, where *Esquire* people hung out and important literary types sometimes showed up.

For their second date, Sally wanted to see an Iranian movie everyone was talking about, so they did that. Afterward, they went to a fancy wine bar/café place where they drank thirty-dollar glasses of wine by candlelight.

For their third date, Jonathan took her to a Knicks game. Sally had played basketball herself in high school and she loved that. She ended up yelling and cheering and spilling popcorn all over herself. This, she considered the breakthrough moment, when Jonathan quit trying to impress her and they both relaxed and actually had fun. "Why is he trying to impress me so much?" she asked. I didn't know. He was the photo editor of *Esquire Magazine*, you wouldn't think he'd be so insecure. She did have a famous dad, though. That might be part of it. And there was the age thing. He was thirty-five. Sally was twenty-four. Maybe men didn't know how to act around younger women, except to spend money and act important.

I had two more meetings with editors the next week. After each, after Will Soren disappeared into a cab, I would find myself standing on an unfamiliar corner somewhere. And so I would walk, letting my jangled nerves settle, letting my feet return to the earth, letting my lungs clear themselves of the rarified air.

There was usually another feeling too, centered in my chest and stomach, a sense that I was now so far up in the clouds, there was no chance of ever making it safely back to earth. I was not going to survive this. I would come crashing down to earth and be destroyed at some point. How could I not be?

Not that anyone did anything wrong. The editors were perfectly professional and utterly considerate of my youth and inexperience. The people at WCM were always polite, kind, quick to answer questions or help. Even Will Soren would occasionally lower his huge head down to my ear and in a few magically lucid sentences, summarize some complicated aspect of the publishing business. But that was not the problem. The person I didn't trust was myself. I was not intended for this. I was an observer of other people's fame and fortune. I was not psychologically equipped to have it myself. My body could not withstand the physical strain.

One night at *In Focus*, I felt so strange and out of sorts, I called Evan and then walked through the cold to meet him at the dumpling restaurant in Chinatown. I got there early, but instead of doing my usual walk around the block, I went inside and sat and zoned out, watching the other people eat.

I was glad when Evan arrived, his bright cheerful face, his expensive haircut, his predictable opinions about the latest movies and books. We ate our dumplings out of steaming white bowls and drank cans of Coke. Because of the cold, the windows had fogged over. Evan told me some funny anecdotes about a car commercial he was working on in New Jersey. He was the assistant to the assistant, paying his dues. I told him what was happening with me. The meetings. Will Soren. It was all so extraordinary I didn't even know how to recount it exactly, and yet Evan with his SoHo apartment and his advertising executive uncle seemed to grasp it immediately. He understood the higher level of things. He was from there.

At his place, Evan rubbed my shoulders and then other parts of me, and we eventually slipped into the clean pressed sheets of his bed. Despite Evan's attentions, I could not seem to relax. I slept fitfully and then at 3:45 in the morning, my eyes clanged open and I lay there the rest of the night, in a mild panic, staring at the ceiling, wishing I was back at dilapidated 191 Wilton.

The next morning I went straight to *In Focus* in my same clothes. Nobody noticed. Nor did I say anything about Evan or anything else, including my book situation. I had told a few people at work about my first meeting, but had quickly seen that a possible book deal at Simon & Schuster was not something I could discuss with my coworkers, in-between their stories of flakey roommates or subway delays.

And so, during the next couple weeks, I avoided workplace conversations and instead went for walks in the winter cold, and when it was too cold, went to the movies or rode the subway up to Sally's, who also lapsed into shocked silence when I told her each new development regarding my book.

Even her father was shocked to hear the high level of editors I was talking to. Nobody knew what to say.

And then we got a new thing to talk about: Jonathan Resnick had a fiancé. Sally learned this accidentally through a friend of a friend at *Esquire*. They'd been engaged for over a year. When confronted, Jonathan assured Sally he was about to break it off, but there were extenuating circumstances. His fiancé was related in some way to his boss. We never got the full story.

This was huge news, especially for someone like Sally, who did not date much, and who had not had a serious boyfriend since high school. I did my best to be a good friend, to listen carefully during the hours of processing, crying, anger-letting and other reactions. But the truth was, I was so preoccupied with my own situation, I could barely stay focused on Sally's. She would often have to remind me of the details of what happened. This I knew, was nearly unforgivable as a friend. But Sally let it go. She knew me so well, she understood I wasn't capable of thinking about anyone but myself at this time. Nor could I fake interest in anything else. I wasn't that sophisticated.

Will Soren called me at work on January 16, 2000. He told me that the two best offers we had were from Ben Weintraub at Simon & Schuster for $175,000 and Cynthia Dunleavy at Montauk Books for $185,000. Will Soren said he had hoped it would be more. But there had been big money thrown at some edgy first novels the year before—half a million, in one case— none of which panned out. So the timing had been bad. Still, the offers were solid. Now, the choice was mine. What did I want to do?

It took me a second to realize he was asking me a question.

Which offer did I want to take? He was waiting. I stammered that I didn't know, which did he think would be best? He pointed out, dryly, that Cynthia Dunleavy's offer was for more money. I said, yes, but she was so scary. He agreed that she was scary and fell silent. Then he told me that I would not be dealing with either editor a great deal. Both would have assistants who would do most of the work. Top editors were more like overseers. But would they actually edit my book? I asked. He said, yes, they would be active in the process. And how were they as editors? They were both excellent, he said. They were the best.

I continued to hesitate. Again I mentioned that I had been terrified of Cynthia Dunleavy. He said that was understandable but added: "Maybe that would be good for you." I didn't know what he meant by that, and I was afraid to ask.

"Think about it," he said, a slight impatience creeping into his voice. "And let me know by Monday."

I hung up and immediately called my mother. She was at work at her school, and for some reason I whispered the news to her in the grave tones of someone who'd been arrested or told they had a horrible disease. She was confused at first, and then brightened when she realized what I was saying. She had read an early draft of *Chicks and Dudes* which I'd emailed her. She had thought it "interesting" and a little bit pornographic. She said it was hard for a mother to read such a story by her daughter, but she was sure it would be of great interest to girls my own age.

My mother couldn't talk at work, so that night I called my parents' house and this time discussed it with my dad. I told him about the choice I had to make. He couldn't help me of course, he'd never known anyone like Cynthia Dunleavy or Ben

Weintraub. Nor did he understand what exactly went into these kinds of decisions. My mother, listening in on the other phone, wanted Will Soren to make the decision. Or at least to advise me. Wasn't he the expert? Wasn't that what he was paid to do? Advise people?

In the end, there was nothing my parents could say, no advice to give, no wisdom to impart. I would have to decide. Of course, once I did, they would support me. And they would love me. And I could call them at night and listen to their familiar voices, talking in their slow Oregon cadences. At least they understood that I was scared. They knew how scared I got. How scared I'd always been. Scared of everything, of good news and bad, of things changing or staying the same. Which was why they were so bewildered when I'd managed to throw myself into the craw of the big city. And now, were even more shocked and amazed by what was happening to me there.

41

THE OTHER PERSON I discussed it with was Naomi. The next night I sat in the kitchen with her—she was on a cooking binge lately—and told her the situation, including the actual numbers involved which I found alarming, but which Naomi shrugged at, as if $185,000 was a completely ordinary amount of money. In general though, she seemed very interested in my situation and thought she might have met Cynthia Dunleavy at an event somewhere. She knew the type anyway, and thought about it for a second before she offered her opinion. The thing about people like that, she explained, was they do get things done. They bust heads to do it, but they achieve their ends. If you become one of the heads they have to bust, that's bad. But if they are busting other people's heads for your benefit, that's good.

I said, "So with her, at least I'd have a powerful person on my side." But Naomi told me not to count on that. She didn't know exactly how it was in the book business, but loyalty was usually conditional in these situations. If my book bombed, I could say goodbye to Cynthia Dunleavy. What it came down to, was how much tension I could stand. With people like

Dunleavy, it could become physically oppressive. But maybe that didn't matter, if I didn't have to interact with her every day. Maybe all that tension and drive would be on the assistants and the publicity people. It would be working for me.

I listened carefully to Naomi. And then as I sat there, deeply absorbed in myself and my decision, she said something else. She said she was moving in with her sister on the Upper East Side. She would be leaving at the end of next month and that I would need to get a new person for the apartment. She had thought about passing on her room to a certain friend, but the friend had found something else. So her room was open. Naturally she assumed I would take it, and Mari would take mine, and someone new would take the small room. But that was for me to work out.

I listened to this, stunned. So now I was in charge of the apartment? There was no way I could deal with that now. But thinking about it more, I might not have a choice. Mari never took care of anything and could barely pay her bills on time. She still brought guys to the apartment occasionally, to everyone's horror and disgust.

"You'll be fine," said Naomi. But now I felt a second wave of dread, this one because I would no longer have easy access to Naomi. Would we still hang out? Could I still ask her questions? She knew things. And I didn't! I needed her for boy advice, for professional guidance, to listen to and feel morally superior to while we gardened on the fire escape.

I stared at her as she removed a quiche from the oven. She cut us both slices and then ate hers, leaning back in her chair, her feet up on the kitchen windowsill, her slender fingers holding the fork just so. That was the other thing about Naomi, she was my standard of New York cool. She had the style, and the presence, and the most important quality of all: she did not care what anyone thought of her. Not one bit.

I called Libby the next day. Had she found a roommate yet? Would she want to move into our place?

She couldn't. She was moving to L.A. in March to work on a documentary about prisons in Brazil. She told me more about that. It was fun to talk to her again. I really liked Libby. More than Carol Smith, I realized. She was a much better friend.

I told her about my book situation and how I had to decide between two editors. She said she would go with the nicer editor. "Life's too short to deal with assholes," she said. Which sounded so sane and obvious as to make me wonder why I'd considered anything else.

Naomi advised me not to tell Mari that she was leaving until I had a replacement, lest Mari find another party girl, like herself, and I end up outnumbered and having stray drunk dudes walking around naked in the apartment every night.

I took this advice and immediately contacted everyone I could think of for possible roommates. My friends at *In Focus,* Sally and her crew, many of whom would graduate and get kicked out of their student housing in May. This added stress was very nearly the undoing of me, as I could not really see myself interviewing prospective roommates, which was what everyone was suddenly telling me to do. Nobody had interviewed me. Nobody had interviewed Mari. But now *I* was supposed to interview people?

Libby called back a couple days later and asked me about Evan. They were old friends, and Evan had confided in her. He really liked me, but he couldn't tell what was going on with us. I told Libby the truth, I didn't have strong feelings for Evan. I couldn't really see myself going out with him. We barely talked when we were together. Mostly we had sex and drank espressos. Libby thought maybe I should try opening up to him more. Just to see. I was like, "I kinda have a lot to deal with right now." Which was the truth.

I decided to accept Cynthia Dunleavy's offer. When I told Will Soren, he chuckled and told me I was brave. I thought, *what's that supposed to mean?* But I didn't dare say anything. Will Soren told me they would begin the paperwork and there would be things for me to sign in a few weeks. And to expect a call from Cynthia's office at some point. Then, since I honestly had no idea, I asked Will Soren what I should do with all that money. "Save it," he said.

That night I stupidly accepted a dinner invitation from Evan. I could tell the minute I walked in the restaurant that he considered this his last chance to save our relationship. We got settled at our table, and Evan asked me how my day was and I saw that I had no choice but to tell him I had just accepted an offer for my book. He immediately got excited and ordered champagne, even as I begged him not to. And then we had to have special food and dessert and by the time the evening was over, I was tipsy and too full and chocolate-buzzed and not myself. I ended up back at Evan's loft, in bed, which was fun but not really representative of the way I felt about him. There was nothing to be done. And so, once again, I woke up the next morning under expensive sheets, in the bright winter sunshine, a perfect Italian espresso with lemon rind at the night table beside me.

· · ·

At work, I emailed Rex and told him about my book deal. It hurt me greatly to send this email. Another nail in the coffin of our friendship, I assumed. He surprised me though by emailing me right back his congratulations. He also announced that he had just been hired at the *New York Post*, to be a book/entertainment editor. Then he reminded me that his wedding was in June and that I was invited and I better be there. I was so surprised by his cheerful email that I asked him out to coffee, without thinking about it, and which he accepted.

We met at a small café off Union Square, and immediately fell to grinning and giggling with each other, like we always did. What a relief! I told him about Will Soren, standing up to do an imitation of his famous saunter as he strode the great halls of publishing. And then the different editors and the different companies and my eventual decision and how weird and scary it all was. But also exciting. Rex thought I had "made it." He thought once they put that much money on the table, they made sure the book did not fail, though I didn't see how that could be true. I read *Publisher's Weekly* every week and lots of books got big advances and went nowhere.

Like Evan, Rex wanted to buy me something to celebrate. We ordered a piece of chocolate cake at the café, which we split. I asked about Rebecca and as he talked, I realized I missed her as much as I missed him. Could we all hang out somehow? Why don't we have a little party or something? A celebratory dinner party, said Rex. Let's do it! They could have it at their apartment. Rebecca would love the idea.

I felt good about that walking home. I had to start being more social and more official in the way I did things. I needed to think about being a public person. I even made Sally come with me to another *Context* party, where Sally made the mistake of mentioning my book deal to Danielle, who's mouth tightened and eyes narrowed. She was writing a novel too, it turned out. I quickly interjected that it was called *Chicks and Dudes* and it was about musicians in Portland, and she lightened up. "Oh, it's one of *those* novels," she said dismissively. "Well, good luck."

After that, Sally and I got revenge on Danielle by being more flirtatious and interesting than her and getting most of the attention from the boys. But it was a hollow victory. The *Context* scene, which had seemed so fascinating to me a year ago, now seemed amateurish. Will Soren would not waste one second on these people. But then he did not waste very much time on me either. In fact, I did not speak to him for weeks after I made my decision. From then on, it was always Liz on the phone, as we processed the paperwork required to turn me into an actual author.

42

MEANWHILE, as Naomi's departure approached, I grew increasingly more desperate about filling our third spot at the apartment. I had pretty much asked everyone I knew if they knew someone. Then a girl from Portland called. Her name was Dana and she had got my number from Nick Pax. She had just moved to New York and needed a place to live.

I had seen Nick during the summer when Crystalline played in Williamsburg. They'd sold out the small club, and I had hung out with Nick the afternoon before the show. He had looked great that day, tanned, new jeans, a new prosperous Nick Pax. He was going to marry Crystal, or that was the plan. I didn't see how that would work over the long term, but it wasn't any of my business and I tried to be happy for the both of them.

Anyway, so my connection with Portland was still intact and I felt some responsibility toward Portland people. Unfortunately, the minute I heard Dana's voice, I got a bad feeling. I told her on the phone I had a couple people looking at it, but she could come by and check it out.

She came on a Saturday. She had that Portland look: pale skin, doughy face, badly dyed hair, with a sleeve of tattoos down her entire right arm. I didn't say anything. I showed her the small room and told her the price. She brightened when she heard how cheap it was. She said she was an illustrator and cartoonist, and had a great job opportunity here. So she'd taken the plunge and was trying her luck in the big city. I nodded and sympathized. I told her how intimidated I'd been at first. I asked her where she went to college or art school or whatever. She said she hadn't gone anywhere. She taught herself. She seemed embarrassed to say this, like other people must have asked her about her education. I asked her where she went to high school in Portland and she named one of the outlying, semi-rural public high schools. That explained her appearance.

Then, as if she'd read my mind, she spilled out her story: she was couch surfing, she was running out of money, she wasn't exactly sure about the job. People had not been nice to her in New York. Not at all. They really looked down their nose at you here, didn't they?

I nodded that they did. Dana sniffled and apologized for venting and thanked me again and said she definitely wanted the small room, and to please please please call her if it was open. I said I would and walked her out. I wished her luck. I did not rent her the room.

Instead, I rented it to Bridget, a friend of Libby's, a blonde, good looking, rich girl from Berkeley, California. What can I say? This was my life in New York. This was what I felt comfortable with. Bridget was sparkly-eyed and talkative. When she came to see the tiny room, she pulled the curtain back, laughed and took a picture of it with her phone and said she would send it to her parents to show them how thrifty she was being. And how bohemian. "Just like when they were young and starving," she said, touching my forearm with manicured fingers.

I told her I had started in that room myself, and gave her what advice and guidance I could about how to set it up. She laughed at that. "I'll find a boyfriend and sleep at his place," she said. "And then one of you guys will move and I'll take your room."

Bridget paid with a check, which she wrote without even taking off her coat. The next day, I put the check in our usual group envelope and mailed it. Later, I called our landlady and introduced myself as the main contact person now, at 191 Wilton.

It took Bridget three weeks to find Evan. She called me one morning at work from her cell phone. She asked me what was happening between us. I said that Evan and I had hung out some, but hadn't seen each other recently, not for several weeks. "Because I'm at his apartment," whispered Bridget, interrupting me. "I hope that's all right."

They'd found each other at karaoke, though they'd first met in high school, at a young filmmakers camp in San Francisco. So it wasn't like she just grabbed him for no reason.

I said I understood, and that it was okay, and probably for the best. Which was a mature way to deal with it. It sure made things easy for Bridget. She and Evan went right to work, fucking each other's brains out. I didn't see her back at the house for a week.

Around the same time, a woman I didn't know at Cynthia Dunleavy's office called to inform me that the first edits of my novel were completed and would be sent to me. I found the manuscript the next morning, outside, on our snow-dusted front stoop in a waterproof FedEx packet. I was late getting to work, so I took it with me to *In Focus*, peeking into it on the subway. The three hundred and eighteen pages were marked up with a red colored pencil. There were also Post-it notes.

This happened to be the same day as Rex's dinner party, so Rex told me to come over early: he wanted to look at the edited manuscript. I did, and the two of us huddled over it, while Rebecca was left to deal with the food. Rex was fascinated by the professional editorial process. There was a one page letter, written by Cynthia Dunleavy herself, which spelled out the major changes she wanted. Then there were her comments on the actual manuscript, in her elegant handwriting, each of which seemed to contain some singular nugget of truth.

I was so glad to have Rex going through it with me. I might have lost my shit, otherwise. Or found something to freak out about. With him though, it was more just exciting and fun and kind of a revelation.

Guests began to arrive. I slid the manuscript back into the FedEx package and helped Rex and Rebecca set the table. A couple from *Context* came, and a single girl from Rebecca's work. A coworker of Rex's from *The New York Post* showed up, and another Oberlin friend who had lived on Rex's hall freshman year.

We drank wine and ate dinner and the mood was cozy and relaxed. Rex told everyone about my book and the edits and we talked about that, and about my book deal in general, which everyone was very impressed by and extremely interested in. The guy from Oberlin was writing a novel too. He'd been working on it for two and a half years but only had 152 pages. I nodded encouragingly, though I couldn't imagine writing something so slowly. How would you even remember what was happening?

For most of an hour, the conversation was about writing and novels and me and my book deal. I wasn't sure what to do about this. I felt so comfortable with Rex there, egging me on, letting me babble about my great success. The single girl eventually got bored and annoyed and whispered to Rebecca that she had to leave. This finally got me to shut up and I apologized for hogging the conversation, but everyone else was like, "No, no, it's so interesting! This is why people come to New York!" Still, the other girl skulked out and I felt bad.

After dinner, the guy from *The Post* got too drunk and yakked his wine breath at me about his dreams of being a *real* novelist. Whatever that meant. The other couple had long since faded into silence and when everyone finally left, the entire evening felt like a failure somehow. It was my ego and my inability to shut up. If I couldn't control myself better, people were going to hate me.

But when everyone else was gone, Rex and Rebecca and I drank the last of the wine and things felt okay again. Rex loved his new job at *The Post*. He was reviewing a new post-modern detective novel told entirely in the voice of someone with Tourette's. And Rebecca was doing well too. We were all happy, on our way up, young and successful. Just like the guy said: This was why you came to New York.

43

IN MARCH, a thin cardboard FedEx envelope came to Wilton Street. I went downstairs and signed for it, not knowing what it was. The return address was WCM who had been sending me things occasionally. I pulled a tab and opened it and pulled out a normal sized white WCM envelope. My name and address were visible through the transparent window on the front. It was not sealed and I opened it and found inside a very complicated-looking check which was made out to me in the amount of $78,625.00.

I sort of froze for a moment, there in the cold sunshine, on my stoop. A city bus went by. Some local kids with sideways baseball caps were standing across the street. I looked at the check again, and the envelope, and the amount.

I turned and went inside, bringing the check up the stairs with me, aware of it's smooth papery feeling between my fingers. Inside my apartment, I set it on the table, the check facing up, on top of the brightly colored FedEx cardboard.

I sat down next to it and picked it up again. $78,625.00 It seemed like such a strange amount. The check itself seemed weird. It had all these watermarks and secret symbols and other intricacies I didn't know a check could have. I kept touching it. I turned it over. There was a place for your signature, just like on a normal check, but even that part was more intricate and elegantly printed.

I put on water for coffee. We'd run out of coffee filters though, so I checked the shelves to see if there were any paper towels. There weren't. So then I went to see if there were any filters in the other cupboard and I ended up digging through a bunch of unused chopsticks and soy sauce packets and then I forgot what I was doing and ended up back in my room staring out the window.

What was I going to do with all that money? Should I move? Where would I move to? Should I quit my job and start writing another book? That's what several people had said to me recently: this is your big chance. This was the opportunity almost no one gets. *Write another book!*

But what would it be about?

I hid the check under my bed, then in my closet, then under some books. I got dressed and went to work. On the subway, I sat in silence as the train wheels rolled and rumbled beneath me. It was late morning, the subway was empty. The doors opened at the next station and then the whole train waited, as an old Polish woman shuffled on board. She sat across from me, working her mouth around, chewing on her gums.

The train began to move again. Twenty feet down, a tall black kid rocked his head to an iPod. Twenty feet past him, another elderly Polish man read a Polish newspaper. The otherwise empty train rattled noisily along.

.   .   .

At *In Focus*, there was a minor drama going on. Veronica was yelling at someone. I went to my cubicle and unloaded my crap. I tried not to think of how much money I would actually make at *In Focus* that day. Not very much. Walter came over to tell me what the drama was about. Someone had sent the wrong layout to the printer. Walter snickered secretly and then snuck back to his own cubicle as Veronica's angry rant continued from her office. I tried to think of my life not working here. I couldn't imagine it. I loved these people. Plus, what would I do all day? Write? All day? For eight hours? It was inconceivable.

After work, Walter and some other people were going to bowling league. *In Focus* had started a team. I had helped organize it. But I couldn't do it tonight. I had stuff to do.

At home, I called my parents. My mother answered and I told her I had gotten my first check for the book. I told her how much it was for. She took a long breath. I asked her what I should do with it. She said I should talk to my father.

My father got on the other line. He thought I should invest it. I didn't like the sound of that. But he told me it would be okay, we'd put it in something conservative, equities, bonds, mutual funds. I didn't know what any of those things were.

It was a weird conversation. My dad even sounded nervous. It was so weird because this should have been this great moment, this great success, but everyone was just scared and talking over each other and then arguing about the best way to mail the check to my Portland bank: Insured mail? Certified mail? FedEx?

After that, I called Naomi and caught her just as she was going to bed. I asked her what I should do with my advance money. She seemed to think investing the money was a good idea. "I'm sure your dad knows what to do. That's what dad's are for."

Other than that, she told me to keep working at *In Focus* if I enjoyed it. And if I had time to write. She would write another book, if she were me. Why not? What else was I going to do?

It was nice to talk to her. I was going to lose her as a friend, I knew that. And I already missed her terribly. "You know what the bad news is?" Naomi said. I didn't. "Guys are gonna hate this. All this money? A big book deal? Nobody's gonna wanna date you. You're never going to get laid."

I let this pass. I asked her if we could hang out sometime. But she said she was pretty busy. Spring was coming. That was big event season. Things were cranking up. But yeah, we could hang out at some point.

A week later, Carol Smith showed up. She flew in from L.A. and stayed with Sally uptown. I was thrilled to hear this. I needed a break from myself, my money, my book deal. I needed some hang out time.

I hopped on the subway and went up to Columbia and the three of us went out for coffee and pastries. Carol had her hair cut in a new way. Or rather, she had actually got a professional haircut. But she immediately began making fun of it and the hairdresser and the whole L.A. beauty culture.

So then Sally told Carol everything that was going on with me. Carol's jaw almost hit the table. She had no idea. But Sally kept saying, "I told you that a month ago!" Not surprisingly, Carol had not listened. But she listened now. She was like, "Wait, you got paid already? You got a check?" I nodded that I did.

We talked about other stuff. Carol had started a new video art project but it had bogged down, thanks to the people she had stupidly agreed to collaborate with. Still, it was fun to hear about. L.A. sounded so ridiculous but also totally fun. I told my couple of stories about Will Soren and Cynthia Dunleavy. After a while, we were all talked out. We sat there with our empty coffee mugs. Then I realized that I could afford to buy everyone another latte. So I did.

Meanwhile, I was continuing to work through the *Chicks and Dudes* manuscript. The most drastic change Dunleavy had suggested, was to entirely eliminate a character named Tom, the drummer of one of the bands. Tom was one of my favorite characters, and I had worried about this since I first read the letter. But when it came time to actually do it, it was quite easy. I put his best lines of dialogue in the mouth of a different character and cut everything else. The resulting space in the narrative had a kind of interesting mysteriousness to it. Like the ghost of Tom was still in there somewhere.

It was strange what was hard and what wasn't. You could always cut things. But adding stuff was a lot trickier. In some cases, even trying to add just one sentence, I found I couldn't match the original tone. It was like my old Portland self had been sealed off from me.

But everything was doable in the end. Thinking through Dunleavy's changes, following her logic, seeing what she saw: it was like having your brain remolded slightly. She was *so smart*. And she saw directly to the heart of the matter, *every time*. Which then made me wonder: why was she so mean and scary? Was that really necessary, if you were that good at your job? Apparently it was. Or at least she thought so.

44

RIDING the L Train to work one morning in April, I saw Dana again. She was coming in from one of the far outer neighborhoods, Bushwick, or one of those places where the most fringe young people squatted or otherwise housed themselves in old warehouse buildings.

She was in my subway car when I got on. I discreetly moved in the other direction, keeping my back toward her so she wouldn't notice me. I stood there as the L made its long several-minute journey under the East River. Everyone fell silent like they do as the train hit top speed and got super loud, filling up with the rhythmic clacks and metallic banging. As the loudest part passed, I snuck a look at Dana. She had fixed her hair, thank god. But she still had her terrible tattoos and was wearing a cheap Army navy shoulder bag where she probably kept her art supplies. She must have had a job or somewhere to go if she was riding into the city. I hoped she did.

A couple days later, a man called me from the *New York Times*. He was writing a piece for the *Sunday Magazine* about the new wave of young novelists under thirty. Could he interview me next week? Sure, I said.

For some reason, I barely thought about this at first. An interview sounded simple enough. It made sense, since I was so young. But the next morning, lying in bed, the words *New York Times* started flashing in my brain. From that moment on, I was interviewing myself in the shower, talking to myself at the store, explaining to the subway pillars my various opinions and thoughts and literary theories.

At the same time, I was getting better at not blabbing everything that happened with my book. And so I managed to keep the *New York Times* interview to myself, except for Sally and my parents and a couple other friends. Naturally, I wanted to hear Naomi's take on the situation. I called her and told her and begged her to meet me for a drink. She finally agreed and I rode the subway up there after work.

I met her at a bar. We talked about her new boyfriend first. She went on and on about that. She was sort of torturing me in a way. Finally I asked her what she thought about the interview, and what should I say? "Nothing," she said. "Answer the questions." But what if I said the wrong thing? She laughed and said it would be a fluff piece. The article would be generic: look at the cute young novelists. Are they any good? Do they deserve all this money and attention? That was the article they would write. That was the article they always wrote. What I said or did would not affect it in any way.

Then she said: "I would worry more about your hair, if I were you." My hair was now long and boring and I mostly wore it tied in a pony tail, or pushed up in a sloppy bun, or down if it was clean. She reached over and touched it with disdain. "They're going to take your picture." I told her they hadn't said anything about a picture and she scoffed and said whenever they do the young novelist article, there's always a picture. That's why they do the article. So they can run the picture.

I rode the subway home that night and wondered where I could get my hair cut. Naomi's parting advice was to go to Tincture, the hot salon of the moment, and throw myself at their mercy. That would cost two hundred dollars, she estimated. But she said it would be worth it. I didn't know about that.

I transferred onto the L Train, rode a few stops and then Dana got on. Right in front of me. There was no avoiding her this time. But it didn't turn out so bad. We said hi and she asked if I'd rented the room. I lied and told her the girl who left had a friend she had promised it to, so she got it. Dana had ended up in a great place out in Bushwick, an artists collective thing. "We have the most amazing parties," she said.

I asked her about her job, and she said she was freelancing. She was kind of closed off now, I saw. She wasn't going to tell me anything. Or maybe she was embarrassed for breaking down in front of me. She was one of those tough Portland girls. I wondered what would happen to her here. I really had no idea.

As promised, Bridget was rarely around the house once she and Evan got together. Or maybe she felt embarrassed about practically stealing him from under my nose. I was not deeply offended by this turn of events, but it did create an uncomfortable tone to our relationship. I was the head of our household in a way. I was older than her. Plus I had lived in New York longer. And yet, she had instantly become superior to me in some way. How she had done that, I didn't know. But it felt weird and not quite fair somehow.

Anyway, as the weather got warmer, Mari was gone a lot too and I found myself alone in the house quite a bit, which I liked. So I went back to one of my favorite activities: fire escape gardening. This had been a running joke with Naomi and I, but now I took it seriously enough to go to the plant store on Manhattan Ave and talk to the Polish guy and buy a small planter thing and some flowers and a tomato plant. The gay guys upstairs—who we never saw—also had a little trough of flowers or whatever on their fire escape. I knew this because they once watered their trough while I had my head out the window and they doused me with dirty water. The dirt was clean, out-of-the-bag dirt, so it wasn't like gross. But I still had to take a shower.

I went to Tincture and got my hair styled. Oh my god, I was terrified. When they got me in the chair and asked me what I wanted, I totally froze and could barely speak. The girl got annoyed and gave me this weird shag thing that I guess was supposed to look seventies. That was happening now that it was 2000, the hipster girls were getting 70s shags, or Dorothy Hamills, or ironic mullets, which looked adorable on seventeen-year-old art students, but I was almost twenty-four and too old for tongue-in-cheek fashion. So now I had this bizarre haircut, that instantly stopped looking like it was supposed to, even though the girl sold me a ton of crap to put in it, and explained the styling process to me three times.

I met the *New York Times* guy on a Friday in Manhattan after work. It had rained earlier, so I wore a baseball hat to deal with my weird hair. I met him in a small, plain restaurant he knew about and we sat in a back room. He was quite young, barely older than me, and good looking in a clean-cut, private school, sort of way. He'd gone to Cornell, he said when I asked him. That was apparently who worked at *The New York Times*, Ivy League grads. It was like a funnel system.

He was totally nice and apologized when he couldn't figure out his new digital sound recorder. His name was James. He seemed to think it odd that I hadn't quit my job. He asked me about it and I said something weird like: "I'd be afraid to be by myself too much." That's how it went. He asked me super easy questions and I squeaked out bizarre random answers that made me sound like a crazy person. Finally, for no reason at all, I babbled out a little diatribe I had rehearsed in my shower, how music was important to young people, but there were never any novels about music or musicians. Most so-called "literary" novels were about middle-aged writing teachers sleeping with their female students, I said. Though I actually only knew of one novel like that, which I hadn't even read.

Throughout, James nodded and listened and consulted his notes. Then, just when I'd relaxed enough to say something coherent, it was over. James thanked me and put away his reporters notebook and slipped the little recorder into his coat pocket.

It was very disorienting. Had I even said anything he could use? On the sidewalk, he told me some photographers would call in the next day or two. He said goodbye and shook my hand and hailed a taxi at the corner. I walked away quickly, in the other direction, as if I had someplace I had to go.

45

THE PHOTOGRAPHERS ARRIVED at my apartment at ten in the morning. I had to take a personal day from work for that, since I'd already stretched my hours around in various ways to get free for different things. Thank God for Veronica. She never referenced my book directly but she had this special attitude toward me of: *I worked with Andy Warhol. I understand the pressures of fame.*

The photographers called from the street. There were three of them, and they had a ton of equipment. I held the downstairs door open and they tromped up the stairs to my apartment, which I'd been furiously cleaning while I waited.

They dragged their bags and cases and lights and screens into my kitchen. They looked around. One of the assistant guys said: "This looks like my apartment," as if he was surprised. I asked what the apartments of the other young writers had looked like and he said: "Not like this."

The main guy asked me what I did here. "Sleep?" I said. But then I got his meaning. I said I cooked and I wrote and I sometimes gardened on the fire escape. He liked the fire escape idea.

He struggled to open the paint stuck window and then held a light meter out into the air. "This is perfect," he said. Then he gripped the window and slammed it upward so hard that a bunch of paint fell off it. But he got it all the way open! Naomi and I had been trying for *two years* to do that!

So then it was totally easy to crawl out there. I did so, and posed on the fire escape, pretending to water my plants. Then I pretended to be thinking. Then I pretended to be writing something in a notebook one of the assistants handed me. It was pretty cheesy. Meanwhile, the three of them stood there, crammed around the window, their arms reaching out: holding things, arranging things, reflecting light onto me, touching my chin, moving me around.

Like the interview, the photo session ended abruptly and left me feeling vaguely violated. One minute a whisp of my hair was the most important thing in the world to these guys. The next, they were thumping and crashing back down the stairs, complaining about the availability of cabs. One of them called a car service on his cell phone. "What's the address here?" he demanded. I told him and they bumped and banged their way out my door and disappeared without even saying goodbye.

That night I had dinner with Benton and Sally at the dumpling place on Mott Street. I tried to be good company but I felt sick with nerves. All I could think about was the photographers and the article and the interview. This was going to be in *The New York Times*!

Later we went to a movie and a new friend of Benton joined us, a tall guy from Wyoming who had just moved to New York to be a grad student at Columbia.

After the movie we went to a bar in the East Village and

played pool and listened to country western music on the jukebox. After a couple beers I was able to relax a bit. I talked to the Wyoming guy. He was homesick. He found New York to be a "monument to egotism." I nodded my understanding. I told him the first year was the hardest. He asked if it got better after that. I said, "Not really."

Later, when the guys were gone, Sally asked me if I liked the Wyoming guy. I had to admit I'd barely thought about him. I told her it was probably pointless for me to think about boys with this other stuff going on. But Sally thought periods like this were exactly the times when romance might bloom. "When you're looking for a guy, you never find one. But when you're distracted and you're busy and other things are happening ... that's when they appear." I nodded and thought of Rex. That's how he had come into my life, when I was totally not looking for anything.

That night I couldn't sleep. This was becoming a problem. I'd lie in bed and fidget around and twist and turn and get myself all worked up. Then I'd get up and quietly creep pass snoring Mari, and Bridget's empty room and light a candle in the kitchen and make tea. I'd put on my coat and open the window and—if it was warm enough—crawl out onto the fire escape. I'd sit there, sighing in the dark, watching my neighbor's windows and the clothes lines and the stray cats wandering around. And I'd drink my tea. And I'd worry.

The "Young Writers" article came out in May 2000. It was the cover story of the *Sunday Magazine*. There were four pictures on the front, one each of the different authors, forming a square. I was in the bottom right hand corner, looking young and confident. The other three people looked exactly the same. It was two boys and two girls. One of the girls was black. One of the boys was Asian. Everyone said the same boring stuff, including me. None of my diatribe against middle-aged novelists was included. For that I was grateful for James and his Ivy League discretion. He had saved me from myself. He had cleaned me up for *The Sunday Times* readers.

My phone started ringing as I read the article. I let the answering machine take the call. But it was Sally and I ran to the phone. She was screaming into the phone. She kept saying, "I can't believe it. It's really happening!" She said Benton had brought the paper over. A bunch of them were reading it at brunch.

Then the call waiting clicks started. I clicked over and it was Bridget. She was at Evan's loft. I had told her about my book but she had apparently not believed me. She kept saying: "I had no idea! You didn't tell me! You're famous!"

The phone rang off and on throughout the day. That afternoon I called my parents and told them and my mother said she didn't know where they had *The New York Times*, but maybe at the mall and she would drive there later to see. That would the mall where I used to work at Banana Republic and later J. Crew. I wondered if my old Portland roommate Kate would see the article. I had not talked to her in years.

Will Soren invited me to lunch. We met at a fancy seafood restaurant in SoHo. He told me that *The New York Times* article had generated interest in foreign rights. Offers for *Chicks and Dudes* had come in from the UK, Germany, Italy, possibly Brazil. The French were playing their usual games but they would come around eventually. I stupidly asked him if we would get paid extra for these foreign editions, and he looked at me funny and said: "Yes."

We didn't say much more, and then I remembered to ask

him a question I had been thinking about recently. What happened to Anna Madsen who had written *Electra Rising*? Wasn't he her agent? He was. He said Anna lived in California during the winter and summered in Provincetown on Cape Cod. I said, "I thought she lived here?" Will shrugged and said she did live here sometimes but she had found the scrutiny to be a little oppressive. She preferred to stay out of the city. He added that publicity was hard sometimes for writers, especially when they developed a certain reputation. I asked what Anna Madsen's reputation was. He shrugged again. "Have you read her book?" he asked. I said I had.

"That's her reputation."

When I got back to *In Focus*, the Wyoming boy had called and left a message on my voicemail. He was very nervous, you could hear his voice shaking. He invited me to dinner at a Mexican place in the East Village. I didn't know what to do about that, but thinking about Sally's advice, that this was actually a good time to meet guys, I called him back. For some reason, my voice shook too.

We went to the restaurant a couple nights later. We ate big heavy plates of refried beans and tortillas. We drank Dos Equis. He was quiet and nervous at first, but then halfway through the dinner, he began to talk about himself. Then he couldn't seem to shut up. Later, he said he was sorry, that he didn't usually babble like that. I said it was okay, I did the same thing.

We walked around the East Village and he did manage to shut up, and I shut up too and then it was a pretty nice time. We window-shopped and looked at different sneakers at a shoe place. Then we got ice cream and sat on a stoop on St. Marks Place and watched people. I suddenly realized my birthday was in a couple days and I told him. He said he had a girlfriend in high school and on her seventeenth birthday, she made him kiss her seventeen times on different places on her face. I laughed and said that was adorable. Then I wondered if he might want to kiss me. But when I looked over at him, he was staring into space, lost in the memory of his old girlfriend, his hometown, his happy life back in Wyoming.

I'D BEEN curious about Anna Madsen, from the moment I'd first heard about *Electra Rising*. I'd looked her up on the internet many times and studied pictures of her and searched out the latest gossip. And of course I'd read *Electra Rising* twice, and continued to re-read parts of it occasionally. I always read anything people wrote about it, even though most commentary was negative, sometimes viciously so. People called her a hack, a slut, an exhibitionist, a spoiled brat. One comment repeated several times was that her only talent was between her legs.

Lately, I'd felt the need to meet her. Not so much to talk to her, as to just see her in the flesh. To see that she actually existed. And to see how the publication of *Electra Rising* had affected her.

And so one day at work when I felt a random wave of courage, I called Liz at WCM and asked if it was possible for me to get Anna's number. "Let me see if I have it," said Liz.

I had tried to be friendly with Liz, thinking she was my age and probably just starting her career too. She seemed like a natural ally. So now, as I waited, I tried again, asking her if she thought it was weird that I wanted to call Anna. She remained neutral, and she said that no, it didn't seem weird. I said I thought it would be good to talk to someone who had been through this first novel stuff. A silence followed and then Liz said in her clipped voice: "Anna can definitely tell you what not to do."

After *The New York Times* article, more interviews came. *The Village Voice* called. A new paper called *The New York Observer* wanted to do something. Several new online "webzines" called. They all frantically tried to convince me that online magazines were as important as actual magazines, which made me not believe them.

Then on Friday, I got five requests for interviews in one day. *The L.A. Times*, *The Boston Globe*, alternative weeklies in Denver and Chapel Hill, and a music magazine in Philadelphia. My own Portland paper, *Willamette Week* called the next day and wanted to do a feature.

As I spent several hours calling people back and trying to write down the times and dates and interviewers, I had a little panic attack. Then I remembered Naomi telling me that the publisher should help me with such things. This was publicity and was not, technically, my problem.

So the next morning, before work, I called Cynthia's office and not knowing who to ask for, got Cynthia herself on the phone. I told her the situation, I was getting a lot of interview requests and I couldn't keep them straight. She said not to worry. We'd have lunch that day and we'd sort it out.

And so I took another personal day from *In Focus* and took a long hot bath and struggled with my hair, which was now too short to put in a pony tail. I rode the subway to the restaurant.

Cynthia was already there with a man named Miguel, who took one look at me and frowned. I don't know what he expected. He was obviously gay, and had his hair dyed and his bangs flipped up in front and also had a tan and big thick glasses.

Cynthia told me that Miguel was my publicist now and that he would help me and to send all media requests to him, though looking at Miguel, I got the feeling he would do nothing of the kind. Or maybe I was imagining this.

After we ordered, Miguel told a long story about another author of Cynthia's who was about to be on Oprah's Book Club. I got the feeling this was to impress upon me that my situation was not so important after all. But then Cynthia, sensing what was going on, said something to Miguel and kind of growled while she said it. Like literally made a low threatening *grrrrrrr* sound with her throat and then Miguel changed suddenly and wanted to hear more about my requests. Fortunately, I'd written the outstanding requests I had on a piece of paper. He unfolded the list and Cynthia put on her reading glasses and they both studied it. They seemed underwhelmed. I guess eight requests isn't that many. And then I felt stupid I'd even complained. So I ate some bread and waited for my roast beef sandwich.

We ate lunch mostly in silence. Then Cynthia paid the bill. Miguel asked me who did my hair. I told him Tincture and he scoffed and gave me a card and told me to go there. It was some private person's name. I was like, okay, though I knew I was not spending another penny on my hair. Still, I thanked Miguel and smiled graciously as I put the card in my pocket.

Cynthia air-kissed me on the sidewalk. Then Miguel freaked out when I told him I didn't have a cell phone. "Get one!" he commanded. Then the two of them stole a cab from some tourists and drove away.

. . .

By the next day, I had three more interview requests, including one from a zine in Portland I had never heard of. This girl asked in her email why I had sold out "the Portland community," and how was I going to defend myself against that? Who made me a spokesman? And why did I think I could speak for her and her friends when I didn't even know them and had gone to Wellington which was a college of rich white elitists.

I deleted the message before any of it could sink in, but an hour later, I started to get the creeps. So I called Sally but she was walking out the door to go see a play with Benton. So then I called Naomi, but hung up after a couple rings. She wouldn't want to hear me complain about my fame. I started to call Rex, but I had the same feeling about him. Also I didn't want to piss off Rebecca. Rex had mentioned a marriage counselor he and Rebecca had seen, who had warned them of the evils of people having nonsexual, emotional affairs outside the marriage. Especially with the opposite sex. Which sounded like he wasn't supposed to have female friends besides his wife. Or at least not the type of friends who called in a panic, in the middle of the night, which made sense in a way.

But who could I call? I dug around in one of my old organizer notebooks and found some numbers from the last three years. Nick Pax's number was there, and the number I had for Todd Sparrow in Portland. I almost called the Nick Pax number but didn't. For all I knew he was married to Crystal Crystalline by now. I still had Kate's old work number. She had been my best friend for those nine months in Portland. I felt a million miles away from that now.

I had Libby's new number in L.A. but I didn't want to sound like an idiot to her, complaining about some weird email. You couldn't do that. And why was I so worried anyway? The truth was, I'd had this panicky feeling in my chest for weeks, months really. And now it was getting worse. Benton had recommended anti-anxiety medication. Naomi had suggested therapy. But what the hell was a therapist going to do? At least they'd have to listen to you. You'd pay them to listen. That's probably what famous people did.

I FINISHED the rewrites of *Chicks and Dudes* and called Cynthia Dunleavy's assistant to arrange a FedEx pick up. That felt good. It also felt a little bit like I was walking off a cliff for some reason. And of course, delivering the finished manuscript meant that another check for $78,625 would soon arrive.

Once that was done, I couldn't help but call Rex. My message was mostly me sighing and trying to string a few actual words together. I finally said: "I will be so glad when this is over."

A few days later, I got another FedEx delivery from WCM. I opened it, and found about twenty pieces of mail addressed to me. Several letters were from fans of *Chicks and Dudes*. Though they hadn't read it yet, these people already related to it deeply. I spoke for them. There were several requests to do readings at different places, colleges, literary festivals, none of which I'd ever heard of. There were also a few requests to donate money to various causes. Two people wanted me to read their unpublished novels. And then there was an invitation to a rave party in Long Island, and some sort of underground movie premiere in Seattle. At the movie premiere, I would be "featured" in some way. I sat down on our stoop, in the sun, and sorted through them. None of them required a response, I decided and I crammed all the torn envelopes back into the FedEx envelope and took it upstairs and stuck it behind my laundry basket where I put all random things I didn't know what to do with.

Around this time, Evan went to Europe to work on a film. So Bridget was suddenly home all the time, trying to cook elaborate meals and not cleaning up after herself. That was annoying. Just as I was beginning to truly hate her, I drank some wine with her one night and spilled my guts about my tumultuous friendship/romance with Rex. Bridget became deeply interested in this saga. She listened carefully, and then methodically extracted from me every relevant detail. After a long discussion, she took my hand, looked me in the eye and told me: "You have to go get him. You *have to*. He is the one you love. And you need him so much. He can nurture you. He can help you. If you were with him right now, you'd be so happy and excited about your book! Not sitting around, moping and worrying like you do. This should be the greatest year of your life. And with him, it would be!"

This little speech hit me hard. In bed that night I lay stunned, my eyes wide open, the obvious truth of what Bridget had said gnawing at my insides. She was totally right. I knew she was. Why had I given up on Rex? Why had I not put up a fight? And most importantly, what should I do now?

What I did was, I got up at 7:45, took a shower and went to work at *In Focus*. I had been doing a terrible job there lately. I was constantly late, constantly adjusting my schedule.

And then Veronica invited me out to lunch, which scared me. This hadn't happened before and I was pretty sure she intended to fire me. But no, she just wanted to see how I was holding up. She had read the *Sunday Times* article and she could see how tired and exhausted I looked. I was deeply tempted to spill my guts to her, about the weirdness of the book, my situation with Rex, all the money I didn't know what to do with. But something told me not to, which was the correct move, as what Veronica really wanted to do was reminisce about her days at *Interview*, hanging out with Andy Warhol and how misunderstood that scene was, how media attention reduces any creative endeavor to a caricature of itself.

When I got back to my cubicle, there was an email from Rex. He was sorry he hadn't got back to me. He'd been dealing with wedding stuff. The ceremony, which they originally wanted to be in Brooklyn, had been moved to Rebecca's family farm in Ohio. This had created numerous complications. Rebecca had flown back there to figure stuff out.

Rex apologized and said he would love to hang out, and had plenty of time now that Rebecca was away. "Call me," he said.

I picked up the phone, then put it down. I had barely slept last night. I had barely slept in general. And obviously, I was still thinking about what Bridget had said, that I should confront Rex, that I should somehow change myself into the type of person that could do that.

I left the office in a daze, heading back to Brooklyn on the L Train. It was five o'clock and my subway car was packed. I leaned against a pole. I was so tired now my vision was jumpy and disconnected. I closed my eyes and dozed off for a second as the car shook and rattled during the under-river crossing.

Then someone squeezed my shoulder. I jerked awake and

found myself face to face with a teenaged girl. She wore big sunglasses and a bright orange dress under a faded military jacket.

"Andrea?" she said, lifting her sunglasses.

It was Brooke Kinney.

We stared at each other. She was bashful now, not the direct, over-serious fifteen-year-old she had been. And the biggest shock: she was *beautiful*. Her skin was amazing, and her big blue eyes seemed to shine, and her hair was *curly*, and adorable, a little lock of it curled down on her smooth rounded forehead.

I stared at her dumbfounded. She said she saw the article in *The Times*. She smiled in her new coy way, and said how exciting it was, and that people must recognize me on the street. I was like, are you kidding? I gestured toward the oblivious subway riders all around us. Nobody recognized me.

She smiled at that and we moved out of the middle of the car, toward the door where we could huddle for a moment. She was going shopping in Williamsburg. That was where everyone went now, all her friends. I was like, what grade are you in? She was a senior. She was going to Barnard in the fall. She said: "I can't wait to read your book!"

That was nice. But I suddenly thought of her dad. Had Brooke known about our affair? In my befuddled brain, I couldn't remember what exactly happened with that. She'd never actually seen us. But she was so smart. And Richard was not the best liar. God, how weird. And yet I couldn't stop grinning at Brooke Kinney. She was sexy. She was interesting. She looked *great*. I wanted to talk to her and hear more about her life, her school, her future. But then I realized she was with friends. A boy and a girl. They were standing apart from us. In the noise and the rush, I hadn't noticed them. Brooke waved them closer and introduced us. They stared at me in wild, undiluted awe. "She's the one I was telling you about!" said Brooke. The fact that she was so proud of me, and excited, that meant she didn't now about me and her dad ... or maybe she did ... or maybe it didn't matter?

They wanted me to come shopping with them, or at least come have a frozen yogurt. I begged off. I couldn't. I had to take care of some things. They were instantly respectful and apologetic for having thought it was even possible. I was obviously a very important person who had many important things to do.

And then in my confusion and my excitement at this strange meeting, I had the random thought: *Life is so short.* Brooke was a completely different person. And so was I! After what, two years, three? And it was going to keep going like this. Things would continue to happen this fast. Maybe faster! And I was going to wake up one morning and be thirty, and wake up again and be forty-five and wake up again ...

And I was going to lose Rex. Not because of my own lack of action, but because of time. Time was going to take him from me. Time was going to take everything from me. It was futile, all of it, none of this was going to matter in the slightest in the end.

Brooke and her friends got off at Bedford Street. Brooke hugged me deeply and the others shook my hand with that same blind devotion in their faces. And then they were gone, this gang of brave children, off to explore the world. I stayed on the train, continuing to the next stop, continuing home, where I would take a hot bath and cry and crawl into bed and sleep until my brain unfogged and I could figure out what the fuck was happening to me.

48

I MET REX AFTER WORK. It was a lovely spring day, fragrant and warm. This was the fateful day when I was going to confess my love to him. Or so I had tentatively planned.

We met on Eighth Avenue below Christopher Street, which was a quiet area of Manhattan Rex had recently discovered, and which I didn't know much about. It was mostly residential, with a school and little shops and not nearly the traffic or people as Sixth or Seventh Avenues. We walked around. There were little kids coming out of a school, their oversized backpacks lurching around on their backs, their nannies or well-groomed parents waiting for them on the sidewalk.

Rex led me to a café he had found. We ordered and sat outside, a feeling of secrecy surrounding us. We barely talked at first. We had to get used to each other again. It had been a while.

I sipped my iced coffee through a straw. Rex gradually began to talk. He was stressed out too: wedding stuff, work stuff, he and Rebecca might move. Her dad wanted to buy them an apartment, as a wedding present/investment. I was like, how much will that cost? He shook his head. He'd been afraid to ask.

I sipped my iced coffee. I asked him if, despite the stress, he was happy about the upcoming wedding. He didn't know. He assumed he was. How could he not be? He thought getting married was one of those passages in life—like applying to college—that was full of stress and uncertainty, but you had to struggle through it, because once it was done and over with, it set you up for the next phase of life. I nodded and agreed. I settled into silence then, watching the few people walk by. It was amazing how quiet and peaceful it was here. It was like you were in a different city.

Later, we walked around. We found a little league softball game going on a few blocks away. "Sal's Auto Repair" it said on one team's uniforms. Rex and I both stood and watched from the sidewalk, our fingers entwined in the chain link fence. The strangeness of such a random All-American activity in this quaint Manhattan neighborhood was captivating. It was at this point that a feeling of peace came over me. I stopped thinking about what I should tell Rex and when I should tell it to him. In fact, I didn't need to do anything. Everything was as it should be. It would be ridiculous to make some grand drama of this. Rex knew how I felt. I'd tried to kiss him the first night I met him. I'd tried to kiss him a bunch of times. His choice was made. And if there was something wrong with him and Rebecca, if for some reason he was really meant to be with me, wouldn't that happen by itself? Didn't love find a way? Or was that just bullshit? Maybe guys were like property, possession was nine tenths of the law.

A gust of wind blew through the trees around the baseball

diamond. Rex looked up at the darkening sky. I looked up at Rex, his jaw line, his thoughtful eyebrows, his scholar's neck. The air bristled with electricity. More heavy clouds swept low across the sky. A pocket of cold air hit us, coming up from the river. A low rumble of thunder rolled over the building tops. The back of my hand grazed the back of Rex's hand as we both turned from the fence and began to calculate the location of the nearest subway station. We ran. A second later, the first heavy raindrops began to splat on the grey sidewalk.

We made it to the subway station just before the true soaking began. Safe underground, Rex and I continued our strange speechlessness. We waited on the subway platform as the first victims of the rain storm began to appear. Wet-haired city girls, shiny eyed, giggling and excited, despite their ruined hairstyles and wet shoes. Bright-colored Keds had become the spring style in 2000: bright red, bright blue, bright yellow. They looked strange, as did most new styles when they first hit the street, startling to the eye and yet perfect in some way that your brain took a minute to process. *Chicks and Dudes*, I murmured to myself, in a blank thoughtless way.

Back in Brooklyn, I got off the L Train first. Rex gave me a quick hug. I looked into his face when he did. But he didn't notice, he was deep in his own world, in his own concerns.

I rode the G Train to my stop in Greenpoint. As I climbed the familiar stairs, a wild crack of thunder exploded overhead. A bunch of us, young people mostly, immediately doubled our pace, running up the last couple steps and then darting off in various directions, thinking we might outrun the coming downpour.

I didn't make it. I got stuck under the awning of the Chinese restaurant. I had no pressing need to be home, so I stayed where I was and watched the heavens unleash their fury on the earth. I crossed my arms over my chest and thought of Rex. He did have things to do. Calls to make. His job. His soon-to-be wife. His wedding.

His apartment was close to the L, so he'd probably made it home and was, at this moment, most likely in his kitchen, dry, comfortable, watching the downpour out the window and stirring a cup of coffee. I was not in my kitchen. I was out here. In the thick of it. Getting cold, getting wet, getting crushed by the bigness of things.

I called Anna Madsen that night. I did it suddenly and without thinking, which was the only way I could call her. When she answered her cell phone, I stammered out who I was and why I was calling. She didn't respond, so then I reverted to flattery and told her I was feeling anxious about my own book and that *Electra Rising* had meant so much to me and that Will Soren had suggested I call her.

"Will Soren?" she said. Then she understood. "You're the girl from the *Sunday Times* article!" Yeah, I answered modestly.

She started chattering away: yak yak yak, about Will Soren and Liz and WCM and her first agent—a nice enough woman, a friend of her mom—and her editor and her publicist and her film agent and the "snake" lawyer she'd hired to get the film rights away from one production company and to another. This was because a certain famous actress who she was practically best friends with, was dying to get *her* hands on it. Anna wanted this, since—as she had just mentioned—they were practically best friends and partied in Spain and went to spas together and talked on the phone until three in the morning and did that funny thing like in high school of "you hang up first ... no you hang up first."

She then asked what I was doing that night. I said nothing, I didn't have any plans.

She said: "You're not going to the *Paris Review* party?"

So I was going to the *Paris Review* party. With the infamous Anna Madsen.

Anna was staying on the Upper West Side with her therapist mother and since the *Paris Review* was uptown somewhere, it was decided I'd go to her house. This avoided any discussion of where I lived.

I spent the next hour ripping through my closet, trying stuff on, and then sending a quick email to Rex telling him where I was going. Already late, I rushed out the door to ride the G Train to the L Train to the 2 Express train to the Upper West Side. It was thankfully not raining and I walked quickly to the address she'd given me and buzzed up.

Anna Madsen came downstairs to let me in. She was newly blonde and wearing bunny slippers and an expensive looking raincoat over old sweatpants and a T-shirt. We both ran up the stairs and into the insanely cramped, book-stuffed bohemian apartment that was her mother's home. It was not that big, but it probably cost a lot. Anna slept in a tiny bedroom and that's where we went while she got dressed. Her mother was in another room, in her office, doing something that could not be interrupted. Anna asked me who I knew from the *Paris Review* crowd and I had to admit, I didn't know anyone. She said I would like it. They were pretentious of course, but whatever. That was their thing. George was cool. He was old now though. It wasn't like in the old days. She had been to one in the eighties when she was like twelve and people had been fucking in the bathrooms. Now it was people in suits smoking pipes and pretending to be smart. But there was still cute guys all over the place. And coke if you knew who was who.

Okay, I said.

49

WE GOT a cab to the party. I was nervous, but going with Anna Madsen was probably the best introduction to this particular world. When we got there though, Anna didn't have any money and I had to pay for the cab. Fortunately, my skirt from the Gap had a little inside pocket and I'd stashed a couple twenties in there. It was weird about money. I kept forgetting how much money I had.

Other people were arriving too and we were barely out of the cab when we encountered two very cute boys in sport coats and jeans. I had worn a blend of Brooklyn cool and Wellington prep: navy blue cardigan, a light blue Gap skirt, black tights, black Chinese slippers and my hair pulled back in a very short pony tail and a bit of lipstick. I was pretty nervous. But when we saw the cute boys, Anna immediately started chattering away with them and they started smiling and grinning and playing along with her "I'm a mess" persona. They picked up her cigarettes which she dropped while arranging herself. Their names were Josh and Jacob. Or Jerod. Or Justin. Or something. I was nervous and couldn't focus.

We entered the actual apartment, which was big and beautiful and you could feel the importance of it instantly. The main thing I knew about the the *Paris Review* was their "Writers at Work" interview series, which they'd been doing forever. I had read millions of those interviews—I'd *studied* many of them—and I guess the stature of the *Paris Review* was pretty embedded in my brain because I suddenly caught my breath at the realization of where exactly I was.

Anna met someone she knew just inside the door: a beautiful middle-aged woman named Haley, who had silver helmet hair and an elegant cream colored dress. She grabbed Anna and wanted to hear about her new book. Anna was like: "It's horrible. I suck. I'm going to kill myself." Haley laughed brightly. Anna did not laugh and said, "I'm not kidding." She introduced me to Haley who glanced at me once and continued to ask Anna questions.

We met more people, most of whom came right up to Anna. She played the same role for everyone: frazzled, fucked up, a failure, in pressing need of a drink. Everyone laughed with her and assured her she would be fine. The second book is always the hardest, said someone. Don't let them pressure you, advised someone else. People brought other people forward to introduce to Anna. None of the people who attacked Anna on a regular basis seemed to be present. Everyone was a fan here at the *Paris Review* party.

Nobody paid any attention to me. Which was fine. But then Anna began introducing me as the young novelist girl from the *Sunday Times* article. This was met with some appreciative *ohs* and a few stone-faced stares. An older woman asked which of the featured writers I was. Anna said: "The one who looks like her! What's wrong with you? Are you blind!?" In another group, a man in a rumpled seersucker coat asked me what my novel was about, "Young people in Portland, Oregon," I told him, which he seemed to find distasteful.

In another group, someone asked the title of my book and I said: "*Chicks and Dudes*." Nobody laughed. They didn't even smile. Instead, the conversation turned to Portland in general. Several people had been there. They commented on the wonderful hiking. And the natural beauty, and the trees, and the mountains.

Anna took me to meet George Plimpton. She glided up to him with perfect nonchalance. She told him my name, and about the *Sunday Times* and my upcoming first novel. His face lit up and he happily shook my hand. He said, "I was just talking to some other young writers about the importance of the first novel." He pulled me forward and introduced me to a trio of nerdy, sour-faced college kids. He then exited. Anna ran for it, too. And I was stuck with the English majors.

Not that I minded so much. It was all new to me. I put in my fifteen minutes discussing narrative devices with the zittiest of the three and then formally excused myself. I headed back toward the middle of the room. Anna seemed to be gone now. Maybe she had found drugs. I stood smiling blandly at no one for a few moments, then sat on a couch and tried to join into a conversation which I never quite got accepted into. So then I walked around more and went up some stairs and found another floor of people that were a little younger and looser and drunker than downstairs. A very confident and well-spoken guy with suspenders and wire rim glasses was arguing with a guy who looked Russian but who was actually a normal person, and who was also super articulate. They were arguing about Raymond Carver of all things, another Oregon writer. I loved Carver and wanted to say something, or join in the argument, but it was pretty far gone at this point and I couldn't find a way to say anything. If only Anna was here to tell them I was from Oregon and I was a writer too! They were probably writers themselves and probably published, judging by how confident they were and how they didn't let anyone else into their conversation.

There was a table of snacks nearby, so I went there and ate carrots and then started talking to a girl who was dressed like me, and who introduced herself as an assistant at *GQ*. What kind of assistant, I stupidly asked. She said an assistant to an assistant to an assistant, and she laughed. I didn't tell her about my book, which so far had mostly been a conversation killer. She told me about her boyfriend who worked at *Spin* but how the internet would eventually destroy the magazine business anyway, and everyone was trying to start their own websites, though nobody would get paid. She was funny and smart about all this and I liked her immensely but then a very good-looking guy waved to her and she ran off and that was that.

By now the party was really going. The downstairs was packed full and what had started as a sophisticated murmur of conversation, had become a full scale roar. Anna reappeared. She didn't mention where she'd been and I didn't ask. She grabbed me and we went downstairs, "to mix it up with the big boys."

We got downstairs and were weaving our way through the packed crowd when suddenly Anna stopped and pointed at someone. "That's Nikki," she said in a low, conspiratorial voice. "She's super important."

Nikki had short white hair and all black clothing and a look of utter disdain and contempt stuck on her face. Anna said I needed to meet her. "She's essential," said Anna, who was acting strange and twitchy and was probably coked up.

She marched me over to Nikki. She was not so smooth this time, not like with George Plimpton. She clumsily broke into Nikki's conversation with a very handsome older man. *Uh oh*, I thought, when the older woman turned toward us. Nikki looked tough. And mean. And like she didn't appreciate being interrupted.

Anna, oblivious, forced her way through the introductions. She told Nikki my name, how I had been on the cover of *The Sunday Times Magazine*, and how my new book was going to be the hottest thing next year. When she told Nikki the name of my book, *Chicks and Dudes*, that sealed my fate. Nikki winced painfully at the sound of it.

She did turn fully toward me though. "Good for you Angie," she said, lifting her face, so she could literally look down her nose at me. "It sounds like you will have a long and rewarding career. Just like your friend here, Anna." Then she turned dramatically away, positioned her back directly in my face, and resumed her conversation with the older gentleman.

Anna gave me a furious look and dragged me away. She then told me her real feelings about Nikki. That she was a fucking bitch, a total snob, a vicious, power hungry, manipulating, psycho monster, etc.

I wasn't nearly as upset by Nikki as Anna was. I could already tell all the literary types were going to hate me. It was inevitable. All these accomplished, sophisticated people, faced with some clueless dolt like me, who was getting the exact thing they thought they were supposed to get? It was a miracle someone hadn't pulled out a knife and stabbed me in the face.

AND THEN SALLY got a job at the *Boston Globe*. Like, a real job. She told me this on my new cell phone that Miguel had insisted I buy. I was sitting in Union Square, eating one of the ten-dollar organic salads I now regularly consumed in my attempt to spend some of the money that seemed to flow into my bank account from every direction. I had just deposited a check for $16,450 dollars for the German rights to *Chicks and Dudes*, the title of which the Germans weren't even bothering to translate.

Sally was naturally very excited and anxious about her new job. And also a little embarrassed as her father had totally arranged it. I was caught off guard by the news, I didn't realize she was looking for something like that. She had been talking about staying at Columbia and doing historical research for one of her professors. But no, an opportunity had appeared and her dad had seized it.

So then Sally said all the things everyone said: how newspapers were dead, how everything would be on the internet now, journalists would never make money again. She was trying to be humble and downplay what a great job it was. Meanwhile, it was slowly dawning on me that Sally would be leaving New York and moving to Boston. I asked her when she was going. She said, "Pretty soon." I was like, "Oh."

So then I just sat there with my phone against my face, on my park bench, with my ten-dollar salad in my lap and the little birds hopping around at my feet. Sally was my best friend. I needed her here. "Oh my god," I murmured.

Sally said, "I know. It's going to be hard."

Bridget was in the apartment when I got home that night. I was still in shock about Sally. Or maybe I was feeling sorry for myself in general. It was hard to understand my own feelings at this point. Maybe I needed therapy. Why was I always so sad?

Bridget was in the kitchen, on her own cell phone and also trying to cook something. She was so not a cook. And she left the hugest messes, which by some quirk in her upbringing, she felt no compunction to clean up. I came out of the bathroom and sat at the little table for a minute and watched her. She had the window open, and the flowers were all pert and healthy outside in the Brooklyn air. Bridget, who probably got her first cell phone on the day they were invented, was talking to her parents. She was complaining to them about her job and about a boy they wanted her to date who she thought was boring. "I can't play tennis all summer," she said at one point. When she hung up, she slapped her phone shut, slipped it into her pocket and instantly grilled me about Rex. What was happening? When was I seeing him again? Had I told him I loved him yet? I couldn't answer her. I couldn't talk. Tears filled my eyes. Without Sally I was going to be so alone here now.

Bridget saw me and got mad. "Now what's wrong?" she said. She assumed it was about Rex. "You have to talk to him," she said. "I'm serious. It's not even a choice. You have to go to him and tell him how you feel, so that he knows and you know and everyone knows."

"Why does everyone have to know everything?" I said

"Because that's how you get what you want!"

Bridget pissed me off. That was the thing. Not cleaning up. Stealing my boyfriend Evan. Acting like she knew everything. She'd always pissed me off, I realized, taking a picture of her room that time, like me and Mari were some big joke to her, that all of this Brooklyn life was a joke, a bohemian adventure, her *salad days*.

How much I disliked Bridget was all I could think about for the next couple days. I went up to Sally's apartment to have dinner and take some stuff she wasn't going to bring to Boston. This was a difficult dinner. I was terribly sad about Sally and mad at Bridget and depressed about Rex. I didn't know what to think about any of it. Sally agreed with Bridget and had said all along: "She's right. You should probably tell Rex how you feel." This would not be Sally's normal advice, she was more like me in such matters, but since Rex was so shy and sensitive, I had to be assertive. It was the only way to clarify the situation.

Still, by now, wasn't it too late? They were already planning their wedding. They were past planning it. They were executing it.

I left Sally's that night with some socks, a couple books and a green sweatshirt that was too big for me. I didn't need any of these things. But they were Sally's and I wanted them even though I didn't have room. I just wanted to keep Sally in my life. *Oh my god*, I thought, *what was I going to do without her?*

· · ·

On Monday I went to *In Focus*. The first thing I did was write Rex an email that I needed to talk to him, it was important. I sent it immediately before I could chicken out.

That afternoon Anna called. She sounded drunk or high. She was both, it turned out. She had been at a photoshoot with a guy she liked, an actor named Dieter Jordan. She talked nonstop about the photoshoot, how the photographer had a ton of coke and how when they finally got rid of all the management types and were allowed to "do their work," they busted out the coke and the champagne and that's why she was so fucked up now, and was riding around in circles in a cab. She was in love with Dieter, and what did I think she should do? I didn't know. She heard the sound in my voice and asked me what was going on with me. I said my best friend was leaving New York. She was like, "Oh Andrea, I'm sorry," which surprised me. I hadn't thought she would care. But she did. She even asked me who it was. I told her about Sally and how she had helped me so much. "It's hard, the whole friend thing," said Anna, with sudden sincerity. "Especially in New York."

When I got off the phone, Rex had answered my email. He could meet tonight. How about we get dumplings at the Chinese place on Mott street?

I emailed him back that dumplings would work.

I DIDN'T WANT to tell Rex how I felt. It wasn't my style. And wasn't that what they always told you about dealings with boys: *be yourself*?

Having one of those "we have to talk" discussions, was so not me being myself.

I wanted to call Sally, and I could, now that I had a cell phone. But I resisted, knowing that I couldn't talk her ear off about any old thing. I would need to ration her friendship and advice and help now that she was leaving. Besides, I knew what she thought. She agreed saying something to Rex would be healthy. Her idea was more, just tell him so you don't have to think about it anymore. Put the burden on him. Get it off yourself.

I was early to the dumplings restaurant since I was coming from work. I killed time by walking around Mott Street, looking at the Chinese toys and knick-knacks on display on the side-walk. I was wearing a $179 summer dress from Anthropologie, which I'd forced myself to buy, since I now had something like $200,000 in my checking account. That was apparently the wrong place to have that much money. Veronica at *In Focus* had recently made me an appointment with an accountant who worked with artistic types. He would help me figure out what to do with my money and how to pay the huge tax bill I had coming. Also, my father had sent me an application for a mutual fund company he said was safe. He wanted me to put my money in there, in the stock market I guess, and so I was supposed to do that at some point, though my gut instinct was to do nothing at all. Which was also how I felt about the Rex situation. And yet here I was …

I went back to the dumpling restaurant and stood outside, watching the last of the sunlight turn the sky pink. I checked myself in the window of the shop next door. I didn't look my freshest, but that wasn't going to matter now. Rex knew what I looked like. There was no feminine trickery to resort to now.

Rex was late. He came striding down the street, apologizing as he came. He was sweatier than I was, and had an acne/shaving rash on one side of his neck. He smelled slightly, but it was, as always, a great relief to see his kind face, the intelligence in his eyes, the general solidness he had come to represent for me.

We went inside and stood by the cash register and waited for a table. We didn't talk. I was trying to get my breath. I wasn't actually nervous. I was just waiting. I was with a friend now. I was with someone who understood me, someone who already loved me in a way. There was no real pressure. I just had to tell him something. He already knew it anyway. But it would be nice for him to hear it. He would be flattered.

We were pointed to a tiny table and we squeezed in around it. Rex flipped through the menu, which was humorously unintelligible as always. We would have the dumplings, he told the waiter. And Cokes. We both smiled and settled into our seats and breathed sighs of relief. Rex had spoken to Rebecca last night and told me the latest wedding stories. He was glad he was not in Ohio. He laughed about Rebecca, the last person on earth who would fall victim to bridezilla syndrome, and yet it was happening, she was reading the magazines, worrying over napkins, arguing with florists. They had registered at Bloomingdale's. There were ongoing arguments with her parents, and his parents, and Rebecca's old Ohio friends, who were obviously not as casual—or ironic—as Rebecca, after her years at Oberlin and in Brooklyn. These native Ohio people had their own ideas about what was appropriate for a wedding.

I laughed along with this and then settled into the same reflective silence as Rex. This was a huge deal, whatever else I thought about it. Weddings. Marriage. Family. Friends. This was the real stuff of life and here was Rex, smack in the middle of it, handling it, being the upstanding guy you knew he was.

The dumplings came. I fumbled to eat them with my chopsticks. Rex had to ask again for the Cokes, doing the hand gesture "drinking from a can," in case there was some misunderstanding. It was a funny thing to do, and made me love him more than I already did.

"So what's up?" he suddenly said to me, in a slightly concerned, already sympathetic voice.

I smiled shyly and touched my lips with my napkin. It took me a second to get my voice. I started to say something about Bridget, that this was Bridget's idea, which was true enough. But I saw that was the wrong approach. I couldn't blame this on someone else. So I stopped and paused and thought about it for a moment.

Rex saw me struggling. "Andrea?" he said.

I thought of Rebecca then, somewhere in Ohio, making wedding plans, sure that her life's happiness was securely in her grasp. This made me sad, deeply sad, and I struggled more and then tears came into my eyes. A surge of love for Rebecca flowed through me. And a surge of love for Rex. And a surge of love for all the people in the world who did things right, who found their soulmates, who married their soulmates, who lived good lives and fought the good fight.

The Chinese man brought the Cokes, cold cans with plastic straws in white paper laid across the tops.

Rex opened his coke and slid his straw through the opening. He mentioned a big summer movie he was reviewing for *The Post*. He still had reservations about his job. But he was glad to have the paycheck. He told me about a coworker who kept not writing her articles and making up excuses. She would probably get fired. She better. It wasn't fair to the other people. How had she even got her job there?

As he spoke, I thought of Rebecca again but in a different way. Her ass was already getting big. She wasn't that smart, really. She would drag Rex away from New York at some point, somewhere she could bake cookies and raise kids and be the Ohio girl she was at heart. Oberlin or not, that's where she was going. I'd gone to Wellington, I knew the type. They kept up the artsy, intellectual thing for a couple years after college. To show they weren't total frauds. But then reality set in and they ran right back to whatever affluent suburb they came from. Maybe this was what Rex wanted. Maybe Rex didn't know what he wanted.

I bit into a dumpling. Rex chopped one of his in half with his white spoon. I chewed mechanically and somehow swallowed. "How's the book stuff going?" Rex asked.

I nodded that it was good. I put more dumpling in my mouth. I couldn't do it. I couldn't tell Rex that I loved him. Why had I thought I could?

We ate in silence. Several other diners stood by the cash register, waiting for tables. Rex and I, not being real New Yorkers, both felt pressured by their presence and finished our dumplings quickly so that they could take our place. Fifteen minutes later, we were outside again.

We walked. We ended up in the small park across from the karaoke bar the USC people always went to. It was now dark, which I was grateful for. We found a bench and sat and again I sighed and tried to relax after the strange tension and confusion of the meal. Rex had not asked again what I wanted to talk to him about.

I settled myself, put my hands in my lap, stared down at my feet, my very temporary flesh and bones, which at that moment rested on the more permanent cobblestones of the great city.

"Rex, I love you and I want to be with you. I don't want you to marry Rebecca."

There. I said it. It was done.

52

"WOW," said Rex. "That's not what I thought you were going to say."

I didn't speak or answer him. But I was glad I'd said my piece. And I believed it. I did love him. I did not want him to marry Rebecca and slowly fade out of my life. Or out of his own life, which I now realized I was exactly right about. If he married Rebecca, he'd end up back in Ohio with three kids, assembling bird feeders in his garage and watching PBS documentaries on TV. I was suddenly, for the first time, absolutely sure of this.

But I didn't say anything. A group of girls in their early twenties walked by on the sidewalk outside the park. They were going to the karaoke bar to sing and drink and laugh and goof around and, if they were lucky, meet the person that they would someday confess their star-crossed love to.

"I wanted to tell you because I wasn't sure you knew," I said. "Even though I was pretty sure you *did* know, it seemed like you might not. So I wanted to say it once, out loud. And make sure."

But that sounded too perfunctory, like I was letting him off the hook. Like I was letting us both off the hook.

So I continued. "I don't know what I can offer you," I said to my feet. "I don't know if I could marry you. Or if I could have kids—"

"—I don't want kids," said Rex.

"Well, you're going to have them if you marry Rebecca!" I blurted, more forcefully than I intended. But that was a good point, a good reason for this conversation. Rex was my friend. Didn't he know what was going to happen if he got married? If he didn't, he needed to.

Rex said nothing for a long time. Then he said: "You're probably right."

"I love Rebecca," I said, softly. "But that's the truth. You know it is."

We tried to say other things. Both of us taking stabs at an actual discussion. But nothing came out right. Rex gave up and lapsed into a troubled silence. I found myself focused on the tops of my shoes.

Eventually, we started walking again. We went south, through the smelly un-touristed streets of lower Chinatown, the blood-stained sidewalks, the half-rotted produce boxes.

Rex jammed his hands in his jeans pockets as he walked. He set his shoulders a certain way. Two women wanted him for their life partners. He had never previously been so in demand. Seeing how awkward it was for him made me want to let him go, let him marry Rebecca, like he wanted to. But at the same time, I was seeing everything from a new perspective. Bridget had been so right about this. The act of telling him the truth had changed everything in a way. I *did* have something to offer Rex. Being with me would make him a different person. It would make him smarter and cooler and more interesting.

Bridget understood the malleability of boys. I did not. But I was starting to.

We ended up at the South Street Sea Port. We went inside the shopping area. In the midst of the noisy tourists, we were released from our tense silence. Rex bought a Miller Lite. I dug a Snapple Kiwi Strawberry out of an ice-filled plastic tub. We went upstairs and sat on the deck chairs facing the East River. The Watchtower sign glowed at us from across the water.

Rex reminisced about our first meeting at the *Context* party. What I looked like across the room. How I seemed to glow. How different I seemed from the others. "You were like a messenger," he said. "You brought news from distant lands."

We joked about the rest of it. Me trying to kiss him on the landing and then Rebecca catching us. He described Rebecca on the subway home, shocked and silent. She had needed reassurance for weeks after that. Her jealousy became a crises point in their relationship. In a way, that incident had inspired their engagement.

These stories, these little fragments and memories, they came out in short bits, with long silences in between. What were Rex and I doing exactly? I guess I was helping him decide what he wanted. He seemed to need that. He had helped me so much, in so many different ways, it seemed absurd for me not to help him through this. But was I supposed to be present while he picked which girl—and which life—he wanted? It felt like cheating.

Despite our talk, no obvious conclusion was reached. At eleven, it was time to go. Rex had turned off his phone. When he turned it back on he had three new messages from Rebecca he needed to return. And I had an early appointment with my new accountant in the morning. We walked to the subway, our bodies far apart now, letting people pass between us on the sidewalk.

There was a deep and ominous silence between us as we sat on the L Train, rumbling toward Brooklyn. I watched the other train riders with their iPods and their books. *Electra Rising,* I saw one girl reading. Despite her detractors, Anna's book had reached people. Would my book be read by people like that? For a brief moment, I was so relieved to think about something other than Rex and I. Maybe that's all I really wanted: to obsess about my career and my book.

We pulled into my subway stop. I didn't know what to say as the train slowed. Rex stood up and we hugged awkwardly. "I'm glad we had this conversation," he said.

"Me too," I said.

"I'll call you," he said.

I nodded. And I got off the train.

The next morning I woke up in an uncomfortable daze, with the sun shining down on my blankets, overheating my body and giving me a headache. My alarm hadn't gone off. I was late to my accountant.

An hour later, I was hurrying into an elevator on West 27th Street. On the fifth floor, I found the not very impressive reception area of an accounting company. A girl pointed me to the small office of Josh Greenberg.

I knocked on the open door and went in. Josh Greenberg was short and much younger than I expected. He looked about thirty. He had a pleasant, open face and curly reddish brown hair that poofed up and sat on his head in a comical, theatrical way.

He gestured for me to take a seat across from his desk. The air conditioning was broken and he apologized for the heat. He redirected one of the fans so it pointed at me. He explained that we were lucky it was an old building. In newer office buildings you couldn't open the windows, which was unhealthy. He talked for several minutes about how buildings were like organisms. They had nervous systems, arterial pathways, digestive tracts. If the skin of a building couldn't breath, certain toxins accumulated inside. The building became sick.

I didn't say much to this. He saw that my eyes had glazed over and he asked me about my financial situation. I had written a book, I told him. I had suddenly made a whole bunch of money. I'd been told I would owe a shitload of taxes.

He nodded thoughtfully. He was leaning back, rocking slightly in his chair. What was the book about? I said: "Bands and music people in Portland, Oregon."

Josh's eyebrows went up. A book about music? He was in a band himself. The Offsets. He played drums. They had played in Portland not six months ago. He knew all about the Portland scene. I asked him if he knew Todd Sparrow. He said of course. And Edith Monroe and Color Green. He even knew Nick Pax and Crystalline, or at least he said he did. He was very impressed I'd written a book about such people. He might have been the first person in New York who was.

Still, he was careful to remain professional. He talked to me about taxes. He would get me some forms. I would have to write some big checks. Was I ready for that? I was like, "Do I have a choice?"

I showed him the application form my dad had sent me for the mutual fund company. He glanced through it, marked it up, showed me how to fill it out. He explained to me, very clearly and helpfully, what a mutual fund was.

He told me musicians usually bought houses when they got "the big payday." He didn't know why. But mutual funds were good too. I would do well with this. He told me which funds to buy. "A little of everything," was his advice.

In general, he seemed to think I was doing great. He wanted to read my book. I told him it was still a long ways away. "September," I said.

"September?" he said, still flipping through the mutual fund stuff. "That's not long. That's three months from now."

In fact, the very next day, a box was waiting for me at home, via UPS. I read on the packing slip what it was: twenty review galleys of *Chicks and Dudes.*

I carried the heavy box up the stairs and dropped it onto the small kitchen table. Nobody else was home. I put my bag down, opened the window and stood there, staring at the box.

I cut it open with a steak knife, pulled the bubble wrap, and there it was. My book. Cynthia Dunleavy had managed at the last possible second to get an Anna Madsen blurb on the cover, which was about as glowing as could be imagined. It ran right across the top, a crucial bit of marketing.

I took out one book and flipped it open, flipped it from the front, from the back, turned it over in my hands. It looked good. It looked professional. Everything about it felt right. The timing, the tone, the funny title. Even the cover was perfect: a sparse, artsy drawing of some young music fans standing around outside a local venue.

I couldn't not call Rex. I scrolled down to his number on my cell, then hung up to think for a second. I walked around the apartment. I looked out my front window at the street outside. Then I got out my phone again and this time completed my call to Rex. "Guess what came today?" I said to him, before he could speak.

"Holy shit," he said back.

53

REX CAME in and went straight for the box of books and lifted out the top copy. "I can't believe this," he exclaimed. "Oh. My. *Gawd*! He turned to me. "I get one of these. I'm reviewing this for *The Post*!"

I was like, "You better!"

"I'm going to launch you!" he said. "I am going to be the unknown critic who first announced the greatness of *Chicks and Dudes*!"

The next night after work, Rex called. He needed to see me right away. I dropped everything and practically ran to his favorite Mexican restaurant to meet him.

Inside, he was sitting in a booth, furious. It turned out his editor had already assigned the review of my book to a different writer, someone who hated articles like the *Sunday Times* "Young Novelist" piece and would trash my book because of it. I said it wasn't that important, but Rex thought it was. This other guy was a jerk and a snob and hated anything that wasn't "accepted as literature," which was the phrase he'd actually used. He'd tear *Chicks* apart and make *The Post* look ridiculous. It was *so typical*, fumed Rex.

He ripped apart his burrito when it came. I suggested it might be good to get some negative reviews. It would get people talking. But Rex didn't want to hear that.

After that we went for a long walk around Williamsburg. I finally got him to stop talking about the review, so then he talked about the *The Post* in general. It wasn't what he had hoped. And newspapers were dying out anyway. He should probably get some other kind of job.

There was no discussion of other issues. Or us. Back at his house, I made an excuse to go home. Rex struggled with this for a moment, then said nothing. He gave me a quick hug. I had intended to do the same, but I found myself holding on to him for a second longer than I intended. This brought a momentary grimace to his face, and I could see the trouble I was causing him. For a moment, I wanted to apologize, for complicating things, for upsetting his happy life. But instead I kept my mouth shut and stayed firm to my basic idea of: I have rights here too. I love him too. I could be with him too.

Two days later, at work, I sent Rex a joking email that since I was the only woman in his life at the moment, I had better feed him.

So he came over for dinner. I managed to make a spinach salad, and boil some pasta and present a passable dinner. Mari was in her room, so that was a little strange, us not being really alone. But in a way it was good. Mari came into the kitchen while we did the dishes and she and Rex joked around like they do—the way they would if Rex and I were a couple. So that was weird, and a little bittersweet.

When he left, I walked him out and then down the street a little ways. We still had not said anything about Rebecca or me or the wedding. At the end of the block, he opened his arms for a casual goodbye hug. I put my arms around him and we sunk into each other. We couldn't help it. It had been building up all this time. We stood on the corner, holding each other, gripping each other, rocking slightly from side to side. The hug itself was like a journey, or maybe a history of our relationship: excited and slightly sexual at first, then more like deep love and affection and admiration, then gradually more tragic and heartbreaking, which made it sexual again.

When we finally separated, we both stood there on the sidewalk for a second, neither looking at the other. "What's going to happen to us?" I finally said. He shook his head. He had tears in his eyes. He said he didn't know.

Sunday, June 6, was the day Sally was leaving. I took the subway to Columbia and helped her sweep out her now empty apartment. Her dad was there with the family SUV. I had never actually met him face to face, so that was nice. He congratulated me on my novel, and I thanked him for all his help. He didn't say much else though. I wondered if he thought I was a bad influence on his daughter. That's almost how he acted. Like he wanted his daughter safely ensconced in a real job, back in Boston and not hanging around with New York sex novelists.

Still, it was good he was there. It kept things cheerful and positive, and prevented me from talking endlessly about Rex. We carried Sally's last boxes down and packed them into her dad's car. The last thing to go was her still-pretty-new futon which we slid down the stairwell and left rolled up against a parking meter in the street.

When everything was ready and the car was full, I stood bravely on the sidewalk and said goodbye to my best friend. She would now live in Boston, right where she started, right near her dad. She would most likely meet some great guy and start a family and eventually fade out of my life ...

Rex called me at work the next day with good news about the *Chicks and Dudes* review. He had wrangled it away from the other guy and was going to review it himself. He had gone into his boss and laid it all out, why the book was important, why it spoke to young people, why we needed to champion it from the start, and be ahead of the curve.

"Wow," I said.

"I know," he said back. "It was Rebecca's idea, actually. She told me to go directly to the top. And it totally worked."

I thanked him for taking a chance like that for my book. And thanked Rebecca too. I said, "So you're talking to her about stuff?" He said he was, but not about *our* stuff. He hadn't said anything about that.

We didn't see each other for a couple days, and then on Saturday Mari and I went to the flea market in Greenwich Village. Rex and I were running out of time. I'd been thinking about that all day. I'd been waiting for him to call me, but he hadn't. So I called him.

He invited me to come over. He said he was cleaning the apartment, since they wouldn't be back in it for three weeks. In a way, that was my answer. He was going ahead with the wedding. How much clearer could it be?

But I still went, getting off the L at his stop and walking the three blocks to his apartment.

He was sweeping when I got there, just like Sally had been. I moved some stuff around. I tried to help. Rex and Rebecca had gotten rid of some of their furniture, the crappy stuff, since they would be getting better stuff after the wedding. Also, the kitchen area was weirdly bare. There was nothing in the refrigerator. And no dishes drying in the rack.

Rex scrubbed the kitchen shelves. I sat in a chair and watched him. It was awkward with neither of us talking. Eventually, Rex asked if I was hungry and offered to order in some Thai food.

I stood up then and came up behind him. He was wearing a button-down shirt and shorts and he was leaning over the sink, wiping the tiles behind the faucet. I put my arms around him from behind and laid my head sideways on his back. He froze and didn't do anything and we both stayed like that for a long time.

And then we had sex. Which was a terrible idea. It was awkward and rushed and when I tried to slow Rex down he seemed to get frustrated and angry. We were on their bed, his and Rebecca's, with all her stuff there, her pictures on the side table and her Pablo Neruda book and her Buddhist Reflections. Rex tried doing it a different way but we couldn't find a comfortable position. Whatever we tried, it just got weirder and more unpleasant. I thought: we're not even fucking this up right. We can't even ruin our relationship correctly.

Afterward, we both lay on the bed, staring up at the electrical wires outside his window. We didn't talk. We didn't touch. We didn't do anything.

54

THANK GOD FOR ANNA MADSEN. She happened to call the next day as I was getting off work. When she heard my Rex story, she immediately changed her plans and got a cab downtown to meet me.

I couldn't bear to go home so we went for drinks in the East Village and then went back to her neighborhood and had more drinks and then walked around and ended up at her house. I fell asleep on their little couch in a fetal position with her designer raincoat over my head. I woke up the next morning disoriented and hung over and totally humiliated, but at least I was in a different place, which seemed to help somehow.

We went shopping that afternoon and then Anna had the great idea to get Will Soren to take us out to dinner. At first I thought she was joking. But she wasn't. I was like, *no no no.* I couldn't be around Will Soren in my present state. Anna sympathized, but also thought the whole Rex saga would be great material for me. She thought it should be my next novel. "I wish I could do something like that," she said. "But everyone sees me coming."

Anna called Will. I really did not want to be associated with this plan. I felt horrible and I looked like shit. But she handled it perfectly, adopting the perfect lightness of tone and charming Will Soren thoroughly. Dinner arrangements were made.

"Don't worry about Will," she said snapping her phone shut. "You are making him so much money right now."

We met him downtown at a beautiful restaurant I'd never heard of in SoHo. Anna waltzed in, her shopping bags bouncing beside her. I had bought some stuff too, but not enough to bounce. We found Will Soren at the bar in his usual suit and tie, a pink shirt, his thinning grey bouffant still flowing lion-like in waves off the top of his head.

Anna air-kissed him. I attempted an air-kiss also, but screwed it up. Will didn't seem to mind, he smiled at my ineptitude and gave me a kindly squeeze on the shoulder.

We followed the hostess to our table, where we settled ourselves. Anna did the talking, chattering about her uptown friends, people her mom knew, people Will was apparently familiar with. It was right out of the pages of *Electra Rising*. Will responded with several hilarious stories from his own work week, each leisurely described in that deep rich voice of his. His stories put Anna and I to shame. Why wasn't he a writer? Because he was smart.

I said almost nothing, but somehow the happy chatter of Will and Anna slowly eased me out of my Rex spiral. I began to smile. I began to laugh. Could it be that these two people were actually my friends? It didn't seem possible. But here I was.

I drove Rex to the airport. A friend of Rebecca's had lent them a car, and so I got up early and took Rex, with two large suitcases full of wedding stuff to LaGuardia for his flight to Ohio. We'd already had "the conversation." It had been more difficult than it needed to be as Rex, in his inexperience, seemed to feel conditions needed to be just right to let me down easy. I nipped this in the bud and told him—talking on my cell phone from the noisy Bedford subway station—that I knew he was going ahead with the wedding, it was okay, the whole thing was my fault, we didn't have to talk about it. He claimed he *did* want to talk about it, but I knew he didn't and it was never spoken of again.

The drive was actually good practice for us, pretending nothing had happened. In a way, nothing had.

He directed me to LaGuardia. I pulled over at his terminal, helped him with his suitcases and then did my best to avoid a prolonged or tearful goodbye. I basically just drove away. But going back, I got lost in Queens and had to call Rex again ten minutes later. He patiently explained how to get back to Williamsburg, but it took forever and left me exhausted. Then I spent forty minutes looking for a parking place and nearly getting into several accidents. When I couldn't take it anymore, I collapsed completely and sat sobbing into my own sweaty forearms, while some plumbing guy in a dented van blared his horn at me.

On Thursday, I went back to Josh Greenberg's offices to pick up my tax forms. Josh was standing in the front area, chatting with the receptionist when I got there. He glanced up, pretending he was surprised to see me. He offered to get the forms himself and did, and then, with a nervous stammer, asked me if I wanted to have lunch. This was pretty much the last thing I needed, but standing there, looking down at his hopeful face (he was an inch shorter than me) I couldn't think of a polite way to say no.

So then I was stuck doing that. A snooty waiter came. I ordered a sandwich. When Josh ordered, he became difficult, getting himself into a pointless verbal tangle with the waiter. Eventually he calmed down. We talked about music, which was easy. We discussed different bands and the New York scene. Josh wanted me to come see a group that night called Socratic Method at the Cake Shop. I said: "Sure ... maybe ... "

On the way home, I called Anna and told her about the lunch. Her ears perked up when I mentioned the Socratic Method show. She knew their guitar player, who had gone to her artsy private high school. She remembered he was quite cute. She thought we should go.

So we went. Anna met me downtown, arriving in her best rock and roll, heroin chic, *Electra Rising* style. I felt underdressed in my cut-off jeans and T-shirt but I found a bright pink barrette clip at a bodega and used it to create a severe hair part, which at least made me look notable, if slightly stupid.

As soon as we entered Cake Shop, Anna began seeing people she knew. Cute uptown boys with preppie red cutoffs or Tincture-styled girls in mini skirts. It was quite an interesting crowd and not the grubby NYU crowd I expected.

The downstairs room was pleasantly packed. Josh appeared with his curly mop top and a black Ted Nugent T-shirt and corduroy pants. He looked cute, in his gritty New York musician way. His little gang of friends looked cool too and he must have told them about my book because they were very polite and respectful toward me. When they figured out who Anna Madsen was though, they got really excited. They had all read *Electra Rising*, or had meant to. So the party was on after that.

· · ·

Socratic Method started their first set with a single piano note, played slowly, over and over. A hush fell over the crowd. Someone yelled. Another person whooped. The keyboard guy continued to play the one note. The drummer made a whispery sound on his cymbals. There was more yelling, someone laughed, a girl screamed from the back. Someone near the front shook up his beer, held it over his head and let it foam down his bare arm. The single note got louder, *dunk, dunk, dunk*. The singer stepped to the microphone and began whipping his long bangs around in the air. The tension grew, the drums started a slow rumble, one of the guitarists began windmilling his arm around. And then someone in the darkness yelled out 1 ... 2 ... 3 ... 4 and then KA- VROOOOOM. The band launched into a thick swirly stomping beat.

Everyone went nuts. It was hilarious. I was laughing and bopping around. It was totally fun in an almost Portland way, but actually better, since people were less intent on out-cooling each other and more just enjoying the punk rock goofiness of it.

"The Method" as people called them, played for two hours, and at 2:30am most of the sweaty audience ended up outside smoking and standing around on the sidewalk. Eventually there was talk of a party and people began walking and Anna and I followed along, not talking, just listening to the voices and the echoing sounds of the narrow downtown street.

The party was in a small, cramped railroad apartment. People spilled out into the hall, and onto the stairs. I hadn't actually talked to Josh, and found my way to him but he was arguing loudly with a girl who seemed more his type, with big tits and a honky Queens accent, though I had to admit, in general Josh's friends had turned out to be pretty great. Even Anna was having fun, flirting and yelling at people.

At one point, Anna and I ended up sitting on the curb outside the apartment, drinking Jack Daniels with two guys who were pretty cute but were trying too hard to take us home. They had coke, which they were doling out to Anna in small doses. Anna became annoyed with them, and when one of them mentioned he never read books, Anna tore into them both with a viciousness that was shocking. I thought she might actually punch the guy. But nothing happened and they gave us more coke and then we went back upstairs where there was still some warm beer in the kitchen.

Eventually, the two of us collapsed into a cab and went back to Anna's place. The sun was coming up as we trudged inside and up the stairs. I was literally falling asleep on my feet and Anna got me onto the little couch and lay a blanket over me.

I woke up dry-mouthed and fog-brained at noon. Anna was already up, reading the *New York Times* in the soft light of the kitchen. She looked beautiful in her trainwreck way, with her expensive underwear and bathrobe and her hopelessly tousled blonde hair hanging in her face.

Meanwhile, I thought I was going to throw up. And my head felt like a dusty cinder block. Anna filled me with Motrin and orange juice and we dragged ourselves to a diner down the street where we picked at scrambled eggs and somehow came back to life as we talked about men and relationships and our careers and the nature of fame. I felt almost normal after we went for a walk along Broadway. Somehow the big city, which had been on the verge of crushing me just days before, had turned itself around and become my best friend again.

On Monday, I went to work. I had to quit my job. That's what people kept telling me. That, and I should get my own apartment. Bridget said it didn't look right for a high-profile writer to live in such cramped and slovenly conditions. It would hurt my reputation. But I suspected she wanted my bigger room for herself, so I took this advice with a grain of salt.

But other people agreed. Anna had this idea that I could sublet a friend's apartment in her building for three months and then bounce around, subletting here and there. She claimed this was a common practice for writers when they had a big book. "You'll be all over the place," she said. "Traveling, moving around. And when you're famous, people will always let you stay in their place for free. Why pay rent?"

But my rent was so cheap, that wasn't a problem. Also, Anna herself had not done that much when her book came out. She'd told me it had felt like a huge letdown really, even when *Electra Rising* hit the bestseller list. "It builds up and builds up and you think it's going to lead to this big final moment ..." she said. "And then nothing happens. And then the phone stops ringing, and Will stops calling, or you call him and Liz gets this *tone* with you ..."

Anna didn't like Liz very much. "She thinks she'll be a big agent herself someday," said Anna. "That's why she treats everyone like shit." I said she'd always been perfectly nice to me. "Of course she is now," said Anna. "But just wait."

PART FOUR

55

REX AND REBECCA'S wedding took place on the last weekend in June. I flew to Ohio on Friday morning. The flight was short and easy and I got a taxi to the hotel, which felt luxurious and a bit indulgent since I could have waited for a shuttle.

At the hotel there was a welcome bag with my name on it. Beneath the ribbons and bright paper, I found a bottle of wine, cheese, crackers, chocolate, organic soap. In a lovely hand-written note, Rex and Rebecca expressed their heartfelt gratitude for my presence. It was all a little corny, but also fun and exciting, and you could feel the love right away. There was going to be a lot of love expressed this weekend.

I unpacked and then went for a swim in the hotel pool to wake myself up. Then I took a long hot bath in the plastic hotel bathtub. I ate some of the cheese and crackers from my welcome bag and put on one of my three new J.Crew dresses I had brought, not being sure what clothes would be required. I didn't know much about weddings, so I had done some research on the internet. Rebecca was having bridesmaids, it turned out, though at first she wasn't. They were a sister, a niece, her best friend from high school and two close friends from Oberlin.

That seemed like a lot of people, and it got me thinking. If relatively straight-arrow Rex could have slept with me, think of all the other secrets that had to be kept at your average wedding, among all those friends, crushes, ex-boyfriends, former lovers. Not to mention the awful pressure of marriage itself. Your last chance to get with so-and-so! Marriage was supposed to clean up your life in a way. Simplify it. But probably in some cases, it just made a bigger mess.

The rehearsal dinner was at 6:30. A shuttle van came to pick us up at 6:00. I met some of the other people in the lobby while we waited. One Ohio couple I had met before, and some Brooklyn people I knew and quickly attached myself to. The group of us chatted and exchanged stories of travel and other incidental events in our lives that could be linked to the wedding. It was all very nice and formal and polite and several of us girls remarked on our inability to shift gears into even the most basic formal dress. Someone mentioned Jane Austen and what it would be like to dress like those people every day. We all recoiled in horror and laughed and felt good about our literary fashion references.

The van came and drove us to an upscale local restaurant, the top floor of which had been reserved for our party. I stayed close to my Brooklyn gang. This strategy worked when Rebecca greeted us and I was able to blend in with the others. I did get a few extra seconds though, as Rebecca looked me in the eye and thanked me for looking after Rex for the time she was away. I joked: "If you ever need a babysitter ..." which sounded weird, and not funny, but Rebecca had already moved on to the next person and didn't notice.

Into the restaurant we went. Rex was there, in a crisp summer suit. My eyes went right to him, just like they had at that first *Context* party. He stood in a crowd of other people, looking competent and alert, kind and warm. He was a deeply good person, as was his bride, Rebecca, which was why this weekend would be so fun. There were no reservations anywhere. Everyone was utterly convinced: this was a perfect match. Would they have felt this way about me? If I was the bride? Me, the author of the "bongs and blow job book," which someone had called *Chicks and Dudes* last week, on a new insider publishing website called *Between The Lines*.

I went to my assigned table for dinner. I was seated next to a striking young man named Ash Crowley, who had just graduated from the Iowa Writers Workshop. Some of the other people around the table seemed to know him, or know of him. They asked him questions about Iowa, which he answered with patience and the faintest air of superiority. He had apparently won a prize for one of his short stories. A collection was in the works, with several publishers interested. Ash was remarkably good looking and wore black plastic glasses that seemed like the exact right fashion statement for an up-and-coming MFA grad, especially if he was headed to New York, which Ash was.

It occurred to me, as the conversation continued, that I had been seated next to him on purpose. We all had. Ours was the literary table. One of the other women had gone to Stanford's poetry program. Another Oberlin grad, had just landed an assistant editor job at Random House in New York. When we heard this, an awkward silence came over the table, as some of the other writers present wondered if this editor might be able to help their careers, or at least help Ash, who was no doubt the most deserving. But alas, the young editor specialized in an academic branch of publishing, and could not help anyone.

Eventually the table broke up into separate conversations. I asked Ash where he planned to live in New York. He said he would probably move to Brooklyn like everybody else. We both smiled knowingly. Ash was quite charming, but the superior air never went away. He didn't mind talking to me, but he also never asked me anything about myself.

Dinner proceeded. The table talked about recent movies, HBO TV shows, and then the one truly important question of our time: would all traditional forms of courtship be replaced by internet dating? As the conversation drifted along, Ash fell into a bored silence. I began to wonder if there was some unpretentious way to tell him that I was a writer too and had a first novel coming out. From Montauk Books, no less. But my experience, limited as it was, seemed to indicate that in all such cases, it was best to keep your mouth shut. When someone at the table asked me what I did, I said I worked at a photography magazine. *In Focus.* Several people had heard of it.

56

DURING DESSERT, several people were called upon to say a few words about the couple and the joining of the two families. Rex's dad, who was very handsome and self-composed, gave a brilliant little talk. Rebecca's mother, who was the opposite of Rebecca, polished and urbane in her conservative Ohio way, told a funny story of Rebecca's first phone call home in which she described a funny "book nerd" she had met, who recited John Keats at keg parties. Everyone thought that was hilarious, Rex most of all. I watched him then, for an extended moment, and he turned in my direction and smiled and nodded to me, not in a personal way, but just going along with the joke, giving me the same look of good-natured humiliation he gave everyone else.

Which was fine. I didn't need anything more. I occupied myself by watching Ash, who smiled mildly at the stories and clapped when everyone else did. I wondered if he really was as superior as he acted. In twenty years, would he have one of those serious literary careers? National Book Awards. Prestigious teaching gigs. A *Paris Review* interview. He was awfully good looking. He probably would.

. . .

After dessert there was more wine, and coffee, and happy conversation. I got up to mingle at some point, I had no choice, as everyone else had left my table except for the Stanford poetry woman, who seemed deeply unhappy about something. She had big worry lines down her forehead and between her eyes. I remembered that type from Wellington, *the anxious faces of the female poet*. It occurred to me that I may never be thought of as a literary writer, not like Ash or this woman, I was more like Anna Madsen, I was going to be a "hipster novelist," a category someone had recently invented on yet another book gossip website. Anna had sent me the link. Anna herself had been listed as number five. Right under Bret Easton Ellis, Mary Gaitskill, Martin Amis and Denis Johnson.

I walked around. I found myself being pulled into a chair next to Rex's father who for some reason knew who I was. But of course he did, Rex had told him about my book. And so I got my fifteen minutes of fame as Rex's cheerful fifty-two-year old father flirted with me, questioned me, and thoughtfully listened to everything I said. He was very cool, I realized, even as he forced me to do most of the talking. What was his job? He was a banker or something. He was one of those perfect people who made a lot of money but remained balanced and open-minded and up to date on the larger world. I sort of fell in love with his long face, his neatly combed grey hair. Then I had the deeply wounding thought: I could have been in Rex's family.

I moved on, standing with some other girls around a table where Rebecca was holding court in her shy, embarrassed way. Seeing me, Rebecca smiled and deferred to me in some way, though I was doing everything in my power to remain as invisible and insignificant as was humanly possible.

I moved on. I met Rebecca's sister who was a senior at University of Chicago but was more like her mother, less hippy, and with expensive glasses, and an oddly shaped designer dress. She was studying political science and journalism. She said, "I'd rather do music stories for MTV and know what's going on in the world, than be another FOX news bunny." I didn't know what that meant exactly, but it sounded like the correct position.

I met other people and stayed out of trouble, though I did end up standing near Rex and some of his guy friends at one point. He seemed taller on this fateful night, in his suit and tie, his hair now ruffled, a nervous exhaustion visible in his eyes. The other guys were teasing him about married life. The word "boss" was used in place of "wife." Everyone laughed. Rex laughed too, but in a different way, his head cocked down slightly. He was a perfectly restrained, self-assured version of himself on this night. He looked great. He sounded great. He was the coolest guy in the room. Him and his dad.

Eventually, it came time to go back to the hotel. A van came and a bunch of us piled in. Ash was in my van this time. He was staying in our hotel apparently. But he was seated far in the back where he was talking about *McSweeney's* with a woman I hadn't met, a singleton apparently. Perhaps handsome Mr. Crowley was going to get laid.

I was in the front, sitting with Charles, a gay guy who had been Rebecca's best friend freshman year at college. He had told a funny story at the dinner about Rebecca and Rex's first date. I asked him what Rebecca was like when she first arrived at Oberlin. But he was bored talking about Rebecca by now. "She was adorable," he said. "She's always been adorable."

I tried to imagine Rebecca and gay Charles as college freshman. And then pictured Rebecca's first encounter with Rex, the "book nerd." That was so not the truth. Or not the whole truth anyway. But if Rex was willing to marry someone who thought of him like that, then maybe that was his true self. Maybe that's what marriage is: you picking out the final version of yourself.

Back in the hotel, I was buzzed from alcohol and caffeine and people and excitement. I went to my room but couldn't sit still. It was weird how alone I was here. Not that I minded. The only person I wanted to talk to lately was Anna. And Sally, when I could.

I took a bath and laid around on my bed for a while, but the cricket-filled darkness of suburban Ohio seemed to taunt me, seemed to dare me to leave my room and come interact with it.

So I did, putting on a pair of dorky shorts I'd bought for the wedding. In the endless hotel hallway, I started to call Anna but then decided her corrupt soul might spoil the mood. So I continued on my own, walking into the main lobby and out the front doors and into the comfortable humidity of the midwestern night.

But the hotel was in the middle of nowhere. Far down the main road you could see an Applebee's and some sort of gas station/convenience store. That was it. So I remained on the grounds of my hotel, walking a slow lap around the parking lot. The grass was the nicest thing. There were acres of it. And the smell of the trees and the June blossoms. I didn't know what kind of trees they were. Ash Crowley probably did. He was probably an expert on different kinds of trees, using their latin names and describing them with amazing adjectives like *redo-*

lent or *concupiscent* or ... well I couldn't think of any other amazing adjectives.

I went around the hotel grounds and then went back into the lobby where I saw the Stanford poetry woman reading on a couch with a cup of tea. I got myself a cup of tea too and went and sat beside her and apologized if I was disturbing her. I wasn't, she promised me. She was just bored and hated watching TV in hotels. She said it seemed like the worst thing to do in a new place, to sit in a room watching cable TV. But everyone did it, so there was no one to talk to, so she had to sit by herself reading.

We talked. She was way nicer than I thought. And at some point I even told her about my book, playing it down as much as possible and saying how people were already making fun of it, calling it the "bongs and blow jobs book," which wasn't even fair because there was only one blow job in it and it was only a couple sentences.

She offered some words of wisdom about the arts and talked about Stanford and the poetry program. I wondered if I could go to an MFA program somewhere and she seemed to think I could, even though I was already getting published. I was certainly young enough, she assured me. She had been one of the youngest people in some of her classes at Stanford.

It was a nice thought, me getting an MFA. It would be a way to back up a little, to make sure that I didn't become Anna Madsen and be the literary "it girl" for a year and then get replaced by the next person and be stuck trying to reinvent myself for the rest of my life. As much as I liked Anna Madsen, I didn't think I was really like her, and I sure didn't want to be a one book wonder, which was Anna's greatest fear, and in her case seemed inevitable, since she couldn't seem to write, or even start another book.

57

I WOKE up the next morning at dawn with a new and terrifying sense of guilt. Rebecca had appeared in a dream, talking to me, explaining why I needed to go with some police-type people who had come in a separate van to remove me from the wedding.

As I came to be more fully awake, I realized Rex had not spoken to me once since I had arrived. Maybe that wasn't unusual. There were a lot of people here. But would Rebecca notice? Did Rebecca know?

It was 4:37am and I tried to go back to sleep. I tossed and turned in my strange hotel bed. I remembered my thought about the bridesmaids and how even among normal people with normal lives and normal friends, there was always an undercurrent of illicit goings on. People slept with each other and cheated on each other and lied to each other and were in love with the wrong person and married the friend of the person they really loved. Stuff went on. You knew it did. My situation with Rex was not the worst offense. And what difference did it make anyway? All these waves of people, moving through time, through schools, through jobs, mucking their way forward, trying to keep their penises and vaginas away from each other and mostly failing at it, as nature intended. (That would be a good next book: *Penises and Vaginas*, or better yet, *Dicks and Cunts*, but I shouldn't joke about that, someone would no doubt make that exact joke against me, if they hadn't already.)

And what about Rebecca? How did we know she was so innocent and virginal? What if she hooked up with one of these Ohio people? What if she'd done it with Ash! He'd probably slept with a million girls. I wondered where he spent the night last night. Probably sitting in a club chair getting a blow job from the *McSweeny's* girl. Sitting there, king-like with his blue blazer and school tie and perfect literary glasses ... and his literary prize. Fuck your stupid literary prize *Ash Crowley*.

Oh my god, but listen to me! The bitterness was already beginning and my career hadn't even started!

I tried to sleep. I needed to sleep. Instead, I thrashed in my covers. I couldn't believe I had slept with Rex. I really couldn't. How had that happened? That was *insane*.

But whatever. It was done. I'd fucked him. That's what I did apparently. I fucked people. Well, I'd rather be like that then one of those girls who never fucked anyone. There was a lot of that going around New York, I noticed. For being the big bad city, there were a lot of virgins or near virgins walking around. That ancient battle still being waged: *the prisses verses the whores.*

And now *Chicks and Dudes* would seal my fate as one of the "bad girls." Jesus, I couldn't believe I was about to publish a book like that. I'd probably be destroyed by it. That was why Anna hadn't written another book. Because people don't like sluts. Or they like them once, for a very short span of time, and then don't ever want to see them again. It was career suicide to publish a book like *Electra Rising*. And now I was committing the exact same mistake. I was walking right in front of the firing squad.

I rolled out of bed and limped into the bathroom and groggily turned the hot water on in the tub. And my parents, my poor parents, they would be forced to watch it happen. My mother, that hesitancy she had shown all along, "it isn't my kind of book." Even my clueless suburban mom could see what was coming: her naive, misguided daughter had run off to the big city where she had promptly been snatched up, manipulated and exploited. The entire country being treated to me and my blow jobs. I wasn't even good at blow jobs! But oh, I was going to be good at them now, as far as the reading public was concerned, I was going to be the "blow job girl," the dumb hick from the provinces who wanted her moment in the spotlight so bad she would literally fling herself, half-naked, mouth open, prone on her knees, onto the national stage.

And Will Soren had seen dollar signs. And Cynthia Dunleavy had seen them too. *A New York Times* bestseller, guaranteed. The only question in their minds: who will be next. Who will be the new Blow Job Girl, after we've all shot our load onto the pages of Andrea Marr?

And what would I do then? When it was over? Where would I go? I couldn't do like Anna, and move back in with my wacky therapist mom and live out my persona going to *Paris Review* parties. Anna could at least go to rehab at some point. And end up on the dinner party circuit. What could I do? Go back to Oregon?

I'd need to save my money. Maybe I could go to Vermont, live in a little town ... but what would I do there? And what about when the money ran out? I needed to buy time. In ten years would anyone remember my name? Probably not. I could go back to school. Get a teaching certificate: maybe teach little kids in some backwater somewhere. Montana or South Dakota. But no, someone would eventually figure out who I was, they'd find my blow job book on the internet. Maybe I could change my name and tutor high school kids, or special ed, people who couldn't read, or maybe I could just get a normal job, a bookstore job, or I could wait tables, or work at Nordstrom. I had experience in retail, I could get recommendations.

I would go home first. I would go home and get my bearings, like I did when I got kicked out of Wellington. Let Oregon heal me like it does. Soak in the rain. Restart my life. Take a vow of abstinence. No alcohol, no sex, no drugs. I could change my diet and develop a meditation practice.

Or maybe I could stay in New York. Stay and write another book. That was one difference between Anna and me. I could write another book. I had been putting that off, of course, but I could do it. I would write a mature book, a literary novel. Maybe read some of Ash Crowley's short stories. See what the MFA types were doing. I could do that. A "high-literary" plot: a mother dying of cancer. Sisters who had never resolved their past. Maybe a brother who drowned in some terrible accident. All of them driving around in Volvos and going to the summer house. A house by the lake ... the buried secrets ... the stepfather who raped them ... with a boarding school in there somewhere. People loved boarding schools.

Ash Crowley. He kept coming into my mind. What a dick. Sitting there holding court at our "writer's table." And how had Rex and Rebecca failed to mention to him that I had a book too? And not some wussy *story collection*. A novel! I'd been on the cover of the *Sunday Times Magazine*! That beat the shit out of some stupid literary prize in fucking *Iowa*.

Ash Crowley. I couldn't shake the image of him from my mind. With his handsome face and those droll eyes, that whole droll thing, that whole *I'm so bored with everything I don't even care who the rest of you are.* Well guess what Ash? You might be curious to know who *I* am, since I have the best agent in New York and just banked a quarter mil and work with Cynthia Dunleavy who would probably not even bother with you, since you're an annoying little literary snob who nobody but a bunch of MFA geeks even gives a shit about. Cynthia Dunleavy would eat you for breakfast, *Ash*. You little twerp! And what kind of name is Ash anyway? What are you, a southern plantation owner? You racist! And I'm sure it doesn't hurt at all to be a *dude*, and be expected to have a long, lengthy career, punctuated by endless awards and honorariums, while us girls have careers that basically amount to "show us your tits." You little shit.

I had worked myself up pretty good and yet despite my rage, I was still half asleep, sitting there on the edge of the bathtub. I turned off the faucet and touched the water and it was way too hot. And I didn't feel like taking a bath now anyway. Anna had offered me sleeping pills. I should have taken them.

I shuffled back to my bed where the bedside clock said 5:25am. I crawled back into my bed and pulled the covers over my head. God, it was so impossible: this life, this world, these people ...

58

THE NEXT MORNING, I woke up late and nearly missed breakfast at the hotel. I hurried down in my flip-flops and managed to talk the lady into giving me some scrambled eggs, even though the hot part of the breakfast was supposedly over. It wasn't too hard to talk Ohio people into things, I noticed. They didn't want any trouble.

So I got some eggs and a bagel and a cup of badly needed coffee. I found a copy of the *Cleveland Plain Dealer* which had someone else's strawberry jam on the front page. I didn't care. I needed some way to focus my spun-out brain.

There were a few late-morning breakfasters scattered around the large dining room. Some I recognized from the rehearsal dinner but nobody I knew. One young couple in a booth were fighting and spoke in terse, whispery tones. "Propose to me now or forget it!" the girl seemed to be saying. But who knows. I went back to my *Plain Dealer*.

And then Ash appeared. He was dressed in blue slacks, a black Lacoste shirt and his Young Literary Lion glasses. He saw me and actually made eye contact, which I returned with a bland smile. He got some food and some juice and then headed toward my table.

Naturally, I was a little unnerved. He asked if I minded some company. I said I didn't. Ash took the place across from me. He looked a little shy suddenly. He folded his napkin in his lap and said he wanted to apologize for not knowing who I was. The Stanford poetry woman had told him about my book, which had jogged his memory. He had read about me in the *Sunday Times Magazine*. Of course he had, he smiled, was there anything of more interest to the students at the Iowa Writers Workshop than the announcement of a new crop of young American novelists?

That did make sense, and I suddenly didn't mind the company of Ash so much. He told me how a tattered copy of that *Sunday Magazine* had circulated for weeks among his fellow students. Which at the time annoyed Ash terribly, he admitted. "I'm sure you never get jealous of other writers' success," he said dryly. "But I do sometimes fall victim to it."

This made me smile. I looked at Ash who flashed his trademark grin: it was part knowing irony, part boyish charm and part infinite confidence that the universe would give him every-thing he deserved. Which was everything.

"So I wanted to tell you that," he said, taking a bite of toast. "And apologize for being so self-absorbed. Congratu-lations."

"Thank you," I said.

"I can't wait to read your book," he added. "I really mean that."

I didn't know what to say back. We ate from our respective plates. He finished quickly and then told me he was probably going to hang out at the pool later, before he got dressed. Some other people were doing that too, if I wanted to come hang out. I nodded that I would.

He disappeared out of the dining room and I put one last bit of bagel in my mouth and chewed it numbly. I stared at my *Cleveland Plain Dealer*. Oh my god, I totally couldn't wait to hang out with Ash Crowley at the pool. And how I hated myself for it.

In my room I dug out my bathing suit, a bikini from a couple summers ago. I put it on and stood in the full length mirror. I'd lost weight recently, and not in a good way. I studied myself: Boney knees. Pale, pimply white skin. Bags under my eyes. My B cup breasts not helping the saggy bikini top in any way. I tried putting a T-shirt over it, but I didn't seem to have packed one that worked for that purpose. Finally my oldest T-shirt seemed the best choice. At least it was faded. Guys like Ash liked stuff that was old and faded, right? WASPS or whatever, they liked old crap that was quality. I remembered that from Wellington.

I fiddled with my hair. I tried it up. I tried it in a ponytail. It looked terrible. But maybe that was okay. It was understood we were killing a few hours before we got dressed up, right? I'd jump in the pool and then I'd just be wet, like everyone else.

I arrived at the pool, a bathroom towel around my neck, which was not what you were supposed to do. They had special pool towels. Okay. I gave them my bathroom towel and took the not-much-different pool towel. When I entered the pool area, I saw that Ash wasn't there. Nobody was, except for some heavy-set people with kids. I took a chaise lounge away from them and sat there and got a book out of my tote. *Slaves of New York*, it was called. It was by another literary "it girl" that was a couple of "it girls" before Anna, according to Anna. It was pretty fun. So I sat there and tried to read it and then put on sunglasses. It was already pretty humid at like 11:30 in the morning in Ohio. I had never been in the midwest, and there were some definite things I was noticing about it. Everything was empty. There were no people in the hotel. No people on the roads. No people in the airport. Though to compensate, when you did see people, they were quite large.

So then Ash showed up. In stylish sunglasses and a striped T-shirt. He looked amazing of course, but he was also loose and friendly and nice. He came over, looked at the cover of my book, threw his towel on the chaise lounge next to me and dove into the water. While he swam two more guys appeared and then a girl. They started to sit a few chairs away from me, but Ash gestured that he was with me, so they came over and introduced themselves. They were Oberliners. They took off their sunglasses for a second to make proper eye contact. That was another thing about midwesterners: they were polite.

We didn't talk much. Ash was so smooth, so cool. This was not a talking time, I saw. This was down time. But I did ask Ash how many weddings he had been to. He said not that many. Five.

I went back to *Slaves of New York*. It was a collection of linked stories about women in their twenties enslaved by their sexist artist boyfriends in New York in the 1980s. Ash and his friends lay in the sun with their sunglasses on and their sunblock and eventually the Stanford woman came out and made a big fuss of dragging an umbrella over to where we were, because she was sensitive to the sun and she was allergic to sunblock. Ash's friends helped her. So then she sat with us, frowning into a book published by Nebraska University Press that was called *The Poetics of Compassion.*

Feeling strangely central in this mix of people, I sat there, trying to read my book, listening to the little tidbits of conversation between Ash and his guy friends. What did midwestern WASP guys talk about? Not much it turned out. They caught up on the news of their classmates. Was so-and-so going to make it by four o'clock? Flying in from LA? He was working on a TV show out there, making the big bucks and getting "mad girls."

After a couple minutes, everyone fell silent. The overweight family with the kids had gone away. And for a moment there was almost no sound at all. The water lapped quietly against the sides of the pool. Ash, his face turned upward to the sky, remained motionless, casually resembling a Greek god.

59

THE POOL TIME was good preparation for the final event. Back in my room, after a shower, I felt clean, clear-headed, relaxed, ready. I put on my best J.Crew dress, my nice shoes. I blow-dried my hair using a Naomi technique, bending all the way forward at the waist, which gave me a bit of a blood rush when I straightened back up. I wondered what Naomi would think of Ash. She'd like his confidence, or she'd hate it. She was, last I heard, hanging out with a forty-year-old sculptor who lived in a trendy new outer suburb, somewhere "on-the-Hudson." You had to take a special train.

A group of us rode to Rebecca's family farm in a van. We walked across the grass toward the picturesque farmhouse and the perfectly trimmed back lawn behind it. Rex's father was there, in a light brown suit, greeting people. I also met Rebecca's edgy teenaged cousin, Lydia, who was dressed in a high formal goth style: lacy black dress, elbow length gloves, eyeshadow and purple-ish lipstick. I found some Brooklyn people to stand with and chit chat. I noticed how being dressed up changed people's posture, the way they acted and spoke and thought even. This was no great revelation, but I hadn't done that many formal things in my life, so it was fun to experience.

I took a glass of iced tea from a caterer and talked to Rebecca's mother. She was shrewd and funny and also philosophical in a non-annoying, old-person way. I liked her a lot. Just like I liked Rex's dad. Just like I liked all the parents and older people who were here. It was like a dream family ... two dream families actually, joined together by holy matrimony.

During a slow period, I discreetly walked out to the barn and called Anna. I wanted to check in with her, and share with someone the unsettling fact that I was at the wedding of a guy I'd just slept with.

She had forgotten all about it. I had to remind her "You know the engaged guy? That everyone told me to steal away from his girlfriend?"

Anna remembered. But she wasn't that impressed. She was in the Hamptons at a music industry party where much worse things were happening.

So then I told her I liked *Slaves of New York*. Anna did too and said she had tracked down Tama Janowitz, the author, a couple years before. "She wasn't even that old," she said. Then I told her about Ash Crowley, describing how handsome and successful he seemed. She said I should marry him because he'd have a long career and I could ride his coat tails and get teaching gigs at prestigious colleges. Which made me a little mad and I was like, "But he hasn't even written a novel yet!" Anna said it didn't matter. "In this business, the boys always win," she said. "You just have to accept it."

The wedding was at 6pm. The ceremony was behind the house in the shade of a beautiful oak tree that someone said was over a hundred years old. Rows of white folding chairs formed neat lines, and there was a little area in front for the ceremony. I sat about halfway back, next to the Stanford poetry woman and then Ash, who had been mysteriously absent the last hour, came and sat beside me on the other side. "Hey," he said under his breath. "Hey," I said back.

The seats filled up and the backyard grew quiet. The music, which had been playing quietly on the sound system was turned up. People gradually came to attention. We sat and waited, looking around at each other. It seemed to take forever, but that was the point I guess: a little glimpse of the eternity of marriage. I caught myself glancing at Ash a few times. And then smiling at the Stanford poetry woman who seemed troubled.

Finally, a little girl came down the aisle carrying a basket of flowers. She was so lovely, so adorable, it made me think that Rebecca would be pregnant within the year.

I braced myself for what was coming next. Rex. A door opened at the farm house and out he came, his face lowered, his shoulders square. I kind of lost my shit for a second when I saw that. I could feel my face collapse slightly. Ash saw the change in my expression and gave me a quizzical look. I smiled like it was nothing. Just getting emotional. Just being a girl.

Rex came closer. The hundred of us turned and watched him approach, the girls beaming, the boys looking on with stoic calm. Rex wore a simple black suit, a black tie. His hair was freshly combed, so that he looked even more youthful and boyish than usual. His older brother was with him. He was several years older than Rex and had lived a strange, disconnected life, which included military service and possibly drug addiction or mental illness. He had done his best to remain in the background, but it was hard not to notice him.

"His brother was in Iraq," whispered Ash, seemingly reading my mind.

"I know, you can tell, right?" I whispered back.

Ash nodded.

And then Rebecca came out. She was on the verge of tears. I couldn't watch her. Or rather, I locked my eyes onto the bouquet she was carrying and didn't look at anything else.

They made their way to the front. The lesbian minister began to speak. I couldn't watch this either. But I kept my face pointed in their direction so as not to give myself away. My eyes filled with tears at several different points. Not for any particular reason. More for the general irrevocability of things. The fact that you don't really have a plan in life, and then one day, your fate appears before you, and that's it. That's your life. Game over.

I endured the ceremony. I remained facing forward, my eyes in the general direction of what was happening, always focusing on some object just to the right or left of whatever everyone else was looking at.

The lesbian minister asked the final questions and then the rings came out and were put on the fingers. Rex and Rebecca kissed and then smiled back at the rest of us as we clapped and hooted our approval. I clapped too and gushed appropriately and did everything that everyone else did.

Afterward, in the fading daylight, Rebecca was the star of the backyard mingle. She wandered around, having her picture taken, crying, gushing over her friends and family. Rex hovered nearby, sometimes bolstering her up, other times tactfully moving away as she tearfully hugged and kissed her friends and relatives. It was obvious there was no avoiding her, and so I slid in with a group of girls that included Lydia, her teenage cousin. As she gushed over the group of us, Rebecca suddenly saw me, suddenly recognized me as if for the first time. Her face froze for a terrifying second and then she collapsed into me, as she had the others, telling me what a great friend I was and how grateful she was to be part of my exciting life, and how Rex loved me so much, both of them did, and congratulations on my book. She hugged me deeply and then quickly moved on to the next person, saying many of the same things, and meaning them all.

And so I faded into the shadows again, into the anonymity of the others, finding my way yet again to the Stanford poetry woman. There, I stood and sipped at another glass of iced tea, and mentioned for the millionth time how beautiful the farm was and what a perfect place for a wedding.

60

AFTER DARK, people loosened their ties and took off their shoes and circulated among the tables. Music played. Ash Crowley appeared at a table I was sitting at, and took the seat beside me. We exchanged notes on the goings on. He asked me if the wedding made me want to get married. I told him truthfully it did not. He said of course not, I had other things going on, I had my book coming out, I had a career. "Your personal life will probably be a disaster," he said. "Like all great artists." I asked him if his personal life would be a disaster and he said he certainly hoped so.

We talked about other things. We made fun of Ohioans. Ash was originally from Chicago. Or a suburb outside it. He wanted to know about New York and I told him about my "starter" apartment, how each new person started in the worst room and moved up progressively, as people moved on to better places or got spit out of New York altogether. He thought that scenario might make a good novel. He wondered if there had been a novel told from an apartment's perspective. Like starting back in 1906 or whenever. It was an interesting idea, I admitted. Ash said, "You can have it. It's my gift to you."

315

Later people danced and I separated from Ash and sat with Lydia, the goth teenager. We had been eyeing each other all day. She was applying to colleges next year and I told her the short version of my time at Wellington. She was like me. She was from a small town in Illinois and she was worried she would not fit in at a posh private school like Oberlin or Wellington. I told her to go anyway. You had to. How else were you going to learn?

Meanwhile, Rex made the rounds. I watched him out of the corner of my eye. He worked the room, shaking hands, not saying much, letting other people tell him about his wedding.

He reached the table where I sat with Lydia. He was excited to see us together. He told Lydia about my book, gushing, saying I would soon be famous and she could tell people she had known me when. The cousin gasped at this and stared at me. "He's kidding," I told her.

A moment later, Lydia ran off. Rex seeing a chance for us to be alone, sat down in the chair next to me. I didn't know what he was doing, and was naturally nervous for a second, though careful to not stop smiling.

Rex had seen me talking to Ash. He liked Ash. Ash was great. I should stay in touch and hang out with him when he moved to New York. But that wasn't what Rex wanted to talk to me about. His tone changed and he looked into my eyes. He told me he valued our friendship. He told me how much Rebecca loved me. How I was practically family to them back in Brooklyn.

I realized, we were having a moment. We were having a *wedding moment*. He looked me right in the eye and smiled in a deeply serious way, and I was made to understand that everything was starting over, that the slate was wiped clean, everything was new again. He loved me as a friend and he trusted me. It was touching. Or would have been, if I was the type of person who actually wanted things like this to be said out loud, in highly dramatic settings, like *weddings*. Which I wasn't.

He caught the skeptical look on my face and he grinned. "I'm jealous of Ash," said Rex. "He's going to get to know you. You guys will probably fall in love."

I didn't answer. We were back to where we started now. Back to me being the cool, jaded one and him being the dorky *Context* guy. He really was a "book nerd" in the end.

So then I had a real drink. A vodka and tonic, like Naomi taught me. And I danced.

Ash was around. Not with me in any confirmable way, but around. At one point an old love song came on and people slow danced, ironically, 1950s style, with the boy's hand on your waist and your hand on his shoulder.

At that point, Ash showed up again. He found me on the sidelines and asked me, with a slight bow, if he could have this dance.

I didn't have shoes on at this point but the grass was cool and comfortable on my bare feet. I followed him into the slow moving, waltzing crowd. Everyone was enjoying the goofiness of the dance. Ash and I did too. But it was also perfect in a way, to move like that, face to face, not too close but just close enough, so that you could smell your partner, and feel the warmth of his body, and of his hand in yours.

As the party thinned out, I ended up sitting with a bunch of people at a table under Christmas lights in a tree. Someone had brought over several large slabs of wedding cake, which people poked and nibbled at with white plastic forks. Rebecca came over and sat for a while, and nobody talked, we all just sat and smiled at her in that profound way. Milestones. Passages.

Ash and I were loaded into the same crowded van back to the hotel. I was forced up against the window in one of the middle benches. Ash was late getting in. "Can I switch with you?" he whispered to the guy next to me. I pretended I didn't notice this maneuver. But I was secretly thrilled.

With Ash now jammed against me, I smiled and looked out the window. "Quite a night," he said to me. I nodded that it was. As more people got in, our shoulders were pressed together. Then our thighs. When it became really cramped, Ash lifted his arm and put it around my shoulders to make a little extra room.

When we got back to the hotel, it was late, but nobody felt like separating and a bunch of us ended up in Ash's room with several warm bottles of our complimentary wine. About eight of us flopped on the beds, or sat on the floor. Someone went somewhere and came back with some wedding food and chips. And so we lay around on the beds. Someone figured out how to make the TV play songs from the eighties. Someone had some pot and a few people went outside and smoked it. Everyone got a second wind it seemed like, and for an hour or two, everyone was chattering away again in full party mode.

Eventually though, the energy lulled and the next thing I knew I had dozed off on one of the beds, me and another girl, with Ash still talking on the other bed, and some other people still awake on the floor. I laid my head down again, shut my eyes and this time, when I woke up, it was dark and I was cold. The room was nearly empty. A couple was asleep on Ash's bed and Ash was now on my bed, also asleep. I had burrowed partially under the blankets and Ash was on the outside of the same blankets but with his forehead close to my shoulder and his body curled around my back, in a classic spooning position.

Before I could think about it, I matter of factly rolled Ash over, included him under my blankets and then spooned with him from that direction, nestling my face into the back of his dress shirt, where I savored each breath of his musky boy-smell until I melted back into blissful sleep.

61

THE NEXT MORNING, brunch was served at the farm. Ash sat with me at the outdoor tables under the oak tree. I had sunglasses on, as did most people.

Ash didn't say much. I didn't either. Others came over, our table filled up. People talked and it was as before, good wishes, warm feelings, shared love among the group, but now with more practical matters interspersed. Travel plans. Airport shuttles. Inner circle family concerns: Rex and Rebecca would fly to Athens that night. A grandparent had to get back to Florida. Lydia, who I had so carefully advised about her future, wanted to drive to Toronto with her questionable ex-boyfriend to see Tool. Her mother would not allow it. Rex was nowhere to be found, and at one point Rebecca came out, wandered around with a worried look on her face, and then went back inside without speaking.

Ash went back to the hotel with a friend. His flight was an hour before mine. Without Ash around I was instantly bored and got the next ride back to the hotel fifteen minutes later. I went up to my room, quickly freshened up, then hurried back downstairs and lingered in the lobby a bit, making a cup of tea from the hot water machine and hoping to perhaps see Ash off. But I missed him somehow. One of the Oberlin girls saw me and guessed who I was looking for and said Ash had left to possibly catch an earlier flight. A bunch of people had gone. I nodded. I dabbed my tea bag into the steaming water.

I flew back to New York in a daze. I got off in stinky, filthy LaGuardia airport and got a cab back to my apartment, where I dumped my crap and walked up the street toward the Thai place. Greenpoint was hot and dirty and uninteresting. Nobody was young or good looking, there was no grass, no barns, no Saabs parked under oak trees. And now no Rex. That would take some getting used to. I called Anna Madsen, who was still in the Hamptons, but she didn't answer. After lunch, I went home and laid down and fell asleep for an hour and woke up sweaty and jet lagged and completely out of sorts.

So I went for a walk to McCaren Park and sat on a bench and drank iced coffee. And cried a little.

I went back to work at *In Focus* on Monday, which was a relief, though some new unspoken separation had taken place between my coworkers and me. A new girl had been hired and she stared at me oddly every time she went by my cubicle. *Sit Next To Me*, another of the new gossip websites, had recently published the advances of all the fall's "hot titles." My advance was mistakenly listed at $250,000. It was only a small website, so I didn't know if anyone had actually seen it or not. Still, it made me paranoid. "Why does she even work here?" I thought I heard someone say in the stairwell one morning. Though I had no proof they were talking about me, or even if they were from our floor.

· · ·

Josh Greenberg called. He was his usual fast-talking self. He asked how the wedding was. I said it was fine. Did I feel like hitting a movie later? I didn't have anything else to do. So I said yes.

I found Josh, slouched in a chair inside the theater. He popped up when I came in. The movie choices weren't so great and we ended up at a new artsy Polish film about runaway girls. It was boring so we snuck into an animated cartoon, which wasn't much better, and was full of little kids. So we bailed out of that and watched the end of a thriller where a bunch of people got shot up in a glass elevator in Asia somewhere.

Then it was back into the summer night. That was nice. Now I felt relieved to be away from Ohio and all those earnest feelings and back in the gritty hardness of the big city. Josh and I walked around for a while and drank iced coffees. He told me stories of being a kid in Queens and coming into CBGBs to see the Melvins. It was not unlike my life in Portland. But also totally different.

Anna Madsen finally got her ass back from the Hamptons. I literally couldn't wait to see her. We went to this new bar that had opened up in the Meat Packing District. These two French film producers started talking to us. They were so good looking they had to be gay, but maybe not, Anna said in the bathroom as she tweaked her look in the direction of "even more slutty."

The French guys took us to a modeling agency party they knew about on the roof of a building in Tribeca. I didn't know who the models were, but there were some people I think were on TV. Several people knew Anna, and came over to her to praise *Electra Rising*, which we both found reassuring. An actress I didn't know then cornered us and said her production company was negotiating for the film rights for *Electra Rising*, which was not true, but Anna Madsen didn't say anything. And of course there were guys around, and Anna and I, not being models and having actual flesh on our bones, enjoyed some attention from the more hetero types around.

Eventually we ended up at another party, at a loud nightclub nearby. This was less fun, and after an hour, I told Anna I had to go. I went outside, but it was suddenly raining so I ducked under an awning and waited for a cab. I wasn't actually in a hurry to get anywhere, so I ended up just standing there, watching the rain fall and the cars drive by and the late night partiers running by in their fancy clothes that were probably getting ruined in the grimy New York rain.

Then Anna appeared. She had come outside the main door so she could talk on her phone. She didn't see me several doorways down. She said "Clarisse?" into her phone. "Fuck yeah, I'm coming over … I told you it would be late … baby, I need to see you …. of course … you know I want to …"

She slipped her phone into her bag and ventured out toward the street with her hand raised. She was so good at that. The cab wave. She was facing away from me, but I made sure to stay out of sight. Not that I was alarmed that Anna was bisexual. I already knew that. It had been in *Electra Rising*. The affair with the loner girl at summer camp, as well as the much discussed chapter describing her and another "straight" friend going to clubs in high school, dancing with guys, making out with guys, getting themselves as worked up as humanly possible and then slipping off to be with each other, thus ensuring sexual satisfaction.

Still, who was Clarisse? Not that it was any of my business. The idea of bisexual Anna did make me wonder about all those times at her mother's apartment when the two of us sat around half-naked. Well, whatever. It didn't matter. It was just one of those things that made an already crazy New York summer a little weirder than it already was. More human complexity for my harried brain to process.

A week later, I went out with Josh again, to a party a friend of his was having at a bar in the East Village. I let him kiss me as we stood against the back wall. He was a good kisser, which I was not expecting and caught me off guard. But I didn't want to do anything else, which pissed him off. He kept trying though, kissing me more and sliding his hands around to my ass, like we were teenagers. He was such a New Yorker. He was always pushing you. Always trying to get a little more.

We ended up arguing and then fighting and then I left, which freaked him out. He chased me down the sidewalk, trying to explain, but also arguing with me more, loudly and right in front of passersby. I got mad and hissed back at him: "I'm from Oregon! We don't fight over every little thing!"

Coming home from *In Focus* one day, there was a postcard from the island Mykonos in Greece. The photo showed the sun glistening on the ocean and a stony hillside dotted with immaculate white houses. The back said that Rex and Rebecca were having a wonderful time and that Greece was the most beautiful place on the planet. The postcard was signed "R&R." I taped it to the wall over my little bureau, but as time went on, it annoyed me and I put it behind my laundry basket.

62

FOR THE FOURTH OF JULY, I went to Boston to hang out with Sally and go see the Boston Pops do their famous Fourth of July show. They were making an extra big deal about it since it was the year 2000. A high school friend of hers came with us, Jessica, and we all sat on a blanket and listened to the symphony and watched the other people around us with their blankets and beach chairs and picnic baskets. We hadn't brought the right stuff, we had a bottle of Pellegrino water and some tortilla chips and when it got cold we had to wrap ourselves, the three of us, in the blanket we were supposed to be sitting on.

Afterwards, we walked around and talked. Jessica was smart and nice, typical of the people Sally always seemed to have around her. I liked Jessica so much, right away, and even when Sally talked about my book, Jessica was nice and interested in what it was like to get a book published, and asked questions, and it was such a relief not to worry about someone getting weird or being jealous or whatever.

Also, you could tell she was excited to be hanging out with

Sally. They were obviously going to be best friends if they weren't already. And Sally had only been here a month! Some people just had good luck finding friends. Sally was herself such a solid person and generous and not someone who thought about herself too much. That was why. She wasn't trying to get anything or be anything. She just was. It was very zen.

So then the next day the three of us went to the movies and then hung out in Harvard Square and met up with two guys Sally and Jessica knew. The four of them were sort of a gang, I realized. And suddenly I felt like I was the third wheel—or the fifth wheel in this case—though everyone was super nice and treated me like an old friend. After that, we went to a barbecue in someone's backyard. Some of these people were from the *Boston Globe*, but they were young, like Sally, so they didn't do anything important yet.

We ate barbecue food: burgers and tofu dogs and salad. I ate too many kettle chips. It was pretty fun. Eventually though, I started to get this anxious feeling in my stomach. I was a little bored I guess. I wanted to be back in New York, being the hot new writer, even if people hated me for it, instead of sitting in someone's backyard in Boston being some girl nobody knew.

I had one more trip that summer, which was one week back in Oregon. This had been planned for months, and was for my nephew Marcus's sixth birthday. Also, my niece Grace was two and a half and I hadn't seen her in a year. These were the kids of my older brother James, who was still living in Seattle with his horrible wife Emily. There had been talk they might break up over James's drinking, but that hadn't happened. Instead, they were all coming down to Portland so everyone could hang out with my parents at the old house, since they were thinking about moving.

This trip was strange from the start. My mom picked me up at the airport. I hadn't seen her since before the book stuff started. She looked okay, a year older, but mostly the same. We hugged and that felt good, but as soon as we were in the car, she started to talk nervously about random things, like where everyone was going to sleep, as if I might object, which of course I wouldn't.

Dad was more normal. He gave me a big hug and joked about "our author." I could see they had the *Sunday Times Magazine* with my picture on it on the coffee table right where you couldn't miss it as you walked in. My mother didn't seem to like it there, and moved it after I'd been home for twenty minutes. I had this terrible picture in my mind of my parents fighting over where the months-old magazine should be casually sitting when friends came over.

My brother arrived shortly with Marcus and Grace in tow. They had been to the zoo. Marcus stared at me. He was a lot bigger than he'd been a year ago. Grace didn't seem to know who I was and came over to me and I picked her up and everyone beamed and was happy that the different Marr generations were bonding. Then Emily, who hates everyone, returned from wherever she was, and wanted Marcus to go wash his hands for some reason. When he wouldn't, she grabbed him and dragged him to the bathroom in a fury.

And so it went. Weird vibes. My brother James was the only one who saw the humor in the book situation. He would look at me knowingly for a few seconds and then burst out laughing. Or he'd high five me for no apparent reason. At one point he joked that I would have to support him and the kids when Emily left him and took his money.

At night, I watched TV with my dad. That was nice and at least relaxing. He had gotten more conservative it seemed like, about politics and life in general, but that was probably just him getting old. And also me living in New York, where no one was like that, and if someone was, everyone freaked out, like conservatives were pure evil and racists and probably child molestors. But my dad wasn't like that. He was just a typical older man who lived in the suburbs and watched too much TV.

I had decided to lie low for those six days and just do family stuff, but eventually I got bored and drove into downtown Portland. I went to Powell's, the huge used bookstore. In high school, my friend Cybil and I discovered our first "cool" books there. Like *The Basketball Diaries* or *Love and Rockets*. It was where I first learned that there was such a thing.

Powell's was pretty quiet on a Tuesday night in the middle of July. There were some quiet book browsers, a few dorky teenagers, a couple classic Portland weirdos, with old sweaters and their glasses taped together. I loved it there. I thought of how fun it would be to come here someday and see my own book. My book about Portland!

Another thing I discovered that night: there'd been a major transition in the local music scene. All the music clubs I knew of were suddenly gone. New places had appeared: The Fort, Blackies, The Egyptian Room. I didn't learn this by actually going to these places, but by reading the new alternative weekly called *The Mercury*. All the bands were different too. As I glanced through the CD reviews, not only had I never heard of the local bands, I didn't even know the national bands they were talking about. I was losing touch with that stuff. I would need to find something else to write my next book about. No more indie rock soap operas for me.

Meanwhile, life at my parents' was annoying and Emily, as usual, could barely stand to be in the same house with me. On the day of Marcus's party, it got so painful I volunteered to go to the store for last-minute party supplies and took as long as possible doing it.

I was standing in the supermarket aisle when my cell phone rang. I was alarmed to see the number was from Cynthia Dunleavy's office. "Hello?" I said. "*Hello!?*" Cynthia barked in her most insistent voice. "Is this Andrea?"

She told me the party date was set, August 24th. I didn't know what she was talking about, but tried to let her know this gradually. "The party ... ?" I said noncommittally. "Your publication party," she barked. "Your *launch* party."

I mumbled something back and Cynthia attacked: Hadn't I discussed this with Miguel? Hadn't I checked my dates with him? "Miguel is your publicist," she said. "It's up to you to coordinate with him. This is your book, you know. Its success or failure is up to you and no one else."

"Okay," I said.

She said more: what about the location of the party? Was I happy with it? Had I checked in with Miguel about the guest list? And what else was I doing? And why wasn't I talking to Miguel on a daily basis? And what kind of contacts did I have in the media? Hadn't I claimed to know someone at *The New York Times*? "I've already been in the *Times,*" I said, and immediately regretted it. "That was six months ago!" she barked. "I would get on that, if I were you."

I agreed that I would.

So then I put down the bag of Snickers mini bars I was holding and dialed Miguel, who of course didn't take my call.

But then a minute later, he did call me back and informed

me we were having the book launch at CBGBs Gallery on August 24, and it would be nice if I could come, if I wouldn't mind, if I wasn't too busy. I didn't take the bait and said, of course I'd be there. I thanked him. And he hung up on me.

THANK GOD FOR ANNA MADSEN. Driving back to my parents, I called her at The Yaddo Writers Colony where she was sleeping with a married guy and trying desperately to start a new book. I told her the story of Miguel. Anna said not to worry, she would take care of it. I was like, "Don't do anything —." But she had already hung up.

She called Will Soren, who called Cynthia Dunleavy, who apparently called Miguel and chewed his ass out, because he called me back an hour later and sounded even more spiteful and sarcastic. He wanted to know which famous musician or celebrity I was having host it. I was like, "What?" He had another call and wanted me to think about it and then of course he never called me back. So I called Anna back, and asked her why on earth Miguel hated me so much.

"Because you're young and talented and he isn't?" she said. She told me not to worry about it. "Fuck that asshole, I'll host your fucking party and we'll invite a million cool people and he can fuck off."

This made me feel a little better and like I could put my

phone away and devote myself to the task at hand, which at that moment was putting a cone-shaped birthday hat on our dog so that James could take a picture.

I couldn't wait to get out of Portland, or so I thought until I was on the plane, waiting for takeoff and then I started crying again. It was embarrassing how often this happened. You'd think someone had died. And then I discovered the two people sitting beside me were newlyweds from a small town on the Oregon coast who were going to New York for their honeymoon. So then I felt obligated to give them New York tips, to share my knowledge, but they weren't really interested, they just wanted to see the Statue of Liberty and go shopping and have sex in their hotel room. So I shut up and left them to look lovingly into each other's eyes and hold hands and then later to grip each other's forearms when the plane started to bounce around in the summer storms over the midwest.

I hit the ground running back in Greenpoint. Rex and Rebecca were back. I got an email from Rebecca at work, inviting me to an upcoming party. There was also an email from Ash. I had been waiting for this. It had been a month since the wedding. He was arriving August first, he had a sublet set up, a one bedroom in Park Slope, was I near there? He would need some things and since I had claimed to be a thrift store shopper, maybe I could help. He was nervous of course, about the move, but excited, and he was looking forward to seeing me, if I could find some time for him.

I didn't understand this email. First of all, why had it taken so long? Hadn't we hit it off at the wedding? Didn't he change seats in the van to sit with me? Hadn't we spent the night spooning? We were two young writers, both on the verge of success! Who else could he want to hang out with besides me?

I ran this email past Anna Madsen. She didn't think much of it. I insisted that Ash was funny and smart and probably very talented. I wanted more than some casual email. Also, how the hell did he get a one-bedroom apartment in Park Slope without even stepping foot in New York?

"I don't like the sound of this guy," said Anna Madsen. "I don't trust people from Iowa."

So then I had Ash Crowley on the brain for the next week. I wondered when he would call and where we would go and what I could show him, or how I could impress him, though technically, I shouldn't have to do that. What could impress a guy like that more than what I had already done? And yet I already felt totally inferior to him: the magically corrosive charisma of Ash Crowley.

Those feelings were assuaged somewhat when Will Soren called me during my lunch break the next day to tell me that Rampart Films wanted to option *Chicks and Dudes* and were about to make an offer. I asked him what that meant exactly and he said: "More money."

Will took me to lunch the next day, to give me updates on everything supposedly, but also he seemed to need someone to have lunch with. He took me to a new Italian place he'd been going to. It was a dark room and the people recognized him instantly and threw themselves at him, kissing his ass, and addressing him as Mr. Soren from the moment he walked in.

We sat and ate and chatted, but Will wasn't as funny as he was when it was Anna and Will and I. I thought: "I'm no Anna, when it comes to conversation." But I hoped that would be okay. Especially if someone might make a movie out of my book.

I tried talking about the wedding, but Will didn't seem interested. He looked tired. Tired and old. How old was he? I looked more closely at his face. He had a lot of secret wrinkles. Was he as old as my dad? He might be.

I stopped staring at him and focused on my pasta. It wasn't the kind I thought it was. I still didn't know how to order in fancy restaurants. There were still so many things I didn't know, it seemed.

Then Bridget, who had been "summering" in various places with her mother, suddenly announced that she was moving out. She hadn't paid her rent yet, and I knew immediately she was going to screw us by the way she told me and the distant manner she took with Mari and I. Maybe it was time for me to move too.

Josh Greenberg called and wanted to take me out to dinner. Since Rex and Rebecca weren't around and Ash still hadn't arrived, I said yes. Josh took me for sushi and apologized for yelling at me on the street. He seemed determined to win me back, though he had never had me, so I don't know what he was thinking.

Two nights later, he texted me from a party in Bushwick. I was bored and sitting on the fire escape with Mari, so the two of us got a car service and went. But once there, we couldn't figure out where the building was, or how to get into it, even though we could hear the party raging above us. Bushwick had become an ongoing experiment in communal hipsterism. It was famous for its huge industrial buildings, rebuilt and reconfigured into elaborate living spaces, with like rope ladders and pirate walkways.

Anyway, so I called Josh and told him we were outside on the street. He came down and found us and we followed him through a dark passageway and then up through this caged-in staircase system and ended up on the roof where the party was. It was a pretty rocking party. Mari was impressed. She always thought of me as an uptight liberal arts bookworm for some reason. She still hadn't read my book, even though I gave her a galley months ago

We got some beer and Mari and I did a tequila shot with Josh and his friends. That sort of woke me up and then we danced and I relaxed and got into it, even though I felt sort of old now, since the kids around me looked like they were nineteen or twenty, which was the optimum age to live in Bushwick.

Then I saw Dana. From Portland. She was hanging out with some skeevy dudes along one side of the roof. I didn't say anything to her. She seemed like she was doing okay. She was still alive. And she was at the right party, with her black eye makeup and her black jean cutoffs and her pale legs and her puffed up mohawk hair thing. It was probably for the best I didn't let her move in. Even though Bridget was going to screw us on the rent.

I felt like I could stay up all night for some reason and so we did, dancing and drinking and goofing around. At four in the morning, Mari and another girl got a car service back to Greenpoint. Josh and I ended up walking through the deserted streets of industrial Bushwick, back toward Williamsburg. Josh kept putting his arm around me, in this casual way which was hard for him since he was shorter than me.

He wanted me to come back to his apartment. I wouldn't. I

knew if I was alone with him, in a bed, he would be all over me, no matter what he said now. I was not up for a battle like that. I would probably never be. I needed to stick with polite upper-middle class suburbanites, like Rex and Rebecca. And Ash. And Bridget who was going to screw us on the rent money.

64

REX AND REBECCA had their official "welcome back" dinner party. Mari and I had become better friends recently, so she came too. We rode the subway to their apartment and Rebecca let us in. Most of the other people were already there. Thanks to the wedding, I knew everyone and we stood around talking and joking and congratulating Rex and Rebecca on their wedding and their honeymoon and on life in general.

And then Ash walked in, fashionably late, of course. I had a feeling he might show up, though I hadn't dared to ask Rex or Rebecca if he was invited. He was by himself, so that was one good thing. He was wearing cutoffs, which didn't look right on him—too informal—and made you wonder if that was for Rex and Rebecca's sake. To counterbalance, he wore a striped polo shirt and dark socks and soft leather loafers of some sort. He looked a little overheated from the walk from the subway, but still very calm and in control, like he always did. He had some expensive goat cheese and artisan bread.

Mari was sure impressed. I had told her the story of our time together at the wedding and how we slept curled up in his hotel room. Now she gave me this look like, *that's him? He's hot!*

And I shrugged, like *I know*. Ash followed Rebecca into the kitchen where he was given a mint julep, and where he effortlessly became the center of attention.

So then we drank mint juleps and everyone got a little drunk, which was fun. One of the cuter guys, Brian, chatted up Mari and me. Mari magically made Brian want to sleep with her like she does. And I magically lapsed into awkward silence like I do. Rex came over and with a totally straight face told me about how amazing Greece was and how you could actually feel the ancient stories and myths around you. Like when he went swimming at night in the Mediterranean, he would imagine Ulysses swimming in that same water, thousands of years before. I was like, "That sounds fun." And then Rebecca came over and joined in our conversation, and she looked at me with so much love and admiration it was weird. She wanted to know what was happening with my book, so I started telling the story of Miguel, my horrible publicist, and everyone seemed very interested in that. I was a little drunk so I went on with it, including the part where I called Anna Madsen and she called Will Soren and he called Cynthia Dunleavy and she called Miguel who got chewed out and then called me and very meanly demanded to know what celebrity I was getting to host my party. Everyone was amazed by this story. I had the whole room's attention now, and, when I looked up even Ash Crowley was listening very closely. "You're friends with Anna Madsen?" he finally asked.

"She's pretty much my best friend," I said casually, and took another swig of my mint julep.

. . .

Eating dinner, Ash was on one end of the table and I was on the other end with Mari and Brian. Brian had become very attentive and was obviously hoping to sleep with Mari, possibly that night, which he actually had a pretty good shot at. I just hoped they went to his place.

Ash was talking mostly to Rebecca. They were discussing Park Slope. Ash began telling everyone his initial impressions of the famously annoying neighborhood: the breast-feeding controversies, the stroller warfare, the organic food debates ... Ash was very funny. With his dry, midwestern wit, he picked Park Slope apart in hilarious and deadly accurate detail. It was easy to see why he had been a star at Iowa.

I also wondered what he thought of Anna Madsen. Probably not that much. But he had to respect her honesty and her courage to bare herself open to the world like that. Even if he was more "literary" than her, he had to acknowledge the immediacy and relevancy of *Electra Rising*.

When it was time for dessert, people abandoned the dinner table and took their slices of apple pie and iced cream and sat closer to the air conditioning in the living room area. Ash came and sat beside me. He wanted to hear about Anna, and I told him about our friendship, how I had called her, and was very intimidated at first, but then we became friends, and she had helped me so much and was going to host my book party, which was now only a couple weeks away. He listened very closely to this. I asked him if he liked *Electra Rising*. He hadn't read it. But people at Iowa had argued about it endlessly. Ash thought it sounded more like a memoir than a novel. He thought a good novelist needed to create characters beyond themselves and their friends. At the same time, he admitted, Anna Madsen had obviously struck a chord with a lot of people. He was looking forward to reading *Electra Rising*. When he added that last part, I knew he was being diplomatic and didn't necessarily mean it. So easily did Ash slip from being casually honest and open to being a literary politician. He would go far, this young man.

I was so in love with Ash. It pissed me off, but it was true. Everyone else was going to be too. He was all I could think about as the night wound down. Naturally, he was the first to leave. He'd been in New York a week and he already had better things to do than hang out with us! As soon as he was gone, all the air went out of the party. For me, it did. Mari and her new boyfriend Brian wanted me to come have a drink with them, but I made an excuse and instead took a long walk home, through the lively summer streets of Williamsburg, which seemed even younger and trendier than usual. When fall came, that's when you'd really see the newcomers. Like at college.

The next morning I got an email from Will Soren which contained the first review of *Chicks and Dudes*. It was from *Publisher's Weekly*.

I had been reading *PW* for a long time now and I trusted their reviews. They were no bullshit, no politics, no showing off. They told you the basic concept of the book and if it worked or not.

I read the review so fast the first time I couldn't figure out if it was pro or con. It was not "starred," but the review itself was pretty good. The best line was: "Marr brings a world of unlikely, and in some cases, unsavory characters to life." I went back and looked at the email and saw that Will Soren considered it "very positive" and had congratulated me on it.

So that was good. And of course I wanted to show it to someone, but I was at work and there was no one to show it to.

Walter and I didn't really talk anymore for some reason. And Veronica, as understanding as she was, never wanted to hear anything specific about what was going with me. Of course I forwarded it to Anna Madsen and got a return email that was a thousand exclamation points filling up my email page. So then I forwarded it to Rex, and then my parents, and then some other people. Then I typed Ash Crowley into the forward email space. I had assumed from the wedding that we were destined to be friends, or at least the kind of writer acquaintances that could send each other things like this. But would he want to see it? I honestly didn't know. I hit SEND anyway. Fuck him if he didn't want to be friends. I would act like we were until he told me otherwise.

65

MY HOURS AT *IN FOCUS*, which were already down to eighteen a week, were further reduced in August to sixteen a week. Everyone was working less. *In Focus* was starting a website in the fall, so we were probably all going to get fired and be replaced by computer people soon enough. The whole nature of photography was changing, as people kept saying. The new digital cameras had pretty much replaced film cameras. And of course people had cameras in their phones now, crappy ones, but you could see where it was going: everyone would very soon be able to take pictures of anything at any time, in any way they felt like it. It was like our brains were being turned inside out. Anything we saw or experienced, would now also be recorded and saved forever. And it didn't cost anything per picture, so you could shoot away, as much as you felt like, which was exactly what people did.

Anyway, on Wednesday, I had one of my 11am to 3pm shifts at *In Focus*. This was the week after Rex and Rebecca's dinner party (no response from Ash about my *PW* review.) So then I was in the city at 3pm, with nothing to do. So I got an iced coffee and started walking and doing something I hadn't done much of recently: day dreaming about my book. Like thinking about what might happen and letting my body really feel it, the exhilaration of it, which I didn't do often, thinking that it would be bad karma to indulge myself.

But not today. Today I let myself fill up with it. *My book was being published.* Nobody could stop it now. Not Miguel, not Ash, not anyone. I didn't let my thoughts get any more specific than that. I let myself be happy and proud and excited and nervous. I took deep breaths and thought about other possibilities, like what if it was a bestseller or what if I was on Oprah or what if it was made into a movie? From there, I let my mind wander into broader things, into a bigger happiness, like just how spectacularly things had worked out, and how amazing it felt to be young and "on the brink" and walking the streets of New York City.

From *In Focus*, I went first to Union Square, which I never got tired of and which I especially loved in the summer because of the cute teenagers sitting on the steps and the skateboarders and the tourists and the way nobody cared about anything because it was muggy and hot and August.

I continued down University Place, and through Washington Square Park where couples sat fanning themselves on the benches. I passed the NYU Law School buildings which I knew about because I went on a date a long time ago with a guy who went there (where was he now?).

I walked through the leafy mellowness of Greenwich Village to Houston street and crossed against the light, since there wasn't much traffic, since it was August. I kept going southward through the narrow streets of SoHo to Canal, which was one of my favorite streets, with the scrappy Chinese people and the electronics shops and the oldness of it, and the hard stoniness of the actual streets and sidewalks.

From there I passed into Tribeca, with its familiar cafés and cobblestone streets and Kinney Publishing, which I usually avoided. Today I walked right in front of it though, and looked at the shiny silver intercom, where my whole New York life began.

By now I had finished my iced coffee and threw it on top of an overflowing garbage can and within two more blocks, needed more liquid because of the humidity. I went inside a bodega and found my way to the refrigerated drink section. I caught a glimpse of myself in a mirror, in my cut off jeans and the red and white tank top I had stolen from Mari because it looked so sexy on her. It didn't look as great on me, but whatever, my face still looked good, and I'd begun to look older, and more mature, like a real writer, which was important. I could be interviewed at the 92nd Street Y or go to a writers colony or something like that, if I had to. Or like if my picture was next to Joyce Carol Oates's picture, or if I married Ash, and we lived in Brooklyn Heights and had cocktail parties, I wouldn't look too out of place. I could pass. Writers always looked weird anyway. And not that I would marry Ash. But I saw that I could maybe be someone like that. I could play that part. I picked out a Snapple and paid and went back outside onto the hot sidewalk.

I passed Chambers Street and continued what had become a lengthy journey, onward toward the great World Trade Towers growing bigger and taller before me. *The great overseers,* I had always thought of them. The great protectors. One time in a cab I had gotten lost, and the driver couldn't understand English and in a panic I had slid around in the seat looking out each window until I found them and confirmed what direction we were going. The great landmarks. The great orienters.

At the World Trade Center plaza, I did my usual thing of standing between the towers and staring up and getting my brain disoriented by the sky and the lines of the buildings, and the height and absurdity of it. Then I crossed over Broadway and entered the tiny narrow streets of Wall Street where my money was now, though I still didn't understand exactly why my balance went up and down, though I had been assured it would mostly go up, over "a long-term time horizon." Wall street was the oldest part of New York, or so I assumed, with my limited knowledge of New York history. Anyway, the buildings looked old and the statues were of people who were from the 1700s and started banks and things.

I kept heading south for some reason and ended up in the Staten Island Ferry terminal, at the very tip of the bottom of Manhattan. The sun was now low in the sky, and I was tired and I needed yet another Snapple, and also risked a vendor hotdog, which I devoured sitting in a plastic chair in the ferry terminal, the flat gray water spread out before me.

I returned to the subway station on my weary legs and hobbled down the stairs and sat with a few commuters on the wooden benches, waiting for the air conditioned train to take me home.

Back in my own neighborhood, it was dark and I went home and took a shower and crawled out onto my fire escape with a coffee mug of white wine. I had apparently purged myself of all egotistical thoughts, as I now seemed to have nothing at all in my brain, and sat there dumbly staring at a clothes line of my neighbor's laundry.

66

BRIDGET MOVED OUT and screwed us on the rent. Not by much, but still. She claimed she had barely lived there that month, and throughout her entire stay, which was true enough. And, as she pointed out, if we were so worried about it we could charge the new person a little extra, which was a common practice in room sharing in New York, screw the new person, but we weren't going to do that. Fortunately, Mari knew a girl named Jenny Hutner, who was starting a teaching job in the Bronx in September. She needed a place immediately, so she paid the extra that Bridget didn't pay and moved in a couple days later, and sure enough everything worked out.

Around this same time, there was an item about Anna Madsen and me in Page Six, the gossip column of *The New York Post*. It was a couple lines about Anna partying in the Hamptons, "… but where was her new best friend, child bride Andrea Marr, whose novel *Chicks and Dudes* will soon scandalize the indie rock set?" This harmless item resulted in a ton of emails and text messages, which was fun, but also reminded me that my day of reckoning, my "pub date," was fast approaching.

Thankfully there was stuff to do, as Anna Madsen reminded me from the Hamptons, like writing out a guest list for my party. This was a pretty paltry list at first, but as I kept working on it, I realized I did know quite a lot of people. Especially when it came to a party like this, where you could invite pretty much everyone. Like all the people from *In Focus*. And Brooke Kinney and her dad and anyone she cared to bring. And Evan and the USC people from the karaoke bar. Sally's friends from Columbia and the *Context* people. And Josh and his millions of native New Yorker musician friends.

Josh called me and wanted his band to play music at the party, since my book was about bands and musicians. I asked Anna and she said that yeah, since the book was about music, maybe they should play, or at least set up their instruments as part of the theme, she didn't want them to play continuously. Just a song or two. And I could maybe go on stage at some point and thank everyone. So then I called Josh back, to tell him this, but he was suddenly all excited because Jules Carpenter from the Contrails had emailed him. Jules had read a galley of my book somehow and wanted to play at the party. The Contrails were the hottest band in New York at that moment, their first record had been huge the summer before. So then I called Anna back and we debated this aspect of the party, and did we want it to turn into a rock show, and Anna kept saying, "one or two songs," since publishing people liked to talk, not listen to loud music, but as she thought more about the prospect of Jules Carpenter being there, who happened to be dating Taylor Harte, a very cool new actress, she thought maybe it would be okay if there was music, and at the end of the night, they could play all they wanted. And anyway Jules Carpenter would pack the place and get us more Page Six mentions.

. . .

Besides Jules Carpenter, other people were starting to read the book. I didn't know how or where they were getting it. It wasn't officially coming out until September 14th, but people were writing me and telling me how much they liked it and what a big hit it was going to be. It was the proverbial "wave of success," which was actually what it felt like: a big ocean wave lifting you up and carrying you forward and dropping you down in a place you weren't totally prepared to be.

Anna finally came home from the Hamptons and we met at her mother's apartment and basically sat around all day, happy to be in each other's company again and thinking about the party and talking. Also, I think Anna was sad in a way. Like all these same things had happened to her two years ago, and now she was living through it again, but not at the center of it, at the side of it, in the wings. And we talked about that a little bit and she questioned her own motives, and asked me if I thought it was weird that she was reliving her success through me, and I was like, "No! No! It's not weird at all! I need you! You're helping me so much!" Which I think made her feel better and anyway, was totally the truth.

So we had our list of people for the party and once Anna made her own list, we had a ton of people, and a lot of important people like Nikki, and people from the *Paris Review* and *Book Forum* and all the more edgy downtown types of the literary world. And also a lot of blog people and website people, since those people were becoming important now. Jules Carpenter was going to be a huge bonus, we both saw, but we still refrained from putting him on the official invitation, but everyone would know about it. That kind of news traveled fast.

. . .

Another night, Rex called and wanted to meet for Mexican food in Williamsburg. It was like ten at night, an odd time for dinner. When I got there, Rex mumbled something about things getting claustrophobic in their apartment lately, even though they'd lived in that same apartment for three years. "Marriage is weird," he said.

So then we talked and he told me more about Greece, not the cheesy stuff, but like how Rebecca got diarrhea and the strangeness of going someplace you've always dreamed about with your new wife. Which was great in some ways. But it was different than if you went by yourself. Like he kept wanting to sit in cafés and write, and pretend to be Hemingway or whatever. But she wanted to do different things like take a tour of some ruins. It was weird, he said. Being married was weird.

So then we talked about Ash. Ash had already had a big dinner party, which was apparently the talk of Park Slope. Elizabeth Dieckmann, a young columnist from *The New York Times* was there, and Ian Colton whose father was the famous British poet and Siobhan Hennessey, who was barely out of Harvard and already had a story in *The New Yorker* and was about to publish a literary novel at Knopf. "Ol' Ash is getting right in there," laughed Rex. "He's not wasting one second."

"And he didn't invite you to his dinner party?" I asked. But Rex laughed. He was the assistant entertainment editor at *The Post*. There wasn't much he could have brought to that table. But I was offended by this. And mad. Rex and Ash were old friends from college. And in the same field. And were supposedly friends! Ash should have invited Rex to his party! But Rex just shrugged.

And then Liz at WCM called me at *In Focus* and told me in her chirpy yet hostile voice to hold for Will Soren. He came on and he was on a plane somewhere. He was calling to tell me the deal was on with Rampart Pictures. They were optioning my book. He told me the details, and how much money it was, and at first I thought I wasn't hearing him correctly. But I was. It was another ridiculous amount of money. I sucked in my breath.

And then more weirdness at work: the next day, I was in the little lounge area making tea when the new girl came in. She was crying. She looked at me like she was going to get in trouble, like I was her manager or supervisor or something, which I so wasn't. Finally, I got mad at her and I said what's wrong? You can tell me. I'm not your boss!

She apologized and wiped her eyes with a napkin and said her boyfriend had broken up with her. But she wouldn't tell me about it and continued to look at me like I was the enemy, I guess because I was the big-deal writer who still worked at *In Focus*, when I was supposed to be uptown having cocktails at 21 with Marjorie Isaacs or something. I was so obviously not like that. So why did people keep acting like I was?

It was so exasperating but there was nothing to be done. I then had the thought that it was time to quit. It was time to say goodbye to *In Focus*. I wasn't even friends with anyone there anymore.

So when the girl was gone, I put my tea cup in the sink and walked down the short hallway to Veronica's office. I knocked on the door. I was totally going to quit. I was determined. I pounded on the door. But Veronica wasn't there. She was gone for the day. Summer hours.

67

THE EMAIL INVITATIONS to the party went out. Brooke Kinney emailed me back instantly and told me she couldn't come because her dad was getting married that same weekend in Colorado. I was like, who is he marrying? She said this woman who owned a bunch of lifestyle magazines out west, like *Aspen* and *Lake Tahoe*. Then she told me about going to college and how exciting it was about my book and we had a great email exchange. I loved Brooke so much. Maybe it was because I'd slept with her dad. It was strange to think I had done that. But I had done it and my relationship with Brooke had been the result. Brooke was my love child.

Other people wrote back. Evan couldn't come, because he was working on a film in LA now, he had written it originally, but now he might direct it too because the other director had gone to rehab. So he would soon be rich and famous, in his own cheesy way, which would surprise no one. There was other news like that. That was a good reason to have a party I saw, if nothing else, you got updates from everyone. Sally was going to come down for it. Thank god. And Carol Smith said she might be in New York then. It was probably good for me that not everyone was going to drop everything to come to my party. It reminded me that I was not the only person with stuff going on. Like Evan with his movie. It was good to be reminded: I just wrote a book. In the larger scheme of things, that wasn't such a huge deal.

And then Rex and Rebecca wanted me to meet this guy they liked for some reason. It wasn't the best timing for a fix up, days before my big party, but I went and had iced teas with them and the guy, at a new café near their apartment. He did research for a historian who wrote bestselling civil war biographies, which sounded sort of fun. He was very smart and nice, but I was too nervous to really talk to him in any focused way. I explained this to him as we were leaving, and told him to call me in a week or two and we could hang out again. This I said in a new responsible adult way. I was getting like that now, very professional and to the point. That was why Miguel had been so annoyed with me. I tended to get shy and bashful when confronted by anything out of the ordinary. I needed to be more like this: super present and more assertive and confident. Like a real author. So even Miguel had been helping me in a way. He was preparing me for things to come.

The day before the *Chicks and Dudes* party, I went over to Anna's and we sat around like we did, Anna in her boxer shorts and a baby tee since it was so hot. She even went to the deli down the street dressed like that, with slippers and her Marc Jacobs bathrobe that he gave her personally when *Electra Rising* first came out.

We went on her computer and answered emails and invited some last-minute people and Anna dug into her vast New York connections and emailed a couple influential insider types, and flirted with them or insulted them or did whatever she thought it would take to get them to come, or at least write about it. God, I hoped there would be people there. I'd been to literary parties and I'd seen how dead they could be. And how even when they were good, they could still be super stressful and super "looking over your shoulder to see if someone more famous was there." But Anna kept telling me it would be great. We'd get drunk and have fun ourselves and whatever. It was just a party. In New York there were a hundred parties every night.

On the actual day, I went to work at *In Focus* from eleven to three but actually left at 2:30. Of course I had been planning my outfit for weeks, but when I got home and laid it out on my bed, I started re-thinking. This was extremely dangerous, I quickly realized. I called Anna and she put me straight. "Wear your black panties, your yellow dress and your red Keds. And nothing else," she said. "And bring lipstick."

When I hung up, I realized I didn't want to waste one more second in my dumb Greenpoint apartment and called a car service and rode over the Queensboro Bridge to Anna's.

I got there at like four-thirty, so we had some time to kill. I was so relieved to be with Anna. She would handle everything from now on. I took off my dress and put it on a hanger and walked around in my underwear and we made smoothies and then Anna took a bath and then I took one, to relax. We also split a half of one of her mother's valium—one quarter each—which just made my arms feel weird and didn't really calm me down. It felt so surreal to be going to a party like this. A party for *me*. At one point I asked Anna if Cynthia Dunleavy was going to be there and she was like, of course, she's paying for it. And Will Soren would be there. And Jules Carpenter. And maybe Taylor Harte. And Rex and Rebecca. And maybe Ash.

God, he better come! And Mari and our new school teacher roommate Jenny Hutner, and Veronica possibly ... My brain was spinning with possibilities and I was getting a fluttery feeling in my stomach, but in a good way.

The time crept by. We had the radio on, to *WINS 1010 News* for some reason, turned up so loud the newscaster's deep voice filled the whole apartment, that and the clacking of typewriters, which they still played between the news stories, even though nobody used typewriters anymore. All the news was about how hot it was. It was the end of August. There wasn't anything else going on.

Anna did something on her computer and I lay on the couch, my bare feet up on the cushions, literally watching the clock hands move. It was like 7:00 now. Anna had said we could not show our faces until 8:30, even though the party started at 7:30. I had not thought we should do this. What if Cynthia and Will were there? We couldn't keep them waiting. But she was adamant. We did not arrive until 8:30. And 9:00 was actually better.

At 7:45, Anna called her gay friend Chase who had been nice enough to go on time, so that he could report back. Chase said that there were a few people there. Not a lot. The "coming straight from work" crowd. People were drinking. Nobody important seemed to be there yet, at least nobody Chase recognized.

So we stayed at Anna's. At 7:50 I started to get really nervous. Anna finally agreed that we should go. But first we had to touch up our makeup. We went in her bathroom but I wasn't doing mine right. So Anna sat me on the toilet and took over. She fiddled with my eye makeup and fixed that and then brushed my hair for a bit, which hypnotized me in some way. She parted my hair and pinned it up with a plastic barrette, which had become my trademark look, unoriginal as it was. But to the publishing world it was very quirky and punk. And I guess that's what I was supposed to be. So whatever.

68

AT 8:15, we hit the street. I suddenly became so nervous I could barely breathe. We walked along the sidewalk toward Broadway. I was already sweating after five steps.

On Broadway, waiting for the light, I found myself watching people: an old lady walking ... a construction worker talking on his phone ... the guy in the pizza place window, in his white apron, rolling the pizza crust ... I envied all of them. These quiet simple moments they were living through seemed infinitely preferable to what I was about to do. I'd have rather bought a slice of pizza and sat in that window than go to this party. Or plopped myself on a bench and watched the pigeons. But I guess what makes the quiet moments so nice, was the exciting moments, the nervy moments, the things like this party.

Anna hailed us a cab. We slid in and I tried to relax, but I was looking at my watch every three seconds. I didn't want Cynthia Dunleavy walking around looking for me and not finding me. Or Miguel, who I remained terrified of. When we got downtown Anna had the cab pull over a few blocks away. It was almost completely dark now, which seemed to be part of the plan. True party girls only came out at night.

We walked down Third Street and Anna stopped at a bodega and got me a pack of Winterfresh gum and herself some new Chinese ginger candies which she was into at the moment. I secretly watched Anna's tough New York face as she paid for the gum and candy. Here she was, helping me, doing everything for me, while her own future seemed so unclear and precarious.

We arrived at 8:47. Which seemed terribly late. I couldn't tell if anyone was there or not. I had come to the CBGBs Gallery a week before, and it was a pretty big room. And so I had feared it would seem empty if the crowd wasn't big enough.

But there were people inside. They were mostly bunched around the entrance and the bar. People turned to look at Anna and I, as we walked in. I saw that Anna was right to doll me up, with the barrette and the lipstick. We were a notable pair, as we were supposed to be.

We went further inside and Josh appeared out of nowhere and grabbed me and excitedly told me that Jules Carpenter and Taylor Harte were on their way. The Contrails guitarist was coming too. And Josh was going to play drums with them!

"Great!" I said, realizing instantly this would be my stock response to whatever anyone said to me that night. "Great!"

Anna got us drinks. I got my vodka tonic like Naomi Cohn had taught me. And then I saw Naomi Cohn. She was right down the bar from us. I started waving at her and when my drink came I hurried down the bar toward her. I was so happy to see

Naomi. She was excited too, and had a super cute guy with her. It was not the forty-year-old sculptor, thank God. So then we talked and babbled and interrupted each other, and she told her boyfriend the story of me showing up at her apartment three years before, dragging my suitcase through the streets of Greenpoint, etc. etc. And now look at me! So then we laughed and I held up my drink and said "vodka tonic" and she looked at me funny and I was like: "It's the drink you taught me. Sophisticated but unpretentious, youthful but experienced!" She didn't remember this, but it didn't matter and we toasted my book and our friendship and secretly Naomi and I were also toasting the guy, who was cute and stylish and seemed perfect for her.

Anna had disappeared, so I walked around, smiling at people and sipping my vodka tonic through my sipping straw, and saying "Great!" People would see me and realize who I was and smile and wave and I would smile back and keep moving around. Sally was supposed to be here and knowing her, she would probably have come exactly at 7:30. So I narrowed my search to just her, and found her finally. She was with Benton and a girl I remembered from Columbia and some other people. They had one of the choice booths at the back of the room. They were all laughing and having a great time, so much so, I didn't want to interrupt. But Sally saw me and started shrieking and actually stood up on the seat and nearly fell, and then everyone gathered around me, which was weird and way more attention than I needed, even though I had to admit, it felt pretty good. Sally gave me the biggest hug. Everyone talked at once and yakked about whatever and then someone asked if it was true that the Contrails were going to play and I said, "I think so," and everyone got super excited, the guys especially. Someone said they saw

Bret Easton Ellis outside on his cell phone. I was like, "Great!"

The room was filling up. I decided I better go find Cynthia Dunleavy, if she was even here, so I started a quick cruise around and that's how I happened to be near the front door when Jules Carpenter and Taylor Harte walked in. The crowd by the door literally parted for them. I ducked over to the side, which was probably not the right move, I was probably supposed to go introduce myself and welcome them—one celebrity to another—since it was my party, but Taylor Harte was insanely beautiful and weirdly small and Jules was such a rockstar: the whole situation was too much and I hid behind a busboy who was gathering empty drink glasses.

It turned out that Cynthia was not there, and had not come. Miguel was there though, he was standing against the wall, frowning, though Taylor Harte had just walked right by him, so I don't know what his problem was. *You wanted a celebrity Miguel, well there you go!* But I didn't hold a grudge. I went over to him and said hi and introduced myself to the nerdy gay guy who was probably his boyfriend. They didn't seem that thrilled to say hi, but I thanked Miguel anyway for all his help and whatever, and he warmed up a little but not much.

I also spotted Liz from WCM at one point and wanted to make my way over to her to see if Will Soren was there, but I was stuck talking to someone at that moment and then when I got away she was gone. She had probably been told to come and so had stopped in for a few minutes, but no longer, because that would not befit an all-powerful future agent at WCM. Still it would have been fun to say hi.

So no Will, and no Cynthia, and a five-minute appearance by Liz. In a way it was a relief. I next got caught in a large group of people that were Mari's friends from her work, and someone brought me another vodka and tonic and then our new roommate Jenny Hutner, chose this moment to try to have a long conversation with me about her inner city teaching job. Obviously, I couldn't have that conversation now. Then Anna came and saved me, and just in time, as the other Contrails guy, the guitarist, had just walked in. And then Josh, who had appointed himself stage manager got upset and started running around, trying to control everything. Anna and I prepared ourselves to go talk to Jules and his bandmate, who were both so gorgeous even Anna was nervous. I straightened my dress. Anna fiddled with her hair. Then we walked over and introduced ourselves. Oh my god, Jules was so amazing to look at. Like so handsome but also shy and funny and this sad distant look in his eyes, like he'd already had enough fame to last a lifetime. But he was there for us, for Anna and me.

I liked him so much. And then Anna and him started talking and realizing all the connections they had. It was like this big meeting of the stars. And then the adorable guitarist guy talked to me and congratulated me on my book. I just about died.

After a moment of standing around, Josh appeared and herded us toward the stage. Jules grinned at me and said he would keep it short. He and his guitar player jumped up on stage and put on their instruments. People immediately started to gather around and suddenly it was like I was back in high school, standing there in front of the stage, watching boys play music, which was an odd way for things to end up, since this was supposed to be my party, for my book, and how did I end up in the audience again? But I didn't care. Nobody cared. They started to play and it was fantastic.

69

ASH CROWLEY SHOWED up later than anyone. Naturally. The music had just ended when he appeared near the entrance, with a bookish preppy girl, who was blonde and beautiful and intense looking. I thought: of course you have to show me up Ash, by bringing some brilliant writer girl, who was probably just named one of the top writers under 30 by *Granta* or something.

I pretty much hated Ash by now. And Anna hated him too. Which reminded me I had to go find Anna and introduce them.

I found her by the bar talking to another Contrails person. He was as good looking as the rest of them. The whole party had taken on a glamorous rich kid New York City feeling. It had turned into an Anna Madsen party is the truth. Which was fine with me.

I broke right in on Anna's conversation, and she could tell I was worked up about something. She separated from the Contrails guy and was like, what is it? I said, "Ash Crowley is here." Her eyes narrowed.

We went to find him. He was stuck trying to get to the bar but he couldn't because it was about three people deep. Where had all these people come from? Also, I noticed that I was a little drunk at that moment. Which was perfect.

Ash was wearing a black blazer and a white shirt and vintage wash jeans and white Jack Purcells. He had, as usual, perfectly blended "Downtown," "casual literary," and *The New Yorker* all in one outfit. I thought: I should throw my drink in his face. I could be on Page Six! Anna wasn't saying anything. It was too loud to talk anyway.

We got to Ash and he saw us coming, and for the first time ever, he did not seem superior or in complete control of his surroundings. He looked a little unsure of himself. Finally! I pulled Anna forward and we squeezed through some people and then we were there: standing right in front of him.

My plan to be mean to him fell apart then. I sucked at being mean to people, and truthfully, I didn't really hate Ash. I liked him. Which was extremely frustrating, but there it was. He introduced us to Sophie, the girl. She was French, from Paris, which explained her superior style. Then we learned that she wasn't a writer at all, but was an economics grad student, a friend of a friend, nobody horrible or intimidating at all, and in fact she was thrilled to be at our party. She couldn't believe Jules Carpenter had just played. She gushed over Anna and I like we were movie stars.

So then Ash started complimenting us too. He had read my book. He said it was great. He thought I had done a lot of interesting things stylistically. And then Anna started talking and Ash was being very respectful to her too, and telling her how *Electra Rising* had been the most talked about book at Iowa during his entire time there. Anna, who was tougher than Ash or me or anyone who did not grow up in New York City, was not influenced by this flattery, but she also saw no easy way to hate him or his starstruck date. They looked so nice and respectful and impressed, it was impossible. And so then, we just stood there for a moment, the party roaring all around us. I looked up at Ash, at his handsome midwestern face and remembered sleeping beside him at the wedding. I had hoped that night might connect us in a way that would transcend the vagaries of our careers, and that we would remain loyal to each other and stay friends, even as he became the next Michael Chabon, and I became the next … Anna Madsen? But it remained unclear if that was possible. Which probably meant it wasn't.

We got pulled away then by Chase and some of Anna's gay friends. We used that excuse to circle back to the bar where we somehow cut in front of everyone and got more drinks. You could now barely move, a whole new wave of people had shown up. The room was packed.

Anna and I tried to confer about Ash. But we could barely hear. So we moved toward the back and found a less noisy corner. But there wasn't much to say even when we could talk. And then these two guys started talking to us. They didn't know who we were and they asked what the party was for, and Anna said, "Some book," and they were like, "We like books," and I was like: "Great!"

Rex and Rebecca had been there for nearly an hour when I finally got to talk to them. That didn't go too well. We stood there awkwardly and couldn't hear over the noise of the crowd. I was drunk now and Rex seemed drunk too, and somehow separate from Rebecca. It seemed like she wasn't that thrilled to be there. She wasn't really dressed right either, in her jeans and button down shirt. Everyone else was more glammed out. But we all smiled and looked around and then when Rebecca got pulled away, Rex and I had a little moment. He was like, "So this is where it ends. All that work. And here you are!"

I shrugged, like *here I am*. And then I wanted to be with Rex again, like be married to him. It was completely irrational and I looked at him and he must have guessed what I was thinking, because he looked down at me and said: "I know Andrea, I know."

I drank more. I couldn't find Anna. A girl knocked into me so hard I spilled my drink on my dress. Thank God it was a vodka tonic. Rex and Rebecca left, Rex coming to find me to say goodbye for the both of them and giving me an awkward squeeze and thanking me and me thanking him profusely, for everything, for all his help with the book, and his moral support—all of this in a drunken party wail that probably didn't even make sense.

So then Rex was gone. And Anna was still missing. And Sally had gone off to get pizza slices with her gang and had promised to come back. Sally was the other person I most wanted to be with tonight. Like Rex, she had been so instrumental in everything that had happened to me.

Then Josh appeared, all pissed off about something. He wanted The Contrails to play another song but he couldn't find Jules Carpenter. I didn't want to deal with him so I went outside, onto the sidewalk, in search of Anna or Sally. The air was nice out there, less sweaty and quieter. I was sort of hungry myself, I realized, and wondered where Sally went for pizza.

Then I spotted Ash. He was with his French student and two other people. There were several small groups outside, clustered around the entrance, but Ash and his friends were further away, down the sidewalk, having a more private conversation. I walked in that direction and then saw who he was talking to: Jules Carpenter and Taylor Harte. The four of them were smiling, joking, laughing with great familiarity. Like they were all the best of friends.

I gasped and turned away. Wow. Ash had come to my party and somehow found his way to the two most famous people in the room. And now they were *his* friends.

I walked away from them, down the street. By the end of the block I realized I was very drunk and I didn't care what Ash did. He could have Jules Carpenter and Taylor Harte. *Go ahead, Ash, use my party to further your own career,* I muttered under my breath.

I walked more and eventually got far enough from CBGBs Gallery that I could safely stop and sit on a stoop. I sat then and took a deep breath and tried to process everything and calm myself down as best I could.

And then, as I sat there, I remembered the Vermont poster. The one from the New Haven train station the day I had officially moved to New York. *Revisit the Simple Life*, it had said. Gazing at that poster, I had pictured myself as an older person, forty or fifty years old. I wasn't that person yet. But I had moved ahead slightly. I was a little closer to that moment when I really would want to *revisit the simple life*. Which was basically what I wanted: to do interesting, exciting things now; to wear myself out; to do everything that I could possibly do; so that the *simple life* would look good to me. It would look like heaven. And then I wouldn't mind when everything was over and I wasn't famous anymore and nobody cared about me or whatever. And I could go to Vermont and have a little house and a cat and maybe a garden and feel at peace knowing that there was nothing left to do. I had done it all. That would be the best thing. I would be very happy if I ended up like that.

70

THE OFFICIAL RELEASE date of *Chicks and Dudes* was September 14. It was a warm day, a sunny day, though people seemed impatient like New Yorkers get in September. They'll take the nice weather, but they've had enough of summer. It's time for the cold and rain, so they can sit in their office and work.

I went back to work myself that morning. I still had my job at *In Focus*. I was down to three shifts of four hours each, but I liked going there, and Veronica had given me some new responsibilities. This was because of a lunch we'd had recently. I'd told her I didn't feel part of the team, didn't think the other people liked me or thought I should be there. She thought that was ridiculous and told me that keeping my job was exactly what I should do, that it would keep me grounded, give me structure, and that fame and fortune came and went very quickly in New York and whatever instinct was telling me to stay at *In Focus* was a good instinct and that I should follow it in the future.

. . .

So I was sitting in my cubicle on the day that *Chicks and Dudes* officially came into being. Of course books didn't actually come out on a certain day. They dribbled out. *Chicks and Dudes* had been in most New York bookstores for weeks. So there was no big unveiling.

In most bookstores it was on the front table. People were sending me grainy cell phone pictures of it from various places in the country, high school friends, music friends, people from Wellington who had no idea what had happened to me and were suddenly shocked to see that I had written a book.

Only a few people knew about the actual release date. And of those people, only Rex remembered to send me an email. "Happy *Chicks and Dudes* day!" it said. I stared at the email. Had I really named my book *Chicks and Dudes*? Those words looked very strange to me now.

Later in the day I got an email from Liz about the film option. I read part of the contract and it said the agreement would be valid "throughout the universe and in all future universes" or something like that. And then Miguel called to confirm several reading dates. I was doing a mini East Coast tour of readings the next week.

But there was nothing to do that day, which I was grateful for. When I got off work, at 3pm, I tried calling Anna Madsen who I had not talked to in a couple days. We had been together so much recently, we had taken an unspoken break from each other. I wasn't sure she remembered that today was "the day," and so I sent her a text. "Book out today" I wrote. She didn't text me back immediately. She had met a guy and was possibly out with him. I was curious to hear how that was progressing, but I would wait until she called me.

· · ·

There had been something funny on my cell phone bill, so my first stop when I got off work was the Verizon place to sort that out. Unlike the other times I'd been there, the guy was actually helpful and nice and explained it to me, showing me on the phone how to turn off the thing that kept trying to connect me to something I didn't want to be connected to. Anyway, they credited my bill and I was glad to get that settled.

So then I went to yoga at this place near Union Square. This was a new thing I was doing with Mari, who was doing it because Jenny Hutner was doing it. So now we were all doing it, though Mari and I were pretty half-assed in our approach, unlike the other women who were like little yoga soldiers. Mari, being small and flexible, was actually good at yoga. I was less so. But it was nice to be there with the other people and feel the wood floor with your bare toes and stare at your thighs and your stomach, which, since I was twenty-four, were not too horrible to look at. That wouldn't last though. Even the yoga instructor who had just turned thirty, had a little paunch. We were all doomed, obviously, and yet everyone at yoga was always cheerful and happy and thinking forward to a slimmer and more flexible future.

After yoga I sat in the little café next door and drank some wheatgrass juice. I felt that nice, post-exercise tiredness. I had done something to my knee though, during the last stretches, and I flexed it a couple times in hopes of making it stop hurting.

I had a vague plan I would go by Barnes & Noble and check on my book one more time. I'd done that pretty much every day that week, but today, since it was the official day of publication,

I felt like maybe I should leave it alone for once. I couldn't hover over my book forever. Maybe it was time to let go.

So I didn't go to Barnes & Noble and instead walked down Fourteenth Street where I stopped in at the new Levi's store. I looked at the jeans, but they seemed very expensive. The salesgirl told me to think of it as an investment, which was the wrong thing to say, since my mutual funds had gone down recently. I had lost nearly ten thousand dollars, the last time I'd looked. That is, if I was reading the figures correctly. Which I wasn't sure I was.

Later that night, on the subway, I had this sudden violent urge to go to Rex and Rebecca's. I hadn't done that in a while. And if there ever was a night I could show up on their doorstep, this would be it. But I felt like they needed a break from me and my book. *God, people must be so sick of me,* I thought.

And so I continued on my way and transferred to the G Train and waited on the heavy wood subway bench. My knee had stopped hurting, so that was good. And then a girl on the platform was reading *The Bell Jar*, and not my book, which was unsettling.

At home Mari and Jenny Hutner were rearranging Jenny's room in a new way that would make it more difficult for us to walk through. We didn't say anything though. She was freaking out about her difficult teaching job and her tiny sleeping space and the grim realities of life in New York. Mari and I had both gone through that. There was nothing to do but humor her and help her push around her futon. I didn't tell either of them this was my official publication day.

After that, I let Mari and Jenny brush their teeth and then took my turn. In the bright light of the bathroom, I looked at my new "published author" self. My face was flattening out. My lips were not as round as they had once been. I was no longer perfectly ripe fruit. I hoped I would look like Anna as I aged, that sharp, intelligent, slightly neurotic, big city look. But I was not Anna. I would look like something else. I would look like whatever I turned into.

I switched off the light in the bathroom and then turned off the lights in the kitchen and then made my way around Jenny's bed and through Mari's room and finally into my own relatively palatial bedroom. I got into bed and clicked off the light. I lay back, looking out my window at the sky and the power lines. Someday I would move. Someday I would live in some other place, in different circumstances. But for now I was here, being myself, doing what I do. And for a moment, for perhaps the only moment in my entire life, everything felt right. There was no need to look into the future, or wonder what would happen, or attach my happiness to some hoped for outcome. I was happy now. Right at this moment. Which was a strange state to be in.

Blake Nelson's many novels include *Girl*, *Recovery Road* and *Paranoid Park* (which was made into a film by Gus Van Sant). He currently writes a travel newsletter at blakenelson.substack.com.